DARK CELEBRATION

A CARPATHIAN REUNION

CHRISTINE FEEHAN

BERKLEY BOOKS, NEW YORK

THE BERKLEY PUBLISHING GROUP
Published by the Penguin Group
Penguin Group (USA) Inc.
375 Hudson Street, New York, New York 10014, USA
Penguin Group (Canada), 90 Eglinton Avenue East, Suite 700, Toronto, Ontario M4P 2Y3, Canada
(a division of Pearson Canada Inc.)
Penguin Books Ltd., 80 Strand, London WC2R 0RL, England
Penguin Group Ireland, 25 St. Stephen's Green, Dublin 2, Ireland (a division of Penguin Books Ltd.)
Penguin Group (Australia), 250 Camberwell Road, Camberwell, Victoria 3124, Australia
(a division of Pearson Australia Group Pty. Ltd.)
Penguin Books India Pvt. Ltd., 11 Community Centre, Panchsheel Park, New Delhi—110 017, India
Penguin Group (NZ), Cnr. Airborne and Rosedale Roads, Albany, Auckland 1310, New Zealand
(a division of Pearson New Zealand Ltd.)
Penguin Books (South Africa) (Pty.) Ltd., 24 Sturdee Avenue, Rosebank, Johannesburg 2196, South Africa

Penguin Books Ltd., Registered Offices: 80 Strand, London WC2R 0RL, England

This book is an original publication of The Berkley Publishing Group.

This is a work of fiction. Names, characters, places, and incidents either are the product of the author's imagination or are used fictitiously, and any resemblance to actual persons, living or dead, business establishments, events, or locales is entirely coincidental. The recipes contained in this book are to be followed exactly as written. The publisher is not responsible for your specific health or allergy needs that may require medical supervision. The publisher is not responsible for any adverse reactions to the recipes contained in this book. Further, the publisher does not have any control over and does not assume any responsibility for author or third-party websites or their content.

First edition: September 2006

Berkley hardcover ISBN: 0-425-21167-3

An application to register this book for cataloging has been submitted to the Library of Congress.

PRINTED IN THE UNITED STATES OF AMERICA

10 9 8 7 6 5 4 3 2

For my beloved daughter, Cecilia, who has always given us reason for celebration!

For My Readers

Be sure to write to Christine at Christine@christinefeehan.com to get a FREE exclusive screen saver and join the PRIVATE e-mail list to receive an announcement when Christine's books are released.

Acknowledgments

Many thanks to Diane Trudeau for her help with the recipes. Cheryl Wilson, you know you are invaluable. Denise, Manda and Brian, thank you for your unfailing support and all of the work you do to help me put these books together.

Dear Readers,

Over the past few years, I have received thousands of letters asking for a reunion of the Carpathian characters. I resisted the idea for a long time, uncertain how one could bring so many vivid and larger-than-life characters together in the same book. It seemed a daunting task. Then one evening, I was sitting around a fireplace talking with some author friends about the mess we'd made of the dinner that night. We'd rented a house together to work, and unfortunately, some of us were a little lax on the cooking skills. (I'm not mentioning names here or raising my hand, but a few of the disasters depicted in this book actually did happen, sadly enough to say.) We were laughing so hard, and the idea of a Christmas party where the Carpathians cooked for their friends was born.

I pitched the idea to my editor as a special thank-you gift book at Christmas time for my readers. I was very excited to have a fun, lighthearted book to write. I was thrilled with the idea of adding in the Dark Desserts, and so many wonderful people from all over the world sent in the most scrumptious recipes. The concept was completely different than anything I'd ever conceived of writing, so it was going to be great fun! And then I sat down and started to write it . . .

First of all, it hadn't occurred to me that there was no hero and heroine, and that I would have to find a way to transition each chapter smoothly. And second, and more important, I don't write fun and lighthearted. My characters tend to take over the book and run away with it, and this book was no exception. No matter how hard I tried, the book turned—yes, you guessed it—*dark*!

Once I called my editor and warned her that the book had taken on its own life and I wasn't going to be delivering that lighthearted book, I simply accepted it and allowed the characters free rein. They took over, and *Dark Celebration* became a huge part of the rich tapestry that makes up the Carpathian world. I had fun revisiting the characters and finding out how they were doing together and what their lives were like as couples as well as what the Carpathian society was like as a whole.

The book turned into something very unexpected, but in all honesty, I thoroughly enjoyed myself writing it, and I certainly hope you have just as much fun reading it. When I write, the characters definitely dictate the story, so several were very forthcoming while others hung back a little more than I would have liked. All in all, in the end I think we caught a glimpse of old friends and what their lives are together. I found myself smiling a lot while writing it and hope you have the same reaction reading it!

Warmest regards,
Christine

THE CARPATHIANS

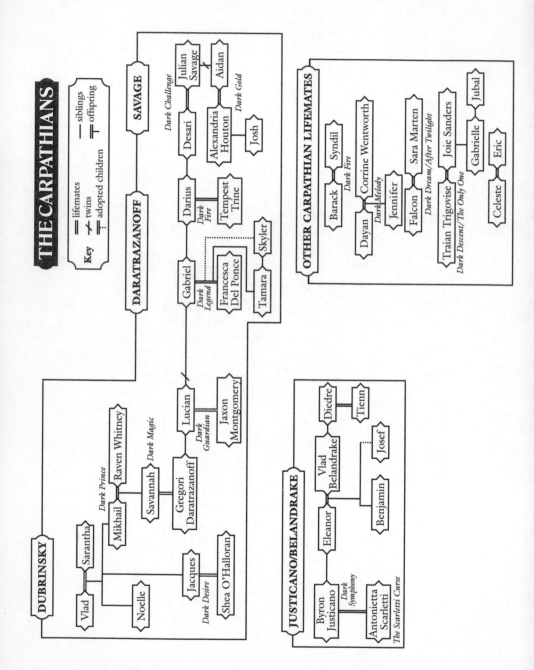

Key
= lifemates
/ twins
T offspring

— siblings
‡ adopted children

DUBRINSKY

Vlad — Sarantha

Mikhail — Raven Whitney
Dark Prince

Savannah — Gregori Daratrazanoff
Dark Magic

Jacques — Shea O'Halloran
Dark Desire

Noelle

DARATRAZANOFF

Lucian — Jaxon Montgomery
Dark Guardian

Gabriel — Francesca Del Ponce
Dark Legend

Tamara

Skyler

Darius — Tempest Trine
Dark Fire

SAVAGE

Desari — Julian Savage
Dark Challenge

Alexandria Houton — Aidan
Dark Gold

Josh

JUSTICANO/BELANDRAKE

Byron Justicano — Antonietta Scarletti
Dark Symphony
The Scarletti Curse

Eleanor — Vlad Belandrake

Diedre — Tienn

Benjamin

Josef

OTHER CARPATHIAN LIFEMATES

Barack — Syndil

Dayan — Corrine Wentworth
Dark Fire

Jennifer

Falcon — Sara Marten
Dark Melody

Traian Trigovise — Joie Sanders
Dark Dream/After Twilight

Gabrielle — Jubal
Dark Descent/The Only One

Celeste — Eric

THE CARPATHIANS

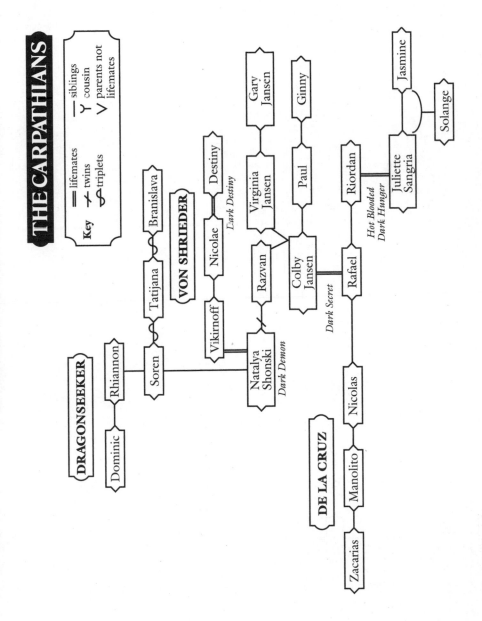

Key
- = lifemates
- ⋌ twins
- ⌔ triplets
- ⌐ siblings
- Υ cousin
- ⋁ parents not lifemates

DRAGONSEEKER

Dominic — Rhiannon

VON SHRIEDER

Branislava
Tatijana
Soren
Natalya Shonski — *Dark Demon*
Vikirnoff
Razvan
Nicolae — Destiny — *Dark Destiny*
Virginia Jansen
Colby Jansen — *Dark Secret*
Gary Jansen
Paul
Ginny
Rafael
Riordan — Juliette Sangria — *Hot Blooded / Dark Hunger*
Jasmine
Solange

DE LA CRUZ

Zacarias
Manolito
Nicolas

1

Stars glittered across the night sky and the moon spilled light, illuminating the trees below and turning leaves a glistening silver. A female owl skimmed the canopy, dipped lower to speed through the labyrinth of trees before rising again just in time to avoid a thick branch. A second, larger owl chased her in a wide circle above the forest surrounding a clearing where a large two-story stone house sat. The female plummeted toward the steep roof, talons extended toward the chimney, pulled up at the last heart-stopping second to race away from the male, wings flapping noiselessly, the wind riffling iridescent feathers.

Raven! Mikhail Dubrinsky warned his lifemate sharply. *That was far too close.*

It was exhilarating.

Raven, you are going to get tired. There was a soft warning growl in Mikhail's voice, as if a wolf lurked inside the body of the owl.

Her laughter bubbled up, soft and warm in his mind as they telepathically communicated. *I'm not a newbie anymore, Mikhail, and after all these years, I think I can handle flying. I love it. It's my favorite thing to do. Are you ever going to get over being overprotective?*

I do not think it is overprotective to watch over the woman of my heart and soul. You always overdo it when you fly. And you risk much more than you should.

That may have been true, but Raven wasn't going to admit it. Once in the body of a bird, she wanted to stay that way for long periods of time. *I feel so free.*

From the moment of her conversion—human to Carpathian—the one thing that had intrigued and filled her with joy above all else in her new life was the ability to fly. She could soar high above earth and see miles of beautiful forest, cool lakes and a riot of wildflowers. Beauty always surrounded her when she took the form of an owl, making her forget, at least for a few moments, the absolute wonder—and responsibility—of being lifemate to the prince of the Carpathian people.

There was a small silence. *Raven, do you not feel freedom when you are with me? I have never caged you, although at times I felt it would be the safest thing to do.*

The female owl circled back toward the male to position herself just under his left wing. *Of course not, silly. Don't you love flying? The wind lifting your body while the terrain below appears so magical?*

There was that whisper of love in her voice—in her mind. Mikhail had come to depend on the steadiness—the absolute steadfastness of her love. *It is so. If you ever are despairing of my nature, I would want you to let me know. I feel your sadness sometimes, my love, the ache in your heart.*

Don't, Mikhail. It's not because of you. Or because of us. Like any woman who has found her true lifemate, I want children. I can't complain. We have our daughter, Savannah, so precious to both of us and much more than many other of our women are gifted with. If we never have another, I have been lucky enough to have one child as well as the only man who could ever make me happy. You and Savannah are enough for me.

Mikhail wished they were home, where he could pull her into his arms and kiss her soundly. He ached with love for her more than he cared to admit, and he could hear—and feel—the desire in her to hold a child in her arms. It was his greatest failure—not only in his duty to his lifemate, but also in his duty to his people. After hundreds of years, he still couldn't protect his people from their greatest threat—not vampires or the mage, not modern society, not even the lack of emotion in the males after two hundred years and the ever-present darkness creeping into their souls. He couldn't protect them from what he was beginning to believe might be the very extinction of their species.

Mikhail. Raven whispered his name in his mind. A soft sound of utter love and compassion. *You will find the answers for our people. You've accomplished so much already by bringing such great minds together in an effort to solve this problem. And three babies have survived in the last few years. We kept Savannah. Francesca and Gabriel have Tamara, and now there is Corrine and Dayan's child, Jennifer. Three girls, my love. There is yet hope.*

Mikhail was silent, wanting to roar his despair to the heavens. Three female children when so many of the men of his species were without hope. To survive, to maintain honor, they had no choice but to find the one woman who would complete their soul—bring light to their darkness. Without a woman, they had nothing but an endless, barren existence.

That's not so, Raven objected. *Many have found their lifemates among my people.*

A handful, Raven. Why can't I find the answer when I have such great minds working on the problem? We need women and children or our kind will cease to exist.

After the assassination attempt on his life, more than anything else, Mikhail feared their enemies would realize just how fragile the Carpathian race had become. With so many against them, it would only take one to realize where the true vulnerability of the Carpathian race lay—the absence of women and children. So far all the strikes had been directed against the men, but sooner or later their enemies would realize that to kill the species, they had only to kill the women and children.

The thought of Raven, his beloved lifemate, or his precious daughter, Savannah, as a target was almost more than he could bear—but it was inevitable. The enemy had joined together with the dark mage and had found a way to hide their presence, making them doubly dangerous. No longer could the Carpathians rely on their ability to read minds and sense a threat. They must be more vigilant than ever. Even now Mikhail scanned the forest below them warily, unable to relax completely.

Mikhail. You have closed your mind to mine.

He forced his thoughts back to their conversation. It was bad enough that he could not console his lifemate over losing a child, let alone stay on track with such an important topic. *You have lived with us only fifty years and already you have suffered the loss of a child. Can you imagine the great sorrow in a hundred years—two hundred? Our women cannot suffer these losses without severe repercussions.*

Shea believes she and Gary are much closer to finding the answers. Gabrielle is now helping as well, Raven reminded him. Gary was human and Gabrielle had been. Recently, to save her life, Gabrielle had undergone the conversion, but she had worked tirelessly even before the change to aid Shea in finding out why Carpathian women suffered so many miscarriages. *With all the training Shea had as a human doctor and her natural abilities as a Carpathian healer, she is an amazing resource to our people. She has worked with Gabrielle, Gary and, of course, Gregori to find the answer as to why our women can no longer successfully carry children.* The few babies born rarely survived the first year. Raven was grateful she had had a miscarriage and been spared the terrible grief of giving birth, holding her child for a year and then losing it. *Shea has already discovered so much. She will unlock this mystery.*

Mikhail believed Shea might be the one to perform such a miracle. She had already proved her tenacity and courage in bringing his brother Jacques back from the brink of insanity, but Mikhail also feared the answers would come too late for his people. Their enemies were banding together, closing in and striking often. Worse, it seemed their oldest and cruelest enemy might still be alive. Xavier, the powerful dark mage, and his grandson, Razvan, were aiding the undead with ancient knowledge.

Raven broke away from him to fly with her usual abandon far too close to the canopy of trees. His heart nearly stopped, and it took tremendous discipline to keep from ordering her back to his side where she would be safe. He couldn't imprison her any more than any of the other Carpathian males could their lifemates, but the need and desire were there, beating at him with ruthless temptation.

Mikhail put on a burst of speed, catching up to the woman who completed his soul, his sharp eyes scanning the terrain below as they flew together. He could feel happiness radiating from her and it helped to ease the burdens in his heart.

You do know, my love, Raven called teasingly, *that you have to play Santa Claus at the Christmas party for all the children.*

Mikhail lost the image—that of an owl—in his mind for the first time in hundreds of years. His body plummeted thirty feet, nearly hitting the top of a tree before he recovered from his shock. Even within the owl's body, he shuddered. *You may rid yourself of that notion at once.*

Raven spiraled down toward their home, her body graceful in flight, landing on two feet on the walkway leading to their porch as she shifted into her natural form. Mikhail followed her, shifting as he landed directly in *front* of her, halting her escape. The lines and planes of his face hardened into a fierce look meant to intimidate. *This conversation is not over.* He couldn't prevent the horrified reaction running through his body. "There are things you should never ask a man to do."

Raven rolled her eyes. "The children will be expecting St. Nick to make an appearance. This is our first big Christmas party, the first real one, and the women have agreed to cook, so the men have to do their part. You have to do it, Mikhail."

"I do *not* think so," he replied. His expression could daunt the most dangerous of vampires or vampire hunters, but certainly did not seem to have the desired effect on his lifemate.

Raven merely huffed out her breath at him, exasperated. "Don't be such a baby. Human men do it all the time with absolutely no fear."

"I am not afraid."

Her eyebrow shot up, the one that always intrigued him, but this time she looked suspiciously as if she might be laughing at him. "Oh, yes, you are. You look terrified—and pale."

"I'm pale because I've expended energy flying without first taking sustenance. I am the prince of the Carpathian people, not Santa Claus."

"That's not an excuse. As the leader of our people, it is your *duty* to play the part of St. Nick. It's tradition."

"Not Carpathian tradition. It is not dignified, Raven." Mikhail swept his black hair to the nape of his neck and secured it with a thin strip of leather. His black eyes glittered at her, making every attempt to intimidate her into submission.

She burst out laughing, completely unsympathetic and certainly not scared. "Tough luck, hotshot. It's your job. Carpathian tradition or not, you promised me we'd have a big Christmas party for everyone. Our people have come from the United States, South America and several other countries to participate in our celebration. We cannot possibly disappoint them."

"It will not be disappointing to anyone if I do not do this ridiculous thing."

Her laughter deepened into a rich, appealing sound that played down his spine and made his stomach do a funny little flip. Only Raven could do that to him. Only Raven could make him want to do anything on Earth to please her.

"Trust me, Mikhail, the entire Carpathian race will be disappointed if they do not see you playing the role of Santa Claus." She stroked his face with her fingertips. "A nice white beard." Her hand ran down his chest to his hard, flat stomach. "A nice round belly . . ."

"You aren't at all amusing." But she was, and it was taking everything he had not to smile at her.

"You promised me you would do everything to make our first Christmas gathering a success."

"I was not thinking at the time. You were distracting me," he grumbled.

"Was I?" Raven asked, blinking innocently. "I can't remember."

Mikhail wrapped his arms around Raven and pulled her into his body. Nibbling on her neck, he tasted her pulse, felt her answering excitement and knew it would always be this way between them. *Raven.* He thought he couldn't love her more, yet each day the emotion grew stronger until he felt he was bursting with it. Sometimes, when she wasn't looking, he could feel blood red tears welling up in his eyes. Who would believe the powerful prince of the Carpathian people would be so enamored of a woman.

He had been born with the ritual words of binding imprinted on his brain as had every other male of his kind. It had been a shock to discover not only that a human woman could become his lifemate, but that she could be successfully turned to his species. More than the complete amazement of all of that was the overwhelming love and hunger he felt for her, that it grew stronger with every moment they shared together. Looking at her could steal the breath from his body.

"You always smell so good."

Raven reached back to circle his neck with her arm, dragging his head closer so she could kiss him. The moment his lips touched hers, fire exploded in his gut and spread low, racing through his system until his blood thickened and his pulse pounded. He pressed his body closer so she could feel the evidence of his desire.

She laughed softly. "You always make me forget what I'm doing. I'm supposed to be cooking the turkey. It's been a very long time and I have to make certain I don't make any mistakes. We've invited the Ostojics and any guests staying at the inn. Even though we can't eat it, we need human food for them and since it was my idea, I couldn't very well pass on the most im portant item on our dinner menu."

"Yes, you could." Mikhail's voice suddenly turned sly.

Raven whirled around to study her lifemate's all too innocent expression. "What are you up to, Mikhail?"

"I'm passing on the duty of being jolly old St. Nick."

Raven put both hands on her hips and tilted her head, narrowing her eyes. "You're up to something very, very bad. I can feel your laughter. What is so amusing?"

"It has just occurred to me that I have a son-in-law."

A slow, answering grin spread over Raven's face even as she gasped in shock, one hand flying to her throat. "You wouldn't. Not Gregori. He'll scare all the children. He couldn't look jolly if he tried."

"We let him take our daughter from us," Mikhail said. "I think as his father-in-law he will have a hard time turning me down."

"And you say I have a wicked sense of humor," Raven accused.

"Where do you think I got it?" Mikhail nuzzled her neck, his voice a husky whisper.

The familiar answering tingle of excitement shot down her spine. Raven loved the way Mikhail's every touch seemed so intimate. "He'll never do it. Not in a million years and you'll still have to, but I'd love to see his face when you ask."

"I have no intention of asking," Mikhail said, straightening to his full height. "I'm his prince as well as his father-in-law and he is my second in command and son-in-law. It is his duty to do these things."

"You can't order him to play Santa Claus." Raven tried desperately to keep her laughter from spilling over. Gregori was one of the most fearsome men she'd ever met. The idea of even considering him in the part of Santa Claus was both hilarious and ludicrous to her.

"I believe that I can, Raven," Mikhail said solemnly. "You ordered me, and I'm the prince."

Raven made a snickering sound. "I suppose you'd prefer I groveled at your feet."

His hands framed her face and he bent to take possession of her mouth. He loved her mouth—her taste—her instant response. *I could kiss you for all time.*

Good thing since you dragged me kicking and screaming into your world. Raven closed her eyes and gave herself up to the sheer magic of his kiss. Her arms stole around his neck and she leaned into him, wanting to feel the imprint of his body so real and alive against hers. There had been too many assassination attempts on Mikhail. Just recently they had lost one of their homes in a fierce battle fighting the combined forces of Razvan, a mage, and vampires. It had been unheard of for vampires to band together, let alone band with any other species.

It frightened her to think there was a conspiracy to murder Mikhail. Her terror of losing him had partly been the reason she'd suggested a huge celebration of Christmas. Although not a holiday usually celebrated by the Carpathians, many of the previously human lifemates, including Raven, missed not having Christmas. She also needed something to take her mind off her growing fears for his safety.

Mikhail lifted his head, retaining possession of her chin. "There is no need for you to fear for my safety, Raven."

The smile faded from Raven's face and she took a step away from her lifemate. "There is every need." She glanced toward the forest, a hitch in her breath. "Someone is coming."

"A youngster, Raven, no one to be afraid of." Mikhail brought her palm to his mouth to press a kiss in the center. "I've never seen you so nervous."

"I try to accept what we cannot change, Mikhail, but as the years have gone by, the danger to you has increased. I try to live as normal a life as possible, but I cannot even now, when it is imperative to protect you, overcome my loathing of sleeping in the ground. My terror of being buried alive makes us more vulnerable than ever." Ashamed, she ducked her head, avoiding his eyes.

Raven. My love. He bent his head once more to hers, his lips brushing hers with a tenderness that brought tears to her eyes. "I made you a promise and I mean to keep it. You do not ever have to sleep beneath the ground. The earth rejuvenates us in our chamber and there is no need to feel you have in any way placed my life in danger. *You* are my life. I cannot allow you ever to be in danger. If I thought sleeping in our chamber was dangerous, I would find another way."

Her eyes searched his, her mind sweeping through his at the same time, searching for the truth. She knew he wove powerful safeguards to protect them, but she still feared that she placed them in danger with her strong aversion to going to ground.

The rustle of leaves on the path to their home broke them apart, Mikhail shifting his body slightly to place his taller frame between the forest and his lifemate. A young woman emerged from behind several leafy plants, looking frightened, but determined. She was average height with tousled, dark hair shimmering with red streaks. She had the skin of a young girl and the eyes of someone far, far older.

Skyler. Mikhail told Raven. *Gabriel and Francesca adopted her. Both Gabriel and Francesca have given her their blood. She is still human, yet carries a powerful bloodline. She is a very strong psychic.*

Raven smiled at the teenager. *She worries about the Carpathian males wanting to claim her now that she is sixteen. She's much too young to worry about such things.* "You must be Skyler. How nice of you to come visiting. Perhaps you'd care to come in and talk to me while I check on the turkey."

"I do not see Gabriel with you," Mikhail said pointedly. This young child represented hope to his race, yet she walked through the forest unescorted.

Mikhail! Don't frighten her.

There are wolves in the forest, as well as the possibility of enemies.

Skyler stopped abruptly, her gaze shifting to Mikhail. For a moment, her dark eyes clashed with Mikhail's black ones defiantly. "Gabriel trusts me to make my way to your house. I'm not a child anymore."

"I can see that. I'm Mikhail and this is my lifemate, Raven. Gabriel and Francesca speak of you so often, I feel as if I know you. Forgive me if I showed my concern for a young woman I look upon as family."

A brief smile flirted with Skyler's mouth. "I have to hand it to you, Mr. Dubrinsky. That should make me feel like a worm, but it doesn't. I'm here because I absolutely want to make it clear that I am *not* a lifemate to anyone."

A shadow passed across the moon, briefly blotting out the light spilling down on the forest. Bats wheeled and dipped in a mad, frenzied performance in the night sky.

Mikhail stood still, searching the surrounding forest with his preternatural senses. He gestured imperiously toward the door Raven held open. They followed Skyler inside. "You are so certain of this?"

The aroma of turkey filled the house, and Mikhail hid his natural revulsion against the scent of meat cooking. Smells from her past often comforted Raven. She was unaware of it, but he sensed her happiness, as if the turkey in the oven had been an important part of her life—a good memory of childhood—so he was careful not to ruin it for her. Raven sent him a small smile as if she might be reading his thoughts in spite of his thin shield. He'd have to watch that. Her skills and powers grew daily.

Skyler looked at the high beamed ceilings and wide-open space before her gaze settled on the three enormous stained-glass windows. Her face lit up and she walked straight over to them. "This is Francesca's work. Isn't she awesome? I helped her with this one." She tilted her head to study the vibrant colors. "I haven't learned how to weave the safeguards into the glass yet. I can do it in quilts, but glass is much more complicated." She glanced at Raven. "Do you ever stand under the setting sun and feel comfort?" Skyler moved an inch to her left. "Right here. If you stand right in this spot as the last rays of light hit, you'll feel it. I did that."

"It's a work of art," Raven said. "If I could, I'd have every window done in Francesca's work. I had no idea you were helping her."

"I have some talent, not nearly as strong as hers, but she's helping me develop mine. I hope to be partners with her one day." The smile faded, leaving her eyes bleak. She reached up to brush strands of dark hair from her face, revealing a small crescent-shaped scar on her temple and drawing attention to the white scars on her hands and forearms. Skyler seemed to be aware of her nervous gesture and folded her hands, her chin raising a fraction. "I've heard rumors of a coming-out party—where the men gather to see if they could possibly be compatible with one of the women . . ."

"We have no women," Mikhail pointed out. "There are no parties and no coming out as we have no women . . ."

Skyler's mouth firmed into a stubborn line as she followed the couple into the kitchen. "Gabriel and Francesca treat me like family."

Mikhail nodded. "They love you as if you were their daughter." He inhaled deeply, drawing her scent into his lungs. "You carry their blood so through love, blood and in every other way, you are their daughter."

"They've offered to convert me when I'm twenty-one and I'm considering it, but I want assurances that you won't try to force me to be with a man—any man."

"No one would force you to do anything," Raven said. "Gabriel is a powerful man. Don't you think he would protect you?"

"Absolutely he would protect me. I don't want Gabriel or Francesca to have to protect me. If I go through the conversion, I do not want someone trying to claim me."

"Are you not aware of the plight of our people? Of our males?" Mikhail demanded.

Raven put a restraining hand on his arm. "Have a seat, Skyler. Can I get you something to eat or drink? We have juice in the fridge."

Without breaking eye contact with Mikhail, the teenager sank into a chair with an almost regal nod. "Yes, thank you, juice would be nice."

She is terrific, isn't she Mikhail? She's terrified but determined that she be heard. There was admiration—and warning in Raven's soft message to her lifemate. Raven poured a glass of orange juice and set it in front of Skyler.

Mikhail's head went up suddenly and he stepped toward the window, his gaze restless as he searched the darkness. He felt the presence of wolves and owls as they hunted for prey, but nothing that would cause the uneasy feeling twisting at his gut. He glanced down at the defiant young teenager, gently probing her mind—and memories. He found Francesca and Gabriel's shields to help distance the girl from the brutality of her life before they had made her their ward, but even with that protection in place, the memories of the malicious cruelty and violence against Skyler sickened him.

Mikhail glanced at Raven and saw the tears shimmering in her eyes as she shared Skyler's past—felt her pain and despair—the utter hopelessness of a child who could not escape from a depraved adult world. Raven hastily crossed to the oven to check on the turkey.

"It smells good," Skyler said.

"I used a wild rice stuffing," Raven said. "I remember it from my child-hood. It took a bit of time tracking down the recipe, but it should be good, although it's been a long time since I cooked anything."

"Francesca lets me cook whenever I want. She trusts me to make my own decisions." Skyler glanced at Mikhail.

"Are you aware of what happens to a Carpathian male without his life-mate?" Mikhail asked, his voice compelling.

Skyler nodded. "Gabriel and Francesca both explained it to me. They lose colors and emotions first. Over hundreds of years, honor can fade and they become dangerous, especially the hunters, any who take lives. And eventually they can become the vampire, the most evil of all creatures."

"And you would leave your lifemate to this fate? You would be that cruel and inhumane? Should he suffer even more than he already has because you suffered?"

"Mikhail!" Raven whirled around, shock on her face. *She's a child. How could you? Giving our daughter to Gregori before she was beyond a fledgling was bad enough, but this child has suffered. And we have no way of knowing whether or not she is lifemate to one of our males.*

She is experienced far beyond her human years, Raven. Allow her to answer.

Skyler carefully placed the glass on the table and stood up, folding her arms as she faced Mikhail squarely. "No, of course not. I wouldn't want anyone to suffer, but I can't seem to overcome the things in my past." She held her trembling hands in front of her. "I don't feel comfortable in the presence of men. I'm not capable of being anyone's lifemate and I don't want to be forced into a position where I have no choice, no say in my life. I didn't come to this conclusion lightly. I love Gabriel and I certainly wouldn't want to think of him dead or suffering or a vampire, but I know I can't ever be powerless again. Male Carpathians are far too dominating, and I would find myself slipping back into that dark place where Francesca first found me."

Mikhail frowned. "Do you believe our women are without power? Is that how you see Francesca?"

Skyler shook her head. "Francesca is loved and returns love. She can do what I can't—and never will be able to do. Gabriel promised me—as did Lucian—that they will never let another force my compliance, but I know a Carpathian male has the ability to bind a Carpathian woman to him. I want to be fully Gabriel and Francesca's daughter, but I don't want to be subject to the laws of your world."

She doesn't know her lifemate could bind her to him in her human state. Mikhail reached out to Raven, suddenly at a loss as to what to do or say to this woman-child. *Why would Francesca and Gabriel and even Lucian keep this information from her?*

"Skyler," he said aloud. "A Carpathian male must put his lifemate above all else. He would see to your needs, have patience with you. You are young yet. You have no idea how you'll feel in a few years."

"I do know."

"And you would sentence a Carpathian male, one who has given many lifetimes of service, to death—or worse—to the undead out of fear?"

"His decisions have nothing to do with me."

"And what of the Carpathian race? Our species is nearly extinct. We cannot continue to exist without women and children. One woman makes a difference. One woman can save a male and give birth to a child."

"I see Francesca struggling sometimes to be true to her nature, and she's a strong woman. Gabriel is very protective and dislikes her going anywhere without him."

Mikhail slammed a barrier in his mind immediately to prevent Raven from reading his mind. Gabriel had to be concerned with their enemies striking at the women, yet he had allowed Skyler to go into the woods. Or had he? "Did you mention to Gabriel that you were coming to see us?"

Skyler scuffed the toe of her hiking boot on the kitchen floor. "I may have forgotten. He was busy helping Francesca bake gingerbread for the house we're making for the children."

Raven basted the turkey in silence, turning over Skyler's fears in her mind. "What is it Francesca struggles against, Skyler?" she asked.

Skyler shrugged. "What do *you* struggle against?"

Mikhail was slightly shocked at the human teenager's reply. She sounded far too mature for her age, and that in itself was a danger he hadn't considered. If Gabriel and Francesca had thought about the potential risks before bringing Skyler to their homeland, they would have mentioned her maturity to him. She was only sixteen—a virtual baby by their standards, yet her experiences had aged her far beyond her physical years. She looked—and spoke—like an adult. Would her voice trigger the terrible needs of the Carpathian male? If so, and she restored color and emotion to her lifemate before she could meet his needs, that might be as dangerous to the male, her not being ready to be with him, as not finding her at all. Often, being a lifemate—and intense sexual awareness and need—came before love or even affection.

Raven touched his hand—a small gesture, but it was enough to lighten his spirits. She smiled at the teenager. "I struggle with the terrible burden of so many lives depending on my lifemate and with the knowledge that so many want him dead. And I struggle with my own inadequacies. There are still aspects of Carpathian life I can't come to terms with, and it could present an added danger to my lifemate."

She smiled up at Mikhail. The stark love shining in her eyes put an unexpected lump in his throat. "I have never, not once, not at any time, regretted that I am lifemate to this man. I think you underestimate your own abilities, Skyler. You're a very courageous young woman. You are far too young to contemplate taking on a Carpathian male, but eventually you will come into your full power and potential. Most of the men have no idea what they've gotten themselves into." She winked at the girl. "It takes time to develop skills and power and most of us were too young, but we learned quickly by utilizing the mind bond."

Skyler nodded. "Gabriel and Francesca teach me by sharing information telepathically, and I've found it's so much more detailed than conversation. I can see how you'd learn so much more quickly."

"How's Baby Tamara doing?" There was a hitch in Raven's voice, and she didn't dare glance at Mikhail. Of course he would notice—he always noticed.

His gaze found hers—sharp—aware, sliding over her body with too much knowledge. She hadn't told him she could get pregnant—that it was the optimum time and if they let this chance slip by, it could be years before it happened again. Ashamed of being afraid, of the sorrow and grief that accompanied taking such a chance, Raven looked away from him. "And sometimes, Skyler, I struggle against my own weaknesses and fears, but never—*never*—against being lifemate to Mikhail."

Skyler, obviously an empath, moved closer to Raven, as if by her close presence she could reduce the sadness. "I guess we all do that, don't we?" She looked to Mikhail for confirmation.

Mikhail touched Raven's hair, his fingers gentle. *Raven, my love.* His voice in her mind was infinitely tender. *Every Carpathian male knows when his mate can conceive. You are everything I have ever wanted. When you are ready—only when you are ready—do we try again.* He smiled at Skyler even as his gaze caressed his lifemate. "You are a very wise young lady."

Dark clouds crossed the moon, momentarily darkening the skies and casting macabre shadows into the large kitchen. The silhouette of a large wolf passed in front of the window, as if a large creature had crept onto the wraparound deck and paced just outside. Instinctively, Mikhail, Raven and Skyler turned toward the second window just over the sink. Skyler gave a muffled cry as a great shaggy head, fur black and eyes glowing nearly red, stared at them through the glass.

"Stay inside," Mikhail commanded as he shimmered—first into transparency—and then dissolved into vapor, streaming across the kitchen to slide under the door out into the night.

The wolf abruptly disappeared leaving the two women staring into the darkness.

"It could have been Gabriel or Lucian checking up on me," Skyler ventured. "They often take the form of a wolf."

Raven shook her head. "They would have come to the house, talked with Mikhail, let you know they were worried."

Skyler put a comforting hand on Raven's arm, a difficult thing for Skyler to do when she disliked being touched or touching. "There are a dozen Carpathian males within hearing distance. If the prince needs help, he has only to call out."

Raven smiled at her, one hand to her throat. "Of course he can. Whatever is out there doesn't really feel like a threat to me." In the form of an animal, it would be easy enough for a skilled Carpathian—or vampire—to hide his intentions, but Raven wasn't going to acknowledge that to Skyler. "Mikhail will let us know if something is wrong. In the meantime, I have this turkey in the oven. Have you ever cooked before? It's been such a long time for me and I could use a hand."

Skyler laughed. "We have a housekeeper. She does the cooking and lets me into the kitchen once in a while, but doesn't really like anyone underfoot. She pretends it doesn't bother her, but I know it does."

"Of course you'd know. You're an empath, you can feel what she's feeling. That must be uncomfortable for you."

Skyler shrugged. "Gabriel and Francesca are helping me to learn how to shut myself off. So far I haven't mastered it yet, but I think eventually I'll be fairly good at it. Francesca helps to guard me during the time she's awake."

"Why do you want them to convert you?"

"They're my family. I want to be with them."

"And they've both exchanged blood with you?"

Skyler nodded. "It will only take one blood exchange for the conversion. Gabriel explained it to me, but he wants me to wait until I'm older. He thinks I need more time to think about it, but I know what I want. As long as the prince doesn't insist on me taking a Carpathian male as a lifemate, then I'm going to try to get Gabriel to do it as soon as possible."

"It's difficult on your body, Skyler," Raven warned. "There's a great deal of pain they can't protect you from."

"I can feel that you're uneasy, Raven. There's something you aren't telling me."

Raven had been completely human, just as Skyler had been, and she was a strong psychic talent. She could feel that the Carpathian blood had already heightened Skyler's awareness and senses. The girl was intelligent and powerful, with well-developed psychic talents. Raven still remembered those days, the sensation of someone else's emotions creeping over her, sharp and terrible. There was a scent to evil and depravity, and an empath as sensitive as Skyler needed to be sheltered from the continual assault on her. It was no wonder Gabriel and Francesca had both given her blood to help shield her.

"I think you already know what I'm not telling you, Skyler. You came here not to ask Mikhail for assurances, but to make him aware of your strong objections. Francesca and Gabriel would never try to hide the truth from you—that your true lifemate can bind you to him whether you are human or Carpathian. If you are the other half of his soul, he can seal you together. You know that, don't you?"

Skyler blushed as she nodded her head. "I'm sorry, I shouldn't have lied. Sometimes I learn more by pretending ignorance. Most people don't give a teenager credit for intelligence or maturity. I can ask for protection against him, can't I?"

Raven studied the too-old eyes. "Have you met your lifemate?"

Skyler shook her head, her gaze shifting away. "I have nightmares. I hear a voice sometimes and I'm afraid." She hesitated. "When I was a little girl and men did things to me, I would scream and scream in my mind. I would hear a voice calling to me. At the time I just thought I was going crazy. But I know he's out there somewhere and he's looking for me." She rubbed the spot between her eyes. "I didn't want to come to the Carpathian Mountains because I was afraid he might be here, but Gabriel and Francesca wouldn't leave me behind. Gabriel said I needed protection at all times."

Raven's heart jumped. "He said that?"

Skyler nodded. "He's been strange lately, not wanting Francesca or me to go anywhere without him. I can see she gets upset, but she doesn't say anything. She works at the hospital and some of the shelters and I often go with her, but he doesn't like her going anymore."

Raven busied herself with the turkey, basting it again, even though there was no need. "When did Gabriel start becoming upset about the two of you going off alone?" She kept her voice casual, but out of the corner of her eye, caught the girl's sharp glance.

"Since the attack on the prince."

There is nothing to fear out here, Raven. One of the males taking a run in the forest decided to drop by, but saw we had company. I am going to see my brother. Do not allow Skyler back into the forest without an escort.

Should I be worried about something, Mikhail?

Raven felt the brief hesitation. *I do not know. I am uneasy, but have no real reason to be.*

Be careful, Mikhail. Be safe. Tell Shea I'll see her soon. What are you discussing with Jacques?

Raven felt his sudden amusement. *The image of Gregori dressed up as Santa Claus surrounded by children.*

2

Mikhail leaned down to kiss Shea Dubrinsky on her cheek. "You look just a little bit pregnant there, lady."

His sister-in-law blew strands of bright red hair from her face. "You think? If I don't have this baby soon, I swear I'm going to explode."

"You're also looking harassed. Is something wrong?" He glanced around the room looking for his brother. Jacques rarely strayed from the side of his lifemate.

A slow smile lit Shea's face. "He's in the kitchen—baking."

Mikhail's eyebrow shot up. "I do not believe I heard you correctly."

"Yes, you did. My back has been hurting on and off tonight and I'm having trouble with this recipe. The worst thing is—Raven, Corrine and I came up with most of the recipes for everyone. They were childhood favorites of Raven's and a few I remembered. Corrine filled in the rest and now I can't manage it. It's a little humiliating to admit, but I seem to be emotional. I keep crying, so Jacques took over the baking."

Mikhail choked and turned away to politely clear his throat. "*Jacques* is *cooking?*"

Her smile widened. "Well—trying to. We aren't having a lot of success at the moment and I think he's learning new words." She tilted her head, the bright red hair falling around her face, emphasizing her classic bone structure. "Perhaps you'd like to give him a hand. Go on in, he'll be happy to see you." She rolled her eyes. "His Majesty has given me strict instructions to lie down for a while."

Mikhail gave her a fierce scowl. "Then do so immediately, Shea. You are not in labor, are you? I will call Francesca and Gregori to examine you."

"I'm a doctor, Mikhail," Shea reminded him, "I'd know if I was in labor. I'm close, maybe the start—but it isn't happening yet." She waved as she started toward the concealed door leading to the basement. "I promise to call them if I need them. I'd never take a chance on anything happening to the baby. I'm just tired."

Mikhail watched her disappear before making his way through the spacious house to the kitchen. He stopped abruptly in the doorway to stare at his brother in shock. A cloud of white particles choked the air and fell to the floor like snowflakes. The powder was everywhere, on the floor, on the dishes and bowls covering the counters and in the sink. Jacques stood at the counter, an apron over his clothes, a dusting of white powder over his face, in his eyebrows, tipping his lashes and coating his midnight black hair.

Mikhail burst out laughing. Even with Raven, who constantly amused him, he rarely gave a deep, roaring belly laugh, but the sight of his usually grim-faced brother covered in flour and sweating bullets was too much even for him.

Jacques spun around, eyes glittering with warning menace—a fierce scowl, which should have intimidated the strongest and most courageous of warriors, on his face. A thin white scar circled his throat and marred his jaw and one cheek, bearing evidence of his past. It was extremely rare for a Carpathian body to scar, as they healed so easily, but Jacques's body bore evidence of brutal torture and probably always would, the thin scar around his throat and the jagged round hole in his chest marking where a stake had been driven deep into his body. "It is not funny."

"It is very funny," Mikhail insisted. It was the first time Mikhail could recall his brother ever looking so disconcerted. Shea had not only saved his life and his sanity, but had brought Jacques back to life with her joy and humor. Mikhail shared the image of his brother with Raven. Her soft laughter filled his mind and poured over him with love woven deep in the rich tones. There was such intimacy with Raven, an intimacy he knew his brother shared with Shea—and it had saved Jacques's life. For that alone Mikhail would always treasure his sister-in-law. "Even Raven finds the situation amusing."

"*Raven*. Do not say her name to me right now. She's the one who got me into this." Jacques blew upward in the hope of clearing the flour from his lashes.

"I believe it is Shea you are helping," Mikhail pointed out, the grin refusing to leave his face.

"Shea was in here crying. *Crying*, Mikhail. She sat in the middle of the floor and wept over a stupid loaf of bread." Jacques scowled and looked around him, lowering his voice. "I could not bear to see her like that."

For one moment, Jacques looked utterly helpless, rather than the dangerous hunter Mikhail knew him to be.

"Who would have ever thought bread could explode? The dough rose up over the top of the bowl and became a volcano, crawling down the sides and across the counter until I thought it was alive." Jacques shook a flour-covered piece of paper. "This is the recipe and it says cover with a tea towel. The tea towel did not have a prayer of containing that horrific bubbling brew."

Mikhail pressed a hand to his side. He hadn't laughed so much in a hundred years. "I can only say I am glad I did not see it."

"Quit laughing and get in here and help me." There was an edge of desperation to Jacques's voice. "For some reason that makes no sense to me at all, Shea is determined to make this bread for the party. She wants it braided and made into loaves and put in the oven. This is my third attempt. I thought people went to stores and bought this stuff."

"You hunt vampires, Jacques," Mikhail said. "Making a loaf of bread cannot be that difficult."

"You say that now, only because you have not tried it. Come in here and close the door." Jacques rubbed his arm across his face, smearing more white flour everywhere. "I need to talk to you anyway." He touched Shea's mind to ensure she was a distance away. His gaze shifted back to the dough, avoiding his brother's piercing eyes. "Shea's been corresponding with a woman who thinks she may be a distant relative."

The smile faded from Mikhail's face. "How long?"

"About a year. The woman found photographs in her attic and apparently is into genealogy. She wrote Shea asking if they could be related. She thinks Shea is Maggie's granddaughter rather than her actual daughter. Shea wanted the pictures of her mother and wrote back to her."

Mikhail stifled the groan that threatened. "Jacques. You know better. How could she have tracked Shea in the first place? We are careful not to leave a trail."

"It is not so easy now with computers, Mikhail, and Shea needs them to do research. The path takes her many places."

"She should never have answered the contact."

"I know. I know. I shouldn't have allowed it, but she's given up so much to be with me. I'm not like the rest of you and I never will be. You know that." Jacques's gaze shifted from his brother and pain rippled in the air between them. "She deserves better and I wanted to give her one small gift. Corresponding with someone who may be a relative and who claimed to have pictures of her mother—how could she possibly resist? And I could not bring myself to deny her."

"You know it is dangerous. You *know* we cannot leave paper trails. Any contact with humans is risky, especially one on paper. It endangers all of us."

Jacques slammed the dough hard onto the counter. "Shea has been researching why we lose babies even as she is carrying our child. She has investigated the deaths of thirty children under the age of one. What do you think that does to her?" His fist smashed into the dough. "She is about to give birth and she is terrified. She tries to hide it from me, but I have never been able to allow her even limited privacy." The admission of weakness shamed him, but Jacques wanted his brother to know the truth. "She carries the burden of my sanity every moment of her existence."

"Jacques, you love Shea."

"Shea is my life, my soul, and she knows it, Mikhail, but it doesn't make it easy to live with me. I cannot stand other men near her. I'm always a shadow in her mind, and I have nearly driven us both crazy worried about this pregnancy—worried about her. If something should happen to her . . ."

"Shea will give birth and the child will be healthy," Mikhail said, sending up a silent prayer that it was true. "Both Francesca and Gregori will see to it that Shea is in good health. I have every faith that you will not allow anything to happen to your lifemate during this time."

"She begged me to promise to stay in the world and raise my child should something happen to her." Jacques raised anguished eyes to his brother. "After her own terrible childhood, you can understand why she would need such a reassurance from me." He rubbed the bridge of his nose, looking tired and weighed down with sorrow. "You know I cannot exist without her. She is my sanity. It is the only thing she has ever asked of me, and I cannot safely comply no matter how much I wish to reassure her."

"What do you know of this woman?"

It was the only apology Jacques could give his brother. By allowing Shea correspondence with a stranger, a human unknown to their species, he had opened the door to endanger their entire race. "The woman, Eileen Fitzpatrick, sent Shea numerous photos of Maggie, Shea's mother, and a woman Eileen claimed was Maggie's half sister. Apparently the half sister is Eileen's grandmother."

"How would she find Shea?"

Jacques shrugged. "The internet. Shea researches genealogy all the time."

Mikhail's eyebrow shot up. "Why? She is no longer human, but Carpathian."

"And apparently genealogy still matters in her research, Mikhail," Jacques said. "Not only for Shea, but Raven and Alexandria and Jaxon—all of them as well as our families too. Gregori and Francesca take care of the Carpathian genealogy necessary for the research into the deaths of our children."

"And this Eileen found her through the genealogy site Shea was working on?" Mikhail prompted.

Jacques nodded, all too aware of Mikhail's continuing censure. "Eileen was born in Ireland, but she happened to be living in the States. I asked Aidan to look into her discreetly. She owns a bookstore in San Francisco and spends a great deal of her time looking up her family history in the library, using their computers."

"So at least this woman is far away." Even as he said it, Mikhail scowled, his dark brows coming together and thunder rolling over his face—cracking in the skies. He read the truth on Jacques's face. "She's here?"

"She will be at the inn this evening. Eileen asked Shea what she would be doing for Christmas, and Shea thought it was natural for a human to be cooking food for the children and having a Christmas party, so she mentioned it."

Mikhail watched Jacques roll a wooden pin over the dough to flatten it. "I like nothing about this party. I should have told Raven no. It has occurred to me many times lately that sooner or later our enemies will strike at our women and children. What better time than now with so many of us gathered in one place?"

"Raven was right, Mikhail. After the last attempt on your life, we all needed something to lighten our spirits. I will admit I have been more uneasy than usual, but I suspect it is because Shea is so close to giving birth."

"Maybe," Mikhail said. "Maybe."

"I do not think our enemies will be able to rally this quickly to launch another concentrated attack on us, Mikhail, but of course we will take every precaution." Jacques rolled the dough out with more enthusiasm than expertise and threw a handful of flour over it, sending another cloud of white particles into the air.

Mikhail couldn't pull his fascinated gaze away from the mess his brother seemed to be making. "Where's Shea now?" He lowered his voice another notch.

"She had better be lying down. She is not feeling very well."

"It is possible the vampires cannot rally, but the society working against us has always found us here in the mountains. They have spies, and it is entirely possibly they have heard of this gathering. One or more of the locals has to be in their pay. And of course, we cannot ever forget that the dark mage is still alive."

Jacques's black eyes glittered with menace, ice cold and dangerous, reminding Mikhail that even with Shea to steady him, Jacques was a lethal and frightening man. The white flour dusting his face and on the tips of his lashes did nothing to soften the threat emanating from him. "We should begin regular sweeps through the town and surrounding areas and see what we can pick up."

Mikhail inhaled sharply, and immediately began to cough as the flour particles entered his lungs. He liked most of the townspeople, had a genuine friendship with a few, and the idea of continually invading their privacy was repugnant to him, even though he knew it was necessary.

Jacques scowled at him. "I can handle it myself."

"You know as well as I do that our enemies have been able to find a way to keep us from detecting them. Continual scanning or taking blood deliberately to monitor them will only rob our neighbors of the privacy they are entitled to. We would not want such a deliberate invasion of our privacy." It was an old discussion, but one he always made to remind himself of right and wrong.

"We have more than a right, we have a duty to protect our women and children, Mikhail, and I shouldn't have to tell you that. You nearly lost Raven three times now."

Mikhail tamped down his own rising beast. It would do no good to turn a useful discussion into an argument. Jacques had a valid point—as did Mikhail, and in the end, they would do what they had to do to protect their race.

Mikhail studied his brother's snarling face. Jacques had been on the verge of insanity when Shea rescued him, and after all the years with her, the demons still lurked very close to the surface. At the slightest hint of danger to Shea, the monster rose quickly, and anyone too close to Jacques could be in danger.

"Jacques?"

They both turned at the sound of Shea's voice. She stood in the doorway, her bright red hair tumbling around her face, drawing attention to her emerald green eyes and the dark circles beneath them. *I felt your need of me. What is it, wild man?* She sounded gently amused even as she wrapped him up in her warmth and love.

Jacques took a breath, calmed his mind, suddenly aware that he had inadvertently tightened his hold on Shea. *I seem so sane to others, yet I am still fragmented without you. I am sorry I disturbed you.* His voice was intimate and gentle, a wash of emotions as he took in the love of his life. Something softened inside, eased the roaring of the demons rising in him—the deep rage that never quite left him no matter how hard he struggled to overcome his past. He would never be easy in the company of humans as his brother was, and he couldn't quite suppress the thought that invasion of privacy was well worth not only his own peace of mind, but his need to keep this woman safe for eternity.

"You look so cute," she said.

Jacques blinked, avoiding his brother's eyes. "Carpathian men are not cute, Shea. We are dangerous. I look dangerous at all times."

"No, honey," Shea insisted, brushing past Mikhail as she entered the room. "You look so cute, I wish I could take your picture and show all the others how sweet you really are."

Jacques turned on her, swooping her into his arms before she could protest, dragging her close, so that the flour rained down on her, looking like snow in her bright hair, coating her clothes and dusting her chin. He buried his face in her neck, deliberately rubbing against her as he nuzzled the warm bare skin, teeth nipping playfully.

Shea laughed, her arm circling his head, protesting even as she held him to her. Jacques's much larger frame nearly dwarfed her, and his long hair, tied with a leather thong, fell down his back in a wild mane in which she tangled her fingers to hold him even closer.

Mikhail felt emotion welling up, choking him. A rush of affection, of genuine respect and love, flooded Mikhail, and he shared that small moment with Raven. Shea O'Halleran had not only saved his brother's life and sanity, but she, with Gregori, had saved Raven and their child. Shea looked so fragile, with her small, delicate features and rounded stomach, but he knew the core of absolute courage and commitment, the iron will that lived and breathed inside her. While human, she had been a renowned surgeon and researcher, a brilliant woman as a human, and now, as a Carpathian, she turned all those skills to her work to try to save their species from extinction.

"In all honesty, Jacques, the flour and the apron does take away from the image of the dangerous predator," Mikhail said, joining forces with her immediately, teasing his younger brother though laughter and jokes were rare between them these days.

Jacques turned back to his brother, far more relaxed than he'd been seconds earlier. Shea's calming influence had the tiny red flames receding from his eyes and the snarl gone from his lips. "Do not encourage her," he protested.

Mikhail winked at Shea. She remained locked in his brother's arms, her head thrown back against his chest, uncaring of the white flour covering both of them. "I do not think she needs much encouragement at all," Mikhail said. "I will leave you to your baking as I have to go. I want to talk to Aidan and Julian."

You are checking on the woman claiming to be related to Shea.

Mikhail barely inclined his head. "Julian was friends with Dimitri at one time, wasn't he?"

"A few hundred years ago," Jacques said, eyes suddenly wary. "Why?"

Mikhail shrugged. "I have not seen Dimitri in his true form in decades. While he has been here, he stays in the body of a wolf. Many of the hunters use the body of animals to aid them when they are close to turning."

He made you uneasy, Jacques said as he nuzzled Shea's neck and pressed a gentle kiss over the pulse beating there.

A little. I am just being careful. We are all a little on edge with this unfamiliar gathering. Too many of our women and children in one place make me feel as if they are all vulnerable. I wish Julian to make contact with him to reestablish their friendship.

It is difficult to monitor one's childhood friends.

Yes, it is, Mikhail agreed with a soft sigh.

"Jacques!" Shea took his hand. "Our baby is kicking very hard. He's been so quiet tonight that I was getting worried."

Jacques placed his palm over her rounded stomach in order to feel the thump of the baby's foot. He smiled at her. "Astonishing. A little miracle."

"Isn't it?" Shea turned her face up to his for a brief, tender kiss. "I couldn't help but be worried. I've been talking so much with all the others working on the problem our people have keeping our children alive, and we all have different theories."

"What is your theory, Shea?" Mikhail asked, his dark eyes compelling an answer.

She pushed back strands of red hair and turned her head to look at him, her face suddenly looking drawn and tired. Strain showed in the depths of her eyes. "Gregori and I both believe there are a combination of things causing the miscarriages and deaths. Soil is our mainstay. It rejuvenates us and heals us and without it we cannot exist for too long. We have to lie in it whether or not we allow ourselves to be completely buried. The composition of the soil has changed over the years. This place less than others, but chemicals and toxins have leached into the richness of our world and just like with other species, I believe it is affecting our ability to carry our children."

Mikhail tried not to react. Soil. His people could not exist without soil for long. Even those who left the Carpathian Mountains sought the richest soil possible in other lands, but it made sense. Birds had problems with their young from contaminations, why not Carpathians? He suppressed a groan— a sudden reaching out to Raven. He wanted her to try to have another child—he needed her to try again—to lead the women after so many had suffered so much. The last thing he needed to do was to discourage her just when she was able once again to conceive. The time came so rarely, and an opportunity missed meant too many years lost.

"You have been testing our soil?" he asked.

Shea nodded. "There are pollutants even here, Mikhail, in our sanctuary. We've been testing every one of our richest deposits to find the best soil possible for our pregnant women. And that is only one piece of a very complex problem."

Hearing the note of anxiety in her voice, Jacques's hand came up to tangle in the hair at the nape of her neck. "You have made amazing progress, Shea. And you will find the answers to this puzzle."

"I believe I will," she agreed, "but I'm not so certain we'll be able to do very much to counteract the problems. And I'm not sure if I can find all those pieces to the puzzle and the answers in time to do us much good." Her hand rested over her unborn child.

It was the first time both men had ever heard Shea sound so defeated. She was very single-minded—analytical. Always determined to keep moving forward believing science could provide answers.

She is tired, Mikhail. She will never give up.

Mikhail forced a small smile, deciding, with Shea so close to her time, it wouldn't be a good idea to bring up the infant-mortality rate. He needed a safe change of subject. "I forgot to mention a very important detail in tonight's festivities. Raven informed me it was my duty as prince of our people to play Santa Claus."

Jacques choked. Shea coughed behind her hand.

Mikhail nodded. "*Exactly.* I have no intentions of putting on a white beard and a red elf suit. However . . ." He grinned evilly.

"What are you planning, Mikhail?" Jacques asked suspiciously. "Because if you think to pass this distasteful task on to your brother . . ."

The shake of Mikhail's head was slow and deliberate, his dark eyes dancing with mischief. "I have decided there is a use for a son-in-law after all. I will inform my dear son that it is his duty to wear the red suit."

Jacques opened his mouth to speak, but nothing came out. Shea pressed her hand hard against her lips, her eyes wide with shock. "Not Gregori. He'll scare all the children," she whispered as if Gregori might hear her. "You aren't really going to ask him, are you? None of the Daratrazanoff brothers can play Santa. It would be . . . wrong."

Jacques's smile widened, and Mikhail felt his heart squeeze hard in his chest.

What is it, my love? I will come to you if you need me. Raven's soft voice filled Mikhail's mind with warmth.

Nothing now that you have touched me, Mikhail reassured her through their telepathic link.

"I want to be a little mouse in the corner watching when you ask him," Jacques decided. "Let me know when you are going to his house."

Shea glared at her lifemate. "Don't encourage him. Gregori is the bogeyman of the Carpathians. Even now, the children whisper his name and hide when he comes near them. I'm not certain I've ever seen the man smile."

"I would not be smiling if I was wearing a red suit and white beard," Mikhail pointed out.

"But you're gentle, Mikhail, and Gregori is . . ." She frowned trying to think of a word that wouldn't be considered offensive.

"Gregori," Jacques supplied. "It is a wonderful idea, Mikhail. You do plan to tell his brothers? They will want to be there when you let him know the important part he will be playing in this night's activities."

Shea gasped. "You two aren't serious are you? Joking is one thing, but Gregori as Santa boggles the mind."

"I must have some pleasure from all of this, Shea," Mikhail pointed out. "Just the thought alone of the look on his face when I tell him it will be his job to dress in this ridiculous manner is enough to improve my mood considerably despite the festivities."

Shea put both hands on her hips. "Carpathian males are such babies."

"I am off to see Aidan," Mikhail announced. "Good luck with the bread, Jacques." He looked around the kitchen. "I trust you do not have to use human ways to clean up the mess."

Shea laughed and waved him away. "The bread is going to be wonderful." When Mikhail left the house, Shea turned to face Jacques. A slow smile lit her face and mischief danced in her eyes. "Did you have fun talking manly Carpathian secrets with your brother? Because you do know you're going to tell me everything he said, don't you?"

"Am I?" Jacques turned her fully into his arms. "I can feel how tired you are, and your back is still hurting. You should be in bed resting." He interspersed his order with small kisses all over her face trailing to the corner of her mouth. All the while his body subtly pushed hers so that she walked backward toward the kitchen door.

"You aren't going to get out of telling me, no matter how charming you are," she warned. "And I'm turning white. How did you get all that flour all over the kitchen? It looks like a war zone."

"It *is* a war zone," he groused. "I do not know how these people do this on a regular basis." He continued to nudge her gently through the hall toward the bedroom, concerned by the way her body—and mind—felt so worn out.

"I promised Raven I'd get the bread done for the party and I'd do it in a human way," Shea reminded him. "I can't let her down."

"First of all, little red hair"—Jacques swept her up into his arms—"you are about to have a baby and Raven would not care if you could not get the bread to bake. Fortunately, you have me and I will get it to work if it is the last thing I ever do."

Shea smiled at the determination in his voice, relaxing against him. "You love a challenge."

"Humans do this kind of thing every day. I should be able to do with it with no problem," he groused, and moved with dizzying speed through the house to the tunnel leading to their chamber beneath the earth.

The room was beautiful, with shimmering light from multicolored crystals layered over the walls. The soil was dark and rich, the best they could find, imported from one of the healing caves. Other than having a dirt floor, and a large dug-out resting place in the soil, the room looked like a regular bedroom. There were candles in sconces on the walls flickering in a multitude of lights, filling the room with a soothing fragrance.

Jacques floated down into the deep depression in the earth and laid Shea gently into the rich soil. He stretched out beside her and leaned over to press a series of kisses along her rounded belly. The baby thumped his mouth and he laughed out loud.

Shea treasured the sound of his laughter, the warmth in his eyes and the love in his fingertips and mouth as he teased the baby into kicking more vigorously. Her fingers tangled in Jacques's long hair as he laid his head against her stomach to talk to the baby as he did every evening.

Come out and join us, son. We have waited long enough.

"More than long enough," Shea said. "I want him where I can hold him in my arms. Tell him that when you're giving him his nightly bedtime story."

Jacques pressed another series of kisses over her rounded tummy. "Your mother is telling you enough is enough. You will have to learn the codes women use, son, when they talk to men."

"We don't have codes," Shea protested with a small laugh. She closed her eyes, savoring the feel of Jacques's strength. The smile faded. "I'm really afraid. I really am. I can't bear the thought of losing him. Already he's such a part of me, Jacques. And I fear I'm the one holding up the process, not him. He wants to be born and I want to keep him safe."

Jacques lifted his head to look at her, nuzzling her neck, breathing warmth over her cold hands. "You carried him when we thought that to be impossible. He wants to survive. We have a strong bond with him. You know we cannot feed our children in the natural way our ancestors have done, and you have developed a formula that has kept Gabriel and Francesca's child alive as well as Dayan and Corrine's little one. You have made great strides, Shea."

She pressed her fingers to her eyes. "I thought Raven was being so selfish not wanting to try again after she lost her baby, but now I understand. Our son moves and kicks and even more. I feel him puzzling things out. We can communicate with him. I didn't know we'd be able to do that—to get to know him before he was born. He knows us just as we know him. If we lost him now, it would be so difficult, Jacques—so difficult—perhaps unbearable, just as I know it was for Raven and all the other women who came before us."

"Don't do this to yourself. Our baby will be born healthy and he will survive."

Shea turned her face into Jacques's chest, closing her eyes again against the pain in her heart. "Will he? Once he leaves the shelter of my body, will he survive, Jacques? And if he does survive, what kind of a future is he facing?"

"Tamara appears to be quite healthy, as does Jennifer."

"And while we go to ground, another has to watch over our children. Does that make sense to you? Why can't our children go to ground as they should? Even if the soil contains some toxins, shouldn't they be able to tolerate the very thing they will come to need?"

Jacques stroked back her hair, sensing the rising fear in her. The persistent ache in her back told her birth was near—was inevitable. She couldn't protect their son much longer. "Our people have gathered in joy for this occasion, Shea." He kissed her soft skin, his hands tender as he continued to tangle his fingers in her brightly colored hair. "Each Carpathian, near and far, has one true purpose at this time—to see to the life of our son. He will survive. The blood of the ancient line runs in his veins."

She rubbed her face over Jacques's heart. "I know. Every day I think about how you survived those seven years—trapped so close to the earth that would have saved you, starving and tortured and so alone—but you refused to succumb." She lifted her chin to look into his dark, tormented eyes. "He has *your* blood, my beloved wild man. And *your* iron will. I'm so grateful that you're my lifemate, Jacques. If anything keeps our son alive, it will be because you are his father." She rolled onto her side and framed his face with her hands. "I feel you in him."

He groaned softly, a small smile flirting with his mouth. "Then God help us when he is a teenager, Shea. Have you ever been introduced to Josef?"

"Byron's nephew? The young rapper?"

"That would be the one. I fear we have been given a brief glimpse of our future."

Shea laughed, the worry fading from her eyes. "Oh, dear. I believe Josef has been practicing to perform tonight."

"It will be almost as good watching Mikhail's face when Josef does his rap tonight as it will be watching Mikhail break it to Gregori that he is expected to play the part of Raven's Santa Claus."

Shea shook her head, her green eyes dancing. "You're a very bad man, Jacques."

"I keep telling you that, but you persist in thinking I am cute and cuddly."

The desire and hunger in his eyes took the breath from her lungs, and Shea circled his neck with her arms. She pressed kisses along the corner of his mouth. "I'll pretend around the others, Jacques, if that makes you feel better, but when we're alone, you'll just have to put up with my thinking you're extraordinarily cute and cuddly."

He heaved a sigh, amusement creeping into the depths of his eyes. "I have no idea how I ever existed before you came into my life."

Her answering smile lit up her face. "I feel the same way about you, Jacques." She laid her head against his chest over his heart. "I wouldn't be able to get through this without you. I've never been so afraid, but you steady me."

He stroked a caress over her shiny ribbon of hair. "And all this time I thought it was the other way around." Above her head, the smile faded from his face, leaving the lines deep and his eyes once more dark with worry. "This woman we are meeting tonight, Shea . . ." He hesitated, trying to choose his words carefully. "You must be very, very careful. We cannot have her suspecting even for a moment that you are anything but a human."

Shea rolled away from him in a small spurt of temper. "You know, Jacques, not all humans are monsters. Look at Slavica and Gary and Jubal. Why should she be suspicious that I am anything but human? Do you think most people go around thinking there are vampires and Carpathians in the world? I thought I had a rare blood disorder for years and I'm a doctor."

His fingers shaped the nape of her neck. "Do not be upset, Shea. I have a duty to protect our people."

"You mean Mikhail didn't like me contacting her."

"I mean I didn't like it. Maybe I have had you to myself these years and the idea of sharing you with an outsider sets my teeth on edge."

She turned her head in time to see his white teeth snap together, very reminiscent of a wolf. She began to laugh again. "I love you very much, Jacques Dubrinsky. I really do." Her hands framed his face. "Are you ever going to get over that silly jealous streak?"

"Is that what it is? I thought it was feelings of inadequacy—that you might suddenly wake up one morning and realize I am more trouble than I am worth." He turned his head to brush her fingers with a kiss.

"That could never happen, Jacques, not in a million years. Don't worry about Eileen Fitzpatrick. I'll know if she's lying to me."

"You want family so much, Shea, maybe you will not be able to tell."

"I have a family, Jacques. You are my family. You and our son and Mikhail and Raven and Gregori and Savannah. I am not deprived. And despite my hormones running amok, I would not endanger our loved ones for a stranger even if she is a relative. I had hoped she would have stories of my mother's childhood, but if not, I will only be disappointed, not devastated."

Jacques turned his face away, happiness bursting through him like the unexpected eruption of a volcano. "Roll over," he instructed gruffly. "I'll rub your back for you." He couldn't look at her, couldn't face her when his vulnerability would be so starkly naked. Men just shouldn't be so dependent on their women, not even lifemates.

"I have a beach ball for a stomach, Jacques," she pointed out. "There's no rolling."

"On your side then," he suggested.

Shea was silent for a long moment before catching his face in her hands and forcing him to look at her. "You're my life too, Jacques, my entire world. All those things you feel for me—I feel for you."

"Even though I can't let go of you and always have to be a shadow in your mind?" He forced himself to look into her eyes—into her heart—to read her mind.

He found unconditional love.

"Especially because you stay with me. I treasure that in you." Shea traced his mouth with her fingertip. "A woman cherishes being loved, Jacques, and you know how to love me."

3

"What is that terrible racket?" Mikhail said in greeting as Aidan Savage opened the door to the large cabin. Mikhail hadn't seen him in several years and he couldn't help smiling as he clasped Aidan's forearms in a warrior's greeting.

Aidan's unusual eyes glittered like two ancient gold coins. "You honor us, Mikhail, with your presence."

"Please tell me Byron's nephew, Josef, is not already here visiting." Mikhail hesitated in the doorway, the lines in his face deepening in disapproval.

"This seems to be the place to gather. Josh has a new video game Alexandria designed and everyone wants to try it. Josef is definitely here," he added in warning as he stepped back to allow Mikhail entrance.

Mikhail paused, one foot in the air. "Perhaps we should have Byron send for him immediately."

Aidan smirked. "You say that as if he's a vampire."

"I would rather face a vampire. I was hoping he might stay in Italy. Byron probably brought him along as a practical joke."

"He is rather entertaining once you get past his exuberant manners," Aidan said.

Mikhail's dark eyebrows drew together. "He draws attention to himself, and does not practice the most basic of our skills."

"I did see him take a plunge off the roof this evening and when he shifted shape, he only made it partway."

"You sound amused," Mikhail said with a sigh. "He is in his twenties. We can no longer afford for our children to take so many years to grow up."

Aidan shook his head. "He's a mere teen in our years, Mikhail. We have lived far too long in the world of humans and have begun to think as they do. Our children deserve a childhood, Mikhail. I enjoy watching young Joshua grow. Josef is happy and healthy . . ."

"Joshua is human. Josef is not. And the world has become a much more dangerous place for our kind, Aidan," Mikhail pointed out. "We are surrounded by enemies and our women and children are the most vulnerable. We need Josef and in order to ensure his safety, he must learn the ways of our people. Can he even weave his own safeguards?"

Aidan nodded. "You are right, of course. I have been concerned ever since the concentrated strike against us, since the assassination attempt on you—that our enemies will decide to strike against our women and children. I will speak to Byron about Josef's training, make certain he is being schooled adequately to prepare for an attack."

"It has occurred to me that our women must be prepared as well." Mikhail lowered his voice, taking Aidan by the arm and leading him to a quiet corner away from the ruckus in the living room. "We have always protected the women."

"They are of the light," Aidan said. "They do not have the darkness needed for the kill."

"So we all thought, but self-preservation and dwindling hunters may bring new needs. Times change, Aidan, and frankly, we are facing extinction. We can no longer rely on the old ways. We have to be prepared to face the new challenges with new ideas."

"The ancient ones may not like your progressive thinking."

A small smile softened the hard line of Mikhail's mouth. "I think the ancient ones are far more progressive and flexible in their thinking than we are. However, I do have some concerns with this Christmas party Raven has insisted on."

"Alexandria thought it was a good idea as well," Aidan said. "It gives her a chance to meet with the other women. She also feels it will aid Shea in giving birth. With so many of us here, there is a better chance the child will survive."

"Shea is close, this night or the next. Raven, like Alexandria, feels the party will create a feeling of family among the Carpathian couples and give hope to the remaining males, especially with the female children and Shea having a successful birth."

"Alexandria is in the kitchen. Joshua and Josef invented a high-speed mixer to help her prepare the dish she is making for tonight's event. I think they wanted out of peeling potatoes. You will have to come in and meet her, although she's a little anxious about meeting you."

"Me?" Mikhail scowled. "Why would she fear meeting me?"

"I have heard you can be intimidating," Aidan said with a small grin.

Mikhail's smile was slow in answering. "These women." He shook his head, then paused, looking suddenly hopeful. "Unless it was Josef . . ." He watched the furious battle taking place on the television screen. Alexandria's brother Josh, curls bouncy on his head as he used a controller, laughed aloud as his character did a backflip over Josef's character. Josef, directing his character with his mind, had the man whirling around so fast he nearly tripped over his own feet.

"Alexandria came up with this game? It is good practice for Josef—for any of our people," Mikhail said. "How did she think of such a thing?"

"Josh and I like to play video games together and we make poor Alex watch us all the time. She still does graphics for a video company and when she realized I could direct the characters with my mind, she came up with this game for Josh and me as a Christmas gift."

"She is a very intelligent woman. Are you thinking of marketing these games?"

"Yes. So many of the others have seen it and wanted it. Alexandria already has ideas for a couple more of them. Because we have Josh, who is human, and Falcon and Sara have the seven children they adopted, she is planning to set the game up to be able to use controllers if necessary. It gives us one more thing we can interact with and appear human. We'll be able to play online with one another as well."

"It is a wonderful idea. Hopefully, it will help bring us all closer when we live such distances apart." Mikhail rubbed his jaw. "I need to speak to your brother about Dimitri. As I recall, Julian and Dimitri were fairly good friends in their youth."

"Yes they were," Aidan said. "Is Dimitri here?"

"He has come from the forests of Russia to join us, yet he remains in the form of a wolf most of the time and is prowling the woods. If you see Julian before I do, have him make contact. I believe he knows Dimitri better than any other Carpathian. They may have even exchanged blood after a battle. I want Dimitri monitored while he is in such close proximity to our women."

Aidan's head went up alertly. "You are concerned that Dimitri has turned?"

"We can no longer count on reading minds and feeling the disturbance of power or evil. The vampires could very well send an enemy into our camp. I do not believe Dimitri has turned, but I am concerned that he is struggling. With so many women close to him, it is possible he will have the necessary hope to continue his struggle, or it will push him in the wrong direction. It is just better to be careful."

"He has long battled the vampires alone in his area," Aidan agreed. "Too many kills so often take its toll on the hunter."

Mikhail sighed. "I cannot save them all, Aidan."

"No, but you do what is necessary for saving our people, Mikhail, and that is all you can ask of yourself. Come meet my lifemate."

Mikhail followed Aidan down the long hall toward the kitchen. "Raven asked me to play Santa Claus. St. Nick. You know, the character in the red suit with the long white beard."

Aidan halted so abruptly that even with his graceful, flowing strides, Mikhail nearly ran into him. "You are going to play Santa Claus?"

Mikhail shook his head, wicked amusement gleaming in his eyes. "That is what my son-in-law is for."

"Gregori?" Aidan's white teeth flashed. The clouds shifted and the light from the moon spilled across the Carpathian turning his hair and eyes to an ancient, antique gold. "I have to be there when you tell him."

"I suspect his house will be overrun with spiders, mice and a few birds," Mikhail said with evident satisfaction. "I would enjoy meeting your very talented lifemate. Lead the way. Just the thought of Gregori in that ridiculous getup has lightened my mood considerably. Alexandria will not find me in the least intimidating."

Aidan hesitated, his hand on the door. "Alexandria first knew of our race through the vampires. She was captured along with her little brother. The vampire chained her and fed on her, wanted her to kill her brother and both would feed on him. She still has nightmares. I catch echoes of them when she is in between our sleep and waking. Joshua no longer remembers, but she doesn't want to hide what we are from him. And that means he has to know we are hunted. It was courageous of her to come here—to put aside her fears and meet the other women."

"Have you discussed having children?"

Aidan shook his head. "Not yet. She is well aware of the mortality rate of our infants and she lost so much so young."

Mikhail nodded. "Gary has mentioned that it is possible that the closer the birth of the baby is to conversion, the less likely it is that we will lose it. He thinks the longer the women are Carpathian, the more likely miscarriages will occur and the less likely there will be female children, but why that would be we have no answers, especially as Francesca had a daughter."

"At least we have Joshua, who is more of a son than a sibling to Alexandria. So far she has been unable to conceive, so there has been no choice for us one way or the other."

Mikhail continued to look at him, straight in the eye, a relentless, driving command. Aidan sighed. "I will discuss it with her."

"You do that. Our people need every child, every female we can possibly get at this point. Our hunters are desperate, Aidan."

"I was one of the desperate hunters, Mikhail," Aidan said quietly. "I know my duty to our people."

"Aidan!" Joshua come up behind him and tugged at his arm. "Aren't you going to play with us? Josef put the game on pause so we could wait for you."

Aidan affectionately ruffled the boy's hair. "In a minute, Josh. Alexandria hasn't met Mikhail yet. He is the leader of our people, a very important man."

Josh's eyes widened and he stared up at the prince.

Mikhail looked down at the boy with his slight build and head of curls, at Aidan's hand tugging at a curl, and he felt a sudden ache in his chest. He wanted another child. One that looked at him the way the boy was looking at Aidan. He wanted a village filled with children, with their laughter and their bright eyes and hope shining on their faces.

His gaze rested on Josef who had followed Joshua, and for the first time he felt kindly toward the boy. Josef had gained a few inches in height, taking on more of the look of the Carpathian male with broad shoulders, but he was still gangly, as thin as a rail, and with his black hair cut into spiky sticks with the tips dyed blue, he looked like a bizarre scarecrow. "Hello, Josef. It is good to see you again."

The boy looked scared for a moment, and then he flashed a cocky grin. "You too, Your Royal Highness. Are we supposed to bow?"

Aidan smacked him on the back of his head with a low warning growl, and Mikhail scowled, his black eyes glittering with sudden menace. The house pulsed with sudden energy and the walls undulated.

Josh pushed open the kitchen door and ran. "Alex! There's someone here."

At the fear in her younger brother's voice and the danger shimmering in the room, Alexandria whirled around with preternatural speed, her body a blur. The high-speed, souped-up mixer was in her hands, still on. Garlic-cheese mashed potatoes splattered onto the walls and ceiling. One glob hit Mikhail squarely on his left cheekbone. Alexandria gasped aloud and stood frozen, holding the mixer upright—sending more potatoes flying around the room. Her horrified gaze remained fixed on the prince.

For a long moment there was only the sound of the mixer and the potatoes striking surfaces all over the room—and the prince's wide chest. Josh giggled. Josef let out a strangled cough, and both boys grabbed their midsections and doubled over laughing. The sound galvanized Aidan into action. He waved to knock the power out of the mixer, and moved across the room with dizzying speed to remove the appliance from Alexandria's hands, placing himself between his lifemate and his prince.

For a moment there was only the sound of the boys' laughter. Alexandria twisted her fingers in the back pocket of Aidan's jeans. *I cannot believe I did that. Whatever is he going to think of me?*

It was obvious she was trying to hold back her own laughter even though she was mortified.

Aidan turned slightly to brush his knuckles down the side of her face gently, all the while keeping a wary eye on the prince. *It was a small accident, nothing more,* he assured her. He could feel his own laughter bubbling up. It was difficult to stand still and keep a straight face with gobs of cheesy garlic potatoes speckling the prince's clothes and his left cheek.

Mikhail's mouth twitched and he covered his lips with his hand. "It is unnecessary to stand in front of your lifemate as if I might incinerate her on the spot for decorating my clothing, Aidan."

"Is that how I look?" Aidan's eyebrow quirked upward.

Josh nodded, still laughing. "Like you're going to hit someone."

Aidan held up the mixer, aiming it toward Josh. "I am thinking about it."

"Point it more toward Josef," Mikhail suggested.

Alexandria cleared her throat, trying to sound sincere when she really wanted to laugh. "I'm terribly sorry," she said aloud to Mikhail. "The mixer got away from me."

"You look a great deal like your brother," Mikhail pointed out as he calmly brushed the potatoes from his face and chest. "Fortunately, I am Carpathian and these things are of little consequence—other than to provide amusement for our younger children." His black eyes narrowed, turned dangerously green-yellow—a wolf's eyes—glowing as his gaze settled on Josef. A low growl rumbled through the room, impossible to tell where it came from—but distinctive all the same.

Josef swallowed his laughter and straightened up, moving away from Mikhail. The prince kept his face like stone, although amusement welled up, threatening to spill over. How long since he'd heard the sound of young children laughing? He needed to spend more time with Falcon and Sara's adopted children. The young always brought hope and the ability to see with fresh excitement the world around them. He needed another child in his home, clinging to his leg and looking up at him the way Joshua was looking up at Alexandria.

Mikhail. Skyler wishes to go home. Do you come back to escort her, or should I? Raven's voice interrupted his thoughts. He had much to do, but so did Raven. "I had hoped to speak with you some more, Aidan, but Skyler is in our home and needs escorting back to her home. I will return as soon as I am assured she is safe."

"I was about to go over to see Desari," Alexandria said quickly. "I can get Skyler safely home. I'd like to walk in the fresh air anyway. I'm a poor cook. . . ."

Joshua snickered. "She's always been bad. Burns everything."

Alexandria tugged on one of his curls in retaliation, laughing softly. "Sadly, it's true. I'm a terrible cook, but perhaps you and Aidan can rescue the potatoes."

Mikhail's hand stopped in the act of brushing the last of the white globs away. "Me? Cook?"

"I can do it," Josef said. "I've wanted to try out the mixer. Watch this, Josh." He waved his hand and the bowl of mashed potatoes rose in the air. The bowl jerked awkwardly as it made its way past Aidan toward Josef and Mikhail, almost head level with the prince.

Aidan caught it before it could get more than halfway across the room. "Alexandria worked hard on this—ah—stuff."

"Stuff?" Alexandria echoed. "And it was Josh and Aidan who were supposed to rescue the potatoes."

Mikhail stepped back and turned to glare at Josef. "I hope you were not thinking to drop that on my head."

Joshua erupted into another fit of giggles. "If Alex made it, stuff is a good word to use, Aidan."

"Hey now!" Alexandria produced a mock glare. "Pipe down or you'll be doing the cooking."

I can escort young Skyler back, Aidan offered.

I need some peace, Alexandria told him. *I love Josh, but the video games, mashed potatoes and Josef are a little much right now.* Her mind brushed up against his with love and warmth. *I'm perfectly fine.* It wasn't altogether true. It was impossible to hide anything from her lifemate, and Aidan was well aware she had faced coming to the Carpathian Mountains with trepidation.

My only love. I will come with you.

You will stay and entertain the prince. I really need some alone time. She loved Aidan with all of her heart, every cell in her body—her very soul, but it was sometimes difficult for her to accept that he could know her every thought. It was bad enough that she felt inadequate at times, and very leery of the other Carpathians—it shamed her. She hated that Aidan knew her smallness.

Not smallness. You have every right to fear for Joshua's safety. Few have been captured by a vampire and survive. Aidan leaned down to press a kiss against the back of her neck. *You are my world.*

As you are mine.

Alexandria flashed a small smile toward the prince. "It's an honor to meet you—even covered with mashed potatoes. Please stay and talk with Aidan. He's been looking forward to some time with you. I'll see that Skyler gets back safely." Before either man could protest, she smiled brightly at Josh. "Would you like to come with me?" She resisted the urge to send a compulsion against walking with her. She really needed the quiet of the night.

"Josef and I are playing the new game, Alex," Josh said. "It's really cool."

"I'm so glad you like it! I thought you would."

"Alexandria . . ." Aidan's voice trailed off. He didn't want to further embarrass her by protesting her going alone. It was a short walk to Mikhail's home, and since quite a few Carpathians had returned and were scanning continually for enemies, she should be safe—*but* . . . Aidan sighed. He didn't like her out of his sight. "I do not mind walking with you."

I just need a little air. I don't know why I'm so nervous around everyone, but I am. I need to work things out on my own this time—please, Aidan—understand. Alexandria sent him a flood of reassuring warmth.

She loved Aidan with all of her heart, but she had always been so independent. In San Francisco, he had seemed more relaxed and easygoing, but since making the trip to his homeland, he'd been on edge. Joshua and Alexandria both were having nightmares, Josh in his sleep, Alexandria just as she was waking. The terrifying dreams were heightening her own fears and that was rousing Aidan's protective instincts, making him try to hold them even closer. She nodded to the prince, blew Aidan a kiss and skirted around the boys, donning her jacket and gloves as she hurried out the door before Aidan could change his mind.

Alexandria dragged in a lungful of cold, crisp air and turned her face up to the sky. Small snowflakes fluttered down, floating with lazy whirls, turning the sky white and muffling the sounds around them. She held out her hands and opened her mouth to let the flakes drop on her tongue. Life with Aidan was unbelievable. He treated Josh like his own son, and her like a queen. She had no idea why, since coming here, she felt sad and inadequate.

Even worse than that was her growing fear. It was silly and very unlike her, but sometimes she found herself looking into shadows, her heart lurching with dread. It had to be the nightmares, the revulsion she felt whenever she remembered the feel of the vampire's touch, the way his tongue felt rasping on her skin and the pain of his teeth as he tore at her neck. She pressed her hand to the spot burning in her throat. He was dead. Aidan had killed him and he would never be coming back. Not for Josh—and not for her. So why was her throat throbbing in the exact spot the vampire had torn open?

Alexandria shook her head to clear her mind. This was Christmas and they were going to have a beautiful one. She didn't get snow in San Francisco and Joshua was thrilled with being in the Carpathian Mountains. He'd met so many of the men online and couldn't wait to see them in person. She wasn't going to ruin it for everyone because of silly nightmares.

Determined, she pushed the too-vivid memories away and began to walk along the faint path leading to the prince's home. She knew the way, had seen it a hundred times in Aidan's head and had memorized every step. He had wanted her to feel comfortable in his homeland and he had shared every memory with her, giving her a virtual map so that she could move around with ease.

The wind touched her face with gentle fingers, flakes coating her hair. She should have drawn up her hood, but she felt free, excited to be walking in the night surrounded by the thick expanse of forest, breathing in fresh, crisp air, peace stealing into her at last.

Skyler was waiting impatiently on the porch. "I think it's ridiculous that

Gabriel and Lucian don't want me walking around by myself," she said. "I managed to make it over here all by myself, before anyone noticed I was gone. No one makes Josef wait for an escort." She wrapped her scarf around her neck and tossed the ends over her shoulders with a small dramatic sniff. "I am *so* not *ever* going to have someone telling me what to do all the time. Gabriel and Lucian are the *worst*."

Alexandria frowned. "Josef contacted you and teased you about this, didn't he?"

"He called me a baby. I walked over here by myself and I certainly can walk back by myself." She dashed her hand across her eyes.

"Josef can be most annoying, can't he? I think you should make it a priority to ask him to show you how he turns into an owl."

Skyler regarded Alexandria with a suddenly thoughtful gaze. "Really? You think I'd enjoy that?"

Alexandria nodded. "I think it will make your day."

A slow smile lit up Skyler's face. "Thanks for the tip. Raven says hello. I think her turkey gravy wasn't coming out the way she wanted."

"Neither did my mashed potatoes. At the moment, the prince is wearing them."

Skyler halted abruptly and blinked up at Alexandria. "Wearing them? The potatoes? Did you throw them at him?" A slow smile transformed her face. "I wish I could have been there."

"I wish I hadn't been there. Josh ran to me frightened and I turned around, forgetting I had a high-speed mixer in my hand, a mixer Josh and Josef had revved up for me. The potatoes splattered all over Mikhail."

She met Skyler's gaze and they both burst into laughter. The sound drifted through the forest, rising upward to meet the floating snowflakes. Somewhere an owl hooted, the sound lonely. A wolf answered, the howl long and drawn out, as if he might be calling to a long-gone pack.

"Alexandria," Skyler said, and abruptly fell silent.

Something in her voice caught Alexandria's immediate attention. "What is it?"

Skyler shrugged, attempting to look casual. "A silly question really. Do you ever hear the earth screaming?"

"Screaming? The earth?" Alexandria echoed.

"I know it sounds crazy. I shouldn't have said anything, but sometimes"—she wasn't about to admit how often since she'd been in the Carpathian Mountains— "I hear screaming."

Alexandria shook her head. "I've never experienced that. Have you talked to Francesca about it?"

Skyler shrugged. "I'm probably being silly. I do that a lot, sort of a left-over childhood thing."

The wolf howled again, and this time another answered it. It sounded like a challenge. Alexandria glanced into the darkened forest interior, a small shiver running down her spine. She began to walk faster.

"I played your new video game," Skyler said. "It was awesome. Josh and Josef and I play late at night online. Some of the men join in too. I'm just as fast as Josef. Gabriel thinks it's because he and Francesca gave me their blood, but I think it's because I can focus so well. I have the ability to just go into my mind and it's like I'm in the game. Josh told me you were working on something special for us. Is it finished yet?"

Alexandria pressed a hand to her burning throat. The nonexistent wound throbbed as if it was still raw and the cold affected it. "Almost. I was hoping to give it to Josh for Christmas, but I wanted to tweak it a little bit. The graphics are almost too real. I think I may tone them down a bit. Do you play with others beside Carpathians on the internet?" She knew Joshua wanted to, but she didn't allow him the contact with anyone on the internet other than the Carpathians Aidan knew.

"Josef does. He plays all sorts of games with people from all over the world. He has a really high ranking. He's really good on a computer too. He can hack into anything—at least he says he can. Once he hacked into some Russian site he swore was a message center for a group of assassins for hire."

Alexandria frowned. "Is he telling these stories to Josh?"

"Probably. Josh really looks up to him because he's so good at video games."

"Great. That's my fault."

Leaves rustled and branches hit together with a muffled clack. The sound sent a shiver down Alexandria's spine. The path to the house where Gabriel and Francesca were staying was little used and much more overgrown than the trail leading to the home of the prince. Alexandria tried to watch the forest, but there were rocks and long stems from wild bushes making the ground uneven and treacherous. If Skyler hadn't been with her, she would have taken to the air and returned home.

"Josef is going to get himself into trouble. Hackers can be traced."

"I told him that." Skyler deliberately stepped on several small puddles so that the thin ice crunched beneath her feet and cracks veined out toward the expanse of snow-covered ground. For good measure she jumped onto the next one, splattering ice and dirt out onto the snow. "He thinks because he's Carpathian he's invincible."

"Well, he isn't." Alexandria tried not to look at the spreading mud over the pristine snow. It looked too much like the long shadowed arm reaching for her—reaching for victims—in her nightmares. She took a deep breath, trying to push down the familiar dread building. Movement caught her eye and she glanced once more toward the forest. She was sure she saw a large wolf slinking along parallel to them.

"What is it?" Skyler asked. She had gone suddenly silent as well, her gaze sweeping the forest as if she too sensed an enemy.

"I don't know, honey, but take my hand."

Skyler swallowed hard, staring at the gloved hand. "I'm sorry. I can't. I never touch people. I feel everything they're feeling and I overload."

Alexandria dropped her arm to her side. "I'm the one who is sorry. Don't look so distressed. I should have remembered that about you. Just stay closer to me. Has Gabriel or Francesca ever flown with you before?"

"Of course. I'm not afraid of it. I like to fly. Did you see something?"

"I'm not certain, but if I did, I want to be able to get into the air fast."

Skyler took a careful look around. "I don't see anything."

"Neither do I—now." *Aidan. I'm a little uneasy. I thought I saw a wolf, but I don't know for certain. I'm going to get Skyler to safety, but meet me at Gabriel's house. I don't want to come home alone.*

I will be there. Aidan's voice was warm, reassuring. *Do not take chances, Alexandria. Gabriel or Lucian will be coming to meet you.*

I don't know them. She sent her preternatural senses out into the region around her, trying to ferret out anything that might be the scent of an enemy. Wolves were abundant in the forest, but stayed away from the Carpathians. Many of the men had a preference for shifting into wolves. See-ing one shouldn't be enough to trigger her alarm system, but it was shrieking at her.

"We challenged the males to a paintball game," Skyler said, continuing walking toward the cabin. "It was Josef's idea and should be fun, but Josh and I can't shapeshift and neither can the other children. I told Francesca we need rules. Like no shifting and no communication between the males; oth-erwise, they have too big of an advantage, don't you think so?"

Leaves rustled again, just a whisper of sound. A twig broke. Alexandria turned her head toward the sound. "There's no wind. Something or someone is moving in the trees just to our left, Skyler. I think we should take to the air. I thought I glimpsed a wolf again through the trees. He was quite large, and moving at our pace, but it could have been my imagination."

"Well, then, we're both imagining the same thing," Skyler said, moving closer to Alexandria. "I sometimes can feel things near. Let me just . . ."

"No!" Alexandria said sharply. "You have no way of knowing if it is a friend—or monster. If you open your mind, you might lead him right back to you. I've called Aidan to us and he is sending Gabriel as well." She spoke as Skyler stepped into another ice-covered puddle. The crunch was loud in spite of the snowflakes, and muddy water spurted out in a long spray.

A shadow fell across the snow, a dark stain looking all too familiar to Alexandria. An arm reaching—stretching obscenely—growing as if made of rubber. Insubstantial—shadow only—yet she could see it reaching toward Skyler, slithering over the rocks and through the shrubbery like a snake. If it hadn't been snowing she would never have seen, but with the white back-ground, the fingers of the hand appeared bony and gnarled, an old hand with talons for fingernails.

To her horror, the dirty water from the puddle moved as well, ringing a tall tree like a dark noose, cutting into the trunk as if it were a garrote.

"Skyler!" Alexandria leapt forward even as Skyler instinctively jumped back. The tree splintered and cracked, the earth rocking beneath them. Al-exandria could have dissolved into vapor, but she refused to leave the teen-ager exposed. She hurtled herself at the girl, intending to use her blurring speed to sweep them both to safety, but the shifting ground split, taking Skyler from her grasp. The best she could do was shove Skyler as far from her as possible, hoping to keep her from being smashed by the tree toppling down.

Even as the tree trunk groaned and splintered and the earth rolled, there was a terrible sound as the tree broke in half, knocking the top from the tree and driving the large, heavy branches straight down on them. Alexandria felt the blow to her head, the branch that picked her up and swept her down with alarming force. For one moment she thought she heard voices murmuring in a foreign language quite close, but she couldn't make out what they said. She tried to turn her head, to see where Skyler was, but the movement brought on pain, a haze of stars that faded away to leave a black, yawning void.

"Alexandria?" Skyler tried valiantly to control the tremble in her voice. *Gabriel! Francesca!* She called her family to her, a shattering cry that swept across the night. *They're coming.* She was pinned down under a heavy branch, her legs trapped, one hurting so much she had to fight back nausea.

Baby. We are coming. Hold on. That was Gabriel, his voice strong and vibrant, a rock to lean on.

You're hurt. Francesca's tone was gentle and soothing. *Tell me how bad.*

They were trying to reassure her, distract her, but Skyler felt danger surrounding her, pressing in on her with a suffocating presence. Her leg was bleeding, spilling bright red blood across the snow. If she moved, bones rubbed together with excruciating pain, radiating through her entire body until she broke out in a sweat.

Something moved in the bushes quite close to her. She couldn't turn around to see what was creeping up on her. Hot breath exploded on the back of her neck and she cried out, trying to fling herself out of reach. Fur brushed her face as a huge wolf pushed through the maze of branches to inspect her wound.

Skyler froze, held her breath as the animal turned to look at her. The eyes were a brilliant ice-blue, startling in the midst of thick black fur. "I know you," she whispered aloud, her heart in her throat. "I've seen you before, haven't I?"

The wolf shifted. The heavily muscled, furred body gave way to a tall, broad-shouldered man with shining black hair streaming down his back. His face was harshly sensual, a carving of stone with lines etched deep and a strong jaw and masculine mouth. His eyes were so blue they seemed to burn over her.

"Why would they allow you to come out alone?" he asked. "It was foolish of them. If they do not guard you better, I will no longer allow you to stay with them."

As he spoke, his gaze held hers, but she could see he had separated himself from his body, becoming a strong dominant spirit. She felt his presence the instant he entered her body. She wanted to scream, to fight, to evade his spirit. He moved through her with speed and purpose, repairing the damage to the nick in her artery, the bone, and lastly the flesh. All the while she shared his mind. Knew his memories, his implacable resolve.

Dimitri. Relentless hunter of the vampire. Protector of wolves and lifemate—to Skyler.

"No!" She shook her head vigorously in denial. She wouldn't be anyone's lifemate, least of all this man with his burning eyes and his dominant nature. She couldn't conceive of being with a man so hard, so utterly certain of himself. Emotions poured into her, colors vivid and bright, so bright she feared she might go blind—or maybe it was his fear, his colors, his emotions. She couldn't separate herself, as if by entering her body to heal her, he had wrapped himself around her insides, burrowing deep to find her soul.

His mind opened to hers, a dark place of haunting sorrow and hundreds of years of dealing death without remorse. He acted swiftly, violently—with absolute resolve. If those deaths were a part of his aching loneliness and terrible sorrow, she couldn't tell. This was not a man to be swayed from his path. He followed his enemies with tenacity and ruthless, unrelenting persistence. Violence was his world and she would never—*never*—go back to that kind of life. She wouldn't survive. As it was, just brushing his mind and finding the darkness, the coiled demon waiting—and willing—to strike, was so terrifying she wanted to retreat to that safe place inside her where no one else could go.

"You will not." He made it a decree, pulling out of her body and back into his own. "You need blood."

She shook her head. "Gabriel and Francesca will give it to me."

He turned his ice-blue eyes on her, his look so cold it burned her skin. Skyler shivered, unable to look away from him, so frightened—of what—she wasn't certain. That this man would change her life for all time. That he would consume her, swallow her whole. That he was harsh and unyielding, a man without compromise. Skyler had fought hard to belong, to come back to life when she had retreated so far. Dimitri wasn't evil, not like her father, but he was a man of violence, of strong emotions and passions, yet capable of turning it all off so that he felt nothing at all.

She shrank away from him when he reached for her mind. Skyler felt the steady, relentless pressure and tried to build a wall, thick and made of steel, impenetrable, but he was too focused and too strong. She raised her arms up defensively as he reached to draw her close to him, a small sound of fear escaping before she succumbed to his control.

Dimitri drew her into his arms, allowing pleasure to burst through him, comfort—even peace. In hundreds of years he had never expected to find her. Necessity had made him cold—brutal even, but the warmth of her body, the sound of her voice, the softness of her skin brought hope where there had been none. He could barely see with the colors so bright—barely think with emotions he hadn't experienced in centuries.

He bared his chest and whispered a command. His blood would replace that which had been lost and it would encourage rapid healing. He sensed the others coming with all speed, but he closed his eyes and gave himself up to the ecstasy of her mouth moving over his skin, taking what he offered her, forging an even stronger bond between them. Because he had so little time, he bent his head to her neck and took what was rightfully his—not enough to convert—enough only to always find her, always be able to reach into her mind.

He raised his head and looked into the eyes of Gabriel Daratrazanoff. Legend. Swift, merciless killer.

4

Gabriel let out a long, slow hiss of anger. "How dare you touch her. She is a child and under my protection."

Dimitri slowly shifted the weight of his body, whispering a command to stop his blood from flowing into Skyler. He rose to his full height, his lifemate in his arms. "She is no child, or she would be unable to restore colors and emotions. She is my lifemate and subject to the laws of our people."

"She is human—a teenager, barely sixteen," said Francesca. "It is true they mature faster than our children, but she is too young." Francesca brushed aside Gabriel's restraining hand and held out her arms. "Give her to me before you bring her out from under your enthrallment. I don't want her to wake frightened."

Gabriel stepped forward, his black eyes glittering with lethal menace. "I remember you, a boy who ran from us many long years ago."

Dimitri turned his head to look at the legendary twin, blue eyes clashing with black like sharpened rapiers. "I am no longer a boy nor do I run from anything—or anyone."

The earth shuddered, rolled slightly. "Have a care, Gabriel," Mikhail snapped materializing with Aidan beside him. "Alexandria is trapped beneath these branches." He searched frantically through the branches of the fallen tree for a glimpse of Alexandria.

Aidan simply burst through the labyrinth, pulverizing the wood into dust until he reached her. She lay still and white, her face turned toward him, blood trickling from her temple to streak her blond hair.

Aidan's heart nearly stopped beating. For a moment there was silence, as if the world itself stopped breathing. Images of Alexandria filled his mind. Her smiling at him, gaze filled with love, her voice teasing him, the touch of her fingers on his skin when he first woke and faced that moment of memory of his life before her existence.

He raced forward like a madman, breaking through branches as if they were mere twigs, his throat tight and his heart pounding. Her skin looked translucent, cold, her lips blue, and she was utterly still, so much so he couldn't detect breath or heartbeat. She had to be dead. He halted abruptly, his hand on his own heartbeat. No air moved through his lungs. His chest refused to rise and fall. His own heart stuttered.

He could not go on without her. There was no life without her. No happiness. Nothing but endless nights that dragged into a black empty void. He couldn't do it again—go back to the place he'd been before he found her.

"Aidan!" Mikhail caught his arm and gave him a little shake. "You look as if you are in a trance. We have to lift the heavier branches off her."

Alexandria moaned. The sound was barely discernible, but it was enough to throw off the chilling fears that haunted Aidan. He leapt forward to smash his way to her side, waiting for Mikhail so they could easily float the remaining branches from her body.

Crouching low, Aidan swiftly moved his hands over her, grateful that she responded to his touch with her eyelashes fluttering. Her lids suddenly opened and he found himself mesmerized by her gaze. "Aidan. I knew you would come. Is Skyler safe? I tried, but . . ." She trailed off in an attempt to turn her head toward the teenager, but she groaned and her lashes fluttered down.

Once again, Aidan's heart reacted, faltering, his breath catching in his lungs.

"She has a concussion," Mikhail said gently, laying a restraining hand on Aidan. The man seemed about to come apart. "Easily fixed, Aidan. Francesca is here with us, one of our greatest healers, should there be a problem." Mikhail struggled to keep from racing away to Raven, certain now his worst fears were confirmed. Their enemies were attacking their women and children. It took centuries-old discipline to remain where he was. He was slightly shocked that Francesca had not hurried to them, offering her services as a healer, rather than blocking Dimitri's path and trying to take the girl from him.

Aidan stroked back Alexandria's hair. "I will heal her myself." He wanted no other to touch her. He had failed to protect her, his greatest and most cherished treasure, and he needed to merge with her, hold her close to him. He needed to watch her closer and see that no harm ever came to her.

Aidan glanced over the top of Alexandria's head to the two men standing so close, the heat of the argument shimmering in the air around them. He closed his arms protectively around Alexandria and allowed his body to slip away, leaving only white-hot energy, pure selfless spirit. He streamed through her with a quick examination before finding the bruise, already swelling, blood pulsing and pushing to leak out. He repaired the damage, making certain that she was completely healed before once again coming back to his own body and the furious argument taking place so close to him.

Aidan held Alexandria in his arms, rocking her gently back and forth all the while keeping a wary eye on the two combatants.

Gabriel took another aggressive step toward Dimitri. "Would you like to tell us *exactly* how this happened and how you came to be here at the same time?"

Dimitri bared his teeth. "Push me too far, Gabriel, and I will take her with me now."

Gabriel's hand shot out, fingers locking around Dimitri's throat. "Do not threaten me or my family."

Dimitri didn't so much as flinch beneath the crushing fingers. His gaze focused on Skyler's face. "You are my lifemate." His voice came out husky, but it came out all the same.

"Stop! Stop, Dimitri. Gabriel, let him go now." Francesca tugged at Gabriel's arm. "He has a blood bond. Before you could kill him, he could take her with him. Please, Gabriel. Show some sense."

"Gabriel." Mikhail's voice was calm. He stood beside Dimitri. "Release your daughter's lifemate. Of course you are protective of her, but this is the man who is the other half of your daughter's soul. If you kill him, you condemn her to a half-life. Be reasonable."

Gabriel didn't feel reasonable. He wanted to tear out Dimitri's throat. The man was stealing his child. The demon rose swift and fast, roaring to be set free. He could feel Dimitri's rising rage in direct proportion to his own.

"We all need to calm down," Francesca said. "Dimitri, give her to me. She's my daughter now, and you have no idea of the things she's suffered."

Dimitri's face rippled with anguish—with torment—for just a split second, and then seemed a stone carving once again. "I know *exactly* what she's been through. She is my other half and when she cried out in fear, in rage and in desperate need, I tried to follow the path to her, but I was too far away and she was merely a child and didn't know I was trying to help. She fought me, blocking my every effort. When she suffered, believe me, I was well aware she was suffering and my torment—my humiliation that I must bear for all time is that I was unable to aid her."

Men touching her. Abusing her. Hurting her. Her fragile spirit retreating until even he couldn't find her. The memories would haunt him for eternity, worse than any kill he'd ever made—his failure to protect the one being who it was his duty—his privilege—to protect. He had been so certain that Gabriel could see to Skyler's safety while he stayed away, making certain not to trigger the demon's need for a mate, but Gabriel had failed in his duty as well. "You did not protect her adequately," he said accusingly.

Gabriel and Dimitri stood toe-to-toe, Skyler still cradled in Dimitri's arms, held high against his chest. "What happened here?" Gabriel demanded.

"You think I did this?" Dimitri asked.

"Didn't you?" Gabriel countered. The branches around them trembled and the air thickened.

"I did not. Her leg was broken and she was losing too much blood. I healed her as quickly as possible and gave her the necessary blood to replace what was lost—not that I owe you an explanation."

"Please," Francesca begged again, struggling not to cry. Her tears would set Gabriel off as nothing else could. The situation was explosive. "Let me have my daughter."

"Do not make her ask again," Gabriel said.

Dimitri's face darkened. "You think to keep her from me?"

The earth rolled and the trees around them shuddered. Small red flames began to flicker in the depths of Gabriel's eyes. "She chooses not to be with you."

"She is too young to know what she wants. It is not a matter of choice and well you know it. If you persist, Gabriel, I will claim what is mine now and bind her to me."

Francesca drew in a sharp breath. "Dimitri, no. She cannot go with you and she would suffer more without you. You cannot be that cruel."

"I will not allow you to keep her from me."

Once more, Gabriel's hand shot out and circled Dimitri's neck, fingers crushing in warning. "Give my daughter to her mother." Each word was accompanied with a hiss.

Dimitri didn't release Skyler, but did release the enthrallment so she woke to the turmoil roiling around her. Instantly, she was aware of what transpired.

"Stop it! What's wrong with everyone?" Skyler shouted. She rubbed her wrist as if it ached. "Can't any of you feel it? Alexandria? Francesca? Something is here with us, I can feel the surge of power. Dimtri, put me down now."

Alexandria suddenly pushed Aidan away from her, stumbled and caught herself, one hand pressed to her throbbing head. "Skyler's right. Something is here." She looked around her at the men with their grim, angry faces. "Can't any of you feel it? Francesca?"

Blood still trickled down one side of Alexandria's face as she picked her way through the branches to Francesca. Aidan stayed closed to her, keeping a wary eye on the others, his body posture more than protectively aggressive.

Mikhail crouched low to study the ground around them. He straightened slowly and held up a hand for silence.

The snow continued to fall, soft floating flakes blanketing them. Small rodents rustled leaves along the ground in an effort to find a hiding place.

There was no wind, yet the branches of the trees around them swayed subtly. Gabriel immediately took up a position in front of the women, Aidan on the other side to cage them in. Dimitri handed Skyler to Francesca as if giving her a peace offering.

Francesca lowered Skyler to the ground, holding her close to comfort her. "I feel it too, Gabriel, a subtle power disrupting the natural flow of nature around us."

"The one thing I consistently have nightmares about is the shadow of an arm with long sharp talons reaching for me," Alexandria whispered. "I saw it on the ground, reaching for Skyler."

Dimitri crouched lower in reaction, his eyes flickering with flames. A soft warning growl escaped.

Alexandria shook her head. "It had to be an illusion. What I feared most. I feel the power feeding us, enhancing our fears, our emotions. Gabriel is angry, so is Dimitri, and the energy is feeding that anger."

Francesca nodded, taking a wary look around her. "I can feel it too. It's very subtle. I can't trace it backward. Can you, Alexandria?"

Alexandria shook her head in frustration.

"I feel it now too," Gabriel said, "through Francesca. I will recognize it again if I come across it."

"Could it be one of the children practicing?" Mikhail asked. "We used to make all sorts of mistakes all the time and accidents happened. Although if it is Josef, I intend to box his ears."

There was a small silence. Skyler took a deep breath and clutched Francesca tighter, all the while rubbing her wrist along her thigh. "They're blocking Carpathian blood. It's hard because I carry the blood, but I'm not fully Carpathian. The flow is coming from the direction of the inn and . . ." She broke off, color stealing into her face. "I'm sorry. They caught me and stopped. I should have been more careful. It was no child. I've been doing this all my life and I can tell you whoever it was is very adept, but I couldn't tell if it was male or female."

"Can you usually tell the difference?" Aidan asked.

Skyler nodded. "The touch is different, but this was too subtle—peculiar." She frowned. "Maybe more than one person."

"Why do you say that?" Mikhail asked.

She shrugged. "Parts of the weave felt different to me, as if more than one hand had woven it or as if the person was split into more than one personality. I'm sorry, I tipped them off and didn't get enough information, but whoever it was is a powerful psychic and they touched me." She glanced at Gabriel. "They knew I was there."

Gabriel spat a Carpathian curse beneath his breath. "We know our enemies have joined, mage as well as vampire. And the society dedicated to kill all vampires has spread worldwide."

"And they can identify you?" Dimitri demanded of Skyler.

She remained silent for a long moment, but the ice-blue eyes burned into her, forcing an answer. "Yes." She backed away from him, her small body trembling. One hand came up to defend herself, and the scars of a lifetime of torture were plain to see, both physical and mental.

Dimiti's face hardened into a mask. Only his eyes were alive, glittering with such intensity Skyler had to look away. "Do not do that," he said. "There is no reason to fear me. We have enemies surrounding us and you have been marked, singled out, yet you turn from the one person who has every right to protect you."

"Dimitri." Francesca said his name aloud to gain his attention. "Now is not the time for this. You are welcome to come to our home and talk about things. I know you have a large wolf preserve and are caretaker of several packs. Skyler is very interested in wolves and probably would enjoy hearing some of your stories."

Francesca! This man is threatening to take our daughter from us. Gabriel bristled, although in truth, he was ashamed to be caught so much in an enthrallment that he had nearly killed a man. Not just any man—lifemate to his daughter.

And you did not use every means at your disposal to bind me? He is acting on instinct. She triggered his response to her and what can he do but try to protect and bind her to him? You cannot forbid him seeing her. After all, he will be your son-in-law.

Gabriel did the mental equivalent of a snort. *Not if he's dead. If he lays one hand on her, I will remove his heart.* It was an empty threat now, and he knew it. He couldn't really fault Dimitri, although he didn't think anyone would ever be good enough for his daughter.

Francesca sighed. *We should have had boys. He is her lifemate, Gabriel. He healed her leg and gave her blood when it was needed. He did not bind her or touch her inappropriately. Now stop trying to intimidate him.*

Gabriel sent her a low, rumbling growl of warning, but remained silent.

"You have no choice but to cancel the celebration tonight," Dimitri said. "Skyler cannot go to the inn when she has been identified. And every one of our women would be in danger."

"Mikhail," Alexandria protested. "You cannot cancel our celebration. The children are so excited. We can take precautions. It isn't like we don't live under a threat every single day of our lives. We don't even know what this is."

"Exactly," Dimitri said. "We don't know what this is."

Mikhail shook his head. "We need to be calm and think clearly. Skyler, if this person or persons uses psychic talent again, will you be able to tell, or can they block you now that they know you are close by?"

"I doubt they could stop me from feeling the disruption in nature, but I carry Carpathian blood as well. I didn't feel it right away when Alexandria and I were walking in the forest. She knew something was wrong before I did."

"Not exactly," Alexandria said. "I felt the effects, and bought into the illusion my mind created, but I didn't realize I was being manipulated."

"Skyler cannot go anywhere near that inn," Dimitri decreed, glaring at Gabriel, his body posture clearly challenging the other man.

Before Gabriel could respond, Mikhail held up his hand. "I'll send Jubal to the inn. He's human and is a very strong psychic. Manolito De La Cruz will go with him. His wounds from the battle are healed, and he is a very powerful hunter. Together perhaps, they can pick up any signs of treachery. We will all be on our guard. As for Skyler, she has Lucian and Gabriel as well as you, Dimitri, to look after her. I doubt with the three of you guarding her, anyone could do her harm."

Mikhail beckoned for the teenager to approach him. "You understand the danger you are in? Because our enemies might be able to find you, everyone in your household is in danger. You must be guarded at all times. Francesca, I suggest you talk to her about what a Carpathian male suffers when he is alone without his other half. She should have some understanding of the situation."

Dimitri, you will learn about this young lady, what she has suffered, the trauma in her life, and you will also avail yourself of Raven's knowledge of human children. Mikhail made it a command, emphasizing what he knew Dimitri was fully aware of. Dimitri had to understand the girl was too young and had been through too much for him to bind her to him. "Skyler is cold and Alexandria needs to get back to her home. Thank you, Alexandria, for your quick thinking in shoving Skyler out of the way. She could have been hurt a lot worse."

Alexandria's gaze jumped to the face of the prince. "How did you know?"

He indicated the ground. "I can read signs just as well as the next person. You pushed her away from the larger branches."

"Thank you," Gabriel said. "We owe you a great debt."

"The debt is to Dimitri," Alexandria demurred. "He saved her life by stopping the bleeding." She leaned against Aidan for support. "Whoever was able to find my fears and amplify them did a good job. I was very frightened."

"What made the tree come down?" Mikhail wondered aloud.

"There was a small earthquake right before it began to crack. I felt the ground roll," Dimitri said. "I did not feel a surge of power. It felt natural to me, but we cannot know for certain."

"I was so scared I think I imagined most things," Alexandria confessed. "I was certain a vampire was hunting us, but Skyler didn't feel it." She couldn't help herself, she had to examine the base of the tree. There was no sign of a garrote, shadow or otherwise. The trunk remained untouched and solid, the top having cracked and fallen in the bitter cold. She looked up at Aidan. "It was my imagination. I should have recognized the flow of power. I feel so foolish."

His hand crept to the nape of her neck. "There is nothing foolish about you. Gabriel and Dimitri nearly came to killing blows and neither recognized the flow of power feeding their anger. And when I saw you lying so still covered by the branches, my emotions swung out of control. For a moment, I wanted to seek the dawn, thinking to join you."

Her breath caught in her throat. "Aidan." She brushed her fingertips down his face. "You thought I was dead?"

"It is my worst fear," he admitted, catching her finger in his mouth. "I always fear I might lose you."

"Well, you won't. I'm strong, Aidan, and my skills are growing every day. I would have turned to vapor, but I needed to get Skyler out of harm's way. It seems I pushed her right into a compound fracture."

"If she had remained where she was, she would have died," Dimitri said. "The heaviest piece of the trunk fell directly over where she was standing. I owe you much." He bowed slightly toward Francesca. "I apologize for causing you distress. I did not feel the subtle disturbance in nature and should have. I was consumed with the need to protect Skyler."

"Women cannot be put in a bubble on a shelf somewhere, Dimitri," Francesca pointed out. "We have to live our lives as well as you men do."

Mikhail interrupted as Dimitri opened his mouth in what obviously was another protest. "We cannot cancel the Christmas party. If we do our enemies might guess who in this region is human and who is Carpathian. By cooking and 'eating' food, we appear as normal as the villagers around us. Now that we know there is danger close at hand, we will be able to keep our loved ones safe."

Dimitri's fangs glistened as he bared his teeth and took a step toward Skyler. "She has suffered enough at the hands of human men. I will not allow this."

Skyler pressed closer to Francesca, gathering her courage to defy a man who seemed too tall, too strong—too invincible with his hard face and burning cold eyes.

Do not rouse Gabriel's anger against Dimitri, Francesca cautioned. *Let us handle this.* She smiled at Dimitri. "Every child looks forward to a celebration such as this. Surely you can watch over her with us and give her this opportunity to relax and enjoy meeting the others as she has looked forward to doing for so long. She needs every good memory, every chance at laughter and a childhood she can have. Remember, Dimitri, she was robbed of that when she was young."

"There is no chance I will ever forget," he bit out between his teeth. He turned the full intensity of his glittering eyes on Skyler. "This is important to you? It is not an act of defiance because your lifemate does not want you to attend?"

She sucked in her breath, feeling the impact of his gaze all the way to her toes. She could *never* be with this man. She wanted to scream her denial. She wouldn't be a lifemate to any Carpathian, least of all this man. He terrified her. Desperation filled her with panic.

At Gabriel's soft warning growl, Francesca squeezed her shoulder.

Skyler forced air through her lungs and clutched Francesca's hand tighter. "I would very much like to go." She wouldn't ask permission. She had done enough begging from men. As a child, she'd had to perform vile disgusting acts for food. She'd had to seek permission to sleep, to go to the bathroom, just to speak. Her life had been hell and she would not return to that—she'd rather be dead.

Never, baby. Francesca's voice whispered through her mind. A pure love, unconditional, a promise that would always be kept. *No one will ever hurt you like that again and live. I am your mother now and will protect you with every fiber of my being. Dimitri seems cruel and unfeeling, but in truth, his emotions are too overwhelming for him to control, so to protect you and all of us, he has to push his feelings aside and become a ruthless warrior. It is what he knows.*

And who he is, Skyler said. *He's violence personified. I've seen into his mind. He merged with me and I could see him killing without thought, without remorse. He thinks to control me. To make me do as he says.*

All Carpathian males think that way. They are control freaks. Even our beloved Gabriel. You are too young and although his every instinct is pushing him to take you now, Dimitri is trying to hold back and give you what is yours—time.

"I will confess I do not like it, but I am probably being overprotective. I cannot bear to see—or feel you suffer." Dimitri bowed slightly from the waist in an old-world gesture. "Then you shall go."

Skyler bit back her retort. She would have gone anyway. She didn't need him—a virtual stranger—telling her what she could or couldn't do.

"I was on my way to see Julian," Mikhail announced, deciding it was time to ease the obvious tension. "I know he loves a good time and I wanted to alert him to tonight's main surprise."

"There is a surprise?" Gabriel sounded wary.

"Raven wants St. Nick to show up, dressed in red," Mikhail said smugly. "The children will be expecting it."

Francesca bit her lip, suppressing a sudden smile when Gabriel actually stepped behind her as if for protection. *Big baby.*

Mikhail is up to something. I am not going to play dress-up in red tights.

Francesca burst out laughing. "Santa Claus does not wear red tights, you nut."

Mikhail flashed her a smile. "Do you think Gregori is aware of that? He is, after all, my son-in-law, and has a duty to do as I ask. Red tights might look good on him."

"You wouldn't," Gabriel said, a slow grin spreading across his face.

Dimitri raised an eyebrow. "Gregori? The bogeyman of Carpathians?"

"He'll scare the children, Mikhail," Francesca objected. "You aren't really going to ask him to be Santa Claus, are you?"

"Yes, of course."

"I want to be there. I think Lucian and I need to go visit our younger brother," Gabriel said. "Be certain to let me know when you are going to his house so I can drop by at the same time."

"That's just mean," Francesca scolded laughingly. "And don't you dare tell him Santa wears red tights. Just the idea of Gregori in red tights is enough to scare everyone."

"There are benefits to being prince after all," Mikhail said.

Skyler cleared her throat. "This is a joke—right?"

Mikhail looked smug. "A fine joke on Gregori, little one. I had better go. I have too many things to do. I have sent the word, Dimitri, to all the others that our women and children must be guarded at all times, especially our Skyler."

Skyler tipped back her head to look up at Dimitri. In spite of herself, she had to admit he was handsome, with the face of man, not a boy. His eyes were so alive, so deeply blue they could either burn or freeze one. He lifted both hands and ran them through his shiny black hair, pushing it back away from his face. Muscles flexed and rippled. He was standing away from her, but she felt his fingers touch her own hair, sliding through the silky strands in a slow, intimate way. Her stomach did a curious flip. Far off she heard a wolf howl. Dimitri turned his head toward the sound.

"He sounds so plaintive—so lonely," Skyler whispered, the mournful howl drawing her instant sympathy. She wanted—almost needed—to find the animal and comfort him.

"He is lonely," Dimitri said. He pulled a black cord from around his throat. "I ask that you wear this, Skyler. For me."

Skyler took a step back, but her gaze fell on the necklace he held out to her. The tiny wolf was exquisite, head thrown back, fur black and shiny, eyes deep blue, like sapphire gems glowing at her. She hesitated only a moment, her hand slowly moving towards his until their fingertips touched. Heat spread through her body, warming her in spite of the cold.

Instead of dropping it into her palm, Dimitri pulled the cord over her neck, lifting her hair and letting it settle back around her shoulders. The cord was still warm from his skin and the small wolf nestled in the valley between her breasts. Dimitri reached behind her where she couldn't see and immediately enveloped her in a soft red cape. The cold receded instantly.

"Now you look like Little Red Riding Hood," he murmured as he bent down to draw the hood over her hair.

She inhaled his scent, wild and masculine and unexpectedly familiar. She felt the touch of his lips on her cheek. He left a burning trail to the corner of her mouth, and her body responded with an odd tingling, a heightened awareness, even a reaching toward him. Even as she stood still with his arms caging her in, she felt something within her rising toward him. Before it could break free and respond, he shifted, once more the wolf, springing away from them to run into deeper forest. Skyler caught the small wolf pendant in her hand and held tightly.

She wanted to chase after him. Call him back. Her lungs seized and her heart stuttered. She knew she didn't want a Carpathian male. All of her life she had known what people really felt, really thought—and most of it wasn't good. Gabriel and Francesca gave her respite, provided a safe haven, but Dimitri would take that from her. She took a deep breath and turned away from the path he'd taken.

"I want to go home, Francesca," she said softly, feeling a coward. "Please take me home."

"Of course, honey." Francesca gathered her close, cape and all, and took to the sky, leaving it to Gabriel to shield them from prying eyes.

"Far away," Skyler murmured, "back to Paris." She turned her face up to the snow floating down in endless silence. The world seemed filled with sparkling gems as the moonlight glinted off the ice crystals and snowflakes. She focused on the treetops and the pristine surfaces as they flew to the house, Gabriel close behind them.

"The baby always soothes you," Gabriel said. "Why don't you go see how she's doing?" Their trusted housekeeper-nanny had come with them and was with the children during the day. He kept his hand on Francesca to keep her from stealing away from him.

Skyler kissed them both and, still wrapped in the hooded cape, went to pick up Tamara and hold her close. The minute she was out of the room, he turned to his lifemate with a deep scowl of impatience.

"Did you see that? Did you see him kiss her? Touch her? He did not simply touch her skin, he left his mark on her. I will not stand for this, Francesca."

"Gabriel." She rubbed his arm gently. "He walked away."

"He didn't walk away. He marked her, he gave her blood, he took hers. It may not have been an exchange, but you and I both know he has imparted a warning to every other male to leave her be."

"As he should. As you or any other male would have done with your lifemate."

Gabriel frowned. "She should have a full childhood. He can wait two hundred years just as all Carpathians did in the past. Sixteen. Who ever heard of such a thing?"

"Savannah was but twenty-three when Gregori claimed her," Francesca reminded him. "It is a different world and Skyler is not fully Carpathian. If he waits two hundred years, she might be dead."

Gabriel scowled. "She will be brought fully into our world. She is our daughter."

"We said it was her decision. The blood exchanges were to help her overcome the trauma, not to take away her choice. You're sounding as bad as Dimitri."

"She is our daughter. I am not about to let her be foolish out of fear. I refuse to lose her to human aging or that inconsiderate lout, who, by the way, is not nearly good enough for her. She is ours, Francesca. I love her as much as I love Tamara, and she is under my protection. All this freedom you keep talking about is ridiculous. We all live under certain rules, and Skyler does as well."

"Dimitri showed great restraint in not doing a full blood exchange with her. He could have taken advantage and did not. Our women, until Savannah, do not become sexually mature so quickly. She is, Gabriel, whether you like it or not." Francesca held up her hand when he would have protested. "Of course she's too young to be bound to him, but that doesn't mean that technically it couldn't happen. She has to overcome her past and who knows if she is going to be able to do that. She has scars in her mind that even I can't erase. I can't even find her memories of her childhood before the atrocities started. He has to know that. He has to be prepared to be gentle and kind and patient with her. It's inevitable that they will be together, Gabriel."

He turned away from her, fists clenched. As he turned, she caught the flash of fangs and he suddenly opened his hands—his fingers curling into lethal claws. Gabriel threw back his head and roared with rage. The sound shook the house and in the next room, Tamara began to cry. He whirled back to face Francesca. "She is not going to be forced by this—this *werewolf* into anything."

Francesca gasped at the insult. "You're acting like a crazy man, Gabriel. Is this how it will be with all of our daughters?"

"No daughter of mine is going to be forced into anything." He turned back to her, black eyes blazing with anger.

"Like I was?" Francesca pinned him with her gaze.

"That is entirely different."

"Why? Because it was you? Gabriel, you have to be reasonable about this. We have to handle this right for both of them. Skyler isn't going to be able to accept him, especially if you act like a crazy father sharpening your fangs."

"Gabriel? Francesca? Is everything all right?" Skyler stepped into the room carrying the baby. "Tamara is distressed. She's never heard her father upset like this before—and neither have I." She looked about to cry. "Are you fighting over me? You never fight. *Never.* I'll do whatever you want me to do."

Francesca went to her immediately and wrapped her arm around the girl's shoulders, baby and all. "Of course we argue, Skyler. Just not out loud. I'm sorry we upset you. Adults often have differences of opinions."

"We wouldn't if you'd agree with everything I say," Gabriel groused.

Francesca rolled her eyes at Skyler and flashed a small half smile. "Ignore him. I'm always right and we both know it. And right now, we have things to do that are fun. *Fun*, Gabriel." She flashed him a small warning look. "Skyler, come help me make these gingerbread houses for tonight's dinner. Gabriel is going to help us."

Gabriel took a deep, calming breath, forcing the air to move through his lungs, to remove the swirling rage that seemed to boil in his veins and churn in his gut. He breathed it away and tried to find his center. The last thing he wanted to do was upset Skyler further or get the baby crying.

"That's blackmail," he grumbled, but winked at Skyler. He held out his arms for the baby, took her and bent to kiss the top of Skyler's head. "We were not fighting over you, little human chickie, only over what is best for you. And it was not a fight, simply a heated discussion. We are both in agreement. No man is ever going to be good enough for you and you need to stay with us forever."

Skyler's look of alarm faded and she burst into laughter. "*Forever?* I think by the time I'm eight hundred you would want to throw me out."

"Never, baby," Francesca assured her, brushing back strands of hair from Skyler's face. She touched one of the crescent shaped scars that had failed, even with Carpathian blood, to heal. And Skyler's worst scars were where no one would ever see. "You will always be our beloved daughter."

"You want to lick the frosting bowl instead of giving it to me, don't you?" Skyler teased.

"Too much sugar for you," Francesca said, laughing. "Come on, we don't have a lot of time to put this together. I hope the instructions are easy. I've never actually constructed a gingerbread house before and Raven wanted several to use as the centerpieces for the tables."

"The pressure is on," Gabriel taunted. He kissed Tamara and winked. "Let's see how the female members of the household do."

"Like you're going to get out of helping us," Skyler said, grabbing his hand and tugging. "I'm going to paint your face with frosting while I'm at it. Tamara will love that, won't you, baby girl?"

The anger was gone, but apprehension at the future had taken its place. Gabriel pretended reluctance as his lifemate and daughters dragged him into the kitchen, laughter bubbling around them and driving away a little bit of the fear of losing them.

Skyler entered the kitchen, inhaling the aroma of gingerbread. The pieces were already shaped into the walls and roof of the houses. They just had to put them together.

There was no warning at all. As she pulled the various colored frostings from the refrigerator, devastating sorrow nearly drove her to her knees. She kept the door open to prevent Francesca and Gabriel from seeing the tears welling in her eyes. Grief was sharp and painful—a blade cutting into her heart. Her throat swelled as the sorrow seemed to expand and take over every cell in her body until she wanted to weep uncontrollably. Rage crept in, dark and terrible, a savage need for vengeance, a need to strike back—to kill. The feeling was so strong, her hands shook and she dropped one of the bowls, shattering it.

"Skyler?" Francesca was there in a moment, wrapping her arm around Skyler's waist and pulling her away from the glass.

The frosting was white, but the bowl had been red and with the shards embedded in the icing, it looked to Skyler like bloodstained snow. She felt the urge to run to the window and check that no one was hurt outside. Her breath caught in her throat and she pressed a hand to her aching heart. Not just anyone—Dimitri. She had connected to him—she was certain of it—and he was suffering.

"Francesca? I have to find him. I have to find Dimitri." Her voice was barely a whisper. She had no idea tears streamed down her face until Francesca touched her cheeks. "He's—it's so terrible. I can't explain it. I have to go to him. *You* have to go to him and ease his suffering."

"I'm sorry, baby, I can only ease your suffering. He has to find a way to live with the emotions he is now feeling. He had knowledge before, but could not feel emotion." She leaned close to Skyler to murmur softly, to ease her burden, "I can provide distance for you and it will help."

Skyler abruptly pulled away. "No." She shook her head. "You and Gabriel always shield me. Not this time. If I did this to him, I want to be able to feel it as well. I need to know these things, Francesca. I am already Carpathian in my heart. I need knowledge as well as emotion."

5

Mikhail streamed through the forest—a white vapor trail concealed by the snow—staying high up in the trees as he tracked the wolf loping across the ground beneath him. Mikhail could see that, in spite of taking the form of the wolf, Dimitri was in trouble. The wolf paused every now in then, shuddering in pain, the shaggy fur, usually so shiny with health and strength, dull and wet with sweat. In spite of the animal form, waves of grief poured off the man, and to Mikhail's horror, small beads of blood were left behind in the paw prints in the stark white snow.

Mikhail dropped down through the canopy to fall more gently with the drift of the snowflakes as he approached the Carpathian male cautiously. Dimitri had gone through hell in the forests of Russia with his beloved wolves. Hunted by vampire and mortals alike, pursued by poachers and superstitious people, he had faced endless centuries of protecting both humans and wolves alone without the comfort of his homeland—the soil—or its people.

The wolf stopped running and stood with sides heaving, head hanging and blood-red tears dripping into the snow. He suddenly threw his head back and howled his unrelenting sorrow to the heavens and whatever deities might hear him. As the mournful notes faded into the night, he resumed his own shape, the wolf falling away to reveal the man. Dimitri covered his face as he sank down onto a boulder.

"You are feeling her pain," Mikhail said softly. "It is both a miracle and a curse for you."

Dimitri sprang up, whirling to face the prince, his fangs exposed in a snarl, his eyes glowing with red flickers of flame. He stood in a fighter's stance, hands up, the air around them charged with electricity—with danger. "I had no idea I was not alone," Dimitri said. "I would not have displayed such emotion."

"Allow me to summon Gregori to you," Mikhail offered. "He could help to ease this suffering."

"No one eased it for her," Dimitri growled. "I knew when they laid their filthy hands on her and I knew when they hurt her, and beat her and cut her. I even knew when they burned her, but I never *felt* it. Not the pain, not the rage, not her despair. When I touched her, drew her into my arms and merged my spirit with hers, it was there, behind the wall Francesca and Gabriel built to distance her from it, but it was all there and this time—God help me, Mikhail—this time I felt it all. Every agony, every humiliation, every depravity. The rage and guilt and I heard her begging—*pleading*—for someone to save her. Where was I?"

"You were doing your duty, Dimitri, as all of us must. Skyler is strong and grows stronger every day. I do not pretend to understand why some men brutalize women and children, I will never be able to comprehend such a thing, but I do know it is common. She is safe now, and happy. Gabriel and Francesca are seeing to her education, and eventually they will bring her wholly into our world."

Dimitri rubbed his hand over his face. "When I saw her, she looked an angel, Mikhail. I never knew what that meant when I heard the description, but there is purity there and goodness. I need her. The darkness is closing in on me and I fear my ability to do the honorable thing."

"Every one of us has moments of weakness, Dimitri. Skyler is your lifemate and as such, you must do what is right for her. Survive and maintain until such time as she is able to come to you. Work with Gabriel and Francesca, not against them. Kidnapping her or binding her will only hurt you both in the end, and I think you know that. At least you have hope where so many others have nothing."

"Hope? When she is a child and I must return to the emptiness of my existence? When I know if I stay I will claim her? When I can feel every brutality inflicted on her and am helpless to take it away?" Dimitri sank once more down onto the boulder and shook his head. "I am lost, Mikhail."

Mikhail crouched down beside him. "You cannot be lost. She must live with what happened to her and as her lifemate, so must you."

"Shamed for all eternity that I could not protect her?"

"You are feeling rage—impotent rage—on *your* behalf, not hers. You should be able to extract vengeance, mete out justice, and because there is only the aftermath, the burden and scars of these terrible crimes, you rail to the heavens for your inability to protect her. She was a child and you were a thousand miles away. You did not know of her existence. You are a hunter of the vampire and you know duty and honor. Behave in an honorable manner. Court her as she deserves. Allow her to heal with Francesca and Gabriel that she might come to you wholly and of her own free will. *That* is the gift that you can give her—and it is much more than most of us have given our lifemates."

Dimitri dragged in a deep breath. "I used to stare up at the stars each night and imagine that she was somewhere in the world looking at the same stars. I tried to picture her, to build an image in my head, but she was so elusive. And then I looked at her with her soft skin and her beautiful eyes and knew I could never have conjured her up, no matter how vivid my imagination."

"Will you allow Gregori to aid you?" Mikhail repeated.

Dimitri ran both hands through his dark, sweat-damp hair. "I have to work this out in my own way, Mikhail. I have been alone many centuries now and it is difficult for me to interact with anyone—even my own people. I spend much time in the form of a wolf, running free with my pack."

"There is danger in that—taking on the wild ways."

Dimitri nodded. "If it becomes too big a burden, I will seek the Dark One. I cannot stay away from her while I am here."

"Do not provoke Gabriel."

"He should not provoke me. I am no longer the shy boy he thinks me. That boy is long gone from this world." Dimitri spread out his hands and curled his fingers into two tight fists. "I am a killer and damned for all time. She saw that in me, you know. She sensed the darkness and retreated."

"You are a hunter. One of my best," Mikhail corrected. "Never think any different. Skyler is now your responsibility and she is tied to your fate. You cannot meet the dawn nor can you embrace evil. You must endure until she is old enough—and strong enough to accept your claim on her." He straightened and looked up at the sky. "I am going to see Julian Savage. He was your boyhood friend. Perhaps you would care to accompany me?" His teeth flashed white, but the smile never reached his eyes. He could feel sorrow for Dimitri and try to aid him, but he could never forget that Dimitri was a danger and always would be until he had bound his lifemate to him. "I thought he, of all Carpathians, would most enjoy knowing I intend to see that Gregori wears the ridiculous red Santa Claus suit."

"Julian always loved a good prank," Dimitri admitted, "but I will visit him later when I am in more control. Isn't his lifemate kin to Gregori?"

Mikhail nodded. "Desari is Gregori's younger sister. She's very talented."

"Have you met the man who kept them all alive when we thought they were lost to us?" Dimitri asked. "He must be a powerful Carpathian."

Mikhail nodded. "Ah, Darius. Elusive. Quiet. Says what he means. Few would ever think to cross him. He is much like his brothers. Confident in his abilities and powers. It is interesting to witness the Daratrazanoff brothers together. There is no jostling for leadership. Each is his own man, yet blends well with the others. It is a strong lineage."

"I heard Dominic of the Dragonseekers had returned."

"He was gravely injured in our last battle with the vampires and the mage, Razvan. Dominic still rests beneath the ground. Francesca and Gregori would very much like to have a healing session for him before she leaves for Paris."

Dimitri stood up, squaring his shoulders. "Tell Julian I will see him later, at the party. I will patrol the forest and try to pick up the scent of our enemies. The wolves may have information for me."

"Be very careful, Dimitri. They followed the trail of energy back to Skyler, but if blood is calling them, remember you also carry her scent as she does yours. You could be marked as well."

Dimitri's mouth hardened into a cruel line. "I would welcome the chance at them. They will not find me as easy a target as they would find Skyler."

Before Mikhail could respond, Dimitri turned and sprinted away, shifting on the run, going to all fours without breaking stride, the movement so seamless and fluid that Mikhail knew no one could have matched him. The ripple of power was breathtaking, and Mikhail stared at the spot where Dimitri had shifted, the tracks in the snow, one moment man, the next wolf. The wonder of his species struck him as it did so often, but as always, on the heels of that wonder came the inevitable burden of responsibility.

My love. You are worried. Raven touched his mind with her warmth. At once the rush of love filled his mind bringing him comfort.

It is nothing. I will be with Julian and Desari. Would you like to join us?

I cannot. I do not like the look of this gravy. It is . . . lumpy.

Mikhail found himself smiling at the annoyance in her voice. If the gravy didn't behave, Raven was going to throw it outside in the snow and use it for target practice. The woman had a bit of a temper, and apparently the cooking wasn't going very well.

I do not find your amusement in the least bit helpful.

Amusement? Mikhail took to the sky, his body reshaping into that of an owl. He winged his way over the forest toward the house where Julian was staying. *I am certain I did not feel in the least amused over you muttering threats to human gravy you are not going to be consuming yourself.*

There was a heartbeat of silence. Alarm spread through him. *Raven? You are not going to attempt to eat human food, are you?*

I'm considering whether or not it would add to the illusion that we are human. Some of the villagers will be there as well as a guest or two.

Mikhail drew in his breath, his wings beating ferociously as he dipped through the trees, the snowflakes on his feathers. *You go too far with this silly feast of yours, woman.*

Her retaliatory amusement washed over him, bringing a flood of warmth. Only Raven teased him like this—unexpectedly, lovingly—daring the wrath of the prince of the Carpathian people. He sent her an impression of bared fangs, but it didn't do much to intimidate her. She only laughed and went back to her lumpy gravy.

Below him, Mikhail spotted Julian Savage running in the snow, his long blond hair like his brother Aidan's—streaming behind him, something tucked under his arm, while a woman chased after him and another man raised his hand, calling out. Julian launched the object into the air and the man caught it, waving it triumphantly over his head. Mikhail landed on the railing of Julian's home and shifted back to his normal form.

"It isn't funny, Julian," the woman called out with a small sniff of disdain. "That's for the midnight dinner." She glared at the other man. "Barack, you give that to me right this minute."

"No one could eat it, sweetheart." Julian circled around her, careful to keep out of reach. "Unless they plan on using it for shoe leather."

Barack flashed a grin. "We could start a new fad with this stuff, Desari. You cook the roast and we'll make the soles of shoes and after they walk for a while, they'll never go hungry."

"Eeeww! That's just sick, Barack. You've been around Julian way too long."

"Seriously, honey, it is much better used as a football."

"Don't you sweetheart and honey me, Julian," Desari protested. "I can't very well have people eating that roast after you've been throwing it around." She glared at the two men, hands on hips.

"Go out for a pass," Barack directed Julian.

Julian took off running and Barack launched the roast high into the air. Julian sprang up and caught it, pulling it into his chest. Before he could land on the ground, Desari began to sing and the notes danced silver in the air around Julian, hooking together to form a net. He bounced as if on a trampoline and slid off onto the ground, landing hard in an inelegant sprawl.

Barack doubled over with laughter, but undeterred, Julian lifted the dried out roast over his head in triumph. "Touchdown!"

Desari sang a few more notes. The silver and gold notes danced and dipped, hooking around one another to form a noose that slipped over Julian's head. Mikhail's breath caught in his throat. In the darkness, with the snow falling, the musical notes were beautiful, shimmering and glowing with life and energy. All the while Desari's voice pulsed through his body, making his heart and mind glow with warmth, happiness and, most of all, the love she felt for her lifemate.

Desari suddenly turned her head to smile at Mikhail. She was beautiful, dazzling even, her voice fading into the night, a part of nature itself. "I suppose I shouldn't strangle my lifemate in front of the prince, should I?" she asked. There was no embarrassment in her voice, only laughter and welcome.

Desari is a true Daratrazanoff. She exudes confidence. He shared with Raven the image of the Carpathian woman with her flowing hair, soft features and her musical voice and the dancing silver and gold notes casting a noose around her lifemate's neck.

And she is beautiful.

There was no edge to Raven's tone, but Mikhail smiled at her through their telepathic link. *Perhaps you should come and join me and leave that gravy to insects—although poisoning any creature is never a good thing.*

You are so funny, my prince.

Mikhail winced. Raven never referred to him as a prince unless he was skating the edge of trouble. He smiled at Desari. "I have always wanted to strangle Julian."

"So has my brother, Darius," Desari said, walking over to him, her every movement graceful.

A slow smile softened Mikhail's mouth. "I can well imagine if Darius is anything like Gregori. Julian used to drive Gregori right up the wall. Even as a boy, Julian had little fear in him. He went his own way and got into more trouble than most of our children could ever conceive of doing."

Julian swept his arm around Desari's narrow waist. "Do not listen to him. I was not the bad boy of the Carpathians. Just independent—and for good reason. I had a vampire using my eyes to spy on our people. I could not very well stick around."

"And you have since destroyed this vampire?" Mikhail asked.

Julian nodded. "I had built him up to be so powerful. As a child, to me, he seemed so, but like most monsters in our lives, once I became an adult, he was not nearly as powerful as I remembered. Looking back, I should have told an adult and perhaps they could have hunted and destroyed him, giving me back my childhood, but I thought he would harm our hunters."

Mikhail shrugged his shoulders. "It is easy for us to look back and say what we should have done, but that is because later we have different information and, of course, knowledge always changes our decisions."

Julian flashed a faint smile. "I would have wanted those years back with Aidan. He has been so good about it, but I know it hurt him to be separated."

Desari reached for his hand in an offer of comfort. "We see him as often as possible now, Julian," she reminded him, and then jerked her hand away to rub her palm on her thigh. "You're all greasy."

"The infamous roast," Julian said, presenting the large, dried up hunk of meat to her with a small courtly bow.

Mikhail covered his reaction with a small cough, turning his face away as Desari glared at her lifemate.

"It's all squishy, Julian, you ruined my roast. What am I going to do now? I have to provide something for tonight's dinner."

"Ask Corrine to help," Barack suggested. "She told Dayan she cooked quite a bit before he claimed her."

"There is nothing squishy about that roast," Julian protested. "It has turned to leather."

Desari made a face at him and then down at the roast. "Disgusting stuff. I think I will ask Corrine to help me make something else."

Barack held out his hands. "Throw it, Desari, we may as well finish our football game."

Mikhail shook his head. "I wanted to let you all know that Alexandria and young Skyler ran into trouble a few minutes ago. We all need to be on alert and give added protection to our women and children."

"Syndil was at the house, thinking she might prepare something for the party. I think I will check on her. If I reach out, she will simply say she is fine." Barack sketched a small salute and immediately took to the sky.

The smile faded from Julian's face. He stepped closer to Desari. "What kind of trouble? Aidan did not send word that Alexandria was hurt."

"She is fine now, but both she and Skyler felt the presence of a subtle flow of power, enhancing emotions to the point of irrationality. Even Gabriel was affected, losing his temper with Dimitri."

"I knew Dimitri had arrived," Julian said. "I can feel the darkness in him growing by the hour. He is unstable and we have to find a way to keep him safe. Gregori gave me a task to keep me going when I thought to give up my existence, and perhaps if one was given to Dimitri . . ." Julian sighed. "He is alone, killing more often than a hunter should have to, and that is slowly destroying him."

"Skyler is his lifemate," Mikhail stated.

Desari gasped. "Oh, dear, she's just a babe. Is he certain?"

"She restored colors and emotions."

"That cannot be good," Julian said. "At best emotions can be difficult to deal with, and in this situation when she was so brutalized, he must be going through hell. I should go to him," he added, "see what I can do. Desari has amazing power with her voice. It might help him get through this."

"He cannot bind her to him," Desari protested, her hand to her throat. "She is much, much too young and from what Francesca said, far too fragile. It takes both Gabriel and Francesca to distance her enough from her past to allow her to function normally. Do you know that she has no childhood memories in her mind they can bring out to aid her? It must be so difficult for Dimitri to suddenly feel all these things. For a time, he will be raw and wounded with her old scars."

"It is a very dangerous situation," Mikhail agreed. "If Dimitri stays near her, he will continue to fight his need to claim her. If he chooses to return to Russia, the danger to both increases." He rubbed his temples, suddenly feeling old. The weight of his responsibilities was wearing on him far more these dark days.

In the midst of the Christmas season, when he should have been feeling joy and hope, he felt tired and the beginnings of despair. How could he save them? Two or three children were not enough. Even if Shea gave birth to a female and the baby survived, it would be years before a male would be saved. Too long to wait in darkness. Too many males. One or two lifemates were not going to keep their species from extinction, especially as their enemies were banding together and becoming bolder and bolder in their attacks.

"We had the advantages for so long," he murmured aloud. "We could scan and know the thoughts of our enemies, but now they've found a way to block us. We could smell the evil stench of the vampire, sense the presence of such an abomination, yet now we can no longer trust our own senses to guide us." He spread his arms out wide. "Before, they would never have come here after us, fearing our power, yet now they chip away at us on nearly a daily basis. Our enemies outnumber us and as we grow weaker— they grow stronger."

Desari glanced at Julian. His amber eyes seemed to glow as he stepped forward to put his hand on the prince's shoulder. He looked very much a warrior, and she couldn't help that small rush of pride in him.

"We grow stronger too, Mikhail. Under your leadership, we have come together when before we were scattered and apart. You have worked tirelessly to get the word to any of our ancients, to continue to look for any lost as Desari and the others had been."

"The women are reluctant to become pregnant and give birth," Mikhail pointed out, shaking his head. "Without children, Julian, no matter our longevity, our species will not survive."

Desari smiled at him. "We *will* survive. This is the season of miracles, remember? I thought you were a believer, Mikhail. Where is your faith?"

There was a small silence. The hard lines in the prince's face softened. "Perhaps this celebration of Raven's is just the thing I need to restore my faith, Desari." He rubbed the bridge of his nose thoughtfully. "Should Josef decide to give us his rendition of *any* carol, please do volunteer to sing. Is it possible your dancing notes can muzzle the boy?"

"Josef's reputation preceeds him," Desari said with a laugh. "I understand he's quite a handful."

"Let us just say I do not envy Byron and Antonietta trying to keep an eye on the boy. They say he is quite intelligent, but not very diligent when it comes to mastering any of our practices. I think he has been spoiled and allowed to mix so much with human children that he has forgotten his duty to our people."

Julian flashed Desari a secret smile at the sternness in Mikhail's voice. As a child, he'd often heard that same edge to the adult male's tones. "He will grow to a fine man," Julian assured him. "Perhaps not a hunter, but we need our society to return to progress once more. We need men who look to business and the arts and especially science."

"I have no doubt Josef will succeed in anything he does," Mikhail said dryly. "But the rest of us may not survive his youth."

"I seem to recall Gregori said the same thing about me—many times." Julian grinned at him, his strange-colored eyes glinting like gold. "The man needs a sense of humor. Now, I am his brother-in-law. Fate has a way of playing little jokes."

A slow answering smile lit Mikhail's face. "I must confess, Julian, I did not think of that at all. His brother-in-law. He is also my son-in-law and as I am Dear Old Dad, I think it is time the man performed some family duties. He will be perfect in the part of Santa Claus tonight."

Julian's eyebrow shot up. "My prince." He bowed low. "I acknowledge you as the master in this game we so often play with the Dark One."

Desari looked from one man to the other. "I can't imagine you asking Gregori to be Santa, and if Julian is endorsing it, that's a bad thing."

"I see she knows you well, Julian," Mikhail observed.

Desari rested her head on Julian's chest. "Was he the resident bad boy growing up? I can well imagine that he would have been."

Mikhail shook his head. "Independent. A smart mouth. He loved knowledge and had little fear in him. But no." He frowned. "There was a young man, a few years older than Julian, who Gregori had to stay on top of all the time. He was far worse than Josef could ever conceive of being. He questioned authority all the time."

"I remember him," Julian said. "He was amazing with weapons even as young as he was. Tiberiu Bercovitz. I haven't heard or thought of him in centuries. Did he come to the celebration? He was good friends with Dimitri."

There was no real inflection in Julian's voice, but Mikhail caught a flare of wariness in the hunter's eyes. The man shifted subtly, but protectively toward his lifemate.

"This is what our lives have become," Mikhail murmured aloud. "We can no longer trust our friends, men who have dedicated their lives to honor, to saving Carpathian and human alike. We treat our best hunters with suspicion."

"It is the way we have always lived," Julian remarked.

Mikhail shook his head. "There was a time, Julian, long ago, when only nature balanced us. There was harmony and peace in our world and we held celebrations such as this one often."

"And we are holding one this night," Desari pointed out. "A unique reunion with all Carpathians welcome to participate, celebrating strengthening our friendship with each other as well as our human friends. We have not done so in centuries. It sends a message to our people that we are once again united, and a message to our enemies that we are strong together, and will continue to grow stronger. It is a start, don't you think? You have given us that gift, Mikhail."

A small smile teased at the curve of the prince's mouth. "Raven has given us that gift. Carpathians never celebrated Christmas before, but she used this time of year as an excuse to bring us all together. I thought she was wrong—but I see that I was."

"We have the chance to get to know one another," Desari said. "My family, well, not the Daratrazanoffs or my lifemate Julian, I mean our band—the Dark Troubadours—was not raised with other Carpathians, and this is truly a unique opportunity for us. We didn't even use the same common mental path as all of the rest of the Carpathians."

"Your brother, Darius, is truly a miracle worker in that he kept so many young children alive when he was merely a babe himself. Shea and Gregori wanted to meet with him to discuss the various herbs and plants he used to keep so many of you alive."

Desari nodded. "All three of them have been together until the early morning hours since we've arrived. I think it is only today that the others have taken a break from research to cook. I heard Shea was not feeling very well. She must be so frightened to be having a baby when our infant-mortality rate is so high."

She flicked a quick glance at Julian, who tried to catch her eye, but she refused to meet his gaze. Julian reached out his hand and took hers, bringing her palm to his heart. *If you choose not to get pregnant this night, so be it, Desari. I would never take away your choice.*

Desari turned her head away from the prince, blinking back tears, rubbing her cheek along Julian's shoulder as she did so. *I do not know if this year is special or if returning to our homeland has caused a leap in fertility, but many of the women have said they can get pregnant, though few wish to try.*

Desari, we will have children when you are ready. If the miracle happens, and I believe it will, it is meant to be. If not . . . Julian shrugged his shoulders and sent her a wealth of love and reassurance. *So be it.* He was not a man to follow the path of others. If Desari didn't want to chance the heartbreak of losing children, he was not going to take her to task, or point out her duty to their people.

Desari smiled at him. She knew he would never pressure her, and she loved him all the more for his patience—for his complete faith in her.

"Julian, I ask again that you reach out to Dimitri," Mikhail said. "I am on my way to speak with Darius. I wish to question him more on how he kept you all alive."

Julian nodded in agreement, and watched as Mikhail shimmered into transparency and streamed upward through the snow toward the house Darius had chosen to stay in. He dropped his arm around Desari's shoulders, sweeping her long hair away from her neck. "We are actually alone."

A slow smile teased the curve of her mouth. "Really?" She quirked an eyebrow at him. "We may be alone, but since you ruined my contribution to tonight's feast, I have to cook. Or better yet, you should do the cooking."

His golden eyes gleamed at her. "I would very much like to oblige." He swept her into his arms, tossing her over his shoulder as if she weighed no more than a feather, and sprinted for the house.

"Julian! You savage!" She gripped him around the waist as he vaulted over the railing and kicked open the front door. "Stop being a caveman."

"Ha ha ha." He brought his hand down on her squirming bottom as he strode through the house toward the bedroom. "As I recall, technically you are a Savage as well."

She laughed and deliberately wrapped her arms around his waist, fingers sliding over the front of his jeans in a stroking caress. The action distracted him immediately so that he nearly stumbled, losing his long strides. Desari took the opportunity to dissolve, leaving him holding empty air as she streamed through the house, a comet of flashing colors. Her soft laughter teased his senses, while her fingers seemed to brush over his face and down his chest.

"That's not nice, Desari," Julian objected, following the prism of colors at a more leisurely pace. "And definitely unfair."

Back off, big boy, she warned, trying to give the impression of a snarl, but instead it came out laughter. *Can I help it if you're so susceptible to a little accidental touching?*

"Accidental? I think not." He raised his hands and wove a complicated pattern in the air. The streaming colors collided with a solid net, and immediately Desari's natural form landed on the floor. She sat at his feet laughing, blinking up at him, her dark hair spilling all around her making her look more alluring than ever.

Julian's heart clenched in his chest. The sensation was so strong that he pressed his palm over his aching heart, drawing in a deep breath. "Every single night I wake up thinking I cannot possibly love you more, Desari. And every single night, when you awaken and look at me, the love I have for you grows stronger—so much so that sometimes I think I cannot contain it."

The bright laughter faded as she extended her hand to him, allowing him to pull her up, to pull her into the shelter of his arms. She framed his face with her hands. She was tall, but he was taller, forcing her to look up in order to meet his burning gaze. His eyes had gone from amber to burnished gold, the hunger there taking her breath away. "You are my beloved, Julian, always my beloved."

"I hold you like this, safe in my arms, your body fitting so perfectly into mine." He turned his head away, ashamed of the welling emotion he could never control in spite of all his centuries of discipline. "And you sing to me as we lie together and there is no other peace in the world like the peace you bring to me."

She took a deep breath, love shaking her with its strength. "Do you want a child, Julian? Do you want to try when we know the heartache that most likely lies ahead for us? Are you willing to take a chance that the greatest sorrow—losing our son or daughter—will take from us what we have?" She had to know the truth before making a decision. There was a part of her that wanted a child, a boy with bright blond hair and gold for eyes—a child who would play pranks on her and tease her, reminding her all too much of the man who was her other half. But the price was so high. So very high.

"Is that what you think, Desari? That if we lost our child, we would lose what we have between us?" He shook his head. "Never. It is impossible."

"Our love is so strong, Julian, the emotions we feel so intense, the sorrow of losing a child would be devastating." The lump in her throat threatened to choke her.

"Any parent knows losing a child is devastating," he replied gently. "The sorrow would be great, yes, but if you're asking me would the risk of that sorrow be worth the chance of having a son or daughter with your eyes and your smile—then I have to say it would be worth it to me. But the decision is yours to make. You are enough for my happiness. A child is a miracle, but I will always survive as long as I have you."

"I'm not a coward, Julian," Desari said, her fingers tangling in his hair. She rested her body against his, laying her head over his heart, listening to the steady rhythm. "I'm not hesitating because I'm a coward."

He stroked a caress down the length of shining black hair. "I could never, for one moment, think of you as a coward, honey. We will have a child when we're ready, not one second before. I have done my duty for my people—a thousand times over—and I will not have a child out of duty. Our child will be conceived in love and wanted more than any other by *both* of us."

Her heart matched the rhythm of his. Her blood heated in her veins. She lifted her face to press kisses along the column of his neck, nipping gently, her tongue tasting his skin. "Well, then, since I would love to have a baby, I say let's go for it. Let's try, Julian, and enjoy every moment of conception and pregnancy and not let worry rule us. Our child will be our Christmas present to one another."

His body was already stirring, his blood heating to match the fire in hers. "You're certain, Desari?"

Her mouth took his, pouring love into him along with her sweet, addicting taste. Every cell in his body responded. He lifted her into his arms without breaking the kiss. *Christmas may really bring miracles.*

Her loving laughter teased his senses. *Don't think this will get you out of helping me come up with something else to cook for tonight's celebration.*

Tonight's celebration is happening right now, he told her.

6

Darius Daratrazanoff glared at his lifemate as she very accurately threw several rounds of snowballs, peppering him in the face and chest. "Tempest, I am giving you a direct order. Come back here now!"

Tempest packed the next snowball tight and launched it at his face. "You and your silly direct orders." She tossed her snowflake-covered red hair and gave a sniff of disdain. "Honestly, Darius, I'm not one of your brothers or sisters who do whatever you tell them. You made fun of me, you snake. Just because I blew up the oven doesn't mean I can't cook." She threw another tightly packed missile, running backward as she did so. "Take it back."

"You cannot cook, and who cares? Certainly not me. The oven, however, blew a rather large hole in the house and I need to repair it, so come back here where I can keep an eye on you."

"Take it back."

"For heaven sake, baby, you set the house on fire. The entire kitchen is black. What did you think you were doing?"

"The oven wasn't working right so I fixed it."

Darius dodged another snowball. "Tempest. It is not fixed. There is a hole the size of our tour bus in the wall and the kitchen is black with soot.

Whatever that purple gooey concoction you were making is, it's now all over the ceiling and walls."

"Okay." She held up her hand, indignation on her face. "That was *so* not my fault. The stove shorted out and blew a hole through the pot and sent berries all over the ceiling and down the walls. I had nothing to do with that. And if you ask me, that probably did something to make the heating coil melt in the oven as well. So *take it back*!" She scooped up snow on the run and packed it into weapons.

"Even if the stove did short out, it does not take away the fact that you cannot cook. You have never been able to cook. Not even when you were on your own. And if you keep going and I lose sight of you, you will be instantly lost. You know you have absolutely no sense of direction."

Her red-gold eyebrows drew together in a furious frown. "First, you accuse me of blowing up the house and setting the kitchen on fire. Then, you tell me I can't cook, and now you say I have no sense of direction! I have a perfectly keen sense of direction."

Darius looked up at the sky to see if lightning was about to strike his lifemate. When none was forthcoming, he chuffed out his breath and changed the subject, afraid if they continued and she told any more whoppers like the last one, they would be in for the strike of a lifetime. "What was the purple sauce all over the wall?"

"Berry pies. I made like ten of them and they blew up." She eyed him with suspicion. "Did you mess with that old stove after I told you something wasn't right with it?"

"I did not go near that kitchen. It was a ridiculous idea. I told you if you wanted the silly things made, I would look at the recipe and reproduce it for you."

"The idea was to *cook*, smart one, you know, like a human."

"It was a stupid idea, Tempest," he said with patient persistence. "Now come here to me this minute." He was beginning to feel a little desperate. His lifemate seemed to be the only one capable of making him feel that way. There were times, like now, when he would much rather face a vampire than Tempest. She was halfway between tears and laughter and that was never a good thing.

She had been an independent human nearly her entire life before he converted her, and he had been the sole commander for most of his. He had been responsible for the safety of his family for so long, the protective urges couldn't be suppressed. In truth, he wouldn't have wanted them to be. He had a good alarm system and it was shrieking at him. He tried to gentle his voice. "Baby, do we really care so much about this dinner? We are not even going to be eating it."

"*Every* woman is bringing a dish." She gestured through the snow toward the house. "And do you think Barack and Julian are going to stay silent about that big mess? I will never hear the end of it."

Darius swore under his breath. He was going to have to do something different, unexpected, completely take her by surprise if he was going to get her out of her mood. He took off running toward her, scooping up snow as he ran, shaping the flakes into loose round missiles. Tempest's eyes widened in shock and as he fired off his ammunition at her, she shapeshifted on the run, her small, compact figure taking on the shape of a snow leopard. Soft gray fur adorned with black-brown spots covered the compact, muscular body and yard-long tail.

"Tempest! What are you doing?" He called gruffly, his black gaze shifting to search the area around them. As often as he scanned, he couldn't find danger, yet he couldn't quite shake the edginess, the need to hold his lifemate close to him. His silly attempt at being playful had backfired on him. Her mood had been mercurial lately, swinging from one end of the spectrum to the other.

The leopard looked back at him and took off, large furry paws making it easy to run through the snow, and worse, with the form she'd chosen, powerful hind legs helping her spring a distance of thirty feet or more with ease. He leapt into the air, shifting as he did so, the male snow leopard landing on the steeper side of the slope away from the trees to follow closely in the tracks of the female. He was a good thirty percent larger, and used his size to shoulder her back in the direction he wanted her to go.

The female snarled, showing her teeth. Inside the cat's body, Darius frowned. He could have sworn that, in spite of the leopard showing temper, deep inside she was weeping.

Tempest. Tell me. Surely these pies are not so important. Tell me what has you so upset. He rubbed his fur along hers as he shifted back to his human form, sitting in the snow, holding the female leopard in his lap. Her teeth were mere inches from his throat as he looked into her eyes, seeing beyond the cat to his mate. *You are my life, Tempest. You know I cannot bear to see you upset. This cannot be beyond my ability to fix.*

The cat shifted in his arms, warm fur giving way so that soft skin slid over his and a wealth of silky hair fell across his face. Tempest circled his neck with her slender arms. "I don't know, Darius. I don't know what's wrong, but I want to cry all the time."

He felt a small shiver run down her spine and gathered her closer, automatically regulating their body temperatures so they wouldn't feel the cold. His fingers fisted in her thick red hair. "How long has this been going on and why did I not know?"

"Because it's so stupid, Darius. There's nothing wrong." She rubbed her face along his chest much like a feline, as if remnants of the animal still clung to the woman. "I'm not used to being around people, so maybe I'm just nervous."

He touched her face and found tears. His heart clenched in his chest. Darius took a deep breath and let it out. "I am going to check you over, Tempest. We do not know what conversion might have done to your body. Perhaps you are ill."

She turned her face into his neck. "Maybe I am. I don't feel very well."

He frowned as he brushed the hair from her face. "You did not want to take any sustenance this evening. I thought it was because of this dinner. After all this time, does it still bother you?"

"Not when it is from you," she admitted. "I just feel tired, that's all. Tired and out of sorts, I guess."

"You should not have tried to hide this from me," he said.

"I didn't want you to worry about me, like you're doing now. This entire time you've been looking around us, searching the ground, the sky, the trees, as if you're expecting trouble. You have enough to do just looking after the security."

"*Anything* concerning you is always and forever my first priority, Tempest." He brushed bright red strands of hair from her face. "I know the adjustment to our way of life has been hard on you."

She shook her head. "It was my choice, Darius. I wanted to be with you. I *chose* you and your way of life myself. You would have chosen differently for me—for us. I've grown to love the others, Desari and Julian, Dayan and Corrine and Barack and Syndil, and I'm getting used to being around them, but this . . ." She waved her hand to encompass the snow-covered mountains and forest where all the homes were hidden from prying eyes. "This is overwhelming to me."

He feathered the pad of his thumb back and forth tracing over her cheekbone. "We do not have to participate, baby. We can walk away from this—go far away and just be together. I thought you wanted to come."

"I do." Her lower lip trembled and tears filled her eyes. "I thought I did."

He bent his head to capture her mouth with his. "Do not cry, Tempest. I would much rather feel the heat of your temper. Your tears are heartbreaking."

She attempted a soft laugh in the midst of their kiss. "Tears are normal."

"Not for you. You are far more likely to throw a very hard snowball at me and call me names than cry."

He kissed her again, and Tempest could taste his desperate need to comfort her. It shamed her that she couldn't stop wanting to weep—and it was so unlike her. She wanted to crawl into a hole and pull the soil over her head. She wanted to cling to Darius, another trait so unlike her. He simply held her, rocking gently back and forth as if she were a child, and when she looked up at his face, his black gaze moved restlessly—ceaseless in his vigil to search out danger around them.

"It's so beautiful here, Darius, it doesn't seem as if we could possibly be in danger. I wish you could find a way to relax and just enjoy life—even if it's only for a day or two while we're here."

He touched one stray tear with his fingertip and brought it to his mouth. Tempest found the gesture curiously sexy. Her stomach did a funny little flip—a sensation she was becoming used to. She secretly found Darius the sexiest, most attractive man in the world, but she wasn't about to let him know that—not with his bossy ways.

"I am relaxed. Being vigilant does not mean I cannot relax. I want to examine you, Tempest. Not because I think anything is wrong, but just so neither of us is worried."

A slow smile drove away the tears. "You mean *you're* worried. Go ahead then. I don't like it when you get upset on my account." He was the most protective being she'd ever run across in her life. Darius could hardly bear for her to be out of his sight. If she did have some kind of strange illness, she'd never have a moment without Darius at her side. Even when the band performed onstage and he was working security, he kept Tempest beside him. If he needed to ease his mind by examining her, she was all for it.

Darius wasted no time, his body simply dropping away from his spirit so that he moved in complete freedom, a white hot light of pure energy entering her easily. Darius took his time, looking at her blood, her heart and lungs, moving lower . . . For the first time in his life he lost his focus and found himself back in his own body, sweat breaking out, his heart pounding. He stared down at her, panic in his eyes.

"What is it? What's wrong?"

His heart thundered in his ears. She looked so anxious, her eyes enormous, but holding such trust it steadied him as nothing else could. "Nothing is wrong. In fact everything is right." He stole another deep, calming breath, gripping her wrists, pinning her tightly against his chest. "What do you know about babies?"

"Babies?" Tempest drew back, shaking her head in adamant denial. "Absolutely nothing and it's going to stay that way. I've never even held a baby. I didn't exactly have parents, Darius, to show me what to do, so if you have a sudden yearning for children, you're going to have to think about finding another lifemate. Of course, then I'd begin immediately taking body parts off of you, but what the heck? You wouldn't need everything for another woman, now would you?"

"Our women always know when they can get pregnant."

Her eyebrow shot up. "How?"

He shrugged, looking confused. "I do not know. I suppose they check. I should have been aware of your breeding cycle."

"Breeding cycle?" There was horror in her tone. "I don't have a breeding cycle. That's just disgusting. Do Carpathians have birth control? I thought you could control that. You control everything else."

"If we are paying attention."

"Well, start paying attention. If you can control the weather and call down lightning, you can certainly keep us from having babies. I'm a mechanic. I fix things. Every time Corrine comes in with her baby, I go out the back door, or hadn't you noticed."

Darius managed another long breath of ice cold air. He tightened his hold on Tempest. "I have been alive for centuries, and in all that time, I never thought once of birth or babies. Once I found you, all I could think of was what a miracle you are to me, not checking for cycles."

Tempest shrugged. "I didn't think about it either. So now we'll just be careful."

"It is a little too late to be careful."

There was a small silence. Tempest pulled back slightly to stare into his dark eyes. "What are you saying?"

"You are pregnant with our child," Darius announced.

She shoved him hard, throwing herself out of his lap to scramble away, struggling to her feet, hands on hips, glaring at him. "Okay. That's just not funny. I don't do babies, Darius. And I'm not in the mood to have you joke with me about it." She pointed a shaky finger at him. "You never once said you wanted children."

"Tempest, I would not even consider joking about such an important thing. You are carrying our child. I saw it in your body, nestled safe and sound, growing every day. I should have been instantly aware, but I have been more concerned with our safety and did not consider that such an event could happen."

She backed up, looking frightened. "I can't have a baby, Darius. Really. I can't be a parent. I'm a mess." She shook her head. "You're mistaken. You have to be mistaken, that's all."

Darius sat in the snow regarding her with a raised eyebrow. "I very seldom make mistakes, Tempest, and certainly not of this magnitude. It is shocking to me that I never noticed the heartbeat. It is very strong. I obviously need to be far more vigilant where you are concerned."

"Is that all you have to say? Darius! Carpathian women are not supposed to be able to get pregnant very easily. I'd better be Carpathian after going through the conversion."

"Baby." His voice was low, a velvet soothing caress. "Of course you are pregnant. It explains everything."

"Everything?"

"Your mood swings, the tears, the temper. I have heard it is easy to have accidents such as the ones in the kitchen."

"Oh you have, have you?" Her teeth snapped together. "There's about to be another accident right here, Darius. I *don't* have mood swings. As for a temper, you're impossibly bossy and would make the easiest going person lose their mind."

"Check for yourself."

His calm, steady tone set her teeth on edge. Just once she'd like him to be wrong—and this was the perfect moment for it. She *needed* him to be wrong. Surely she'd know if she was going to have a baby? And he would have known. He knew everything. Tempest took a deep breath and let go of the physical world around her.

There it was. A tiny heart beating, little more than that, but definitely a new life. Tempest observed in total amazement and awe. This tiny creature lived inside her. A part of her—a part of Darius. "How come I didn't know?"

She was barely aware of Darius standing beside her, wrapping his arms around her and holding her close. "I should have known," he said gently. "It was my responsibility to watch over your health at all times. I was so busy worried about enemies, it did not occur to me to think about pregnancy, but I should have."

She leaned into him, murmuring aloud, more to herself than to him. "What in the world are we going to do? I have no idea how to take care of a baby." She looked up at him, afraid to be happy, afraid of the love and joy already growing. "You know me, Darius. Other than you, I've never really gotten attached to anyone."

"That is not entirely true. You are very attached to the others in the band. I can feel your affection for them."

"It isn't the same thing as having a child. I could drop it. And I have no idea how to be a Carpathian, let alone a Carpathian parent. This is so scary. What are we going to do?" She clutched his hand, feeling desperate.

"I guess we're having a baby." He feathered kisses down her face to the corner of her mouth. "We can do anything together, Tempest. By the time the baby gets here, we can figure it out."

"Aren't you terrified? Just a little, Darius?"

"I kept Desari and Syndil alive. We will do just fine." Few things terrified him. The possibility of losing Tempest was the only thing he could think of offhand. He had never asked for a single thing in his long, difficult life, until she had come along. She was a miracle to him with her brightness. She was so alive—her moods mercurial, her laughter often and contagious. There was no existence for him without her and he wouldn't lose her, not to an enemy, not to accidents and certainly not in childbirth.

She was trembling. "I thought the conversion took care of all that. I mean, I didn't have a cycle anymore so I just stopped thinking about it. And it didn't seem like anyone ever got pregnant. Corrine was pregnant before she became Dayan's lifemate. And isn't there some kind of time-out for newbies?"

"It does not seem so."

"You're not even upset," she accused. "You're the man. The man always gets upset when the woman gets pregnant. It's practically tradition."

His face always seemed carved in stone, a ruggedly sensual face with no expression and eyes that were flat and cold and held the promise of death—until he looked at her. Tempest loved the slow smile that occasionally curved his mouth and lit his black eyes. She especially loved the way he looked right now—with love heating the ice and flooding her with warmth.

Her lungs found the rhythm of his. Her heart beat in perfect time to his. "You're really not afraid, Darius?"

He shook his head. "This will be a good thing. Our child will grow up with Dayan's child. They will not ever be lonely. It is important, especially if they are male, that they have someone they can count on—have a strong bond with. As the years pass, sometimes it is only remembered friendship that holds us to our honor when we are without a lifemate."

"Don't tell anyone I'm so afraid. There have to be books on parenting. I'll just sit around and read."

He brought her hands to his mouth and pressed kisses along her knuckles. "You're shivering. We should get back to the house."

"You mean before someone notices the great big hole in the wall?" She managed a small smile. She stepped away from him and took off with confidence, walking back in the direction of the house, shoulders straight, head up, determined to make up for all her shortcomings. If Darius could handle having a baby, then so could she. Of course, she wasn't touching it until it was at least three years old. She chewed nervously on her lower lip and glanced back at Darius. He just stood there shaking his head. "What? Are you reading my thoughts again? I told you never to do that. It's bad enough that I have to try to follow what I'm thinking. And it's only fair for you to handle the baby until he's three, and then I'll take over."

"Really?" He caught the back of her jacket and tugged her around. "The house is in the opposite direction. That way leads into deep forest."

"I knew that. I was just making sure you were on top of things." She grinned at him. "The snow's a little disorienting."

He took her hand and led her in the right direction. "I noticed you said 'he.' You think we're having a boy?"

"If we're going to do this, Darius, it *has* to be a boy. I definitely wouldn't know what to do with a girl. And the poor thing would be a prisoner. You'd never let her out of your sight and you'd scare any young man who came near her."

He growled low in his throat, and Tempest burst out laughing. "See? Just the thought gets you riled up."

"I never get riled up. It is a complete waste of energy."

Tempest stepped in front of him, stopping so abruptly his body bumped up against hers. One slender arm circled his neck and she leaned close, pressing her soft breasts into his chest, and lifted her mouth to his. Her long hair spilled over his arm as he instantly responded, fingers curling around the nape of her neck to hold her to him, deepening the kiss until she thought she might melt the snow all around them. She broke it off, her eyes sparkling at him. "You get riled."

His heart slammed hard in his chest, a sensation only Tempest seemed to create. "Around you maybe."

She waited this time, taking his hand again so they could stroll back through the gently falling snow to the house.

"Someone is close by," Darius announced as they emerged from the trees into the clearing where the house stood. He inhaled sharply. "It is the prince. Stay behind me, Tempest."

Tempest dropped back a foot, rolling her eyes at what she considered unnecessary protection. She slipped her hand into Darius's back pocket. *I thought
the prince was the leader of the Carpathians. Are we supposed to fear him?*

Darius's warning growl met with soft laughter. He glanced back at her. *I
do not know him as the others do and I prefer to ensure your safety.* He turned
back to greet the prince, who seemed to be inspecting the damaged wall.
"Mikhail, I was just about to fix the house."

The prince arched a black brow. "Should I inquire as to what happened?"

"Better not," Darius advised. "Some things are best left mysteries. Give
me a minute to repair the damage and we can go inside, out of the weather,
to visit."

"The hole appears larger than I remember." Tempest peered around
Darius to scowl at the blackened ruin of a kitchen. "I think someone's been
here adding to the wreckage. It didn't look like this when we left it." She
flashed a tentative smile at the prince. "The house is really nice. Thank you
for lending it to us."

Mikhail turned away to keep the couple from seeing the laughter in his
eyes. Raven's idea of having the Carpathians cook dinner for the guests at
the inn was turning out to be more fun than he had anticipated. "Raven and
I are more than happy to lend you one of our houses. We hope you are able
to stay for a long visit and maybe look upon this place as your home when
you are not traveling."

"Thank you," Darius said politely, without committing to anything.

Hands on hips, Mikhail stared at the gaping hole in the wall of one of
his most beloved dwellings. "I have always wanted a small alcove there. I
thought the room was too square and needed an intimate conversation
area."

Darius nodded. "I believe you are right, and it's very easily done. Is this
what you had in mind?" He waved his hands and the sides of the house
moved into a series of curves.

Mikhail studied the structure and nodded. "Something like that. More
on this line." He added to the curves, making them serpentine, so that the
house appeared to be a giant snake. "What do you think?"

Tempest shook her head as the two men remodeled the kitchen. It looked like a competition to her rather than a repair job. She sighed and rubbed her hand over her stomach. The idea of having a child had never occurred to her. After she had gone through the conversion and her normal bodily functions ceased, she simply didn't give a thought to birth control. It was a stupid mistake, and one she couldn't take back.

Darius seemed fine with the idea, maybe even pleased, but nothing ever rocked him. He was a dangerous, lethal man, completely confident in his abilities, and the confidence was born of experience. She had been on the run most of her life. She had no family and didn't know the first thing about children.

We will do fine. Darius brushed the words through her mind like caressing fingers, his voice so soft and warm she could feel him inside her.

Not if you keep changing the house. It's making me feel dizzy, not to mention it's ugly. Stop competing and let's go inside. Sheesh! You're like a couple of schoolboys.

Darius cleared his throat. "Tempest would like to go in. That particular shape is obnoxious, but we can live with it for the brief amount of time we will be here if it is what you desire."

Mikhail burst out laughing. "It is obnoxious. Raven would think I had lost my mind. I could not resist."

Darius took Tempest's hand, his thumb brushing a subtle caress over her inner wrist as they entered the house. "I hope you are not here to check on how the cooking is progressing. We are not quite ready for tonight's celebration."

"I have no interest in cooking, although I do not think the others are faring much better than you two. I just dropped by to get your opinion on a couple of things."

Darius waved Mikhail toward the most comfortable chair. "What can I do for you?"

"Well, before we get too deep in serious things, I thought you might like to know, Raven has decreed someone must play Santa Claus."

Darius stiffened, but his face remained without expression. "The jolly man in the red suit."

"Exactly. I can see that your reaction is much the same as mine. Fortunately, I have a son-in-law and I feel it is his duty to take on this . . ." He paused searching for the right word.

Something very close to amusement flickered in the depths of Darius's eyes. "Honored task," he supplied.

Mikhail nodded. "I could not have found a better description."

"I will be more than happy to accompany you when you tell my older brother you are bestowing such a privilege on him."

"Strangely enough, quite a few others wish to be there as well."

Tempest looked from one solemn face to the other. "Are you both crazy? That man could scare the devil."

"That is what you say about me."

"Well, you could too," Tempest pointed out. "But he isn't telling you to play Santa to a bunch of children."

"And I sincerely thank you for that," Darius said. The amusement faded from his eyes as he continued to study Mikhail's face. "You are worried, and not about my brother playing the part of St. Nick. What is it?"

"I am uneasy over the gathering of our women in one place. While I think it is a good thing for all of us to get together, it has occurred to me that our enemies will figure out that it would not take much to wipe out our species."

Darius nodded. "There are so few women and children. Get rid of them and the males have no hope. Very soon chaos would reign and many would choose life as the undead over death."

Mikhail nodded. "I fear it is so. We had an incident a few minutes ago in the woods. A subtle influence none of us felt immediately. Skyler tried to follow the path back to the sender, but they realized she was on to them and shut down. But they now have a direct path to her."

"The other women?" Darius was already checking with and warning Desari and Julian, Dayan and Corrine and lastly, Barack and Syndil. Each responded with a quick touch to assure him there was no threat to them at the moment and they understood to be careful and alert.

"There have been no other incidents and I have sent men ahead to the inn to ferret out any enemies, but we must be vigilant at all times and keep our women and children close and protected."

Like you all don't already do that? Great, he's just giving you more ammunition to be bossy.

Darius ignored her. "The child—Skyler. Is she safe? Gabriel and Lucian are my brothers by blood. Skyler is blood kin."

"We will all see to her safety. You probably don't remember Dimitri—he was much older than you—but he's returned from Russia and is Skyler's lifemate. It is a complication we did not expect."

"Gabriel is protective of her."

"Yes, he is—as he should be. She is invaluable to us." Mikhail leaned toward him. "I know you have been talking with Gregori, Francesca and Shea about how you kept the other children alive after the massacre. They were only babies. You were merely six years old."

"Unfortunately, I do not remember very much. It was centuries ago. We were on another continent, in an unfamiliar world. I did not remember much of my homeland other than the war and the massacre. I inadvertently instilled a fear in the others of these mountains and we avoided the area completely."

Mikhail nodded. "It is understandable, but perhaps you do not realize the miracle you achieved. The greatest minds, our most talented healers, are not able to do what you have done. In order for our species to survive, we must find the answers to why our women miscarry. Why so many of our infants die in their first year. And why we have such a high percentage of male over female births."

Tempest gasped and went completely pale. "Darius?" She framed his face with her hands, forcing him to meet her terrified gaze. "Is this true? Did you know this?"

"Yes." Lifemates did not lie to one another.

"Miscarriages? The child dies in the first year?" She refused to look away from him—refused to allow him to look away from her. "You knew this all along?"

"Our race is dying," Darius said. "We have too few women and even fewer children."

"But you said . . ." She trailed off, dropping her hands as if touching his skin scorched her. "You should have told me this immediately."

"What good would it have done? The decision is made for us. Our child grows within your body. We have already created a life. There is no alternative for me but to ensure the child survives. I refuse to consider any other possibility." His voice was mild, his face carved of stone. His black-black eyes never left hers.

"You should have told me," she repeated.

"Several of our women have been successful in carrying babies," Mikhail said, standing. "There is always hope. Especially now. I will need to discuss this further with you, Darius," he added.

Darius continued to hold Tempest's gaze. "Yes, of course. I am at your disposal." He waited until the prince left before he tunneled his hand in the mass of bright red hair. "We will not lose our child."

"Because you decree it?"

"If that is what it takes. My will is unyielding. I did not lose Desari, or Syndil or Barack or Dayan. They live because I decreed it—because I fought for their lives and used every ounce of will and skill I possessed to ensure their survival. Do not think I would do less for my own child—for our child."

"That's why they all have such confidence in you—why they expect so much of you. Without you they would have all died."

It was the simple truth. He had been six, but already, the Daratrazanoff blood was strong in him and his will grew and grew until he refused to allow defeat into his mind no matter the odds.

"I didn't think I wanted to have a baby, Darius. Now, when I think I may lose it, I know I want it desperately. Shea must be so frightened. She's close to labor. If I were her, I would not want to allow the baby to leave the safety of my body."

"She has Jacques to keep them both safe, Tempest. You have me."

Tempest slid onto his lap, laying her head against his chest. "Then I'm not going to worry."

He kissed her gently, lovingly. "I will believe that when I see it."

"For that, you can bake the pies."

"Pies?"

"The gooey purple stuff. You said you would do anything for me and I need those pies baked."

"You think I cannot do it."

"I think it will be very funny to watch you try." She leaned in for another kiss, laughter beginning to bubble up.

7

Barack, in the form of an owl, circled the house he was occupying with Syndil. There didn't appear to be a disturbance, but his heart was still in his throat. Something didn't feel right. He reached out to her on their private, very intimate telepathic band, but she didn't respond. He felt her presence, felt her focus—her entire concentration elsewhere—a good sign as Syndil would have been broadcasting waves of fear had she been frightened.

He dropped down fast, shapeshifting as he plummeted, and he hit the porch nearly sprinting, needing to see her. She was still so emotionally fragile and their relationship was very tentative at times. She had a tendency to retreat even from him. Ever since the brutal attack by Savon, a trusted family member who had turned vampire, she'd had problems with trust and especially intimacy.

"Syndil!" he called out to her, striding quickly through the small cabin.

There was no answer, only the sound of his own heart thundering in his ears. He inhaled sharply, scented the two leopards and . . . He stilled, fighting for calm. He inhaled again. Blood. Not just any blood—Syndil's blood.

He shoved open the door to the bedroom to find the two large cats, Sasha and Forest, curled on the bed. They both raised their heads and gave him a long, slow appraisal. Sasha bared her teeth while Forest openly snarled.

Barack's heart jumped. The leopards always traveled with the band and never acted aggressive toward any member of the band, not even when they were in a bad temper.

He snarled back at them, closed the door and whirled around, racing back out into the night. He inhaled again and found her scent—the direction she'd taken. At once he shifted on the run, taking to the air to move more swiftly, his heart pounding in fear for her. He followed her scent through the forest until he came upon a clearing of scorched ground. A terrible battle had been fought here. Trees were bent and twisted, leaves shriveled, and in places the ground was scarred from the acid burn of the unholiest of creatures—the undead. He caught sight of her and his breath stilled in his lungs.

Barack watched the woman kneeling on the blackened ground, her arms spread wide, palms hovering just above the earth. Snow fell softly over her, coating her hair and clothes so that she appeared to sparkle. From his angle he could see the concentration on her face, her eyes closed, long lashes forming two thick crescents. She appeared serene, her entire energy focused on her task. She looked beautiful—a little fey, her black hair gleaming beneath the coating of snow, flakes on her long lashes and her sinfully perfect mouth whispering a crooning song of hope and encouragement to the barren land.

He stood, his heart pounding in his chest, the terror of not finding her safe in their home receding while love stormed in to fill every part of his heart and soul until there was no longer room for any other emotion. Syndil. His lifemate. Of course she would be healing the earth. She would have heard it moaning in pain, the evil spreading slowly through the soil, poisoning and burning every living thing. She was the most beautiful woman he'd ever seen—could ever imagine. Beneath her hands, green grass sprang up through the snow. Small shrubs and trees pushed their way to the surface as she sang softly, coaxing growth.

Desari, with her pure, incredible voice, could bring peace to people. With just her voice she could wrap an audience in satin sheets and candlelight, and make them remember old loves and tarnished hopes. Syndil's voice also held great power, but hers was bound to the earth. Scarred and damaged lands called to her. She could never ignore their summons. Few could hear the screams and cries as she did, and even fewer could heal where blisters and lesions lay raw upon the land.

Syndil astonished him with her power. He watched as she shifted left, then right, moving up the slope, touching a badly damaged tree, enticing new growth, expunging the hideous results the undead had left behind in the soil. She stood and turned toward the small creek—the water no longer running, but standing still even though the creek bed was filled to capacity. Dark brownish-red stains covered the surface of the water, and tentacles spread out from a discolored gelatin-like ball altered the composition of the water. Thousands of tiny white parasites made up the round globe, and many used the tentacles as tiny arteries and veins moving out away from where the rest congealed in a large mass.

Lifting her hands, Syndil began to sing, oblivious to Barack's presence, her entire focus on the damage to the land. He always knew the moment she was near, yet she hadn't the slightest idea her lifemate was close by. It should have upset him, but he couldn't help the surge of pride in her. Whenever she committed to healing the earth, she was totally, unswervingly focused, often expending far more energy than she could afford. Just as a healer of people was left drained and swaying with weariness, so was Syndil when she healed the earth.

Her voice swelled with power, and the parasites writhed as if in pain. The jellied mass shook ominously. Barack moved into a better position to defend his lifemate. The air reeked, the smell so noxious, in spite of the falling snow, the foul odor nearly gagged him. Barack inched closer to peer at the congealed mass. The creatures looked almost like maggots, but much smaller. The stench of evil permeated the entire area.

He looked around him, quartering the area with every one of his senses, scanning for signs of an enemy. Was this the aftermath of the vampires who had died here during the attempted assassination of the prince? Or was it another, much newer threat? He stepped closer to Syndil, stretching out his hand to her, but as her voice filled the night with her strength, the small parasites began to explode, much like popcorn, leaping out of the jelly ball in an effort to get away from her voice. Once in the exposed air, they burst.

Barack's hand fell to his side. He looked at the trees, twisted, bent and blackened, the sap oozing out of numerous lesions, congealed with the same brown-red gel. Parasites bubbled up from half-a-dozen trees to drop lifeless to the ground. Barack waved his hand toward the sky. At once the wind picked up and the air charged, crackling and snapping. A whip of lightning flicked across the layer of carcasses in the snow, turning them instantly to black ash. With a howl of fury, the wind scattered the remains in all directions while the snow rained down and once more covered the earth with a pristine white blanket.

For the first time, Syndil turned her head, her large, dark eyes soft—almost liquid. A ghost of a smile curved her mouth, drawing his attention to the beautiful shape of her lips, and his heart clenched, a vise squeezing hard enough to hurt. All those years he had spent with her, never once realizing she had been driving his need for sex. Never once had he looked at her any way other than as a foster sister, yet all along she had kept his emotions safeguarded. It was no wonder that not once had he been satisfied with another woman. It had become laughable over the centuries, the terrible need clawing at him until he thought he might go insane if he didn't touch a woman's skin, bury his body deep within hers. There had been so many willing, yet he was trapped in some kind of mindless torment, needing them—yet none could fulfill his desires.

At times, Syndil still felt he had betrayed her, but at last he understood the endless cycle that had been happening to him. Looking at her, inhaling her scent, the brush of her hair or fingers turned his body into a hard painful ache that only she could assuage. He'd had a hard-on for so many years he could no longer count, and looking at her only made it happen all over again. Only now she was his—a gentle, sexy woman he didn't deserve, but who somehow managed to love him all the same.

"What are you thinking about, Barack? You look sad."

One did not lie to one's lifemate. In any case, she had only to touch his mind to know. "I remember the precise moment I realized that it was *you* arousing my body to such a painful ache. You stood by a stream brushing out your long hair. I found myself fascinated with every stroke of the brush and wishing I could feel your hair against my bare skin. I wanted to lose myself in all that silk, and I knew you had been the one I wanted all along—it was you I'd been searching for among so many women."

"How long ago was that?"

"We were in France."

"That was fifty years ago."

He nodded. "I thought what I felt was wrong. We were children together, a family. It seemed—distasteful. I was afraid I was tainted in some way. I would watch you after that; every move you made seemed sensual, seductive. And I hated the men watching you—coming close to you."

"But you still went off with other women."

He shook his head. "I kept up the illusion, but I already had had too many unfulfilled nights. What was the use? Other women no longer drew me once I figured out what was happening."

"I saw you." There was pain in her voice, and it made him wince.

"You saw me flirt and walk off. I took blood and left them with false memories. The nights were torment, Syndil. Sometimes I thought I was in hell." He reached out his hand to her. "I had a terrible secret and I could never share with anyone. I lusted after you to the point that I could not let you get too close to me. I was always afraid someone would discover the way I felt about you. At the time I would have given anything that it was just lust, easily satisfied. It was so much more—is so much more."

"Why didn't you tell me?"

"A Carpathian male should always—*always* be in control of himself. We wield too much power to be ruled by anything but our brains. I could not control my body or my thoughts when I was close to you." He ran his fingers through his hair. "I know everything about you, Syndil. The way you tilt your head just slightly when you're considering whether or not you are going to participate in a conversation. You tug on your left earlobe when you are worried. You have the most beautiful smile I've ever seen. I know you're so fragile and yet at the same time, you are incredibly strong."

A slow smile chased the worried frown from his face. "I always walk behind you to the stage so later, when I'm alone, I can feel the sway of your hips and the brush of your hair."

"You never told me this."

He rubbed his lower jaw. "It is a little humiliating to admit I have been obsessed with you. And when I knew I couldn't take it anymore, that I had to admit the truth, even if it meant leaving our family, you were attacked by Savon, our trusted brother."

Syndil glanced away from him, back toward the stream. The water ran cold and clean, all traces of the poison gone. Barack followed her gaze and as always, when he saw the result of her work, it left him feeling humble and proud of her.

"Syndil, there is no one in this world who can do as you've done. Do you have any idea how amazing you are?"

She looked out over the blackened ruins of the battle-scarred land. "There is much to be done here. Our enemies left their poison in the ground to work its way beneath the soil where we rest. If they can turn the earth against us, they have won."

Barack's head went up alertly. She sounded so weary. The energy needed to heal large sections of land destroyed by fire or foul vampire magic was enormous, and he had very little idea of the toll it would take on her to heal what the undead had wrought here with the size of such devastation. She looked pale, her eyes almost too large for her face. She pressed her hands to her chest as if her heart ached. "Syndil." He reached out his hand to her. "Come here to me."

He waited. His heart beating, a small part of him praying she would step forward, eager for his touch, for his aid, but as always, there was that tiny, brief moment of hesitation, the wariness in her eyes, the shadow in her mind she could no longer hide from him. She crossed the distance to him, reaching out. His fingers closed around hers, and he drew her with exquisite gentleness to him. In spite of the fact that Carpathians could regulate body temperature, she was cold, shivering a little. He enfolded her in his arms, shielding her from the snow with his larger frame and using his own body heat and energy to warm her. He drew her scent into his lungs and smelled blood.

"What happened?" His drew her arm down so he could look at it.

She frowned, her body losing some of its stiffness to sink more fully into his. "Sasha and Forest were lying with me on the bed, sweet as usual, and then Sasha began to get agitated. Within minutes, Forest followed suit. They began pacing back and forth, sending out distress calls. I scanned, but the most I could do was feel a hint of power in the air. Not good or evil, simply power."

"That does not explain these scratches, Syndil. They are deep." He bent his head to her bare arm, his lips feathering kisses up and down the lacerations, tongue swirling over the wounds, taking away the pain with his healing saliva. He kissed her arm again and raised his head, one hand cupping her chin so she couldn't look away from the censure in his eyes. "You should have called me immediately. Your well-being comes before all else."

"There was nothing to tell you. With so many Carpathians gathered in one place, there is bound to be power in the air at all times. I just assumed the leopards were reacting to the different feel. They're used to us, but not to the others. They were fine with me until I tried to leave the room. I'm sorry. It's just that I couldn't think of anything else but taking care of this." She swept her hand in a graceful arc to take in the blackened land. "I had been hearing the screaming of the earth since I awoke, and I could no longer ignore the call. I knew it would be difficult and draining, but I didn't expect . . ." She broke off and looked over his shoulder at the huge area destroyed by the battle with the undead. "It's so large, Barack, so much damage."

There were tears in her voice—in her mind. "You're just tired, sweetheart. You need to feed." There was both sensual invitation and dominant command in his voice.

He tried hard to suppress the rougher side of his nature as much as possible, particularly when it came to anything sexual with Syndil. She was with him—and that was the most important thing in the world to him. Whatever time she needed to develop trust in him—years, centuries, perhaps longer—it mattered little. She could have all the time she needed; he just had to control the dominant nature so prevalent in the males of his species. He wouldn't risk ruining the fragile trust developing between them.

He opened his shirt with a single thought, and Syndil turned her face to press against his chest. The rub of her soft skin against his, the feel of her lips moving just above his heart, her hair brushing over him like silk, all sent urgent need slamming hard to pool in his groin in a painful ache. His fingers tangled in her hair and he cradled her head in his arm, his body clenching in anticipation. There was a heartbeat—two. She kissed his chest, teased with her tongue, scraped once, twice with her teeth. His heart went into overtime. His body hardened more, jerked with eagerness.

Syndil's teeth sank deep, the pain giving way to instant pleasure, his body flooding with ecstasy. He shifted to rock his hips against her. It only inflamed his senses more. Syndil unexpectedly—and for the first time without his prompting—merged her mind with his, feeding him her own sexual desires, the flare of heat, her blood running hot, the erotic pictures of her leaning over him, hair cascading down to pool on his skin while she . . .

Barack groaned aloud. *You cannot do that to me and not expect reprisals.*

Her laughter was low and sensual—a definite invitation. He closed his eyes, savoring her response to him—the acknowledgment of her need for him. He simply lifted her, cradling her to his chest while she fed, and took to the air.

Syndil licked his chest, closing the tiny pinpricks, and lifted her mouth to his neck. Her hands slid inside his open shirt. "Where are you going in such a hurry?" she murmured against his skin. "I have always wanted to make love in the snow. What's the use of being able to control our temperatures if we can't utilize it for our enjoyment?"

Barack didn't care where they were. If she wanted snow, there was a perfectly good spot he could see that looked somewhat protected from the elements. He dropped down fast, his mouth already on hers, fire flaring between them. His need of her was always hot—shattering—yet he kept his hands gentle and his aggression controlled, not wanting to frighten her. She panicked when she was beneath him, and never once had he assumed a dominant sexual position.

She pushed his shirt aside, shoving it down his arms as if she was in such a frenzy to get to his skin that she'd forgotten she could brush the offensive material away with her mind. He watched the rising desire on her face, the burning intensity in her eyes, as she spread kisses across his chest, up to his throat, caught his mouth with hers and returned to his chest with teasing bites.

Never had she acted this way toward him, and he couldn't stop his body's response, his own desire building faster and hotter than ever before. Syndil wanting him, initiating their lovemaking, was more of an aphrodisiac than anything else could ever be. She'd never shown a hint of the same urgent need he always felt when he touched her.

Of course I feel it. Her teeth tugged at his ear. Her tongue swirled and played and danced over his skin. *I just don't know how to show you properly.*

Was there a touch of shame in her voice? He hoped not; she had nothing to be ashamed of. He would spend eternity trying to take away the betrayal and memory of Savon raping her—and there was a part of him that would never forgive himself for not being there to protect her.

You show me just fine. He put all the fierce love he had for her into his voice, his hands coming up to tangle in her impossibly long hair. She always wore part of it up, and he loosened the pins to let it all fall free. Her hair was so sensual, and right now, with her mouth doing sinful things to his body, he craved the warm silk of her hair spilling over him. He didn't want her to ever stop, but he needed her clothes gone.

Then take them off.

He smiled at the impatience in her voice. He always asked permission so as not to alarm her, but maybe—hopefully—they were past that now. He waved his hand and she stood before him, stark naked except for her long hair, a silken cloak to frame her soft skin and luscious body. As always, when he looked at her, his heart pounded, his lungs seized, and he felt tears burning in his throat. No one would ever be more beautiful to him.

She lifted her head as she followed suit and whisked off his trousers and shoes, leaving him naked in the snow and starkly aroused. "I want to be past that now," she whispered. "I love you so much, Barack, and I need to be able to show you. More than that, I need for you to show me. I know you have to hold back and I don't want that for you—for us—anymore." Her fingers whispered over his thickened shaft and his breath left his lungs in a heated rush. "I just have never wanted to start something I couldn't finish." She kissed her way down his belly, her hands caressing and stroking until he was afraid he might go out of his mind. *Do you understand what I'm saying to you?*

I always understand you, my love. There is no need to warn me. He was proud of her for her boldness, but he feared he might not make it through this night. She was reading his mind, feeling the fire building in his groin as she wrapped her fist around his heavy erection and bent her head to breathe warm air over him.

She was the most beautiful sight he'd ever seen, her body perfect, breasts full and ripe, her long black hair a stark contrast to the white snow. When he saw her intention, the erotic image in her mind, his body hardened even

more. He waved his hand and the sky rained rose petals alongside the drifting snow. "Sweetheart, you don't have to do this."

But she did. She wanted it nearly as much as he did—he could see it on
her face. Just once, he wanted her like this—enjoying him. Wanting his
body as much as he wanted hers. No, more than that. Needing him in the
way he needed her. Desperate to touch him, to taste him, to feel his body
moving in hers, his heart beating the same rhythm as hers. Just once. Mostly
he needed to see the dark hunger in her eyes, feel it in every touch of her
hands. He needed to see eagerness and enjoyment when she looked at him.
Just this once—that was all he would ask for.

He closed his eyes briefly as her fingertips trailed lightly over his shaft,
sending small electrical charges whipping through his bloodstream. She
looked up at him and smiled as her tongue slid over the broad head in a curling dance that took his senses to an entirely new level. A soft growl escaped
when she raked her fingernails along the inside of his thigh. Before he could
stop himself, he reached out and tangled his fingers in her silky hair, gently
pushing it over her shoulders. Looking down at her kneeling before him,
with that small, mysterious half smile on her face and that too-hot look in
her eyes, nearly was his undoing.

He kneaded her shoulders for a moment, eased the tension from the
nape of her neck and then slid his palms over her soft skin to her breasts—
all the while breathing deep to stay in control. His thumbs found her nipples, brushing them into hard peaks, his caresses drawing a gasp of pleasure
from her. His hands cupped her breasts, fingers stroking and caressing with
an expertise of knowing her body so well.

Syndil cried out with pleasure as the sensations swamped her. As always, with one touch of his hands, she was on fire. She knew he could shatter her, bring her to a fever pitch with just the strong pull of his mouth or
the scrape of his teeth. He knew everything about her body, every way to
bring her pleasure, and he always did—unselfishly and wholeheartedly. He
always put her pleasure before his own. It wasn't fair. She desperately wanted
to bring him to that same fever pitch, sweep him away on a tidal wave of
passion, bring him the kind of ecstasy he always brought her.

Her fingers tangled in his hair. His mouth and stroking hands sent vibrations humming through her bloodstream and quickening her pulse. Her womb

clenched, and she felt the familiar urgent need gathering deep in her core. She forced herself back in control, her fist closing over the silky-hard length of his erection, deliberately sending warm air over him to distract him.

His breath caught in his throat and he straightened, throwing his head back when her mouth closed over him, tongue sliding and curling as all the while she kept the suction tight. He rewarded her with a groan, thickening even more.

Pleasure flashed through her. She kept her mind firmly merged in his, reading his every thought, every image, making adjustments to push his pleasure higher, until his hands gripped her hair, his hips thrust helplessly and guttural sounds escaped his throat.

She felt his body tighten, the rush of fire spreading from his toes through his body straight to his groin. She took him deeper, finding the perfect rhythm so that he shuddered and muttered an expletive she'd never heard him use.

"You're killing me," he whispered hoarsely.

In a good way, Syndil knew. Her entire body reacted to the knowledge that she was pushing Barack to the very edge of his control. She wanted to shatter it, to do to him what he did to her. The power felt incredible, and the satisfaction even more so. She was almost euphoric with happiness, kissing her way up his belly to his chest, his throat, urging him over the top of her, so frantic to have him buried deep inside her she couldn't think of anything but pleasing him—pleasing herself.

She fell back into the rose petal-covered snow, dragging him with her. Skin pressed to skin, hearts beat the same rhythm. She felt his weight settle over hers, his hands hard on her hips, his knee nudging her thighs apart. He thrust hard, entering her body, joining them together in one fiercely primitive stroke. Her nails dug into his shoulders. Lightning streaked through her body, and she cried out with drowning pleasure.

He moved in her, hard, sure strokes, filling her emptiness until she felt as if she were soaring free. His hair slid over her skin, a sensuous silk brushing her already hypersensitive breasts. Her body tightened, muscles clenching and gripping as her hips rose to meet the fast rhythm of his. She moved slightly, adjusting her position, and his hands gripped her hard, holding her down.

At once she was aware of her surroundings, of the man on top of her. Syndil looked up at the face, almost savage in his desire, red flames flickering in the depths of his black eyes. She could see his teeth, already lengthened, the muscles clearly defined in his arms.

Syndil tried desperately to hold onto the passion that seemed to always be locked away inside her. It poured out on occasion, but somewhere, somehow, just when she thought she had conquered her fears, a door slammed shut and dammed up her needs, her physical desires, behind a wall of terror. She fought it, fought the rising panic and the memory of teeth biting at her, of brutal hands hurting her, of something obscene and unnatural ripping through her, taking her virginity without love or thought for her innocence. He had been family, a loved one, yet he had attacked her, nearly tearing out her throat, beating her, raping her in every way possible. She had fought until the bones in her hands were broken and her flesh was saturated with blood and she thought he would kill her.

This wasn't Savon, her attacker, this was Barack, the man she loved above all others, yet she couldn't separate the two when Barack covered her body with his and held her down. She couldn't breathe, couldn't think, couldn't hear him trying to soothe her. She could only feel the weight of him crushing her, feel the grip of his hands, see the glow of red flames in his eyes.

"Stop." She whispered the word, tears beginning to form in her eyes. Her throat swelled, threatening to choke her. "Stop. Oh, God, Barack, you have to stop." Her voice swung toward hysteria as her control shattered, her mind seemed to fragment and she couldn't distinguish past from present. She began to fight him, hitting hard, clawing at his face, pushing at his chest.

She drew blood before he caught her wrists, shaking her head back and forth to avoid his mouth when he bent close. He whispered something to her, but she couldn't hear him, caught up in the deadly illusion she couldn't seem to escape.

Barack groaned and rolled off her, to lie faceup in the snow, staring at the flakes as they fell from the sky. He slung one arm across his eyes to hide his expression, shielding his mind so she couldn't see the anguish and frustration filling him. He wanted to roar with rage to the heavens, but he stayed silent, struggling to bring his body under control. He heard her choke back a sob, and turned his head toward her.

Tear sparkled like diamonds in her eyes, trailed down her face to drop into the snow-covered ground. "I'm sorry, Barack. I'm sorry. What's wrong with me?" She covered her face with her hands and wept as if her heart were breaking.

"Syndil, there's nothing wrong with you." Barack came up on his knees and reached for her, keeping his movements slow and gentle. "Come here to me, baby, let me hold you."

She could see the scratches on his face and chest, down one forearm, even a long thin scratch on his hip. Tiny drops of blood beaded up, criss-crossing his skin so that he looked as if he'd been attacked by a cat.

"What have I done?" Ashamed, she tried to struggle, to break his grip on her arm. "I have to go away. We can't keep doing this. Let me go, Barack. I'll go back to leopard form and stay in the earth until this passes."

"I don't want to hear that. You aren't leaving me. You have a duty to your lifemate, and it isn't sex. You stay aboveground, with me, in your natural form, do you hear me, Syndil? I expect nothing less of you." This time he didn't hide the Carpathian male. He made it a command, and bared his white teeth to emphasize he meant business.

"Why? Why would you even want me? I can't keep doing this to you and live with myself. How long is your patience going to last? How long before you turn to another woman for the things I can't give you?'

"Another woman?" he echoed, so shocked at the suggestion it showed on his face. "Syndil, you aren't making sense. There is no other woman for me. What aren't you giving me? I make love to you all the time."

"*You* make love to me. I should be loving you back."

"You do love me back." He raked a hand through his dark hair, clearly agitated. "So you have a small problem with one position. *One.* Do you think it matters to me?"

She didn't respond, simply shook her head, covering her face tightly with both hands. Tears leaked out and her shoulders heaved as she fought for breath through the sobs.

"Syndil, I love you. You're my life. We have years, centuries to get this right. You matter to me, not sex." He gave her a little shake. "Look at me,

Syndil. If you never can let me lie over the top of you, so be it. Why is it so important to you? You don't see that image in my mind. It doesn't matter to me what position we make love in, not now, nor will it ever. Damn it, look at me."

He caught her hands and pulled them from her face, staring into her eyes. "I love you more than life itself. So we can't make love with me on top. Is that some sort of red badge of courage to force yourself into a position you feel threatened in? Do you honestly, for one moment, think what position we have sex in is important to me?"

"It is to me," she whispered, ducking her head. "I'm so ashamed I can't love my lifemate the way he deserves. I can heal the earth after the worst of battles, but I can't heal myself. I can't be a decent mate to you. I try so hard, Barack, I really want you. I love the way you make me feel as if I'm the only woman in the world, as if no one else could ever please you, but I can't do it. I can't."

He swept his arm around her head and dragged her against him. "You're an idiot, Syndil. You love me and that is all that matters. The rest of this is just silliness. I'd make love to you standing on my head if that was how you wanted me." He caught her chin and forced her head up. "Do you really think I can't look into your mind and see how much you love me?"

"But you have to suppress your own nature all the time, Barack."

He burst out laughing. "Being a dominant, overbearing male isn't always best, Syndil. Don't you think Darius has to occasionally suppress that side of him for Tempest, and that she might wish he'd do it a little more? And Julian definitely has to work at it for Desari. The same with Dayan and Corinne. It's our nature to be in command, but you are the light to our darkness. Unrelenting dominance has to be balanced by you."

"But you were never like Darius, Barack. You get bossy, but . . ." She trailed off, but there was hope in her eyes when she framed his face with her hands.

"Because all of us allow Darius to lead us does not mean we do not have these natural traits. You didn't see them in me before because we did not share minds. Darius is a strong leader. We are content in his leadership." A small grin flashed briefly on his face. "He does most of the work, and that suits me just fine. But in the end, we all have the traits nature dictated to us. The point, my beautiful love, is that you, as my lifemate, bring me balance."

"I do?"

He bent his head to press a small kiss over each eyelid. "You do," he assured her. He trailed kisses down her face to the corner of her mouth. "And I am grateful. Darkness spreads and we have to fight it every day."

"But it wasn't in you—not like the others," Syndil said.

"Because of you. Even before I made my claim on you, you were already providing a balance for me. Syndil, you aren't just my lifemate. You're my life, my only love, my world. I have known you since you were a babe, I watched you grow into a remarkable, talented, unbelievable woman. Look at what you do with the earth. Who else can work such a miracle?" He kissed the tip of her nose, feathered his lips over hers and slid his tongue along the seam of her mouth. "I was in love with you long before I ever knew what a lifemate was."

"Are you sure, Barack?" There were still tears gleaming in her eyes, but her lips moved against his. "You have to be sure."

"That is the only thing I'm sure of." His mouth found hers and he lifted her gently, settling her over his lap, waiting for her to settle over him like a sheath over a sword.

Syndil's breath caught in her throat. He filled her, fit so snug, so exquisitely tight that the silky friction sent fire dancing once again through her veins. One moment she was in tears, the next he was lifting her toward the heavens. She linked her fingers behind his neck and eased back, her body moving in a familiar rhythm as she began to ride him. She couldn't imagine how she had gotten through her life without him. He made her feel beautiful and extraordinary when she was certain she really wasn't.

"I love you, Barack." She pulled back to look into his eyes. "I really love you."

The sight of her took his breath. Her full breasts swayed sensually, her nipples peaked and hard in sexy invitation. Her small waist and hips undulated, eyes slumberous, mouth swollen from his kisses.

"I know you do," he murmured, and brushed a kiss across each eyelid. He could barely speak with the sizzling heat rising so fast, so ferociously, with every bit of pleasure that more dominant position had given him. Deliberately he shared his mind, shared what she did to him body as well as his heart. "You're my life, Syndil, and I don't want you forgetting it again."

She moved with him, a counterpoint to each thrust, driving their pleasure ever higher. Barack was her world and his acceptance of her meant everything. Maybe she couldn't lie beneath his body, but she could enjoy other sensually arousing positions and she could make the most of each and every one of them.

Barack's arms tightened possessively and a small thrill went through him that she didn't protest, or pull away. Her muscles clamped around him, squeezing like a fist, so slick and hot and tight that he couldn't hold on a second longer. He threw back his head and yelled to the night in joy, feeling her body ripple with pleasure around his. For a while neither could breathe properly, or even speak—just feel.

Barack recovered first, kissing the top of her head, her ears and finally her soft mouth. "I love you, Syndil."

"I'm beginning to believe you really do," she said softly as she rose with her usual grace. She held out her hand and he stood beside her, a tall, strong man who loved her enough to give her space and time.

Dressing in the easy manner of their people, they strolled, hand in hand, back through the snow to the little cabin. It looked inviting, cozy even, and Syndil picked up the pace, drawing him with her. "You will help me cook something, won't you? Corinne assured me the recipe she gave me was easy and fast."

"I have my doubts about that," he teased, "but I'm willing to try."

As they walked up the narrow path to the cabin, the smile faded from his face. Barack frowned and took a careful look around, the back of his neck suddenly itching with unease. He paused before pushing opening the door to the small cabin, sweeping Syndil behind him with one arm. "I don't like the feel of this. The silence."

"It's snowing. It's always quiet when it snows."

"Maybe." But something was wrong. A whisper of movement from inside had him closing the door firmly and pushing her away from the cabin. "Get to safety, Syndil. Hide yourself in the trees while I figure out what's wrong."

"Are the cats all right?" she asked anxiously.

"I'm about to find out."

She caught the waistband of his jeans, curling her fingers around the edge. "I'll be afraid out here alone. Let me go in with you. Even if something waits there, I'd rather be with you and know what's going on."

He cursed under his breath for being weak. He could deny her nothing when she was afraid. "Stay behind me, Syndil, and do exactly what I say."

She nodded and moved closer. "Does it feel like a vampire?"

He shook his head. It felt like danger—trouble—something out of sync.

"Not in harmony," Syndil said suddenly, going very still. Her grip tightened on his jeans. "In the house. The cats. I reached for them and they are—crazy."

He turned back to her, pulling her close to reassure her. "It's all right, honey." He felt the leopards prowling within the walls of the cabin, enraged for some reason he couldn't fathom. He tried to reach out to them as he'd been doing since they were young, to calm them, but neither responded. He had to get them into their cage, both for their safety and the safety of any person coming in contact with them, until he could figure out what was wrong.

He slipped inside beneath the door, streaming in as vapor, swirling through the rooms until he found the cats, very conscious that Syndil was right behind him in the same form.

Forest, the male, lay stretched out on a bed, while Sasha, the female, paced back and forth restlessly. The moment he entered the bedroom, Sasha reacted, snarling, showing her teeth, tail twitching as she paced, her eyes darting around the room as she detected his presence. Forest launched his body from the couch, going from a prone position to a full-out attack, claws raking through the insubstantial vapor in an effort to get at Barack.

He streamed away, out of reach, trying to push the cat's mind back toward sanity. Leopards were notorious for their tempers, but this savage behavior was way out of character for either cat. The leopards had been with the Troubadours since they were born and had never behaved in such a manner. Sasha kept looking at the window, acting as though she might break through the glass to escape.

Something is terribly wrong with them, he told Syndil. *I can't control them.*

Syndil remained silent, listening to the earth. *There is a subtle flow of power—of energy. It's upsetting the leopards. There are so many Carpathians here. Most are probably using energy for shifting and other tasks. Maybe the cats are too sensitive to be here.*

Maybe. Barack doubted it, but he was going to cage the animals. *I'm going to get them to follow me to the cages. I can't direct them inside, so I'll have to trick them.*

How can you do that? There was trepidation in her voice.

I'll just use myself as bait.

Syndil drew in her breath sharply, fighting back the protest welling up. *I was afraid of that. Be careful, Barack.*

He touched her mentally, his vapor circling hers for just a moment as if he could brush up against her in reassurance. Barack shimmered into his human form right under the female's nose, shifting back almost immediately and streaming through the house, leading the cats to the smallest bedroom, where the heavily barred traveling cage was kept.

He reached out to open the door of the cage, shifting for just seconds so he could use his hand. Forest leapt, raking Barack's arm, tearing deep gouges in his skin before Barack could shift back to mist. He streamed toward the back of the cage, leading the two leopards inside. They followed, raging at him.

Behind them, he waved the door closed. Both threw themselves at the bars, snarling a protest. Barack didn't wait for them to settle down, sending word to Darius and the other band members before taking his natural form.

Syndil was already reaching for him, stroking her fingers down his arm, leaning into him to use her saliva to heal the wounds. "You need to be faster," she told him, her large eyes chastising him.

A slow smile lit his dark gaze. "I don't know, sweetheart. Then I wouldn't have your sexy little mouth all over me, now would I?"

Her eyebrow shot up. "Actually, yes, you probably would."

8

Mikhail flew low over the forest, making several passes, quartering the region in an effort to ferret out any danger that might be lurking to harm his people. He touched Raven's mind often, could feel her happiness as she prepared whatever dish she was making for the celebration dinner. He had had no idea she missed cooking, and it shamed him. He had been her lifemate for years, yet he still was discovering things about her. She enjoyed the preparation of a meal, the presentation, the pleasure others received from it.

He felt the mental brush of her fingers over his skin. Felt her smile, the warmth in her eyes.

Yes, I do enjoy cooking for others, but it certainly is nothing I need in my life—as you are. My life is full, Mikhail, and I have no regrets.

Her voice filled his mind with love, kept even the memories of the terrible, haunting loneliness at bay. No Carpathian male who had lost emotion and the ability to see in color and then had it all restored by finding his lifemate would ever give her up. At that moment, he ached inside with love for her. It helped ease the terrible burden of knowing that some of the unattached warriors who had returned for the celebration, men of honor and integrity, would eventually lose their battle with darkness.

You are worried about Dimitri.

I feel—uneasy. There is trouble in the wind, but I cannot find it. Dimitri does concern me. None of us can forget the loneliness we felt before we found our lifemates, but at the same time, we also remember the darkness spreading, taking over, the demon calling for freedom. There was both worry and warning in his voice.

Dimitri will be fine because he has to be. You can only do so much, Mikhail. The others have responsibility too. You did not create the species.

No, but my people were left in my hands and I intend that they flourish. I refuse to allow nature or our enemies or even our own natures to triumph over us.

Raven went silent for a moment, contemplating. *You don't believe Carpathians are targeted for extinction simply through a natural process, do you? Because whatever has caused this is not natural.*

Mikhail smiled to himself. Raven always fiercely supported him and his people. He brushed mental fingers tenderly down her face as he flew high above the forest and began to drop lower and lower in a wide circle. Snow drifted down, lighter now, but still steady, turning the entire landscape a glistening white. He liked the snow; it always reminded of him of daylight, pushing the night aside briefly so that the world glittered a beautiful silver.

Mikhail flew over the area of blackened ruins, now covered in snow, that had once been some of their richest lands. The battle between the Carpathians and vampires had left the land scarred and damaged. He had noticed lately that more and more after the undead departed a region, they left behind the beginnings of a barren wasteland that sometimes seemed alive, creeping out to destroy the areas around it. It was one more thing he had to address—and very soon.

Something caught the sharp eyes of the owl, and he dropped lower to skim between the trees to inspect the battleground. In one section, tiny new shoots had pushed through the snow-covered soil. The trees were no longer bent and twisted, but stood proudly, branches raised to the sky. Shocked, Mikhail landed on the ground, shimmering into human form as he did so. Everywhere he looked small green shoots appeared, the stalks healthy and growing thick and wild in spite of the snow. He crouched low to examine the soil. Instead of the toxic mess that had been there, the soil was dark, rich with nutrients—a virtual miracle. The sound of water caught his attention.

Clear. Cold. Clean. Running over rocks once again. He sank down beside the small creek just to listen to the sound of hope. *Raven!* He couldn't hide the excitement in his voice—the sheer wonder. *I remember this from my childhood.* He sent her the image. *There was a woman in our village. We have forgotten the old ways. We had a society, artisans—craftsmen—scholars as well as healers. Not only did we have healers for our people, but there was a woman. I only saw her once and I was but a young boy. I remember very little, only that green sprang up around her wherever she went and that she was present at all births. Perhaps Lucian can tell me about this art. He and Gabriel are among the most ancient. They might remember.*

There was a small hesitation on Raven's part. *A healing of the earth?*

Shea and Gregori seem to think some of the problems with our women and children start with the soil. If we have a healer of the earth among us, can she not provide our pregnant women a safe haven to rest in? To birth in?

Was this done in the past?

He rubbed his temples trying to reach into his boyhood memories. It was so long ago and even back then, things were already starting to change the ways of their race. He had been a child, but he was certain of seeing the woman. *The soil is some of the richest I have ever seen. When I plunge my hands into it, I can feel the difference.* He tried to keep his excitement contained.

Who has done this?

I do not know, but I intend to find out.

Mikhail. Raven hesitated. *This probably sounds silly, but last evening when quite a few of the ladies got together in the caverns with the pools, we all went swimming, remember? I told you about it.*

He did remember vaguely. Some of the women had gathered together in an effort to get to know one another. *You said you had a good time.*

We go there often; it's beautiful and the soil as well as the water is rich and rejuvenating, but this time it seemed even more so. I remember thinking how the cavern looked renewed and the soil darker and richer, the water in the pools amazing, but I thought it was just me—that maybe I was just very happy to be with everyone.

And? he prompted hearing her hesitation.

You're going to think I'm crazy, but when I woke tonight and knew I could conceive, my first thought was that I should have stayed out of the water.

His heart jumped in his chest. He reached down to touch one of the budding branches from a young sapling that hadn't been there a few hours earlier. *Who was there with you?*

Savannah went with me. Desari, Syndil and Tempest were there, and Corrinne and Alexandria. Sara dropped by briefly. What are you thinking?

The impossible. And because he needed to give more thought before voicing hope, he changed the subject. *How is your meal coming?* He was feeling much better about tonight's celebration. If this gathering resulted in finding a woman who could heal the earth and help protect their pregnant women and infants, giving their healers more time to find answers, he would be eternally grateful—and their species would truly have something to celebrate. And what if—just what if . . . He hardly dared to hope that the water or the soil had encouraged the women to be able to conceive. He didn't dare hope, but it was there anyway for the first time in a long while, refusing to be suppressed.

Better than fine now. Christmas always seems to bring miracles. We just have to look for them. Find this person, Mikhail. If she can do what you say, she is more valuable than any of us realize.

Mikhail took to the air once again, his heart pounding in his chest. Far below him, he glimpsed a couple wrapped around one another, oblivious to anything but each other. Once more he quickly scanned the region, needing to ensure the safety of each of his people. Again, although he had that same edgy feeling that kept his alarm system prodding him, he could find nothing that indicated an enemy was setting a trap. He sent a small warning to the male, a slight hint of censure reminding him to keep alert for enemies, and flew on until he found the small remote cabin Lucian had chosen for his stay. Several wolves called a warning as he shifted into natural form and stepped up onto the verandah.

Lucian materialized almost right in front of him, and still, after all the years of power and command weighing on his shoulders, Mikhail felt awed by the man. His black hair flowed down his back, his shoulders were ramrod straight and his eyes blazed with the dark promise of death.

Lucian and Gabriel Daratrazanoff were twins, legends unsurpassed in Carpathian history, and it showed in the set of Lucian's shoulders and his stern face. Mikhail found Gabriel much more approachable. He always found it humorous that other Carpathians feared Gregori, Mikhail's second in command, best friend and son-in-law, but found his older brothers so approachable when they were at least as dangerous, if not more so.

Lucian gripped his forearms in a warrior's greeting. Gregori's older brother looked fit and strong, his eyes gleaming, piercing through Mikhail straight to his soul as if he could read inside any man.

"It is good to see you again after all this time, Mikhail. You have grown into a powerful leader since I last saw you. Your father would have been proud."

Mikhail clasped the man's arms, feeling the solid strength there. "You may tell your woman she can put away her weapon now."

A slow smile warmed the bleak, cold eyes. "She will not be pleased that you spotted her. She is a cop and definitely prides herself on her abilities. Being Carpathian has only added to her skills."

"I do not actually know where she is," Mikhail admitted. "Only that she is close by and pointing a weapon at me. I have heard she does not stay home where she belongs."

A choking sound came from above him and a young woman materialized, a gun in her hand, glaring daggers at Mikhail. "Where she belongs?"

Her hair was the color of platinum and gold, a shorter length than most of the women wore, but attractive, framing her pixie face. Her eyes were dark, a startling contrast to her pale skin and hair.

Lucian casually removed the gun from her hand and leaned over to shove the weapon in her boot. "You cannot shoot the prince, Jaxon. It simply is not done."

"I wasn't going to shoot him," she objected, and sent Mikhail a quick, mischievous grin. "At least, not unless he was going to insist that women stay home while the men have all the fun."

"You call slaying the undead fun?" Mikhail asked.

She shrugged. "If it isn't housework, it's fun. I like action, not sitting at home waiting for my hero."

"You like to stir up trouble," Lucian replied, amusement in his velvet voice. "But at least you admit I am your hero."

Mikhail had forgotten how mesmerizing and powerful a weapon Lucian's voice was. Everything about Lucian seemed to be a combination of "compelling" and "weapon." The man's face could have been carved from stone, yet his eyes were more alive, more intense and more lethal than Mikhail had remembered. "It is good to see you again, Lucian. And good that you have found your lifemate." He sketched a slight bow toward Jaxon. "I could not resist teasing you as I have heard you are fiercely protective of Lucian," he told her. "We are grateful to you. He is a legend among us."

"She insists on guarding me," Lucian said.

"Well, of course I do. Any Carpathian hunter shot by a human after being warned *repeatedly* to be careful needs a babysitter—um—bodyguard."

Lucian bent to brush a kiss on top of her head. "No respect." The deep love on Lucian's face was mirrored on Jaxon's as she teased him.

"I can see that," Mikhail acknowledged. Somewhere deep inside he felt happiness for this couple—for all the couples—but this one in particular. Lucian had been alone for so long and he'd fought too many battles, sacrificed too much. This small pixie seemed fragile until Mikhail looked into her dark eyes. She had seen too much, was wise beyond her age and had that same strength of will her lifemate possessed.

She flashed a warm smile at Mikhail, even as her fingers tangled with Lucian's. "Thank you for allowing us to use one of your homes. Lucian's home was so far into the mountains we would have spent all of our time flying back and forth and wouldn't have been able to visit."

"Please come in." Lucian held open the door, stepping back to allow Mikhail to precede him. "We have much to discuss. I thought, at first, when I heard of the celebration, that it was a foolish indulgence and far too risky, but now I see I was wrong. It has been good to see everyone and to be home once again. I have stayed away far too long and there is a sense of community here once again."

"I hope we are doing the right thing," Mikhail agreed as he stepped inside the snug little cabin.

It had been years since he had entered the old house. The walls had been repaired where gaping chinks between the wood had allowed the wind to sweep in. Lucian and Jaxon had fixed the cabin up so that the interior was bright and welcoming. A fire crackled in the old stone fireplace and the furniture was inviting. Lucian waved him toward the couch, and Mikhail seated himself opposite Lucian's chair.

Jaxon hesitated briefly, glancing at the windows, wariness creeping into her expression as she assessed whether anyone could look in and easily see them through the glass.

"I do not actually bite," Mikhail said, and gestured toward the empty end of the couch he occupied.

Jaxon perched on the arm of Lucian's chair, one foot swinging free. "I'm perfectly comfortable right here, but thank you."

"She insists on guarding me," Lucian explained. "Or at least she pretends so. The real reason is she cannot bear to be apart from me."

The foot swinging free arced just a little more and she drove her toe into his calf.

"I can see that," Mikhail said dryly. "I am certain Raven is the same way—hating to be apart from me." He shared the conversation with his lifemate. Immediately, he felt the warmth of her laughter brushing at the walls of his mind. "Before I forget, I thought you might like to know, we need someone to play the part of Santa Claus for the children."

The smile faded from Lucian's face, leaving his eyes shadowed and wary. He stiffened slightly. Beside him, Jaxon stirred, and he put his hand on her thigh to prevent her from speaking aloud. *Do not dare to volunteer me.*

You are such a chicken. They are just children.

It is a red suit and beard.

And you'd look so cute and cuddly.

Mikhail put him out of his misery. He sat back in his chair with a little half smile. "I thought my son-in-law would be the best man for the role. As he is your younger brother, tell me what you think."

Jaxon choked back a squeak that could have been between laughter and horror. She nearly fell off the arm of the chair, only Lucian's steadying hand preventing her from landing on the floor. "You're kidding, right? Gregori would be every bit as bad a choice as Lucian would be. One look at him and the children are going to either run like rabbits or burst into tears."

Lucian's thumb swept over the back of her hand in a small caress. "Never underestimate a Daratrazanoff, little one. We can rise to any necessary occasion and I am certain Gregori will enjoy the role." He sent Mikhail a wolfish smile. "Let me know when you are going to tell him what honor is in store for him and I will be happy to accompany you."

"Oh, you two are just plain bad," Jaxon said. "You like stirring the pot. Gregori is bound to get you both back, you know."

A glimmer of a smirk flitted across Mikhail's features and was gone. "It will be well worth it."

Lucian nodded and reached for his twin, automatically sharing the information. Gabriel responded on their private mental path. *Mikhail was here earlier and I could not resist allowing him to give you the news.* There was laughter in his voice. *I certainly plan on being present when our prince makes his first demand as a father-in-law.*

Lucian's fingers tightened around Jaxon's. That small shared moment of amusement, of love and laughter, was due to his lifemate. He had been without emotion for so long—loving his twin, yet never actually feeling the emotion. Over the centuries the memory had begun to fade and it had been alarming. He had walked in darkness without hope, until she came into his life.

Jaxon leaned down to brush a kiss on the top of his head in a rare public gesture of affection. Even with her stepfather dead, she still couldn't get over the reticence she had developed to protect those she cared about. Lucian was always the one to make the first move, to take her hand, put his arm around her, and her first instinct was always to look around her with wary eyes—stiffen—and pull away. He was slowly getting her over it, and every small demonstration of affection when others were around was a huge step forward.

Lucian rubbed his chin. "I think we should commemorate this event with pictures. It would serve us well in the coming years if we had such a thing documented."

Mikhail leaned forward slightly, his small smile softening the hard lines in his face. "Surely you are not considering—blackmail."

"Well, yes, as a matter of fact. We could hold this over his head for centuries."

"Poor Gregori. It isn't fair to conspire against him this way," Jaxon objected. She frowned. "Although come to think about it, maybe he does deserve it for being such a male chauvinist."

Mikhail's eyebrow shot up. "And Lucian isn't?"

Her mischievous smile lit up her eyes again. "He tries desperately, but fortunately he has me to straighten him out."

"Lucky me," Lucian said dryly.

She sent her foot swinging against his leg a second time. "You *are* lucky. I keep telling you, but you keep forgetting."

Lucian laughed softly. Mikhail had never pictured the warrior laughing and relaxed, and for some reason the sound lifted the burden on his shoulders just a little more. Good things were happening with their species. Maybe it wasn't happening as fast as Mikhail liked, but change was taking place.

"I wanted to ask you about something I barely recall centuries ago. I was just a boy and remember very little."

"I cannot promise to remember, but I will try."

"In the old days, there was a woman who lived in the village. I do not even remember her lifemate or if she had one. I was too young to really care about such things. She healed the earth. Do you remember her?"

Lucian frowned. "I did not stay in the villages much, even when you were a boy, Mikhail. To remember one person—a woman . . ." He shook his head. "The villagers, especially the women, avoided Gabriel and me, often fleeing when we were sighted."

"Try, Lucian," Mikhail urged. "She would not have fled in fear from you. She was powerful in her own right. She would walk and flowers and grass would grow beneath her feet. It could be very important to us."

Lucian nodded slowly, his frown deepening as he tried to pull up the ancient memory. The village busy with people living life—a life he never thought he could ever have. Families. Laughter. He had avoided it all as much as possible.

Jaxon's hand slid into his hair, teased the strands of hair along the back of his neck, sending a shiver of awareness down his spine, spreading warmth through his body and into his heart.

He forced his mind back to the old days, searching through bittersweet memories until he found the village where Dubrinsky had lived. Children ran together in small groups. So many nameless faces he had tried not to notice turning away from him. A serene face smiling at him, nodding, acknowledging him even as the children trailed after her. Life sprang up from nothing beneath her feet, green stalks, bright colored flowers, a rich tapestry forming on the ground while the little ones stared in awe.

"She came from a rare and much respected lineage. There were few with her talent. She was beautiful, her hair long and dark, and she always stood tall and straight and looked men in the eye."

Jaxon smacked him on the back of the head. "I doubt he needs those precise details," she said. "And just why would she need to be looking you in the eye?"

Mikhail tried to hide his shock. Every Carpathian alive was in awe of this man, but his lifemate treated him—exactly in the way Raven treated the prince of the Carpathian people. He swallowed his smile and glanced away as Lucian reached up to circle her waist and drag her from the arm of the chair onto his lap. She struggled for a minute and then subsided, allowing him to hold her.

"I remember watching her walk into a barren field. Within minutes foliage sprang up everywhere around her."

"Did she attend births? Or treat the soil before a child was to be born—or even conceived?" It was a long shot, but Mikhail was ready to grasp at the smallest of chances.

Lucian's dark eyebrows shot up. "What are you thinking, Mikhail?"

"Shea said something about the soil being riddled with toxins earlier this evening. As I was flying over the battleground scarred and poisoned by the undead, I noticed one section had been healed. The soil was the darkest, richest soil I have seen in centuries. And then Raven mentioned that she and several other women got together last night in mineral pools and the soil and water were different. This evening she is able to conceive. I have heard whispers that other women have experienced the same."

Both men looked at Jaxon. She held up both hands, palms out, shaking her head adamantly. "Not me. Don't even think about it either. I'm just getting used to this lifemate thing. And in case you think I can heal the earth, think again. I've killed every potted plant I've ever tried to grow both before and after the conversion. I'm not your earth healer."

"Have you heard anything about this, Jaxon?" Lucian asked. His fingers curled around the nape of her neck in a slow massage. "Have any of the women mentioned it to you?"

"No, but I can ask Francesca. She seems to always be in the know about everything. I don't know how she does it all with a baby and a teenager."

Mikhail scrubbed a hand over his face suddenly looking tired. "It was a long shot anyway. I cannot remember who the woman was or her lineage, nor do I remember if she aided with birthing."

"I will ask my brother and the other ancients if they remember more of this woman, but truly, Mikhail, if there is such a woman in our midst, we have only to ask her to step forward."

"The answer cannot be so simple."

"Maybe it is one piece of a puzzle we must work out—a very important piece."

"If we find this woman and she is as important as I hope she is, this celebration will be the best thing we have ever done."

"You are worried. The attack on Skyler and Alexandria?"

Of course Gabriel would have kept Lucian informed. Mikhail nodded. "I have been uneasy for a couple of evenings now. It has definitely put me on edge."

"We went out there and looked around," Jaxon said. "Someone had come from the direction of the inn on a sled and was in a snow blind—a very clever one, manmade—about half a mile from where Skyler and Alexandria were hurt. The feeling of power lingered, but it didn't feel Carpathian." Jaxon bit at her lower lip, puzzling it out. "I've been really trying to get a feel for the different energy fields. That's all Carpathian magic really is, a manipulation of energy, and this felt off to me."

A small smile lit Lucian's eyes briefly at the flare of surprise on Mikhail's face. "Did I mention Jaxon is a *great* cop? She tracks nearly as well as I do now."

"You said something felt 'off' to you," Mikhail prodded. "Off like vampire?"

"There was an evil taint to it," Jaxon admitted. "Lucian felt it through me, but couldn't on his own, and that really bothered me. If they've found a way to block their identities from the hunters, all of you could be in real trouble."

"They have been doing that for some time," Lucian reminded her, his hand sliding down her thigh in a small gesture of assurance.

"Not like this, Lucian," she objected. "You felt the difference. It wasn't completely vampire—but still stank of evil." There was worry in her tone.

"It has occurred to me that if our enemies strike against the women and children," Mikhail confided, "then they would have the best chance for eradicating our species altogether. I do not know how much you know about the group of humans dedicated to wiping out our species. We always refer to them as the society. The vampires have tricked them, infiltrated their ranks and used them as puppets. The dark mage Xavier may be alive as well as his grandson. If that is so, Razvan is the first Dragonseeker to ever turn, and he is something we have never faced. His sister, Natalya, tells me he is a brilliant strategist when it comes to planning a war. No doubt he's already come to the same conclusions I have regarding the best way to strike the most devastating blow to our race."

Lucian nodded. "I have believed for some time it is inevitable they will begin to strike against our women."

"And still you allow your lifemate to hunt and destroy the vampire."

Lucian's fingers tightened around Jaxon's in warning when she would have protested. "What better way to keep her safe than to teach her how to survive when she is attacked? Jaxon has remarkable skills and natural instincts. It would be a crime to stop her from learning how to kill the undead. And before you object, I do not think all our women should be out hunting vampires. But Jaxon is a special case, as are Natalya and Destiny. You cannot suppress their instincts, and let their abilities go to waste, so I have done all I can to prepare her for the hunt."

Mikhail sighed. "In the old days, those with lifemates did not hunt the vampire. Now it is a necessity."

"I have hunted for centuries, as have most of the ancient hunters—and Gregori. We know no other way of life anymore. It is not just a necessity, it is who we are."

"Why did the lifemates keep them from hunting if they were more experienced?" Jaxon asked.

"Because even when we had women and children, we knew how precious they were," Mikhail explained. "If we lose the male, we also lose the female, and that was not an option for us. Now we may have no choice but to allow our women to fight as well."

"Not all the women, Mikhail," Lucian reminded. "Only those who have the skills and the desire to fight. Women like Jaxon and Destiny."

Mikhail sighed. "And Natalya. She was in the thick of the battle. She told me that her twin brother, Razvan, fathered several children. Colby, Raphael's lifemate, is one of his daughters."

"The Dragonseeker women always were unpredictable. They always will be. If Razvan had other children besides Colby, we need to find and protect them. I take it Dominic will be going out as soon as he is healed to look for his kin."

"It will take time to heal his wounds. Even with our best healers, it has been difficult. Francesca will try again soon and if we find this woman who can heal the earth, perhaps she can help by enriching the soil where he lays."

Mikhail stood up. "I must go. The celebration is in a couple of hours and I have several visits still to make. I know I have no need to remind you to be on the alert, but still—I feel I would be remiss if I didn't."

Lucian stood as well, and once again gripped Mikhail's forearms in a gesture of respect. "You have my full allegiance, Mikhail. Should there be need, call to me—I will fight at your side, always."

A brief smile failed to take the shadows from the prince's eyes. "The Daratrazanoff family has always been at the side of the Dubrinskys. We fight as one."

Jaxon lifted a hand to the leader of the Carpathians as he left the house. "He seemed so sad, Lucian, I felt like crying," she said. "And I never cry." She pressed a hand to her aching heart. "Sorrow came off of him in waves."

Lucian swept his arm around her. "You're always so sensitive to other people's feelings. Mikhail has a heavy burden to bear—to keep our species from extinction. He still remembers the old ways, gone now for all time. Back then our people thrived and lived together in a society. It is his responsibility to guide us into a new life, one where we can survive and live in harmony with other species around us. Like me, he cannot help but look back at what we had and look into the future with worry. I do not envy him his task. It is a terrible weight to carry on his shoulders."

"Do you really think our enemies are going to go after the women and children?" She swallowed hard, closing her eyes against the memories flooding her of her own brother murdered by a mentally ill man. Her heart pounded at the thought of finding young Skyler or one of the infants brutally murdered.

"We will watch over them."

"But we already know Skyler has been targeted," she protested. "I tried not to care for her, but it's impossible. She's wonderful—and so young and old at the same time. Gabriel is worried about this Dimitri claiming her, and now this." She swept a hand through her hair, clearly agitated. "I feel like locking her up."

Lucian burst out laughing, carrying her hand to his mouth to press kisses into the center of her palm. "Now you know how I feel—how every male feels about protecting his lifemate and his children."

She scowled at him. "I don't need protection, Lucian. I'm capable of looking after myself. Skyler's a teenager. What if this Dimitri character tries to carry her off?"

"Dimitri is added protection for Skyler. I do not understand how she triggered his instincts at such a young age, but she has and he can do no other than to ensure her health, safety and happiness. It may take him a little while to conquer the demon, but I have every faith that he will."

"Why?"

"Dimitri has always valued honor and responsibility. He rarely even bent the rules in his youth. He may want to carry her off, but in the end, unless something terrible happens, he will do the right thing by her." He shifted her into his arms, holding her close to comfort her, her memories now so fresh and distressing. "On the other hand, it is always better to make certain."

She tilted her head to look up at him. He always made her feel safe. She had never known that sensation before he entered her life, certainly not as a child and not as a young woman. Lucian had changed her entire life and given her back hope and promise and dreams. She slipped her arms around him. "I want for Skyler what you've given to me. She deserves—and needs happiness, Lucian."

He nuzzled the top of her head with her chin. "I know, little one. With Gabriel and Francesca looking out for her, and the two of us as well, Skyler will be just fine."

Jaxon wrapped her arms around his waist, pressing her cheek against the steady beat of his heart. "Have I told you today that I love you?"

"Not yet, but I was going to get to that. A little prompting on my part usually gets more than satisfying results." He inhaled her feminine fragrance. *Jaxon.* The woman he could never do without. She was so small, so fragile looking, but with the strength of steel and a will of iron.

"Well, I do," she replied.

"What?"

"You know very well what."

Lucian lifted her with ease, bringing her up to his hungry mouth. "Say you love me and say it right now, woman."

She wrapped her arms around his neck and her legs around his waist. "Or what? Are you threatening to punish me in some despicable way?"

His teeth nibbled at her pulse, scraped and teased, while his tongue danced a seductive rhythm. "Say it, stubborn woman."

"Your head is already far too big." Her fingers stroked his long hair. "If one more person looks at you as if you are the bomb . . ."

"The bomb?" His eyebrows shot up. "Where do you get such slang?"

"I'm hip, baby. Totally hip." She laughed at his expression. "Actually, Skyler told me I was the bomb and I couldn't wait to try it out on you." Her smile faded into a small frown. "Maybe we should go find her, make certain she's really all right."

"It sounds like a plan. I wanted to run with the wolves anyway and if we do that, we may have a chance of finding and talking with Dimitri."

"Why is there a 'but first' in your tone?"

Clothes floated to the floor, leaving her bare breasts pressed tightly against his chest and his hard shaft pressed against her already slick entrance.

"I want to make love to you."

"You always want to make love. And you did this evening three times. I think you need help. You're a sexaholic." She squirmed, pressing her most feminine core against him, rubbing slowly back and forth to entice him as she kissed her way up this throat. She lifted her body several inches to poise just above him.

"You attacked me this morning," he pointed out.

"Did I? I'd forgotten. Well, maybe I did." She slid down his body, impaling herself on his hard thick shaft, feeling him slowly, inch by inch, invading, filling her. She began a seductive ride, moving over him, muscles tight and hot, slick and silky with desire.

He caught her hips in his hands and took over the pace, so that their movements were perfectly synchronized and they moved as one, the now familiar fire building between them. She tilted her head, wanting his kiss, the sweet explosion of his commanding mouth taking hers, tightening every muscle in her body, sending darts of fire racing through her bloodstream.

Making love to Lucian was one of the few times when she ever relaxed her vigilance—and she knew it was the same when he touched her. Her teeth teased his lower lip, slid over to tug at his ear, all the while the pressure kept building and building deep inside her—in him. "I do love you," she whispered, the sound barely audible over their combined heartbeats and heavy breathing, over the sound of joy escaping his throat in the form of a growl. But he heard. She knew he heard. His fingers tightened possessively as he swept them both into a world of pure passion.

9

Skyler sat on the railing of the porch and stared out into the glistening world of white. Pain vibrated through her body—through her very soul, until she felt so weighed down by it she could barely breathe. Inside the house she could hear Gabriel and Francesca laughing as they played with Baby Tamara. Every now and then she felt their light touch, as they assured themselves that she was close by.

She made certain that they only touched the surface she presented to them, a teenage girl in a strange, exciting new place looking forward to a Christmas celebration. The Carpathian blood they'd shared with her made the façade easier, and a lifetime of hiding her emotions from others made the task simple.

She bit hard at her lower lip and studied her long fingernails. She bit them all the time, but they grew back quickly, stronger and better than ever thanks to the Carpathian blood Gabriel and Francesca had shared with her. She still couldn't touch people without reading their emotions. If anything the blood had enhanced her abilities, and it could be dreadfully uncomfortable. She disliked attending school, and preferred the tutors Francesca provided, although she knew her adopted parents thought she needed the company of younger people. She didn't. She needed to be alone.

"Skyler? Are you all right?"

The male voice jerked her head up. Josef stood in front of the railing, hands jammed in his pockets.

Biting down hard on her lower lip, she was careful not to let the misery show on her face. The pain was making her sick to her stomach. Even her vision seemed blurry. "Sure." She could barely manage to get the word out, and she didn't bother trying to flash him a false, cheery smile.

This wasn't her pain. Somewhere out there in the forest, the man who claimed to be her lifemate was suffering agonies. She wanted to ignore it, but she couldn't. Guilt clawed at her insides. She knew pain intimately—and despair. In spite of everything, she was intrigued with the man. He was way old, of course. And too dominating. He would definitely expect her to obey him, and that wasn't her style at all. She conformed to the wishes of Francesca and Gabriel because she loved them, not because she had to.

"Skyler." Josef's voice broke again into her thoughts. He hopped onto the rail and crouched close to her. "Look at me."

"Why?"

He dragged a handkerchief from his pocket and wiped her face. "You have little drops of blood on your forehead." He pretended not to notice when she winced away from him, refusing to allow his fingers to brush her skin. He simply wiped, careful not to touch her, and drew back to huff out a long stream of air. "What's wrong?"

"Nothing." How could he not feel it? How could Francesca and Gabriel not feel the pain and sorrow weighing so heavily in the forest? The wolves did. She could hear them off in the distance, their mournful song filled with sadness and distress. Didn't Josef at least hear the animals?

Skyler wiped her hand over her face, as if she could draw a veil over the truth. That man, so invincible-looking, so stern and cold and bleak, a man with ice in his veins and death in his eyes, had looked at her—looked right through her—and touched her somewhere no one else had ever been. She pressed her hand hard against her aching heart. It hurt. It shouldn't, but the feeling was like a vise squeezing with a steady, relentless pressure.

"It isn't 'nothing' when you're sweating blood, Skyler. We're friends, aren't we? You can tell me what's wrong."

Skyler didn't know if she had friends. She trusted her adopted parents and Lucian and Jaxon. Other than that, she never allowed herself to be alone with anyone. Francesca thought time was going to heal her, but Skyler doubted it. In order to preserve her spirit—her sanity, she had retreated from the world as a child, and perhaps she'd stayed away too long. She didn't know how to be a friend—or a partner.

"Yes, of course we're friends," she said, giving the obligatory answer. Over the years she'd found if she just said what people expected to hear, they went away happy and left her in peace.

Josef relaxed visibly. "Why didn't you come over to Aidan's and play the new video game? It's way cool."

"I was helping Francesca make the gingerbread houses for tonight." She wrapped her arms around herself protectively.

"Antonietta's making some cool thing for this dinner tonight. You should come over and help. I'm heading back there now."

"I've met you a dozen times already and know you from online, but haven't met Antonietta. It's intimidating to think about meeting her. She's so famous."

"She can play the piano," Josef conceded, "but she isn't stuck up or anything. She was blind before she was with Byron, but I don't think she sees much better even now." He grinned, white teeth flashing against the dark outline he used around his lips drawing attention to his tongue-piercing as well as the hoop in his lip.

"I thought when one is converted, all the scars and imperfections disappear." She touched the crescent-shaped scar on her face. "And how can you be pierced? Doesn't your body heal itself?"

Josef sighed. "It's a real fight," he conceded. "I don't wear them most of the time because the holes are always closing up within minutes, but I have to keep up my rep, so I just concentrate on it all the time around everybody and I can keep the piercing with no problem."

"Is that why the skin's grown over the diamond on your nose?" Skyler asked, rubbing her chin along the top of her drawn-up knees. She stared out into the sparkling white world. It seemed a fairy tale, all crystal and ice. Cold—like she was. She closed her eyes briefly against the sorrow pressing down on her, trying to listen to the wolves, trying to sort out their song. She'd always loved them, always had such an affinity for them, and now the sound called to something lonely and primal in her.

Josef clapped his hand over his nose. "Not again! I hope it wasn't like that when the prince saw me." He regarded her with a narrowed gaze. "You are coming over, aren't you? Antonietta's really nice. Byron is too, but he doesn't want me to know he is."

Skyler shook her head. "I can't right now. I'll catch up to you later." She needed to be alone, to think things through for herself. She liked Josef, but he was a distraction and he didn't have a clue that she was upset. *Dimitri would have known.* The thought came unbidden and filled her with shame—with regret. With anger.

"Come on, Skyler, don't be a big baby. Just because your parents think you need a babysitter doesn't mean you can't come with me. I'm over twenty-one."

She glared at him. "Really? I thought you were Joshua's age. You aren't going to goad me into doing something wrong, Josef." Which made her feel even guiltier. He might not be able to goad her, but she intended to disobey her parents. The terrible weight in her chest pressed harder, the sorrow nearly choking her. She had to make it stop—make Dimitri understand it wasn't about him or her rejection of him. It wasn't personal. She would have rejected anyone. He had to move on.

"You're just angry because I made fun of you having to wait for an adult before you could walk home," he said. "I was only teasing you. There's no need to be upset."

"I'm not a baby," she snapped, pressing both hands into her wildly churning stomach. Maybe if she threw up on him he'd go away. "You didn't have to tease me."

"Sure I did. That's what friends do."

That brought her up short. They were friends—of a sort. She liked Josef. She just didn't like being alone with him—with any man. With anyone. She swept one hand through her hair and tried not to cry.

Josef, reading her expression, tried again. "The prince came by while I was at Aidan and Alexandria's and he said he was going to have Gregori play Santa Claus tonight. Man, that's gonna freak out all the kids. It ought to be fun."

"Freaking out a bunch of little kids isn't funny, Josef. Especially not when it comes to Santa Claus. You could traumatize them."

"You're beginning to sound more and more like Francesca." He didn't make it sound as though he was complimenting her. "I'm not traumatizing them. Gregori is—and I didn't choose him—the prince did."

"Tonight, make sure you don't help scare the children, especially Tamara."

They glared at one another for a long moment in silence. When Josef went to turn away with a sullen expression, she cleared her throat. "Can you shapeshift?"

He puffed out his chest. "Of course."

She glanced toward the house. "Do you think someone who is only part Carpathian can actually shapeshift?" She avoided his gaze by rubbing her chin thoughtfully on her knees as if in deep contemplation. Josef might act like a dork around adults, but he was as sharp as a tack and he might be able to read her expression.

"Well . . ." He frowned. "That's a good question. Natalya turned into a tiger, which was very cool by the way, but I've never heard any of the adults mention anyone else who could do it."

"How do you shift?"

He shook his head. "Don't even think about it, Skyler. It isn't that easy. I practice all the time and I still make mistakes."

"You don't practice all the time. You play video games all the time." With another surreptitious glance toward the house, she slid off the rail into the snow. Unlike Josef, she couldn't regulate her body temperature and she was stiff from sitting on the railing with the cold wind adding to her chill. At least it had stopped snowing—she glanced up at the ominous sky, laden with heavy clouds—for the moment.

Josef scowled at her. "Hey! I can shift. Watch this." He backed up a few steps and stood, arms out. Feathers began to sprout over his body, his face reshaping several times until he had facial discs—dusky white with gray-brown mottling bordered by black. His irises turned a bright yellow, and his developing bill was gray-green with tufts of bristly feathers around its base. His body compacted, shifted, slowly shrinking with a few stops and starts until he was sitting in the snow in the perfect form of a very small owl. The body of the owl was gray-brown with an intricate pattern of stripes and bars and even spots in places. It sat very still, the body so small she was really awed that Josef had managed. The large eyes blinked up at her.

Skyler walked around the tiny creature. "Amazing, Josef. How did you get it so tiny? Can you actually fly? Or should I just have you stuffed for ornamental purposes?"

The owl issued a whiny note and hopped several times, wings extending and flapping until it awkwardly took to the air. Josef flew around her several times, rose higher and darted back, straight at her head.

Skyler threw up her hands and ran out into the snow, scooping snow from the edge of the porch to fling it at the errant bird. "Stop it, that's not funny, Josef."

The bird rose again and circled her, once again building speed for the attack. Skyler ran back toward the house, close to the structure as the bird rushed her. She ducked and covered her head just as Josef swooped on her. The little screech owl hit the side of the house and fell like a stone onto the ground. The bird lay perfectly still, its little feet pointed straight up, just like a cartoon.

Skyler let her breath out in a slow hiss of displeasure. "That's not funny, Josef. Get up." There was an ominous silence. She lifted her head and took a step toward him. If he was trying to scare her—as usual—she was going to wring his neck. The little owl remained motionless, feet stiff. Her hand fluttered to her throat as fear crept in. She was afraid to move, afraid to examine the small little creature.

"Josef!" She hurried over, dropping to her knees in the snow to reach for the screech owl. Just as she went to lift it, the huge eyes popped open, the bill yawning wide and wings flapping. Skyler couldn't stop the startled scream that escaped.

"Gotcha!" Josef sat up laughing.

Skyler leapt to her feet, her heart pounding. She wanted to smash something over his head and she never had violent tendencies—well, almost never. Josef just brought out the worst in her. He loved pranks and she seemed a great target. "You're not funny."

The smile faded from his face. "What's wrong with you lately, Skyler? Screech owls often fly into things and knock themselves silly. People think they're dead, but they're just out. I read about it and thought it would make you smile. Honestly, you're no fun." He jumped up and backed away from her. "We're not grown up yet. There's nothing wrong with laughing about stuff."

He walked off without a backward glance. She told herself she was glad to see him go—that he was being ridiculous, but inside the loneliness grew stronger. She didn't laugh like other kids—she didn't know how. Online, when she talked to Josef, she could be different, be someone else. No one could see her or touch her and she could just relax and have fun. But here . . . everyone was too close. She could feel every emotion, and it ripped at her skin and clawed at her heart until she felt so raw she thought she might just cease to exist. Sometimes, even the earth seemed to scream in pain at her.

In the distance, a lone wolf howled mournfully. The single drawn out note struck at her. The wolf was as lonely as she was. She reached up to wrap her fingers around the pendant lying between her breasts. Suddenly, it felt warm instead of icy cold, almost pulsing in her hand. She knew better. She was going to get in such trouble if Gabriel and Francesca discovered she'd taken off again, but she *had* to go. She couldn't stop herself.

Skyler drew her white, fur-lined parka around her and took off at a light jog in the direction from which she'd heard the wolf. Was it Dimitri? Her heart jumped at the thought. His eyes had been so blue—so intense—and so filled with pain. She knew pain intimately—she knew people. They hid terrible inclinations, terrible secrets beneath falsely smiling faces. Was she any better than the rest of them, leaving the man to suffer because she was afraid?

She shivered in spite of her jacket. Gabriel would be furious with her and she didn't like it when he was really angry. Mostly he just gave her a look, but if he was angry, he insisted on punishing her. That usually meant she had to spend time with other kids. For others, it would have been easy, but it was always the most dreaded of all retributions. Her feet dragged in the snow and she halted, glancing back in the direction of the house. She couldn't see it anymore, having entered into the tree line. The wolf howled again, a plaintive note this time, as if he too searched for answers.

Skyler squared her shoulders and set out once again, picking her away through the snow drifts as she tried to follow a shallow trail that wound along the streambed. The tip of her nose grew cold along with her ears. She pulled the hood closer around her, trying to keep the cold out. It was impossible. She stumbled and nearly fell. The abrupt action rattled her enough that she shook her head hard, trying to clear out the soft pitiful cries of the wolf that just wouldn't let go of her.

For so long she'd thought her answer was to live in the Carpathian world, but she'd realized she couldn't relate any better there than in the human world. She brushed at the tears that should have been in her eyes, only there were none there. She felt them burning deep inside, locked away like her memories. Only Francesca and Gabriel seemed to be able to accept her with all of her differences—all of her shortcomings. She was never going to overcome her past—or her psychic abilities. She might have more control than she used to, thanks to her adopted parents, but it wasn't enough to allow her to be like other people.

She tripped on a branch buried in the snow, and glanced around astonished to realize she had been walking the entire time and had no idea where she was. She turned in a circle frowning. Which way was home? She could call out to Gabriel, but he'd be furious with her. It would be so much better to find her own way home. He'd still be upset with her when he found out, but his anger would be somewhat tempered by the fact that she was safe.

An almost humanlike scream of agony shattered the silence sending chills down her spine. The hairs on the back of her neck stood up, blood nearly freezing in her veins. She gasped for breath, looking wildly around. It was close, so close she could hear the accompanying snarling and snapping of a wolf in distress. Propelled by something outside herself, Skyler ran, allowing the reverberation of the struggle to guide her.

Beneath a large misshapen tree a huge male wolf, reddish in color, fought with the clawed vise clamped around his leg. Blood sprayed across the snow, and the wolf chewed at his own paw in an effort to free himself. As she skidded to a halt, the creature whirled around to face the new threat, lips drawn back in a vicious snarl, yellow eyes gleaming with malice as he warned her off.

Skyler backed away, keeping a safe distance as the animal lunged at her. The trap brought him up short and he yelped, spun and bit at his leg again, before whirling to keep a wary eye on her. His sides heaved and sweat made his fur even darker. His entire body shuddered. She could feel the pain rolling off him in waves. It wasn't Dimitri. The wolf couldn't be a shapeshifter or he would have freed himself. It was truly a wild animal caught in a vicious snare. Looking into his eyes, she realized his freedom was gone, but his spirit refused to surrender. He snarled at her continually, showing his teeth, salvia dripping from his mouth, and all the while, his yellow eyes never left her face.

Had she already given up when this magnificent animal held on valiantly? When it was willing to chew off its own paw to survive? Skyler couldn't turn away from the beast, her compassion rising quickly. She held up one hand, palm outward. "Just relax," she soothed, trying to calm her rapidly beating heart. She drew in a deep breath and let it out.

The wolf rumbled deep in its throat, but stopped growling. She nodded as if they were conversing. "That's it. That's good." Sometimes she could hold an animal, even a wild one, while she checked injuries, but she'd never tried to hold a wolf to her. It took a touching of two spirits, and that was never easy in the best of times. She concentrated on the animal, calling silently, relentlessly, to the very essence of the beast.

The wolf grew silent, staring at her with intent eyes. She stepped closer, feeling the warming tingle that always spread throughout her body and mind before she connected solidly. Her stomach unexpectedly knotted and her throat burned. There was a bitter taste in her mouth. A shadow slipped against her spirit, something oily, slimy and evil. Her soul shuddered and drew back.

Horrified, Skyler lifted her head to stare at the wolf. She saw the paw reshaping, the animal's body twisting and contorting, the muzzle elongating into a hideous bullet head sitting atop something half human and half wolf. The mouth pulled wide in a parody of a smile showing stained, pointy teeth.

Her breath froze in her lungs. She couldn't move, couldn't form the thought to call Francesca or Gabriel. She could only stand there waiting for death to come for her.

A large black wolf burst from the trees, running full out, using ground-eating leaps that covered several feet at a time. The animal struck her with its shoulder, driving her away from the vampire. Ice-blue eyes burned with glacier cold as the black wolf whirled in midair and sprang for the throat of the shifting vampire. Heavily muscled, the wolf drove the creature backward before it had a chance to change fully into one form or the other. Powerful jaws clamped around the exposed throat and tore.

Look the other way.

The orders rang sharp and clear inside Skyler's mind. She squeezed her eyes shut tight, but that didn't begin to drown out the sound of ripping flesh, high-pitched screams and the snarls and growls of the undead. The voice slashed at her brain, cutting deep. She felt droplets like white-hot cinders burn through her gloves and skin to her very bones. It was impossible to keep the small cry of startled pain from escaping.

The snarls grew louder, the shrieks more violent and terrible. Skyler covered her face with her hands to try to keep from looking, but she couldn't stop the morbid terror and spread her fingers enough to peek through. Dimitri was once again a man—no—not a man. He was fully a Carpathian warrior, his eyes blazing with fury, his mouth drawn into a cruel, merciless line. Muscles rippled in his back and bulged in his arms as he slammed his fist *through* the vampire's chest and wrapped his fingers around the blackened, wizened heart. There was a terrible sucking sound and the shriek rose higher. Blood sprayed in a black arc. Skyler's hands protected her face, but this time blood splattered across the backs of her gloves, melting the material and skin instantly.

Skyler gasped with pain and pushed both hands into the snow, staring in horror as Dimitri extracted the heart and tossed it some distance from the vampire. The undead clawed and bit, fighting viciously, tearing deep lacerations in Dimitri's skin. Acid burns streaked the hunter's neck, chest and arms as he called up a storm and lightning sizzled and crackled overhead.

Movement caught her eye, and Skyler turned away from the mesmerizing sight of a vampire to see the blackened heart wiggling across the snow-covered ground in an effort to get back to its master. As it rolled along the path back toward its master, the heart drew close to her hands buried in the snow. With a cry of terror she dragged her hands clear, turned away and was sick, her stomach heaving in protest at the abomination.

A whip of lightning streaked from the sky to incinerate the heart. The lightning separated at the last moment, forming two tendrils to strike at the vampire while it also hit the heart. Noxious fumes filled the air and black smoke rose, along with the wailing shriek that faded along with the vapor.

In the ensuing silence, Skyler heard her heart thundering overly loud in her ears. She lifted her face to meet Dimitri's eyes, and her heart abruptly skipped a beat. He looked so strong—so invincible. His eyes were so cold, so blue, yet they burned through her skin to her bones, branding her. He moved and she blinked, the mesmerizing spell broken. Skyler backed away from him, his anger washing over her in waves. The force was so powerful she hunched, nearly driven to her knees. A sound of distress escaped her throat, instantly drawing his intent gaze to her pounding pulse.

At once the anger was gone. He held out his hand. "Come here to me. You're injured. Don't be afraid, Skyler. I couldn't harm you, no matter the circumstances."

She swallowed hard and stepped back another step, her mouth going dry as he crooked his finger at her. Why couldn't she scream for Gabriel or Francesca? They were her lifelines when terror invaded and her spirit retreated. Physically, she was incapable of running away from him. She had learned a long time ago that all that brought was swift reprisal. She could be beaten into physical submission, but her mind could go where no other could follow. She could stay safe, huddled far away in a place inside her mind.

Dimitri could see stark fear in his lifemate's eyes. Every vestige of color drained from her face, leaving her so pale her skin looked translucent. The anger he was holding in check receded as protective instincts he didn't know he had rose sharp and fast. He wanted to gather her into his arms and shelter her there, but he could actually feel her soul shying away from the wild need in his. He had never imagined anyone could be so fragile. Approaching her called for a finesse he wasn't certain he possessed.

"Listen to me, little one." He made a supreme effort to gentle his voice. He was rarely around people and his throat felt rusty. "You shouldn't have had to witness that. The killing of a vampire is always a messy and violent business. I want only to heal the burns on your skin. Will you allow me to do so?"

She didn't answer, simply stared at him numbly.

His heart shifted in his chest. "If I frighten you too badly, I will call Francesca to you. She is a great healer, but it must be done soon. Vampire blood burns like acid. This one had recently turned or it wouldn't have been so easy to . . ." He hesitated wanting to avoid the word "kill." "Destroy."

Skyler swallowed several times. "How?" The word came out barely a whisper.

He touched her mind, found her hands throbbed and burned. She looked as if she might faint, even felt faint in her mind.

"It won't hurt. I'll be very careful."

She took a deep breath as she lifted her chin and forced herself to take a step toward him. Her body trembled visibly. He could see the effort cost her dearly, but he was proud of her for the attempt. He didn't make the mistake of going to her. He was too tall, towering over her diminutive frame, and he knew it would only frighten her more if he moved. He waited, holding his breath still in his lungs, regulating his heartbeat to hers in an effort to help steady her. She took a second step and then a third, reaching out with both hands so he could see the streaks of acid burn where the vampire's blood had melted the material of her gloves. Her hands shook as she placed them in his open palms.

"Would you rather I call Francesca?"

She shook her head. "They don't know I followed the call of the wolf. They'll be angry with me." She raised her eyes to his. "Disappointed in me."

His call. Inwardly, Dimitri swore. He had not bound her to him, but his blood—his heart—his very soul called to hers. Of course she had answered. No lifemate could resist her other half in need. And he needed her desperately. He closed his fingers around hers.

"I'll do this then. I cannot call down the lightning as you are not fully Carpathian, so I must use my own healing powers. It can feel—intimate. You'll have to trust that I am not taking advantage, but only doing what is necessary."

He lowered his head, inch by slow inch, giving her plenty of time to change her mind. His gaze held hers captive, refusing to allow her to look away from the familiar act he was performing on her. His lips moved along the streaks, feather light, just skimming, brushing small caresses over the burns. His tongue stroked, velvet soft. She jumped and nearly pulled her hand away. Instinctively he tightened his fingers, holding her skin against his lips.

Surely you know our saliva heals.

Skyler nodded, still unable to pull her gaze from the deep blue of his. *It doesn't feel the same as when Francesca or Gabriel have healed cuts on me. It feels . . .* Intimate. Too intimate. Sexy. Erotic even. Faint color stole into her cheeks at her thoughts. She couldn't control the rush of heat in her bloodstream, or the way her womb clenched in anticipation when his lips touched another long burn. She was so mesmerized by him, she didn't even notice she'd used the most intimate form of speech of all—mind-to-mind on a private path only the two of them shared.

His tongue swirled, taking the sting from the burns. It felt like seduction—and as if he were stealing away more than the pain. She could see every detail of his face, the strong jaw and nose, the shape of his mouth, most of all, those glacier-blue eyes she couldn't escape. His lashes were heavy and very black, just as his hair and brows were. The color of his eyes was more dramatic, more intensely alive, with the contrast. She felt almost dizzy, as if she were falling into his intent gaze.

She drew air deep into her lungs and found his scent. Her heart matched the rhythm of his. Her mind actually relaxed its guard and allowed him to slip inside. His soul brushed up against hers. He didn't push, or take, merely touched, so light she barely felt it, barely felt the merging, her soul reaching instinctively, yearning for his—for him.

She wanted to snatch her hand away, to tell him she'd have Francesca help her after all, but she couldn't. Nothing had ever felt so right in her life. In that brief moment there was no past or future, only this moment and this man.

Dimitri was careful to find every burn on her skin, every thread the vampire's blood had left behind. They could be like spoors, spawning the most malevolent things if not eradicated. Fortunately, the vampire had been one that was more recently turned and hadn't yet grown fully into the power of evil. Dimitri took his time, brushing the pad of his thumb along her inner wrist, savoring the feel of her skin and the fact that for this one small moment in time, she relaxed a little with him.

It was with great reluctance that he lifted his head and allowed her hands to slip through his fingers. "There. It is done."

"What about your wounds? I can't heal you."

"I can do that myself." But he couldn't breathe without her. He looked away from her before she glimpsed that in him—the need to gather her up and take her far away where she had no choice but to accept him. The beast struggled to rise, demanding its mate. Ruthlessly, he pushed it down. Nothing would mar this moment with her.

"I wanted to see you again. I needed to talk to you."

He bowed slightly from the waist and reached out with that same slow deliberation, giving her plenty of time to object. When she didn't, he tucked a stray strand of blond hair behind her ear. "I am at your service."

Her smile was tentative—an olive branch. "I needed to tell you that it isn't you. It's me. I know what a lifemate is and this is a mistake. I'm—flawed. I can't be like other women—not ever." She ducked her head, avoiding his gaze. His eyes just seemed so alive, almost burning her skin, yet so cold she shivered.

"It takes a great deal of courage, little one, to tell me these things. I thank you for making the effort." He kept his voice gentle, resisting the urge to drag her into his arms. She was utterly adorable standing there trying to reject him and not hurt his feelings. They were all wrong—Francesca and Gabriel and even Mikhail. She wasn't too young. Even now, when she should have been little more than a girl emerging from her childhood, he knew she was already an adult. His soul had brushed hers. She had been ripped from her childhood, and the young woman so close—so elusive—was simply too fragile. So beaten down, so sensitive with her enormous psychic talent—the atrocities committed against her had driven her spirit too deep, too far, and she was barely able to stay in the world. "Time will sort this out for us. In the meantime, allow me to escort you back to your home."

"Aren't you angry with me?"

"Because you are not yet ready for my claim?" He took her hand, his fingers warm and sure when she was so uncertain. "Of course not."

Snow plopped down from the nearest tree and both turned toward the sound. Branches swayed as a small owl took to the air, wings outstretched, body wobbling as it launched itself into the air. The screech owl dove straight at them.

Dimitri leapt to place his body between the creature and Skyler. He timed his attack, swatting the bird from the air even as she yelled, panic evident in her voice.

"No! It's Josef. It has to be Josef." She tried to get around Dimitri, her protective tone raising the hackles of the wolf, triggering the response of his beast at the idea that she would shield another man. He moved without seeming to do so, keeping her from rushing around him.

The owl shook, the movements jerky, arms breaking through where wings had been. It fell into the snow and a young man sprawled out, all arms and legs, looking slightly shocked and very scared, but determined. He scrambled to his feet, balled his fists, and glared at Dimitri. "Leave her alone."

Dimitri might have overcome the instinct of his species, but he felt Skyler's response to the stranger, the instant flash of amusement tinged with admiration. He bared his teeth, a snarl rumbling deep in his throat, a challenge to the other male. At once the small clearing was ringed with the pack, the wolves pacing, eyes glowing, answering his snarls with agitation and aggression to match his own. Fire burned in his mind, his heart, raged in his soul and was reflected in his eyes, now a fiery red.

Skyler tried to push past him, but he caught her arm, his grip like steel. "Who is this man to you?"

"My friend. Don't you dare hurt him." She would fight for Josef when she couldn't fight for herself.

The wolf pack bared teeth, edged closer, narrowing the circle. Skyler could make out the large shaggy animals, all in good health, all focused on Josef.

"You do not need to have male friends," Dimitri bit out, his strong white teeth flashing, showing a hint of his lengthened canines as well as incisors. His muscles rippled beneath his skin, crackling and popping as he fought off the change.

Frightened, Skyler began to back away from him again, sensing the wild rage rising, the animal taking over. But something, maybe desperation, pain, sorrow, *something* gave her pause. She touched him, her palm flat on his chest, looking up into his eyes. Even in the guise of a wolf, his eyes were always going to be blue, and right now they were turbulent and stormy. "Dimitri. He's a friend. Not a boyfriend." She shouldn't have to make excuses, but she couldn't stop wanting to soothe him. The need was every bit as urgent and strong as the desire to run.

He caught her hand, carried it to her lips and waved his hand to the slavering wolves. The circle opened reluctantly. "Go. Go now," he bit out, "while I'm still in control."

"I'm sorry," she whispered.

Skyler and Josef ran, careful not to touch each other, Skyler with a heavy heart and guilt clawing at her. She ran with tears streaming down her face wondering where they came from, feeling inadequate and a coward. She ran from Dimitri's pain and her own fears. Was there never going to be a safe refuge for her?

10

Music filled the small confines of the room, spilled out into the hallways and drifted outside. Antonietta Scarletti-Justicano turned her head toward the sound. Two pairs of footsteps approaching. She sniffed the air, easily distinguishing the familiar scent of Josef and the unfamiliar scent of his companion. Female . . . young . . . and very distraught. It took a second to get past the girl's radiating fear to feel Josef's matching alarm. She lifted her fingers from the ivory keys and turned toward them.

"Josef? What's wrong?"

Skyler realized instantly Antonietta couldn't really see them. It was almost unheard of for a Carpathian to be anything but perfect physically. She tried to recall what she knew of Josef's aunt. She'd been a famous pianist before Byron had claimed and converted her and she'd been blind most of her life. Skyler moved closer to her in an attempt to make it easier for her. "I'm Skyler Daratrazanoff, Francesca and Gabriel's daughter." She didn't make the claim often, but she loved saying it out loud.

"It's lovely to meet you, *cara*," Antonietta said, her voice as musical as her fingers. "Please tell me what is upsetting you both."

"A vampire attacked Skyler," Josef burst out.

Antonietta reached out toward her. Instinctively, before she could stop herself, Skyler stepped back.

"I'm all right. Dimitri killed it."

"And then he touched her. Licked her." There was disgust in Josef's voice. "We barely got out of there alive. He had a wolf pack with him and the wolves would have killed us."

Byron! Antonietta summoned her lifemate immediately. "Josef, are either of you hurt in any way? Have you called Gabriel?"

"No!" Skyler protested. "Please don't do that. Neither of us is hurt. Vampire blood splashed over my hands and burned through my gloves. Dimitri was healing the burns when Josef saw him. Josef misunderstood."

"I didn't misunderstand him baring his teeth at me, Skyler," Josef snapped. "You didn't see him. There was death in his eyes when he looked at me."

"He saved my life," Skyler declared.

"Your heart is pounding very fast and loud," Antonietta pointed out. "I think you were far more frightened than you wish to admit."

"Of the vampire," Skyler insisted.

A tall handsome man strode into the room. "Vampire?" He glanced from his nephew to his lifemate, and circled Antonietta's waist with his arm.

At once Antonietta could see the others in the room. Most of the time, when she wasn't tired, she could see shadows on her own, enough with her other heightened senses to know who and what was around her, but sometimes she simply didn't bother. She was used to a world without sight, and unless Byron provided her eyes for her, it was difficult to continually remember and maintain her vision. *A vampire attacked this young lady and Josef seems to think Dimitri, her rescuer, then behaved inappropriately, although she claims he was healing her hands.*

Byron immediately reached out to the other Carpathians on their common telepathic path of communication to spread the news of a vampire attack. Gabriel's answer was sharp and instant. "Your father is on his way," Byron announced aloud, even as he reached for Skyler's hands, grasping her fingers before she could pull away and raising them up for inspection. Old scars crisscrossed the skin, running up her forearms in what were obviously defensive wounds. The sight of such abuse on a young female sickened him. On the backs of her hands were newer marks, recently healed, faint, but telltale.

Skyler jerked her hands away, visibly trembling. "I told you, he healed the burns." She put her hands behind her back, out of sight. "It was awful."

Gabriel materialized in the room without preamble, reaching for her, yanking her against him, his hands sliding over her checking for damage. "You have a lot to answer for, Skyler Rose."

"She's had a terrible fright," Antonietta said, interceding.

"Some stranger was all over her," Josef said, frowning in disapproval. He drew himself up to his full height. "I followed her because she was acting funny and a vampire attacked her. Before I could do anything . . ."

"Such as call for me?" Byron interrupted. "I don't recall a summons or a cry for help."

"I did not get one either," Gabriel said, retaining his hold on his daughter. "The threat of a vampire getting his hands on you, Skyler, is enough to put gray streaks in my hair. What were you doing out in the open without protection? You were warned earlier that you were in danger, yet you chose to ignore it? You ignored a direct order from your mother and me."

Skyler clung to him. It the midst of such a chaotic world, he was a tower of strength—always and ever her rock. "I'm sorry," she whispered. *I couldn't stop myself from going to him. There was such pain. I know pain and I couldn't be the cause.*

A slow hiss escaped him. His fingers stroked a caress even as he buffeted her from his fatherly anger. Part of him wanted to shake her hard, the other half wanted to hold her to him and comfort her, keep her safe. *You did not think to confide in Francesca—or me? You could have asked us for help in dealing with this, Skyler.*

Was there hurt in his voice? Was she destined to hurt everyone who mattered to her? "I'm so sorry," she said aloud a second time. "I couldn't think clearly." It was the truth—and the only excuse she had to offer.

"Tell us exactly what happened," another voice said. Skyler looked up to see Mikhail and Lucian standing close. Both looked grim. "If Dimitri assaulted you, Skyler, you must tell us," the prince added.

"No!" She shouted the word, a surge of adrenaline rushing through her

bloodstream. Everyone was staring at her, crowding close. She could barely breathe, barely speak. "He tried to help me. Why won't you listen to me?"

"If you value your lives," another voice interrupted, "you will leave my lifemate alone. I can feel her distress radiating through the forest and yet you surround her, pressuring her to tell you tales you should be asking of a hunter." Dimitri stood tall and straight in the open doorway. His long hair blew in the slight breeze and a few snowflakes dotted his head and shoulders.

Gabriel pushed Skyler toward Antonietta. "I believe I will take you up on your explanation," he told Dimitri through clenched teeth. "Antonietta, if you would be so kind as take my daughter into your kitchen and make certain she drinks something sweet such as orange juice. It must be natural."

"Gabriel," Skyler protested.

Go with her. It is my duty and privilege to ensure your safety and I intend to do just that. We will discuss this later.

"He saved my life," Skyler said defiantly, looking around at the room filled with Carpathian hunters. "He saved my life."

Antonietta ignored the small automatic hesitation on Skyler's part and put her arm around the girl. "I think your man can hold his own with this group." *Be on his side, Byron. Please. He seems so alone.* She flashed a confident smile at Skyler. "I can see when I work at it. I won't give you something like olive oil to drink instead of orange juice."

Skyler went with her, but halted in the hallway leading to the kitchen. She looked back, her troubled gaze meeting Dimitri's.

It will be all right, lyubof maya, *go with the woman and let me make things perfectly clear to these men—and your father.*

Please don't hurt anyone—or get hurt. I couldn't stand that. She glanced at Gabriel. He was watching her—not Dimitri, and he had a frown on his face. She was disobeying him again. She ducked her head and turned to follow Antonietta.

We will come to an understanding, Skyler, your father and I. I thank you for defending me. And stay away from the boy. He is jealous and capable of starting trouble he cannot conceive of.

Skyler didn't know what to say to that. Josef had acted jealous, but he wasn't enamored of her. She thought it more likely he was lonely—just as she was—and he didn't want to lose a friend.

It was dark in the kitchen and Antonietta forgot to turn on the lights, so Skyler tried to do so unobtrusively. "Gabriel's really angry with me this time. I did go off like an idiot, but my mind was so foggy. I could only think about getting to the wolf."

Antonietta pulled orange juice from the cooler. "The wolf? Or Dimitri?"

Skyler frowned, rubbing at her temples. "I don't know. I thought Dimitri, but I followed the cry of the wolf."

"And Dimitri wasn't the wolf?"

Skyler shuddered and shook her head. "The wolf appeared to be trapped in a steel claw, the leg bleeding. I wanted to help it, but then it changed into something hideous and Dimitri came and fought it."

"That must have been terribly frightening." Antonietta conveyed the information to Byron so he could tell the others. "It doesn't sound right to me," she informed Skyler. "Here, sit down. You're still shaking."

Skyler pulled out a chair and sank into it, shocked that her legs were so rubbery. "I tried to resist, but I didn't call Gabriel or Francesca for help and I should have."

Antonietta sat opposite her. "It sounds a bit like a compulsion, don't you think? But how could a vampire have targeted you? He would have had to have access to your mind—your thoughts—in order to trap you with something familiar to you."

"Earlier, I tried to trace a surge of power. It came from the direction of the hotel, so we all thought it was someone there, but whoever was using energy caught me, and maybe they touched my mind enough to know I love wolves." She bit at her lip. "And that I was worried about Dimitri."

They did not believe a strike would come so soon—or that it was a vampire. They believed someone from the human society was baiting a trap for her—at least that is the explanation they are giving her lifemate. He is angry and rightly so. He has the right to demand she be protected at all times, sheltered more than any other if they refuse to allow his claim at this time. Mikhail has no choice but to accede to his wishes. Byron exchanged the information with Antonietta, knowing she didn't like to be kept "in the dark" over anything. For so long her family had kept secrets from her. He refused to do so. His lifemate would have whatever knowledge he had at all times. He sent her warmth and love, reassurance that the child wouldn't be harmed.

I can feel her growing fear, Byron. They all need to be gentle with her. She nudged the glass of orange juice closer to Skyler's hand. "Drink. You'll feel better."

Skyler sent her a small smile. "You're easy to talk to. The others just bellow and no one really listens. Josef was brave to interfere, but he isn't exactly telling the truth. He isn't lying, but he's making it sound as if Dimitri was doing something wrong."

Deep inside, she shivered, remembering the feel of Dimitri's mouth against her skin, his tongue stroking velvet caresses over her wounds. Heat rushed through her veins, sent awareness into her deepest feminine core. Tiny sparks of electricity skipped over her skin and her breasts tingled. She blushed, grateful Antonietta couldn't see very well.

"Do you like Dimitri?" Antonietta asked.

"He confuses me. For one moment he seemed the most gentle man alive, and then he was like a demon, dangerous and ready to kill in an instant."

"When he was fighting the vampire?"

Skyler shook her head. "I think I could have been okay with that, but no, with Josef. Josef is—just Josef. He's sweet and funny and way smarter than anyone gives him credit for. He would have fought for me and Dimitri is—big, strong. You saw him. Still, Josef thought to rescue me."

"He should have called Byron and you should have called Gabriel," Antonietta pointed out.

"I know."

"Josef is going through a difficult period in his life. He spends far too much time interacting on the internet instead of with people. He needs better social skills. Meeting you and Josh after so many months of continual communication—it was like he had friends already."

Skyler found Antonietta more difficult to read than most, but she was certain the conversation was about her and the way she hid from life as well as being about Josef. "Well, at least I won't have to worry about the vampire. He's dead now, so I'm safe and everyone, Josef included, can breathe easier." She hoped the fact that Dimitri had destroyed the threat to her would keep Gabriel from being so angry.

She is very certain the threat to her is gone, Antonietta shared.

I very much doubt it. She was definitely targeted and this is the second time. Dimitri said the vampire had to have turned only a month or so earlier, that he hadn't grown into his powers. Most fledgling vampires are used as pawns by one far more powerful. We know they are in this area, and no fledgling would try to take on so many Carpathians. He was sent by someone else testing the waters.

Antonietta's hand fluttered gracefully to her throat. *Then young Skyler is in more danger than ever. Surely someone will tell her. It is unfair to allow her to think she is safe. Really, Byron, I would want to know.*

No doubt they will tell her when this mess is settled. I would not want to go up against Lucian and Gabriel, especially when they are united, but Dimitri has grown into a force to be reckoned with. He has taken on the Daratrazanoff brothers and invoked his rights. He won't back down at all, or give any concession. He blames Gabriel for allowing Skyler to be in danger, and truly, Antonietta, what can Gabriel say in response? It is his sole responsibility to keep her safe, as his daughter and certainly as Dimitri's lifemate. Whatever has taken place over the centuries, it has shaped Dimitri into a strong, lethal warrior. He means to force an order from Mikhail—or take her with him.

She's too young—too hurt. She needs time to heal, Byron.

I think Dimitri is aware of that. He's not pushing his claim to bind her, only that they comply with his every wish.

"You're talking to your lifemate, aren't you?" Skyler guessed shrewdly.

"Byron," Antonietta supplied. "Yes, he's sharing information with me. We have a partnership. He promised me he would always treat me as an equal, and he does even when others think he shouldn't. I am used to a certain way of life and Byron has never asked me to give it up."

"He makes you happy?"

"Very much so. I cannot imagine my life without him. I would have no life without him."

"So what is going on in there? They're all pretty angry. None of them are working very hard to block their emotions." Skyler raised her gaze to Antonietta's. The woman was looking back at her and *seeing* her—seeing more than Skyler wanted anyone to ever see. "It's because of me, isn't it?"

Antonietta's smile was gentle. She shook her head, drawing attention to the thick rope of hair plaited intricately. "It's because they are men. A vampire attacked one of their women and blame must be placed, strategy worked out. Mostly, it is a lot of hunters in close proximity to one another. They should just tell you they are going to have to guard you every moment and leave it up to your good sense to know they are right."

"But—isn't the vampire dead? I saw Dimitri incinerate the heart." Her pulse was pounding again. She was *not* facing another vampire.

"He was too easy to kill. That usually means another sent him out as an expendable pawn. If he got you, all to the good, but it is a distraction to draw our attention away from the real attack."

Skyler took a small sip of the orange juice. It was never easy to eat or drink. Things always smelled good, but her stomach often rebelled. "Thank you for not treating me like a little kid. I'll be very careful. But you know—even though they've twice targeted me, it might simply be because I was convenient. They had a trail back to me. They knew what would trigger a response and they used it. Everyone is hovering around me, but they could be after the prince—or someone else important."

Out of the mouths of babes. Byron responded when Antonietta relayed Skyler's comment. *We will double our guard on Mikhail. It won't be easy, he doesn't like it.*

"It's hard to know there is so much evil in the world," Antonietta said. "I think most adults want to protect their children as long as possible from that knowledge."

Skyler fiddled with glass, turning it first one way and then the other. "I learned it early and it isn't like I can go back and pretend it all away. I didn't want to do this—this Christmas thing. I've never had a Christmas."

"With a tree and a pageant and Santa Claus coming?" Antonietta was astonished. "It is so much fun. A wonderful reason to bring the entire family together and celebrate life. Any excuse is great, and this is a perfect time of year."

"That's what Francesca said." Skyler leaned her chin into her palm, her clbow propped on the table. "Gregori is going to play Santa Claus. Have you ever seen him?"

"I've met him a few times. Byron and Jacques are good friends and Gregori visits Shea often. She's going to have her baby any time and everyone is very anxious about it. He doesn't seem a likely candidate to play the part."

"That's an understatement." A small smile slipped out for the first time. Skyler made a little face. "Wait until Sara and Corrine hear Gregori's going to be playing Santa. They've been getting all the children prepped for sitting on Santa's lap."

Antonietta burst out laughing. "Oh, dear. That could be bad."

"There's going to be a few crying children tonight," Skyler predicted. She inhaled deeply, for the first time relaxing enough to notice her surroundings. "What is that I smell? It's wonderful."

"My housekeeper gave me the recipe for a wonderful creamy pasta dish." Antonietta laughed invitingly. "Josef and Byron helped me prepare it. You should have seen us. I couldn't really see the ingredients, so Byron read each off and Josef handed them to me."

"Oh, no." Skyler's smile flashed again, this time wider, reaching her eyes. "He probably didn't know what they were."

"Neither did Byron. I didn't think about the fact that they wouldn't know what seasonings or anything else was for that matter. Our first attempt ended up in a hole in the backyard."

"Francesca and I made gingerbread houses and we insisted Gabriel help us. It was fun to see him look so helpless. He's always so invincible."

"That is a good thing, Skyler," Antonietta pointed out. "I think the men are finished with their quiet and well-ordered discussion."

There was a moment of silence, and then both women broke into laughter. Skyler waited a heartbeat and Gabriel was beside her. He held out his hand and she took it immediately. "I'm sorry, Gabriel. I really couldn't stop myself."

"I know, baby. You are not in trouble, although I am thinking of tying you to my side. Francesca needs to see you. She's very anxious."

Skyler nodded. "Where's Dimitri? You didn't fight with him, did you? You really do know that he saved my life?"

"It is difficult for one Carpathian to mislead another. Dimitri spoke the truth. He thought it best if he didn't upset you further." Gabriel flashed a smile toward Antonietta, reached to take her hand and bow low over her fingers. "Antonietta, as always, it is a pleasure to see you. Thank you for looking after my daughter."

"It was my pleasure," Antonietta said. "She is welcome anytime."

"Are we going to hear you play this evening?"

"They've asked me to play. I am not certain the children will appreciate it, but as I hear Gregori is to play the role of Santa Claus, it may be the only thing that soothes them."

Josef raced into the room, tried to skid to a halt and knocked into Gabriel, who caught him by his shirtfront and steadied him. Josef didn't seem to notice. "Skyler! I was afraid you'd already left. Paul and Ginny are expecting us over at their house. We have to hurry. We promised Sara we'd help her with the costumes."

"Skyler will have to meet you there," Gabriel said firmly. "I'll bring her myself," he added before either could protest. "Francesca wants to see her."

Josef scowled. "You don't think I can take care of her."

"No one needs to take care of me," Skyler protested, glaring at Josef. "I'm not a baby."

"He only meant keeping you safe from any outside harm," Antonietta hastily intervened. "Josef, Skyler will meet you there in a few minutes. You be careful as well." She smiled up at Byron as he materialized beside her, having escorted the other males out. He slipped his arm around her ultra feminine, curvaceous figure and dropped a kiss on the top of her head.

They followed Gabriel and Skyler to the door to wave. Byron pulled Antonietta into his arms. "What is it? I could feel you becoming agitated, but I couldn't read why." His hands framed her face, thumbs sliding in a caress over her skin. "I'm sorry our house was invaded just when you were composing. I know it's very important for you to have quiet while you work."

"That's not it. And besides, Josef is never quiet." The young Carpathian stayed with them most of the time. He enjoyed Italy and the palazzo where they resided. Mostly, Antonietta thought he admired Byron and wanted to be close to him. There were times he got the exact same expression on his face and imitated Byron's gestures. Byron paid attention to him, worked with him on his Carpathian skills—showed an interest.

He exasperates me no end.

You love him and he feels that. He needs you.

Byron made gave an inelegant snort. "Josef, if you think for even one moment your life is in danger, you call me and every other male in the vicinity. You have no business taking on a vampire at your age. You may have the courage, but not yet the skill." He eyed the younger man with a stern eye. "Do I have your word?"

Josef nodded. "Yes." He started out the door, then turned back toward Byron, tears glittering for a brief moment before he managed to control them. "I nearly got her killed, didn't I? I should have reached out the minute I saw the trapped wolf shifting. It all happened so fast." He ducked his head. "I couldn't move. At all. I don't have courage, Byron. I was afraid."

"You are supposed to be afraid. No one does everything right in their first encounter with a vampire. Dimitri is a hunter and a damn good one. He's been at it for centuries with no help, but I can assure you, his first vampire, he most likely froze just as you did."

"Did you?"

A fleeting smile crossed Byron's face. "Jacques and I were together and feeling pretty cocky until the thing came out of thin air and showed us a mouthful of black, pointed teeth. I think we both had a heart attack on the spot." He ruffled Josef's hair. "You did fine. And you did your best to protect her from Dimitri."

"He wasn't just healing her," Josef said. "It was blatant seduction."

"He is her lifemate, Josef. You have to respect that."

Josef scowled and slammed the door. Byron sighed. "So much for being any kind of good parent. I wish to hell my sister would take charge of that boy."

"No, you don't." Antonietta leaned into him, her soft breasts brushing his chest, fingers moving through his hair. "You love being an uncle."

"He drives me crazy. I can't remember ever being that young."

Antonietta twined her fingers through his as they made their way back through the house to the cozy den where they enjoyed sitting in peace together. Their household in Italy held a tremendous amount of responsibility. Antonietta's family resided with them and there was always drama.

"I feel the jaguar, Byron," Antonietta confessed without looking at him. She pressed her hand to her chest. "Deep inside of me, she's there, responding to something in the air. She's—*clawing* at me. My eyesight is worse than usual, but I can see with jaguar eyes."

Byron knew the Scarletti family—Antonietta's ancestors—came from a direct line of jaguar people. The cat had always been strong in her. He leaned forward, took both her hands in his and brought her fingers to his mouth. "When did this start?"

"A few hours ago. At first I just felt restless and edgy, but now it feels more like moodiness, wanting to strike out, a wildness I can't really adequately explain." She looked miserable. "I thought I was through with all that."

"You are Carpathian, Antonietta, and everything jaguar isn't evil. There are some that make it that way, but right now, what's more important is what is stirring up the cat in you." He glanced out the window to the storm clouds. "It's only a couple of hours until we meet the villagers for this pageant and meal at the inn. We have to be ready for any danger coming our way."

She swept a hand through her hair. "I've always been able to control the jaguar, but she's fighting me, trying to escape, and I think . . ." Her eyes met his. "I think she's dangerous."

"You'd never hurt anyone, Antonietta," he assured.

"You don't understand. She's trying to hurt *me*. I'm not letting her out and she's angry."

Byron's gaze narrowed and he sat up straighter. He sent every sense flaring out into the night, scanning, reading, trying to find a subtle strain of power influencing the part of Antonietta that was jaguar. He could feel a small stir in the air, but with so many Carpathians together, it was impossible to tell if the shift in the air was manipulating the cat in his lifemate.

"I heard a rumor that the Dark Troubadours are having trouble with the leopards they brought with them," he said. "The cats attacked one of the band members and threatened several others. They've caged them and they've never had to do that. Even Darius is having trouble controlling the cats' behavior."

Antonietta frowned. "What would do that? And what of the others? Isn't one of the Carpathian males with a woman who is fully jaguar? What's happening to her?"

"Yes, Juliette. There is also Natalya, Vikirnoff's woman. The tiger is strong in her." Byron pulled Antonietta into his arms to comfort her. "Come with me."

"Where?" He was moving her toward the door and her heart fluttered in fear. "Byron, I don't want to chance it."

"The cat will know where the power is coming from. She can trace it straight back to its source."

"But I'm not certain I'm strong enough to control the jaguar." In all her human years with the cat inside her, always fighting to come out, she had never been afraid of the animal. Until now. She shivered. The snow once more was beginning to drift down, but it was fear more than cold that made her shiver.

"We can control it together. Keep your mind merged with mine at all times, even if the cat resists," he said.

For some reason, memories of the conversion washed over her. It had been particularly difficult and painful, the jaguar fighting the Carpathian blood. Sweat broke out. "Byron, are you sure?"

"If you are afraid we cannot control this thing together, I'll call Jacques. Together, nothing will defeat us. You cannot go to the party under an influence we know nothing about."

She reached for Byron's mind with her own, sliding in with ease. It was an extremely intimate thing to do, and as always, her body reacted to the closeness. She was woman enough to enjoy his erotic thoughts and images of her, the way he viewed her full curves with lust rather than wishing for a thinner, more modern woman. He loved her hair, the thickness and color. He especially enjoyed taking out the elaborate braid just before he made love to her.

It took a moment to adjust to two minds vying for supremacy, but they merged naturally and Antonietta reached for the beast, embracing the jag-

uar, allowing it freedom. It sprang forward, claws unsheathed, with a chaotic need to bound across the snow-covered meadow for the trees. Byron
paced easily beside her, ignoring the warnings rumbling from the female.
He was not about to let Antonietta out of his sight.

The female jaguar slowed to a walk, placing each paw delicately in the
powdery snow, but moving without hesitation deeper into the woods. They
were moving in the general direction of the inn, but were still several miles
away. To Byron's knowledge, there were only a couple of homes in the direction they were going. Gregori's home was high in the mountains, surrounded
by a grove of trees and large boulders. It was protected from weather and
enemies on three sides, and even a hiker walking within yards of it wouldn't
be able to spot it. Gregori had woven safeguards around it to further distort
the image from any potential enemy.

Jacques and Shea lived in the second house. It too was very secluded.
Jacques still needed a space between him and the rest of the population.
Shea and Savannah were close friends and often visited each other, but even
their homes were miles apart. Jacques had built a very elegant house almost
into the mountain itself, so even from the air, it was impossible to see.

The cat lifted its head and scented the air several times. *She is searching
for a particular scent.*

What is it? Byron could feel the urgent compulsion in the cat, but he
couldn't find the thread driving it.

Antonietta didn't answer him right away, and when she did it was with
some reluctance. *She is hunting prey.*

The female jaguar pushed off with her hind feet and sprang up onto a
fallen log, pausing for a moment to look toward the mountains, toward Gregori's home, and then turned her head in the direction of the other house.

Deep inside the body of the jaguar, Antonietta gasped. *Byron! Did you
feel that surge? The eagerness?*

What is she after?

*The baby. She's after Shea's baby. That means Darius's leopards are being
pushed to attack Shea. Whoever it is doesn't know about me. The compulsion is
directed at the cats.*

Byron reached out on the private link he shared with his childhood
friend. *Jacques. Hear me now.* He shared the information, the feelings Anto-

nietta was experiencing as well as their fears. *We have to give this information to all Carpathians, but once we do, Shea will hear. Do you need time to break it to her gently?*

Byron hated to add to the couple's stress level. Both were terrified of the upcoming birth—and rightly so. Now they had to worry about an enemy who could manipulate animals and was doing so with the specific intent of harming their child.

Spread the word, Byron. We must find this enemy before Shea gives birth. I fear it will be this night. There was a small silence, and then Jacques sighed. *She is already fighting it, wanting to keep our son safe inside the womb.*

You are certain it is a boy?

Yes. I have a son. He is strong and wants to come out into the world, but Shea has been holding him back. Knowing an enemy has specifically targeted our child makes it more difficult.

She has my protection as well. I stand by your side, ready to fight.

We thank you, my old friend. There was weariness in Jacques's voice. *Please thank Antonietta. It must have been difficult for her to get her cat to reveal this information. Without her effort we would not know an enemy is about to strike. Shea sends her thanks as well.*

Byron shared the response with his lifemate as they both exerted pressure on the jaguar to turn back toward home. Immediately, the warning went out to all Carpathians on their common path of communication, and he felt a surge of pride in Antonietta.

The female snarled, resisting the order. Byron moved in closer, and at once Antonietta responded, catching his thought. There were much more pleasant ways to distract the cat than fighting it. Byron quickly shifted forms. The male jaguar shouldered the female, rubbing his chin along her back, and the female sprang away from him, throwing an enticing look over her shoulder. They raced back to the house, heat overcoming the need for prey.

By the time they shifted back to their own forms, their arms were wound tightly around one another, mouths welded together, and his hands were deftly pulling the intricate weave from her hair.

11

Juliette De La Cruz paced restlessly back and forth across the kitchen tiles. Her body felt too tight for her own skin. It was impossible to control her mind as it flipped channels, a chaotic whirl from subject to subject. She couldn't seem to stay focused on anything at all—not even the fruit and melon salad she was making for tonight's celebration.

She missed her sister and cousin. This would be her first holiday without them. She'd invited them, but as always, they'd refused to have anything to do with the De La Cruz men. It wasn't as if she blamed them, but Juliette could have used their company. Outside the window, the snowflakes drifted, turning the world around her into a peaceful, quiet realm, but her body and mind were out of control.

It was hot. Too hot. She unbuttoned her blouse and tied the ends together in a knot beneath her generous breasts. She lifted the heavy fall of hair from her neck and paced around the small kitchen once again. *If you don't come home soon, I'm going for a run. I need . . .* She reached out to her lifemate, but she didn't know what she needed. Her body wanted his—but it always did. She just couldn't become calm.

Deep inside, she felt her cat moving, struggling for supremacy. Juliette was part jaguar and even after the conversion, her cat was strong, but she was always able to control her. Now even her cat wanted out—wanted freedom.

Breathe. The word was whispered in her mind. Soft. Intimate. Warm. *You always forget to breathe.*

She knew she was alone in the kitchen. Her beloved lifemate, Riordan, had gone to see his brothers. Riordan and Juliette had traveled from South America and had arrived in the early morning hours. Riordan hadn't had a chance to see his brother, Manolito, who had been injured in a battle.

I'm breathing. I wish you were here. There was a blatant invitation in her voice. Riordan was very good at putting the heat in her blood with one whisper of his seductive voice. "I'm making this fruit salad. You're supposed to be helping me." Her breasts tingled and seemed heavy and aching. She had the full, curvy figure of a woman. Her waist was small, but her breasts and hips were generous and right now every square inch of her skin burned. She wanted him. Right there. That moment. He had to come back or she was going to have to throw herself in the snow to cool down.

I am on my way. Let me make my good-byes. It must be the fruit salad you are making. I think fruit turns you on.

Only what one can do with it. Juliette laughed, but there was little amusement in her. Her body was too edgy. The De La Cruz brothers seemed to be very sexual creatures, and she fit right in, needing Riordan, welcoming the many inventive ways he made love, but she'd never felt so edgy, so desperate.

She ran some water and dribbled it down the valley between her breasts, glancing out the window as she did so. No one was there. She was completely alone. She scanned often as Riordan had taught her, but she still felt as if someone watched her. Juliette tried to shake off the feeling, fearing it was leftover paranoia from her days kidnapping women back from jaguar males. She would never get over the constant vigilance needed to stay safe in the jungle. Looking out the window, she scanned again, just to be certain, taking great care to track any movement in the area around the cabin—even animals—but there was no one even close to her house.

Juliette? Jacques sent the word that someone is trying to use the leopards to attack Shea and her unborn child. Whoever is doing this is unaware of the jaguar strain running in some of the women. It is strong in you. Are you having trouble?

Juliette sighed with relief. She could handle her jaguar if the cat was what was causing her to be so moody and edgy and paranoid. *Yes. But I've been dealing with my cat all my life and I'm in control of her.* When her cat went into heat, it was especially difficult to maintain control and that could be the unexpected problem. She should have thought of that.

Be careful, Juliette.

She smiled to herself as she gathered up the melon peels. Of course he just had to have the last word, to give her some sort of a command. He'd spent too much time alone with his brothers in South America, or maybe the De La Cruz brothers were all just plain bossy with their women—well, okay—with everyone around them. They liked their women submissive, yet neither she nor Colby, Rafael's lifemate, were in the least bit unassuming. From her perspective at least, that made for a fiery and very interesting sexual relationship.

Catching up the bowl of rinds, she carried them outside into the thick grove of trees surrounding the house. The moment she stepped into the night air, the cat inside her stirred, unsheathed claws and looked up toward the mountains—toward Jacques's residence. She reprimanded the cat with a warning snarl and pushed it ruthlessly down. The cat tried again, rubbing against her insides, spreading a fire that only Riordan could put out.

So that's the way it is. We've been too long without our mate.

Her hair whipped across her face with a strong gust of wind. She pulled down the thick, dark strands and tossed the rinds for the deer. Everything in her froze, the smile fading abruptly as she stared down in shocked horror at the track marks in the snow. Her mouth went dry as she took a cautious look around. Her heart began to slam hard and for one awful moment, her legs went rubbery.

Riordan? How far away are you?

What is it? He felt her fear more than heard it, and already he was striding through his brother's house, calling to the other men, ready to take to the air.

Jaguar tracks. Male. How can that be? I was throwing melon scraps out for the deer and the tracks are all around the house. He was staring in the window while I was making the salad. She stayed still, almost afraid to move, her gaze quartering the area, paying particular attention to the trees.

The Dark Troubadours brought their leopards, Juliette. His voice was soothing. *Perhaps you are mistaken and one of the leopards was investigating our house.*

She brought her teeth together in a sharp snap. *Don't patronize me! I know the difference. I've tracked jaguar all my life and I don't make mistakes. I know a jaguar track and I know when a male has been in the vicinity. I can scent him as well. I'm telling you one of them is here, in the mountains, and there's only one reason he'd be here.*

Get in the house. I'm on my way, coming to you now.

No, the tracks lead away from the house. I'm going to follow him. Antonietta has the ability to shift into a jaguar as well. I don't know if any of the other women can as well, but if they can, they could be in as much danger as I am. It stands to reason that several of them carry the blood whether they can shapeshift or not. It would explain their strong psychic abilities.

Juliette. He put warning into his voice, displeasure.

She ignored him as if she hadn't heard him. *I can't believe one of them came here with so many Carpathian males around. They must be getting desperate. What if they followed us? What if I brought this danger on these people?*

Don't panic. I'll be there soon. Go into the house. He repeated it, this time making it a command. *Not all jaguar males belong to the group kidnapping females.*

You and I both know if he's here lurking around the house, he's after a woman who can shapeshift. I'm not allowing what happened to my baby sister to happen to anyone else. I'm tracking him.

Already, she was calling up her cat for the change. Before her conversion to Carpathian, the change from human form to jaguar had been slow and painful, but it was much easier now. Before, she could call on her jaguar heritage only for short periods of time and shift, but it was always difficult, and even more so to hold that form for very long. Now she could do it effortlessly for hours on end.

If someone is influencing the cats in an attempt to get them to attack Shea and her unborn child, it may be too dangerous for you to use that form. You said you were having trouble. He used any excuse he could think of to stall her.

I've been restless and edgy, and yes, my jaguar has been clawing at me to let her loose, but no jaguar male could influence us that way.

He could if he was psychic.

I would know. I spent my life fighting them in the jungle, Riordan. In any case, I'm perfectly capable of controlling my cat. I've been doing it all my life—even when she's edgy and needs a mate.

You better never let her loose when she needs a mate—unless you're coming to me. Now wait for me.

She reached for her wild side, allowing her jaguar to completely take over her body. Spotted fur slid over her skin. Muscles and tendons contracted and stretched, stiletto-sharp claws sprang from her curving hands and her face elongated to accommodate the jaguar muzzle and teeth. She dropped to all fours, already running smoothly. Roped muscles and a flexible spine allowed the stocky jaguar to leap from boulder to log and even take to the tree branches when necessary.

I forbid this, Riordan bit out, his hiss of anger sliding into her mind with a black swirl.

Then it's a good thing no one can boss me around. Juliette had fought most of her life against the jaguar males. They kidnapped women with the ability to shapeshift and stole any child resulting in the union. Juliette had stayed in the forest working with other women to try to help, but in the end she'd lost her mother and aunt to the jaguars, and eventually they had captured Jasmine, her sister. She couldn't allow any woman to fall into their hands.

Riordan was a strong Carpathian male and had lived for centuries in South America, adopting the Latin possessive and protective nature toward women, which compounded the already overbearingly dominant traits of his species. She knew he was furious at the idea she could be in danger and he wasn't with her, and he was also angry with her for her refusal to do as he ordered.

Rafael will come with me. We will find this male.

Good. Then I'll have backup. I suggest you hurry.

He sent her a low growl and the impression of strangling her. Juliette ignored him and raced across the snow as lightly as possible, covering the male's tracks, scenting the forest air. Her jaguar fought her for a moment, trying to turn in the direction of the mountains, but she held the cat to its course, moving fast in an effort to overtake the male.

How long had he been outside her house watching her make her fruit salad for the party? She had been insistent that Riordan go visit his brother since Manolito had been injured. It had never occurred to her that she might run into a jaguar male here in the Carpathian Mountains—especially with all the protective males surrounding the women and guarding them as if they were all precious treasures.

You are a precious treasure, Juliette, although I'm considering beating you into submission.

I would cut off body parts when you slept.

That would be a problem. In spite of the gravity of the situation, amusement welled up between them.

Juliette felt a surge of love. She had never thought she would find a man—least of all a very dominating one—she could love and respect. Her life had been all about fighting men, but Riordan valued and cherished her. He always put her first, even when he was attempting to order her around. And in truth, it was nice to be able to rely on someone. Riordan was totally reliable. He would come and he would bring others.

She moved with confidence, staying low, aware the jaguar male could be luring her into a trap. Where there was one, there were often more, especially if they had come for a female—and that was likely. The male had veered toward the south, moving quickly through any open spaces, trying to stay to the trees for cover.

I cannot detect him when I scan.

Riordan swore. *Juliette, get out of there. I'm telling you to break off and wait for us. We're so close, but you could be running into a trap.*

I cannot allow him to get near the other women. He's circling around now and heading toward Rafael's house. Go back, Riordan. Colby has her brother and sister and their friends there. Panic edged her voice. She was still a distance away and she was fairly certain Riordan and Rafael were coming toward her. They would miss the jaguar male and he would have free access to the women and teens at the house.

Colby will protect the children. She is aware of the danger and is taking precautions. Just stop where you are, Riordan coaxed.

Juliette hesitated. What would be the best thing to do to ensure the male didn't grab anyone? She turned slightly, standing in a lower dip, lifting her head to scent the air again. Instantly the musky odor of male cat filled her lungs. Her head swung in the direction, but it was far too late. He was a mere blur, rushing at her with full speed. The much heavier male slammed into her side, cracking ribs and driving her from her feet. He was on her in a second, going for her throat, claws raking her sides, tearing deep lacerations. She tried to use her teeth, sinking them into the jaguar's leg, but for some reason, her teeth didn't really penetrate. She couldn't get a grip on him. The blood was hot, stinging and burning the inside of her mouth and muzzle.

She had fought many males, but this one was incredibly strong. Even with her amazing agility, she couldn't get out from under him. She kept her throat protected, but he raked her chest, dug at her soft belly with his back paws. She tried a roll, her smaller body squirming out from under his, but his teeth clamped hard on her shoulder, the long canines puncturing her skin to tear through muscle and tissue.

Submit to him. Riordan snapped the order.

No! Never. She'd force the male to kill her first. *I'd rather die than let him put his filthy hands on me.*

Riordan swore and gripped her mind, ruthlessly taking control. He was far stronger than she'd ever expected and he forced obedience, the female jaguar lying still beneath the male's raking claws and teeth. *Look at him. Look him straight in the eyes.* Even as Riordan gave the command, he was forcing her compliance, dictating to her brain what he wanted the female jaguar to do.

Juliette lay in the snow, bleeding from dozens of wounds, her sides heaving, her ribs on fire, staring into the triumphant yellow gaze of pure evil. There was cunning intelligence looking back at her. She let the submissive terror of the female jaguar show in her eyes, although deep inside she felt Riordan waiting for the perfect moment to strike. She wasn't alone, she could do this. Riordan could destroy him through her. One less jaguar male to terrorize the females. She waited for the male to touch her, shuddering with distaste, but willing to be the sacrifice if Riordan could put an end to his life.

The male jaguar leaned closer, bending over her. His face contorted, chest and arms beginning to change. His muzzle receded to be replaced by a bullet-shaped head, skin pulled tight over a skull. The slash of mouth yawned wide revealing brown-stained teeth, razor-sharp and pointed.

Juliette's heart skipped a beat, then began to pound in utter terror. She felt Riordan's shock, heard his warning broadcast to the other Carpathians. Not jaguar—vampire. Instantly she began to shift, bringing up both legs up to kick hard. Her feet, in the midst of the change hit the vampire in the chest. Nothing happened. He didn't even rock back. It was like hitting concrete, and the shock jarred her entire body. She tried to roll away from him, but one contorted hand caught her, sharp talons driving through her shoulder like spikes, pinning her to the ground.

He rose above her, a dark oily thing of utter evil, smirking at her in a macabre way. One finger lengthened into a talon. He breathed on it, and leaned down, all the while grinning with deliberate malice, tracing a smile around her throat. She felt the wash of hot blood gush over her neck and down her chest. Then the burn started, a fiery acid invading her skin and tissues, swelling until the pain became agony. The vampire bent and began to lick at her throat. He lapped greedily, then bit down hard, sinking long spiked teeth deep into her skin, growling as he tore at her flesh.

Pain blurred her vision, but Juliette never took her gaze from the top of her attacker's head. It was the only part of him she could see as he bent over her. She could feel Riordan concentrating, focusing, coiled and ready to strike. She knew that others were close, but only Riordan was within striking distance through her. She felt energy gathering, building until the air around her fairly crackled with it. Beneath her the snow began to melt. The vampire was too busy, feeding at the gushing well he'd opened.

Riordan struck with tremendous force, the blow hard and decisive. The vampire's skull cracked in long thin lines, splitting with a terrible crunching sound. Maggots poured out and the vampire screamed, leaping away from her, his eyes red-rimmed, his face smeared with her blood. Spittle spewed from his mouth as he raged at her. He kicked at her body, sending her flying across the snow. She hit a tree and dropped into a crumpled heap. She couldn't drag air into her lungs. Every part of her body felt on fire.

Juliette tried to push herself up, knowing he was coming for her. She couldn't quite get her legs under her, so she tried to crawl away, dragging herself toward the trees, nearly mindless with pain.

Hands touched her throat. Pushed something into the gaping wound. She looked up into the face of her brother-in-law. Juliette couldn't stop the tears. She bit down hard to keep from crying out as Rafael gathered her into the safety of his arms.

"It is all right now, little sister. Riordan will destroy it."

It took a tremendous effort to turn her head toward the vampire. Her neck and throat, in spite of the soothing pack Rafael had placed on her, felt raw and on fire, but she needed to see the vampire killed or he would haunt her dreams for all times.

Riordan dropped out of the sky straight onto the vampire's back. The beast rose up, snarling, fighting, a whirling demon of claws and teeth, shredding skin, and trying to crack bones. Riordan was far calmer. He locked his legs around the vampire's neck and slammed his fist deep, punching a hole as he drove through the back toward the heart.

The undead contorted, tried to become insubstantial mist, but Riordan was already locked on him. The vampire threw himself over backward, slamming Riordan into the ground, nearly breaking his neck. Riordan had no choice but to evaporate beneath him, streaking around to the front, already reshaping as he plunged his fist toward the heart, this time through the chest.

The vampire retaliated in kind, desperate to get away, striking the hunter's chest wall, cracking bones, breaking through skin.

Juliette, locked with Riordan, felt the blow to her own body, pain spreading fast, robbing her of breath and sanity. Just as abruptly, it was cut off and she was no longer merged with Riordan, but left alone with the agony of her own wounds and fear for her lifemate uppermost in her mind.

A second male arrived, then a third. She recognized the family features and knew one of the men must be Manolito, Rafael and Riordan's brother. The other was definitely Mikhail Dubrinsky, prince of the Carpathian people. She coughed, trying to talk. "Help him." She was certain she managed to get the words past her raw, gaping throat, but no one rushed to aid Riordan. They seemed more concerned with her.

"We are helping him," Rafael soothed. "Your life is too important to take chances with and Riordan is quite capable of killing the vampire."

"We need the richest soil possible," Mikhail said. "Someone has healed a portion of earth where the battle recently took place. The soil there is dark and lush with minerals. Get that and bring it to the healing cave. If someone can locate the woman with the talent to heal the soil, bring her as well. I've sent word to Gregori and Francesca. They will meet us there."

No one paid attention to Riordan and the vampire. Juliette felt desperate to reach him—to touch him with her mind. She could no longer see her lifemate, Rafael was taking her through the air to some cave she didn't want to be in. As hard as she tried to, she couldn't find her voice again and she didn't dare distract Riordan by using their telepathic link.

Carpathians began arriving, crowding close, answering the call to aid one of their kind. It was frightening to be among so many strangers—so many males. She had done this—with her headstrong nature. The vampire had used her worst fears against her and she'd fallen right into the trap. Had she broadcast her fears? How had he known she would follow a jaguar male? And now Riordan was in danger and no one seemed to care. She shoved at Rafael, tried to struggle, but her arms felt like leaden weights. Where was her strength? And why was her vision so hazy? Everything seemed vague and far away to her.

"Juliette!" Rafael's voice was sharp and commanding.

She'd always thought him far too overbearing, and would have told him so, but she seemed to be drifting, her surroundings cloudy.

"Juliette." He hissed her name. "Riordan needs you. Come back now!"

That brought her up short. Of course she could focus for Riordan, but why was Rafael holding her to him instead of allowing her to go to her lifemate? Nothing was making sense and the pain was too great. She closed her eyes, wanting to let go and just drift away.

"I've got her now." That was Riordan. She recognized the safety of his arms, the warmth of his body, the shape and contour of every part of him. His long hair brushed her face as he bent over her, the sensual touch so familiar to her. She smelled his blood, felt him wince when she snuggled closer.

You're a mess. I need to take care of your wounds. She whispered the invitation to him, turning her head in an effort to inspect his chest.

The healer is here, my love. He will do for me what is necessary. Right now, you stay merged with me. Riordan could feel her spirit sliding away. She'd lost so much blood, but Rafael had packed the wound and they were preparing for the ritual healing ceremony. It wasn't happening fast enough to suit him.

She was too pale, her mind confused. She didn't even seem to realize her very essence was moving away from him, growing weaker with each passing minute.

"Hurry, we don't have much time."

Gregori arrived, a tall, wide-shouldered man with long flowing hair and a man's face. There were no soft edges to him anywhere. He bent over Juliette without preamble and glanced back at the tall, slender woman who entered the cave after him. "Francesca. Hurry. She is far gone from us."

Riordan wanted to protest the assessment, but he knew it was true. He was holding Juliette in a ruthless grip, caging her spirit when it wanted to drift away along with the tremendous blood loss.

A wave of the healer's hand and aromatic candles sprang to life all around them. Riordan sat between the two healers, Juliette cradled in his lap, watching as the male simply shed his body and became a white light. The energy was strong, Riordan had to turn his head away. Almost immediately, Francesca did the same. He felt them enter Juliette's body, moving quickly to her neck and throat, examining the great tears in the veins located there.

You have lost too much blood, Riordan, and need healing yourself. Have your brother give her his. He is ancient and strong and his blood will help speed the process, Gregori dictated.

Rafael immediately stepped forward and offered his wrist. Riordan had no choice but to force Juliette. She was too weak to feed on her own, and he doubted if she would willingly take from another—even his brother.

Raven, Mikhail's lifemate, began to chant softly and all around him, Carpathians filled the cave of healing and those not present, joined in from afar to aid Juliette. The ancient words were beautiful as the voices rose in a melodious throat chant. Riordan knew the healers were deeply concerned because they were using the Great Healing Chant, one designed to bring back a lost soul already moving to the next world. He felt tears in his eyes, feeling the power of the unified people, all working toward one purpose—bringing his lifemate back to him—bringing their sister back to them. His voice rose with the others, so many now, like in the old days, using their ancient language, a language secret with rituals almost as old as time.

Ot sisarm ainajanak hany, jama.

Me, ot sisarm kuntajanak, pirädak sisarm, gond és irgalom türe.

O pus wäkenkek, ot oma śarnank, és ot pus fünk, álnak ekäm
ainajanak, pitänak sisarm ainajanak elävä.

Ot sisarm sielanak pälä. Ot omboće päläja juta alatt o jüti, kinta, és
szelemek lamtijaknak.

Ot en mekem ŋamaŋ: kulkedak otti ot sisarm omboće päläjanak.

Rekatüre, saradak, tappadak, odam, kaŋa o numa waram, és avaa owe o
lewl mahoz.

Ntak o numa waram, és mozdulak, jomadak.

Piwtädak ot En Puwe tyvinak, ećidak alatt o jüti, kinta, és szelemek
lamtijaknak.

Fázak, fázak nó o śaro.

Juttadak ot sisarm o akarataban, o sívaban, és o sielaban.

Ot sisarm sielanak kaŋa engem.

Kuledak és piwtädak ot sisarm.

Sayedak és tuledak ot sisarm kulyanak.

Nenäm ćoro; o kuly torodak.

O kuly pél engem.

Lejkkadak o kaŋka salamaval.

Molodak ot ainaja komakamal.

Toja és molanâ.

Hän ćaδa.

Manedak ot sisarm sielanak.

Alədak ot sisarm sielanak o komamban.

Alədam ot sisarm numa waramra.

Piwtädak ot En Puwe tyvijanak és sayedak jälleen ot elävä ainak
majaknak.

Ot sisarm elä jälleen.

Ot sisarm weńća jälleen.

My sister's body is a lump of earth close to death.
We, the clan of my sister, circle her with care and compassion.
Our healing energies, ancient words of magic and healing herbs bless my
sister's body, keep it alive.

But my sister's soul is only half. Her other half wanders in the nether
world.
My great deed is this. I travel to find my sister's other half.
We dance, we chant, we dream ecstatically, to call my spirit bird and to
open the door to the other world.
I mount my spirit bird, we begin to move, we are under way.
Following the trunk of the great Tree, we fall into the nether world.
It is cold, very cold.
My sister and I are linked in mind, heart and soul.
My sister's soul calls to me.
I hear and follow her track.
Encounter I the demon who is devouring my sister's soul.
In anger, I fight the demon.
He is afraid of me.
I strike his throat with a lightning bolt.
I break his body with my bare hands.
He is bent over and falls apart.
He runs away.
I rescue my sister's soul.
I lift my sister's soul in the hollow of my hand.
I lift her onto my spirit bird.
Following up the Great Tree, we return to the land of the living.
My sister lives again.
She is complete again.

Francesca worked to repair the large cuts to arteries and veins while
Gregori went after Juliette's spirit. Riordan was reluctant to turn her over to
him, afraid she would go the opposite way and be out of his reach forever.

She fears other males. She hides it well, but her past has taught her men are
not to be trusted.

Do you trust me? Gregori asked.

Riordan drew back. Gregori. The Dark One. Second in command to the
prince. He was a straight-up killer, but then, weren't they all? The De La Cruz
brothers had always questioned authority, always fought restrictions, and were
powerful, dominating men. They expected—and received—deference from

all those around them, and they were always just a little bit harder on their women. Riordan felt it took extraordinary women to stand up to his—and his brothers'—personalities, and it took extraordinary men to get the De La Cruz brothers to follow their lead. Gregori was such a man.

I have complete faith in you.

Do not allow her any chance at resistance.

Riordan had no problems being ruthless. He should have forced obedience earlier when he knew Juliette would go after what she thought was a male jaguar. If he had done so, she would not be at death's door right now.

Juliette's spirit flinched from Gregori's strong personality; the terrible white-hot light that shone on her drew her upward, back toward pain and suffering. She retreated, but Riordan was there, blocking her path to the other world, forcing her back toward the healer. She tried to struggle against Riordan, somewhat hurt that he had sided with a stranger, but she was weak and it was easy to force compliance.

Pain hit her—him—a raw, fiery burn that tore through her body. She screamed and screamed, pleading with Riordan to make it stop. She fought him, her spirit fought him, but he grimly held on, blood-red tears tracking down his face while Gregori and Francesca did their best to work fast in her resisting, struggling body.

This vampire's blood not only carried acid, but also parasites, and he had licked her wounds and punctured her throat with his teeth, depositing the hideous creatures into her bloodstream. They immediately moved to invade every cell—every organ, an army bent on destroying her.

Gregori. Francesca's normally calm voice was filled with alarm. *Look where the concentrated attack is.*

Riordan couldn't see, the light was too bright. Gregori swore softly in their language. *Tell me what is wrong,* Riordan demanded.

Our enemies are becoming more sophisticated in their attacks. The parasites are after her eggs. Gregori delivered the news on the Carpathian common path of communication.

The chanters faltered as the enormity of the news struck them. The men looked at one another, and several put their arms around their lifemates.

"Can you save her children?" Mikhail asked.

Raven slipped her hand into Mikhail's waiting for the answer.

We are trying.

Gregori left Francesca to work on broken ribs and the lacerations and burns while he attacked the parasites, driving them away from their prize. It was daunting to see the damage they left in their wake. He could tell Rafael's blood made a difference, giving her starving cells a chance, flooding tissue and organs with strength to help combat the vampire's poison. He worked fast, destroying the parasites where he found them, chasing them when they fled.

When Gregori was certain he had killed the last one, he began to work on the damage, first repairing the ovaries, ensuring no egg had been penetrated. The parasite would attach itself, replicate and feed off the internal organs. They had voracious appetites. It seemed hours, when in reality it was far less with both healers working together, before Gregori was able to regain his own body. Francesca swayed beside him, pale and exhausted. They had worked a miracle in record time.

"She needs more blood and good rich soil," Gregori said, "but she'll be fine." He inspected Riordan. "You, however, need a little help."

"The soil will aid me," Riordan said. "I can't thank you enough for saving her life. She was far gone from us."

Mikhail held up his hand for silence. "There is one among you able to heal the earth. Would you step forward?"

The Carpathians looked at one another. Over in the corner where the Dark Troubadours had gathered, Barack took Syndil's hand and led her to the front. "Syndil is capable of healing the earth."

Mikhail let his breath out slowly. The woman was one of the children Darius had saved, her Carpathian lineage strong and true. She looked nervous, but stood quietly waiting. He smiled at her. "So you are our miracle worker. I saw the land after you worked on it."

She spread her hands out in front of her. "It is my calling. A small talent, but strong."

The prince shook his head. "I do not believe it is a small talent. We would give this couple to Mother Earth to heal. If you could choose, where would you put them?"

"Here," Syndil pointed to a spot without hesitation.

"The soil is rich there, no toxins?"

She frowned, holding her hands over the spot. "It is the best in the caverns, but I can make it better." She glanced at Riordan. "If you don't mind waiting."

"Not at all," Riordan replied. Gregori was healing him even as Mikhail was watching the woman prepare the soil. "I am grateful to you."

Syndil knelt and closed her eyes, palms down toward the earth. She sang softly, calling to the soil, encouraging the wealth of minerals to double.

Mikhail tightened his fingers around Raven's. *My God, Raven. She's the real thing. She can do this, enrich our soil for us.*

It takes its toll on her. Look at her.

Syndil swayed, pale, much like Francesca and Gregori, when she stood. Barack reached for her, circling her waist to steady her. Mikhail nodded. *We will all aid her as best we can.*

Syndil stepped back and smiled at Mikhail. "There. The soil should really help both of them."

Riordan, holding Juliette to him, floated down into the bed of rich loam. Around them, the dirt filled in to cover them. Rafael stepped forward and began to weave safeguards while the Carpathians drifted back to their homes.

Mikhail bowed to Syndil. "If I asked you, would you consider choosing the birthing place for Shea? I could take you around and have you look at various sites we're considering. I would greatly value your opinion."

"I know nothing of birthing."

"But you know much about soil."

Syndil glanced at Barack, who nodded. "Of course, although I doubt I'll have time to make anything for the dinner tonight."

"Believe me, this is far more important," Mikhail assured.

Raven agreed. "I have the dinner well in hand. Shea's birth is the most important thing we have going and our biggest reason to celebrate."

I think this very humble woman is our greatest reason to celebrate, Mikhail declared.

12

"We're in for it now, Ginny," Colby De La Cruz said with a small sigh as she braided her younger sister's hair. "Rafael is going to be crazy now. He hardly lets me out of his sight as it is. And I was just making progress too." She cast a quick glance at Rafael, her lifemate, pacing furiously the length of the room, every now and then casting her a smoldering, warning look.

"Why is he so upset?" Ginny asked.

"Your Aunt Juliette was injured."

Rafael spun around, his dark eyes flashing with anger. "Your Aunt Juliette *disobeyed* a direct order from her lifemate. She ignored her own safety and nearly got both of them killed."

Ginny gasped, one hand flying to her mouth. "Are they all right, Rafael?"

"They're both fine," Colby answered, glaring at her lifemate. "There's no need to try to scare her to death."

"There's every need," Rafael declared, reaching out a hand to tangle it in the mass of red-gold hair surrounding Colby's face. "And just who are these kids—that *boy* over here? What do we know about him?"

"You mean Josef?" Ginny asked. "He's nice."

Rafael's scowl deepened. *She does not need to be thinking that boy is nice. I do not want her around boys at all.*

Colby sighed. *Ginny is not yet in her teens and she's human. I hardly think Josef is going to look at her that way.*

I looked at you that way.

I'm a grown woman and in any case, Paul is with Josef. You know her brother would never allow anything improper.

I'm going to go show my teeth to that young man. If he knows what's good for him, he'll go home. Rafael stalked from the room, his face set in harsh lines, his jaw stubborn. "And wear your hair down tonight for this thing. I like it that way."

Colby rolled her eyes at Ginny. "That man has way too much testosterone. He's going to scare Josef."

"Why?"

"Because Josef might look at you wrong. Lord help you when you get old enough to date, Ginny. I think he'll have ten bodyguards—all female—surrounding you."

"All my friends are afraid of him," Ginny conceded, "but he's always sweet to me. And Paul spends most of his time with Rafael."

"I know, baby, he's really great, but he does love to order us all around."

"Not like his brothers. Well, except for Uncle Riordan. He's nice, but the rest of them are scary."

The half smile faded from Colby's face. "Scary how? None of them are mean to you, are they? They are sworn to protect you and Paul. Rafael promised me." It was difficult to integrate her human family with her Carpathian one, but Colby thought they were working things out fairly well. Unfortunately, Rafael had four brothers and only Riordan had found his lifemate. And that meant the other three brothers were extremely dangerous. Manolito was close by. Zacharias and Nicholas were in Brazil overseeing the ranch near the rainforest. Colby was certain neither trusted themselves around so many others. They were too close to turning.

"They aren't mean to me," Ginny denied hastily. "I just don't like to be around them very much. They're just scary. It was kind of nice coming here because they didn't come with us. They're always watching me."

Colby sank into a chair at the kitchen table. "Baby, you know if you're unhappy, all you have to do is say the word and we go home to our ranch in the United States."

"No! I love living in Brazil. I can even speak the language—a little. Paul's helping me and so are my uncles. I love the ranch and the rainforest and all the animals. I don't want to go back—really."

"Hey chick-a-dee." Paul strode in and pulled his sister's braid. "Why are you hiding in here with Colby? Everyone came over so we could all get to know each other."

"Are they having a good time?" Colby asked.

Paul grinned at her. "Well, we are now that Rafael came in to scare the heck out of Josef. He's sharpening a knife, but Josef isn't paying attention and all the kids think it's funny."

"Oh, dear."

"I'm going to go see," Ginny said cheerfully, and skipped out of the room.

Paul sat opposite Colby. She studied his face. Some of the lines that shouldn't have been there were smooth again, but he still looked too old for his seventeen years. "What is it, hon?"

"You know how Mom was always so smart? I mean really smart. Not ranch smart, but book smart? Chemistry, physics, that kind of smart?"

"Which you have clearly inherited."

"What do you know about her family? There's a man here with the same last name as our mother and he looks like her. Well, she's prettier, but they really do look alike and they say he's really smart. He's human, Colby, like me."

"Does it bother you that I'm Carpathian and you're not? Rafael allowed you to keep all your memories because that's what you wanted, but if it makes you feel too different . . ." She trailed off. There was no way for Paul to become Carpathian. As far as she knew, he had no psychic ability whatsoever. Ginny hadn't displayed any either. Colby had a different father and one who had come from a direct line to the Carpathians.

Razvan. She didn't want to think about him, didn't want to ever admit that he had been her birth father. Razvan was grandson of the dark mage Xavier, mortal enemy to all Carpathians. Long ago, Xavier, the most powerful mage, had taken on a gifted Carpathian student, Rhiannon. He murdered her lifemate, kidnapped and impregnated her, igniting a terrible war. Triplets were born, Soren, and his two sisters now lost. Razvan and Natalya were Soren's children. Razvan had betrayed his Carpathian blood, blood of the famed Dragonseekers no less, betrayed his twin sister, succumbed to the lure of black magic, joined with the vampires and led them in a plot to assassinate the prince. It shamed her to think she carried Razvan's genetics, especially now that she had come to the Carpathian mountains and met so many of Rafael's people.

"No, I like that you're Carpathian, Colby, it's kind of cool." Paul raked a hand through his hair. "And I love where we live and Dad's brothers, but if this man, Gary Jansen, is related in any way to mom, I want to know him. And I want to know why we were never in his life."

"Have you asked around about him?"

Paul nodded. "Rafael told me his name and said that he's friends with Gregori. Apparently, he does a lot of research. You're older than me. Do you remember Mom ever talking about her family? Did you meet any of them?"

Colby shoved both hands through her thick mass of hair in agitation. "I remember a little bit, Paul, and none of it was good." It was painful to remember the past, and even though Colby had thought those days of feeling inadequate were gone forever, finding out that Razvan was her father had made them all come back.

"In what way?" Paul persisted.

Rafael appeared beside Colby, tall and strong; his face could have been carved from a statue, finely chiseled with great care around his sensual mouth. Every evening when she woke, when she saw him like this—a warrior, her lover—she always felt such a rush of emotion, almost overwhelming. Rafael looked at the world with ice-cold eyes and at her with hunger and love. For a woman who never quite fit in anywhere, it seemed a miracle. His arms now circled her, pulling her right up out of the chair, his larger frame nearly completely engulfing hers as he tucked her into the shelter of his body.

I do not like these thoughts. You did nothing wrong as a child. It is best not to think of these things when it brings you so much pain.

Paul has a right to know certain things.

About her. About her father. About their mother. She laid her head against Rafael's chest. It was all so complicated, and her background was rather humiliating. She didn't want Paul to be ashamed.

She had been the one to insist on coming to the Carpathian Mountains for the big celebration. She thought it was important to get to know other Carpathians and be just a little more social. The ranch in South America was isolated, enormous, and the De La Cruz brothers were treated like royalty—feared, but still given far too much deference. Colby thought it would be good to remind them they weren't the only ones in the world with gifts and duties. Now old wounds were being torn open on the very night when she had hoped to solidify their place in a community. She had to delve into the past and tell Paul the truth about their mother's family.

Rafael hissed his displeasure in her ear. "You do not need to prove to anyone that you are worthy of belonging. You belong with me."

"I know." She rubbed her face against his chest. "I just want Paul and Ginny to feel they belong."

Rafael caught her chin and lifted her face to his. "They have always had a sense of belonging. With you. You provided for them when no one else would, gave them a home and love and security. Few could have done what you did at such a young age."

Paul came around the table and put his arms around both of them. "Colby, did I upset you with my questions? I'm not looking for another family. I love the one I have. I don't understand what's wrong with you, but you've been acting upset and restless for the last hour. I've been afraid to leave you alone for too long." He looked at Rafael for confirmation.

Colby took a deep breath and pressed her hands against her churning stomach. "Everyone has secrets, Paul. I never wanted you to feel different. I've watched you and Ginny for any signs of being unusual—especially you—but you both seem to be very normal, without psychic gifts and without any ability to shapeshift." Her fingers clung to Rafael's shirt.

He brought up one hand to the nape of her neck, strong fingers easing the tension out of her. "I always thought shapeshifting was normal," he said.

"Well, it's not for us," Colby said. She was near tears. Paul had so much to contend with. He was a young teenage boy, yet he had worked a ranch nearly all of his life, hard, backbreaking work. They'd lost their mother and eventually Paul and Ginny's father to an accident, and the three alone had kept the ranch going.

"I started showing signs of psychic ability very early. I could sense dangerous things, especially if I was upset," Colby confessed in a little rush. "Mom admitted to me that my father was 'different.' That's all she said at first. But then later, when I was about thirteen, she told me she was 'different' too. And that we had to be very careful. We could never let anyone see the things we could do and that I always had to watch you, Paul, to make certain that you didn't behave irresponsibly."

"What does that mean?" Paul demanded with a small frown.

Colby took a deep breath. "It means we carry jaguar blood. Our family, hundreds of years ago, were shapeshifters. The men didn't stay with the women and eventually the species began to die out. There are very few who can actually shift into their cat form now, but many people carry the genetics. Some of the men still able to shift have been hunting for women to keep the line as pure as possible. They aren't very nice men."

"And Mom thought I might be one of these guys?" Paul was clearly offended. "I respect women. I'm always respectful."

"I didn't mean it like that. I'm not saying this very well. Mom wasn't married to my father when she had me. Your father's family didn't want anything to do with her—or me—because of that." She broke off abruptly.

Rafael took over. "Colby has never felt accepted in any world, Paul, and she didn't want that for you. Neither did your mother. Your mother hid her differences, and Colby did the same." He gestured around him. "Here, being atypical is normal."

"Do you really think anyone feels normal?" Paul asked. "I didn't know all this—that I have jaguar blood—although that could be cool especially now, but look at Josef. He's a Carpathian, can shapeshift and do all sorts of neat things. He's brilliant. You should see the things he can do on a computer, and he's a math whiz. He just is kind of nerdy around people. He doesn't feel good about himself at all. He knows the adults don't like him and he feels uncomfortable around all of us teenagers. Skyler is beautiful, but she's uncomfortable too. Ginny and I are the only 'normal' ones and we should be the outsiders."

"Sometimes you're brilliant, Paul," Colby exclaimed.

"I think it doesn't matter much about what we are or where we came from, Colby," Paul replied. "I think we all feel uncomfortable when we're young."

"I didn't," Rafael said.

Colby smacked his chest. "You're so arrogant."

"I don't think he was actually ever young," Paul said. "I'm not even sure anyone gave birth to him. They found him under a rock."

Rafael caught Paul around the neck and pretended to strangle him. Colby watched the two of them laughing together and found the tension ebbing away.

You did a great job raising this boy, Rafael told her.

She nodded. *He's wonderful.*

"So do you think most of the psychics are descendents of shapeshifters?" Paul asked. "I could do some research on that. I'll bet Josef would help me."

Rafael shrugged. "It is possible—even probable—but any time you do research, you leave a trail for someone else to follow. We are most careful of tracks leading to the discovery of our species. And you're making me feel guilty over this Josef boy."

Paul flashed a grin at his brother-in-law. "Don't worry, he didn't notice you were sharpening your knife for his benefit. I told you, in social situations he doesn't have a clue." He burst out laughing when Rafael looked disappointed. "I noticed, and so did Skyler and Josh. We all thought it was very scary."

"You don't sound convincing," Rafael grumbled.

Colby laughed softly. "You should be happy you didn't scare the boy."

"I want to meet him," Paul said abruptly, as if he'd just managed to screw up his courage. "If Gary Jansen is my uncle, I want to meet him."

"We don't know that he is. Lots of people have the same last name," Colby pointed out, the smile fading from her face. Instinctively, she moved closer to Rafael, her body brushing up against his.

"But it's likely, Colby. This is a small community of people. He's part of it. Quite a few of the women here seem to have jaguar blood. Maybe he does too and that's what drew him in the first place."

Rafael rubbed her arm in a comforting gesture. "Maybe. All right. Give me a little time to finish things here first," Colby said.

Suddenly, her kitchen was too small. She needed the open range and a good horse to ride. Her mother had always feared jaguar blood, feared producing a male child. Jaguar males weren't always the nicest of men, and Colby didn't want Paul exposed to any more danger—or rejection. And she certainly didn't want anyone influencing him in the wrong direction. Raising children was definitely not easy.

Paul leaned over to kiss her cheek, then sauntered out of the room, calling for Josef and Ginny.

"You can't protect him forever," Rafael said gently. He wrapped his arms around her, nuzzling the top of her head with his chin.

"You say that, but you try to protect me—and Ginny. I just don't want him hurt anymore. I see it in his eyes sometimes. He wouldn't let you or Nicolas take his memories, and he remembers how the vampire took him over and used him to try to kill me. I know he still has nightmares about it. I just want him to be happy, Rafael. He's such a great kid."

He tipped her face up to his. "He is a great kid and he's going to be fine. We'll look after him together."

Her gaze slid away from his. "I couldn't bear to tell him the truth about me, about Razvan. I thought this would be such a good idea, coming here, meeting everyone, but now, I'm not so sure. Someone is bound to tell him who my birth father was."

"Do you think your brother would care about that?" Rafael scowled at her. "Paul loves you for who you are, not who your father was."

"You don't understand. He's asking about his past for a reason, and once he starts delving into it, he'll find out about me. I couldn't take it if he rejected me too. And how could I ever blame him? He's had so much to contend with because of me. If Mom hadn't had me, Paul and Ginny would have been accepted by the Chevez family and raised on the ranch in South America. He would never have been exposed to a vampire. Now he knows about the jaguar blood and once he finds out it isn't always so cool, he won't be happy about that either. And someone is going to tell him about Razvan." She shuddered, looked around and lowered her voice when she said the name. "I can hardly face any of these people, let alone have Paul and Ginny find out that such a terrible man is my father."

Rafael's hand came up to burrow his fingers in her hair. "You are his victim just as his sister was. Do not be ashamed of who your father was. You bear the mark of the Dragonseeker, and that is an unbelievable boon. The Dragonseeker clan is one of the most revered of all Carpathian lineages and it is *your* line. I hope that each of our children bears that mark. You should be proud of it, not ashamed."

"My father came from the same lineage and he tried to assassinate the prince," she pointed out. "He betrayed Natalya, his twin sister. He has children—like me—scattered across the world, and he intended to use us like blood banks. I have family I've never met, all victims of this man. His blood runs in my veins. Do you really think I want Paul—or anyone else—to know I'm related to him?"

Rafael gathered her closer to him. "*I* know you're related to him. Carpathian males perhaps have more understanding than most for those who become wholly evil. It is a path we all go down, and some touch a little closer than others. Before you came into my life, Colby, I could not always tell the difference between good and evil."

"Razvan nearly killed the prince," she repeated. "He took blood from little girls. It was why he got my mother pregnant in the first place—in order to use my blood to sustain his life."

Rafael could hear the horror in her voice. Colby still had trouble accepting the evil in their world, and he loved her all the more for her innocence. He took her hand and tugged, pulling her from the openness of the kitchen to the stairs leading to the privacy of their chamber belowground.

"We can't leave the children," Colby protested.

"You're always so responsible. I've directed Paul to be a good host. You need a few minutes without all the noise."

"I need our ranch. Wouldn't you love to go horseback riding in all this snow?"

"Is that what you'd like to do?"

She shook her head. "We don't have time. The dinner is in just a little while. And we're supposed to be entertaining the kids."

He reversed direction. "If you want to go riding . . ."

"It's snowing, silly." There was a wealth of love in her voice. Rafael, for all his domineering ways, always tried to give her whatever would make her happy. "And horses don't see that well at night."

He laughed softly and leaned down to place his lips against her ear. "I am Carpathian, *pequeña,* and I can provide whatever you want. Come with me."

Colby went because she could never resist Rafael or the way his black eyes burned with such hunger for her. As she stepped outside, he wrapped her in a fur-lined full-length hooded coat and boots. Just outside the walkway, standing by the porch, a horse sidestepped, tossing its head, eager to be running. The animal was at least seventeen hands, with hooves made to run in the snow. Rafael swung onto its bare back and reached his arm down to her.

"This is a night rider, Colby, and he loves to run."

She took his arm, allowing him to swing her up in front of him. "Go fast, Rafael, I want to fly across the ground tonight."

His arms caged her in and he bent his body protectively over hers, whispering a command to the snorting animal. The horse took off, powerful muscles bunching as he leapt forward. After the first explosive burst of speed, the horse's gait settled into a rhythmic gallop and they raced flat out across the open meadow. Snow hit their faces and the wind whistled past them. Clouds spun overhead and it should have been dark, but the snow made the world a bright, sparkling dream of a place.

"This land is breathtaking," Colby said. "Do you miss it?"

"At first, all of us did, but we've been so long where we are that the rain forest and the heat and humidity are our home. This is beautiful and wonderful to visit, but it no longer feels like home to me."

Colby turned her face up to the night sky. Rafael loved the rain forest, but he would have given it up—given up living with his brothers on their ranch—had she wanted to stay in the United States. Though she hadn't believed it when Rafael first claimed her, now, knowing his every thought, she realized just how much power she wielded when it came to her lifemate.

He gave her total acceptance and unconditional love. She pressed back against him allowing the rhythm of the horse to soothe her.

The animal knew his way, and twice leapt effortlessly over fallen logs and splashed through a small creek bed. He slowed when they were near the woods and hills, where she could see the ferns and shrubbery poking through several drifts of snow.

The world was silent here. Only their breathing could be heard in the night. There was only the feel of Rafael's arms around her and the crystal world with gently drifting snow—almost surreal.

"It doesn't seem possible that danger could be lurking so close, does it?" she whispered, afraid if she spoke too loud it would break the spell.

"There is only the two of us, Colby." He kissed the back of her neck. "Just us, alone in this world. Nothing evil and no shame, only a man who loves you above all else." His arms tightened around her as if he could keep her safe from anything—even her own feelings of inadequacy.

Colby fit her body more closely to his. Why did she feel inadequate? Was it what Paul had said? That most people just did? Or was it the fact that she'd never had a childhood? She suddenly sat up a little straighter. "Rafael. I'm like Josef."

He snorted, began to choke, sputter and cough all at the same time.

Colby swung around to look at him over her shoulder. "No, I am. I never developed social skills at all. I worked all the time and I had to hide who and what I was. Don't you see? I'm still doing it. I don't want anyone to know about Razvan, so I hide away, feeling ashamed. I don't have to go out and meet all these people—people you know and grew up with. People I'm afraid might wonder why someone as talented and gifted as you would choose to be with someone like me. I'm a teenager, struggling to find myself. That is just plain pitiful."

"I think this is all a conspiracy to make me feel more guilt because I tried to scare that boy. I'm not apologizing to him. He shouldn't have been ogling Ginny."

"I'm sure he didn't ogle her. He wants to be friends."

"Men never want to be friends, Colby." His hands slid under the coat to cup her breasts, his thumbs brushing her nipples as the horse circled back toward the house. "Our minds are too preoccupied with other much more pleasant things than friendship."

"You mean *your* mind is," Colby answered. She closed her eyes and savored the feeling of his hands caressing her body. Both of them were highly sexual, and Rafael rarely went too long without sliding his hands possessively over her body. He couldn't walk past her without his palm cupping her bottom, or brushing her breast. Sometimes, she leaned against him and rubbed enticingly like a cat, loving the feeling of his body growing rock hard and knowing it was all for her. Like now.

The motion of the horse created a wonderful friction with her wedged between his open legs. Her gaze met his, and instantly she felt a thrill run down her spine. He was looking at her with that urgent hunger, so intense, so in need, everything in her body reached out in response. She tilted her head so she could nibble at his chin, further provoking him.

For a woman who had done nothing her entire life but be responsible, it was wonderful to have no inhibitions, to be able to just be whatever she wanted when she was with Rafael. She reached behind her and deliberately stroked the hard bulge forming in the front of his trousers.

Maybe she wasn't so sure of herself with others, but that wasn't the case when she was in her own home. Rafael was an extremely dominant man, yet she could stand up to him and knew always that he loved and desired her. She had Ginny and Paul and they both loved her for who she was. Maybe it was time to stop hiding from herself. She was no longer afraid of her own power. She knew what she wanted and she knew she was strong enough and determined enough to go after it. Razvan may have fallen a long way from grace, but he had passed on a legacy of gifts she couldn't deny. And so had her mother. She had to give Paul and Ginny the opportunity to embrace those gifts—not run from them.

"You'll do the right thing," Rafael murmured against her ear. "You always find the right answer for them. Jaguar traits are not all bad, and you want them to love that part of themselves. They may have great gifts and we can help them develop them, and if there are things that are difficult to deal with—well—we both know about them too. We can guide them together, Colby."

"Thank you," she said softly.

"I haven't done anything."

"Of course you have. You knew I needed to work this out to do the right thing for the kids and in order to do that, I had to believe in myself."

"I took you for a ride on a horse."

"You gave me a dream."

He was silent for a moment, urging the horse back toward the house, listening to the sounds of the hooves crunching the snow. "So this other boy. This Josef. Tell me about him."

Colby hid her smile. Rafael liked to be such a tough guy, but deep inside he was a marshmallow.

He leaned forward. *I caught that thought. I am going to make you pay for that.*

Excitement zinged through her body and heated her bloodstream. *I always so enjoy your little punishments.* She turned her head to lift her mouth to his. It was more than awkward kissing on a horse, but they managed it, and as always, liquid fire poured through her veins and love seemed to flood her mind to the point of spilling over.

"Josef is Byron's nephew. He seems young for his age. I think he's barely out of his teens."

"That is a babe by our standards," Rafael pointed out, his fingers anchoring in her hair. "Where did Paul and Ginny meet him?"

"Online. They all correspond. Skyler, Paul, Ginny, Josh and Josef. Some of the adults play video games online with them. But they've all become great friends. They were very much looking forward to meeting in person. I think Josef has a difficult time because he is a little older in age, but not maturity, yet everyone expects it of him."

Rafael sighed. "I suppose it wouldn't hurt to try to get to know the boy."

"You really are a marshmallow," she teased, knowing he would retaliate. Wanting him to. Anticipating it. Her body was suddenly pulsing with energy—with need. Rafael exuded sex, his mouth sinfully sensual, his good looks wickedly masculine. She loved the way he wore his clothes, his hard stomach flat and his hips and the columns of his thighs encased in denim. His eyes were heavy-lidded and black as night, holding a seduction all their own.

Immediately, she felt overheated and sensitive, her body flooding with urgent need. His hand cupped her neck, drew her head back so his mouth could claim hers. She sat in the cradle of his hips, his erection pressed tightly against her buttocks, his arm over her breasts and his mouth rough, his tongue a velvet rasp of excitement, stroking and teasing, licking at her skin, teeth nibbling gently.

Just like that her body responded, heat spreading like liquid gold through her veins. She wanted him so bad she could taste it.

I want you too. But you deserve to suffer a little bit.

Beneath the fur-lined coat, her clothes were gone, leaving her body exposed and vulnerable to his wandering hands. He slipped his hands inside the coat, guiding the horse with his legs. His palm slid along her thigh, and her breath hitched in her throat.

"What are you doing?"

"Whatever I want." His voice had turned husky, almost hoarse, and the heat from his fingers was in direct contrast to the chill in the air.

Her blood heated instantly, her core pulsing with excitement. His fingers began a slow, almost lazy circle, occasionally brushing her most sensitive spot. A low moan escaped. The fur slid along her skin, sensitizing her nerve endings even more. He kissed her again, lifted his head, but held her face toward his with one hand while the other moved over her damp curls.

"Look at me, *querida*. Keep looking at me," he commanded.

She always loved that about him. He wanted her to know who possessed her—who loved her—who drove her out of her mind with pleasure. And she loved to look at him, to see his fierce hunger, his stark desire for her, the lines of lust etched deep, the burn in his eyes as he took her.

His finger sank deep, drew out creamy honey. "I love how you get so wet for me. You're always so tight and hot and wet." He licked his finger with a slow seductive stroke of his tongue, never taking his gaze from hers, and returned to burrow his fingers deeper in her feminine channel.

The horse stopped moving, simply remaining still while Rafael pushed his fingers deeper, filling her so that she gasped with pleasure. He stroked her over and over, teasing the tight folds, caressing the inner knot of nerve endings until she was gasping, crying out for release, but then the wicked fingers retreated. He caught her in his arms and slid off the horse. Setting her feet on the ground, his arm locking her to him, he talked softly to the animal and then sent it on its way. They watched the horse gallop back up toward the hills.

Colby blinked and looked around her, still dazed and still pulsing with a terrible hunger. She wanted him so much, she was afraid she couldn't take a step. Rafael simply swept her into his arms and moved with the blurring speed of his kind through the house to their underground chamber.

Heart pounding when he set her free, Colby looked around at the room designed not only for sleeping, but for playing. She stood in the middle of the room dressed only in the coat, the edges gaping open to reveal her full breasts and the red curls at the junction of her legs. She was so damp, so hot. So in need. She could barely breathe with her need.

"Come here, *pequeña*. I have waited too long for your body." He held out his hand to her.

She always felt so mesmerized by him, so willing to do whatever he asked of her. She loved the feel of his hands on her far too much. "I think I'm obsessed with you." She put her hand in his and he jerked her to him, spinning her around, pushing her back against the wall and trapping her between his body and the hard surface.

"It is good for you to be obsessed." His fingers trailed down her face, across her neck to her throat. The pads of his fingers teased her bare skin, sending little flames dancing through her body. Without warning, he yanked the coat from her body, exposing the soft creamy flesh beneath. "You always wear too many clothes."

Her heart began to pound in response to his intensity. He could always do that to her, take away her balance when it came to their sexual encounters. "Would you like me to go naked in front of all of our company?"

He growled low in his throat, bared his teeth, then leaned forward and gently bit down on her nipple, dragging his teeth back and forth until she moaned. "If I had my way, I would choose a time in history when I could simply lock you up, keep you safe and to myself, never share you." He pinned her wrists together above her head. "I would keep you in shackles, chained to my bed, completely naked waiting for me, always wanting me."

His hands cupped her breasts and lifted them as he bent his head to feast. His mouth was already hot, his tongue lapping wickedly, his teeth scraping and teasing, his mouth suckling strongly. Most of the time, he took great care to pay attention to every nuance of her mind, ensuring everything he did was exactly the way she liked, but sometimes, when his demons and petty jealousies were riding him just a little too hard, he allowed himself the freedom of taking her body the way he wanted. Fast and hard and rough.

Excitement always coursed through her mind—and maybe a little fear. He would never hurt her, but he always demanded submission—he always pushed her sexually. He was greedy for her. He wanted to know she would love him no matter what, that she would give him everything, that she would hold nothing back. But in the end, nothing mattered to him so much as her pleasure and he always—always—gave that to her tenfold.

Rafael dropped to his knees, hands pushing her thighs apart and dragging her hips forward so his mouth could devour her. His tongue stabbed deep, drew out cream, and he began licking and sucking while her hips bucked against his mouth and her hands tangled in his hair. She screamed as the first wave rushed over her. The almost desperate sounds he made drove her right over the edge. Spasm after spasm rocked her.

He tumbled her to the bed, following her down, skin to skin, thrusting his knee between her thighs to keep her open to him. He surged forward with one hard stroke, burying himself deep, driving through the soft velvet folds until he hit her womb. He tilted her hips, pushing deeper, forcing her to take all of him. He swore softly as her body, so tight and hot, grasped his, squeezing and milking and sending fire racing down his spine. Lightning sizzled in his bloodstream and whipped through his body. He began to piston, driving with his hips, sinking deep into the refuge of her body, reveling in the way her muscles tightened like a fist, holding him to her.

He thrust hard, over and over, ignoring her helpless pleas as he took her higher and higher, building the pleasure until she was whimpering for release, pleading with him to take her over the edge. She began to throw her head back and forth, struggling against the terrible sexual tension, but he held her still, plunging his body into hers, taking them both to a fever pitch of need. Then she was screaming, as her body shattered around his, as jet after jet of heat filled her and her womb convulsed with shocking pleasure. It spread through her like a tornado, taking her body by surprise, ripping through her vaginal walls, down her thighs and up into her stomach.

She lay gasping for breath, staring up at the man she loved above all else in the world—the man who loved and accepted her for who she was. Bloodlines or not, Rafael loved her and that was enough for her. She could feel confident in herself no matter what because he loved her unconditionally.

13

The wind began to pick up in strength, blowing snow around even as more began to fall in earnest. Mikhail hesitated just outside the large house. Traian Trigovise had designed and built the house for, not only his lifemate Joie, but to share with her brother Jubal and sister Gabrielle. Now that the vampire who had taken Traian's blood was dead, Traian felt he could once more live in the company of other Carpathians without endangering them all.

You're being such a chicken, Raven teased.

Traian's in-laws are visiting. And Gabrielle has risen. There are going to be questions I would rather not have to answer at this time.

Because she is in love with Gary Jansen.

Not exactly. Mikhail knew he was hedging. He didn't want Gabrielle and Gary to be in love. As humans it was perfectly fine, but now that Gabrielle had been converted, he knew there would be tremendous problems. And with Gabrielle's parents there to celebrate Christmas, there would be more questions than normal. *I think I will skip this visit.*

Mikhail Dubrinsky! You knock on that door. As the prince, it is your duty to welcome Joie's parents. And Gabrielle needs your support as well.

My duties as prince seem to be getting larger and more complicated as time goes on. Maybe I should pass this duty along to my second in command.

Raven laughed softly. *Don't you dare.*

Mikhail heaved a tortured sigh and knocked on the door. It swung open immediately and a woman with bright eyes and a ready smile greeted him.

"Please come in. I'm Marissa Sanders, Joie, Jubal and Gabrielle's mother."

"Mikhail Dubrinsky." He identified himself, and sent Raven the image of him throttling her. *I'd rather face a vampire than a mother-in-law.* Her answering laughter wasn't in the least sympathetic. *I am going to have to explain to you the finer points of lifemates. You seem to be missing them.*

"Oh! The prince." Mrs. Sanders stepped back to wave him inside. "Lovely to meet you. I have so many questions."

He bowed slightly. "I will try to answer what I can for you."

She stopped in the hall so abruptly he nearly ran into her. "Prince of what? Are you in exile? Everyone just refers to you as the prince, but they never say of which country. I imagine there are quite a few princes thrown out on their royal . . ." She brought herself up short, and swung back to continue walking down the hall.

Mikhail nearly groaned out loud, but managed to suppress it. *Traian!* He issued the summons sharply, and in that moment he didn't give a damn whether the entire population of Carpathians heard the panic in his voice or not. He was not answering this woman's questions.

She showed him into the large living room, and immediately took the chair opposite his and leaned forward eagerly. "I've just come from Sara's. You'll be happy to know the seamstresses are on track."

"Seamstresses?" he echoed faintly. *What seamstresses, Raven?*

I have no idea. Ask her.

Mikhail nodded, trying to look wise. "That is good, Mrs. Sanders. Uh—er—which seamstresses would that be?"

Her eyebrow shot up. "You obviously dropped the ball on that one. Good thing I was here to pick it up. The children needed costumes for the pageant."

"Costumes?" He seemed to be repeating her words, but he couldn't help it. He ran a finger around the neckline of his shirt. *Traian, get in here before I do something like send an earthquake rippling through this house.*

"Did you expect to simply produce the outfits out of thin air?"

"I suppose I was, yes."

Mikhail! Raven's voice reprimanded him sharply before he could speak. *Don't you dare say another word and I mean it. That poor woman has two daughters who are now Carpathian. She deserves a little respect.*

Mikhail closed his eyes briefly. Of course she deserved respect, but he shouldn't have to deal with her. *Where is my second in command? It's your job to protect me at all times and distance me from these unpleasant tasks.*

Gregori gave a derisive snort. *I think you are capable of handling one little woman. I have my hands full at the moment with your daughter.*

Mikhail struggled between self-preservation and prank, and the prank won. He was not going to pull out his son-in-law card. He could handle this woman no matter what she threw at him. It would be well worth it to see Gregori prancing around in a Santa Claus outfit.

"Just like a man. You order a huge celebration and then expect it all to get done on its own." Mrs. Sanders crossed her arms over her chest and regarded him with a stern eye. "Just what has been going on with my daughter Gabrielle? Joie and Traian said she was with you. I certainly hope you aren't the kind of prince who believes in harems because, and let's get this straight . . ." She leaned forward to look him in the eye, bent on intimidating him. "I'm not the mother to stand for it."

Mikhail choked. Coughed. *Traian! I'm commanding you to get into this room immediately.*

Sorry, Mikhail. I am on the way. Joie and I were just a little bit occupied.

Mikhail heard Raven's soft laughter at the admission. *They don't need to be enjoying themselves while I'm stuck with this woman.*

Maybe they're making a baby. Do you really want to disturb them? Raven breathed in his ear, teasing his senses and stirring his body.

Yes! And stop that. I need my brain to actually function around this woman.

We are occupied with Gabrielle, Joie hastily added, clearly embarrassed.

Mikhail sighed. *Forgive me. I should have known you would be with your sister.* It wouldn't be easy for Gabrielle to rise and know she needed blood to survive. Newly converted Carpathians always seemed to have difficulty with the concept. He could never understand the big deal. Carpathians weren't flesh eaters like humans and they didn't kill like the vampire, yet they were reviled for their need of blood.

"I won't have my daughter regulated to the status of a—a—*concubine*. I won't allow it. I know you're married, so don't bother to deny it. You don't even have a country that I can see."

Mikhail let his breath out and reached for the woman's mind, uncaring if it was impolite. He could make her forget all this nonsense and simply go into the kitchen.

Her mind collided with his, as if she were reaching for him at the exact same time. Thunder rolled. Lightning sizzled in the sky and the clouds roiled impressively. The two minds impacted, slamming against one another, hitting hastily erected barriers. Mrs. Sanders jumped to her feet, her face pale, both hands clutching her head in pain.

Puzzled, Mikhail rose as well. He bowed slightly. "Forgive me, Mrs. Sanders." It took a moment to recognize the unfamiliar brain patterns. It was no wonder her children were so gifted and such phenomenal psychics—all three of them. "You have the undiluted blood of the jaguar."

"And you are Carpathian." She looked around the house, took a deep breath, closing her eyes for a moment. "Of course. That explains a lot. Traian is Carpathian, isn't he?"

Mikhail felt the flicker of another's presence. Her husband stood silently in the doorway, his mind trying to assimilate what was being said. It was obvious that Mrs. Sanders was capable of telepathic communication. Her psychic abilities were very strong, and she had called her husband to her in her distress. Mikhail continued the conversation as if there were only the two of them present. "It is essential for Carpathians to pass as humans at all times."

She sank into a chair. "I have never heard that a human can become Carpathian, but Joie is, isn't she? That's why she looks different—a subtle difference, but it is there. And you really were going to make the costumes out of thin air."

To Mikhail's alarm, she looked as if she might cry. "I am very sorry, Mrs. Sanders. You can understand why Traian couldn't simply give you this information. It is necessary to protect our species at all times." He studied her averted face. "You haven't revealed your lineage to your children. They have no idea, do they?"

She shook her head. "I didn't want them to know. I was afraid for them.

My husband knows, but he's very protective of me. When I need to let the cat out, he goes with me and I run in the hills. He stands by to make certain no accidents happen."

"Can any of them shapeshift?"

She shook her head. "I never taught them. I've seen them all grow restless and moody at times, but I didn't want them to carry that burden. I don't know if I did the right thing or not. But having a son and trying to raise him right is a big responsibility when he is jaguar. His instincts . . ."

"Jubal is a fine man. He's very protective of his sisters." Mikhail reached out a hand and touched her.

Immediately she calmed, blinking the tears back, regaining the control she thought lost. "Jaguar males are very dangerous."

"I am centuries old, Mrs. Sanders. I will admit I did not have a lot of contact with your species as we resided in separate parts of the world, but I remember many of the males were wonderful people. Need and fear often cause people to do things they would not ordinarily do. Jubal was born a good man, and will remain so throughout his lifetime. Should he be forced into extreme circumstances, I believe he will rise to the occasion with his mind and strength and the gifts given to him, not fall back on primitive means."

She took a deep breath. "Thank you for that. It's my worst fear."

He had glimpsed that small piece of information clearly, as it had been in the forefront of her mind before she had slammed the barrier down. "You have remarkable children, Mrs. Sanders. Joie is a treasure we all seek to protect. Jubal has been helping with vital research—as has Gabrielle."

"Gabrielle met a young man, Gary Jansen. She says she has been working with him on a huge research project. Is he Carpathian too?"

The half smile faded from Mikhail's face. "Gary is human—a friend and protected by all Carpathians. *Always.*" If there was one human in the world the Carpathians would go to war for—it was Gary Jansen. But now . . .

"What is wrong with Gabrielle?" Mrs. Sanders asked. "I know there is something, but even Joie and Jubal have refused to discuss it with me." She shook her head. "My family has too many secrets, yet you seem to know them all. Gabrielle is alive, isn't she?"

Mikhail rubbed his hand over his face, hating to be put in such a position. This woman deserved answers—deserved the truth about her daughters. "Just as Joie was converted to our species because unless she was she would have died, so was Gabrielle converted."

Mrs. Sanders made a small sound of despair and turned her head to meet her husband's gaze. He stood in the doorway, tall and straight, his face an expressionless mask. "Rory. Oh, honey. I'm so sorry. This is my fault. All my fault."

He hurried to her side, dropping down on one knee to take both of her hands in his. "Don't do that to yourself. You've done nothing wrong."

"Is it so difficult for you to know your children are Carpathian?" Mikhail asked. "They will always be treasured. Always be protected."

"Joie, yes, but what of Gabrielle? She's different, not adventurous in the same way Joie is. She has a love of research and home. This life isn't for her."

"It is *life,* Mrs. Sanders. She would have died and we gave her the choice. It is what she wanted. Our healers are with her now and they will assist her in her new life. She is tied to a lifemated Carpathian, Vikirnoff Von Shrieder, and to me. We will always see to her happiness and safety."

Mrs. Sanders took a deep breath and gripped her husband's hand. "At least I do not have to worry that a jaguar male will get their hands on either of my daughters. That has been a huge worry, especially with Joie traveling so much." She attempted a small smile for her husband. "I don't mind Carpathian or human, but no jaguar blood."

"I thought there were very few," Mikhail said.

"Purebloods, but of course, there are many descendents and I don't want either of my daughters near a male jaguar."

Mikhail didn't point out that Jubal was a male jaguar, or that he didn't tolerate prejudice toward any race or species. The woman feared the male jaguars and with good cause. He had impressions of a past she kept locked away. Mikhail held out his hand to her husband and introduced himself just as Traian and Joie rushed in. Mikhail had relayed the conversation to the couple, urging them to come quickly to ease Mrs. Sanders's tears.

"Mom!" Joie said. "I'm so sorry I didn't tell you about Gabrielle. I wanted to. I didn't know how."

Mrs. Sanders hugged her daughter tightly. "Have you seen her? Is she all right?"

Joie bit her lip and sent a quick glance to Traian. "She is apprehensive. And it isn't as easy for her. I had Traian to guide me. And when I need to feed, he provides for me and it isn't so horrible. But Gabrielle is in love with someone who isn't Carpathian and he can't give her the things she needs."

Mrs. Sanders's hands fluttered helplessly to her throat. "Who provides for her?"

"The man who saved her is named Vikirnoff Von Shrieder. He and his lifemate, Natalya, have been with Gabrielle often, talking to her and working with her to accept her new life. She won't take blood from Traian or me, but she has from both of them. They're good with her, Mom. And she's trying."

"I want to see her."

"We both do," Mr. Sanders said firmly.

Joie hesitated. "Mom, she's very emotional. Her entire life has changed. Fortunately, there is a woman visiting here with us. Her name is MaryAnn Delaney. She's a counselor for battered and abused women, and she's dealt a lot with trauma victims as well. Gary has her with him and they're talking to Gabrielle right now. I really think it best to let them work with her. You know Gabby, she's a fighter. It's just the initial shock of waking up so different."

"I'm her mother. I should be with her."

"She's promised to come here as soon as possible." Joie looked up at Traian and he wrapped his arm around her shoulder. The trauma of her sister nearly dying had taken its toll on Joie. She adored Gabrielle, and had brought her into this life, exposing her to vampires and Carpathians, and it weighed heavily on her that Gabrielle had been converted.

"This man, Gary, is he the one she's so crazy about? The one she stayed here in the mountains to be close to?" Mr. Sanders asked.

Joie nodded. "She doesn't talk much about their relationship, but they're obviously drawn to one another. Gary has been beside himself over this and has gone to her rest . . . Gone to be close to her daily since this happened."

Mikhail reached for the comfort of his lifemate. Tied to Gabrielle the way he was, he could feel her unrelenting sorrow. None of them had considered the larger picture. Gabrielle was now fully a Carpathian female. The other males would be desperate for her to be a lifemate to one of them.

Gary's attentions to her would not be welcomed by any of them. It was possible for Gabrielle to be a lifemate to one of the men without being in love with him. Affection often came later, after the raw sexual need and the intimacy of being lifemates. Conceivably, Gabrielle could love Gary and still be a lifemate to a Carpathian male. The potential for explosive trouble was building inside the already complicated world of Carpathians.

She is in love with him. Raven's voice was gentle. *He deserves happiness after all he has done for us. You know he has earned his place in our world.*

Mikhail sighed heavily. *I know this, but logic does not dictate to a male near the end of his time. If she is a lifemate, she must give up whatever affection she feels for Gary and embrace her new life fully.*

There was a small silence. *You would force her to choose a man she does not love? That is wrong.*

There is only one lifemate. Her love for Gary will fade with time and if she truly gives her new life a chance, she will find happiness with her true mate.

Raven sniffed in exasperation. *You have no idea what you're going to do about this situation, do you?*

Mikhail raked a hand through his hair. *He loves her so much. Whenever I am with him I feel it. And he has spoken to Gregori often of his feelings for her. Since her near death, he has rarely left her side, holding vigil until she awakened. None of us could get him to eat. This is going to be bad, Raven.*

Raven sent him comfort, camaraderie, a soothing touch of her fingers trailing down his face. He wanted to leave this house with all its complications and go to where there was joy. In the midst of all the problems, with the enemies coming at them from every side, there was Raven and her ready smile, her warmth and ability to bring happiness and laughter to those around her.

"They're here!" Joie announced. "Mom, be gentle with her," she added, clinging tightly to Traian's hand.

"You don't have to tell me that," Mrs. Sanders said with a small frown.

Mikhail rose intending to excuse himself. Jubal came in, flicking a warning glance at his mother and father, then stepped aside to allow Gabrielle into the room. She looked beautiful, tall and dark-haired with gray eyes and a full mouth. Her skin was pale and she trembled visibly, but the man at her side slipped his arm around her for support.

"Mom. Dad. It's wonderful to see you." Tears swam in Gabrielle's large eyes, turning them charcoal.

Her parents rose, taking several steps toward their daughter. Mrs. Sanders stopped abruptly, the color draining from her face. She lifted her face and sniffed several times, testing the air. One hand went up defensively and she screamed, backing away from the couple.

Gabrielle's skin went dead white and she turned her face into Gary's shoulder at her mother's rejection. Joie and Jubal sprang in front of their sister, blocking her from her parents' view. Mikhail moved with blurring speed, putting his body between the hysterical mother and her daughter. Gary swept Gabrielle into his arms, holding her close, and Traian stepped between Joie's parents and his sister-in-law, shielding them with his larger frame.

Mrs. Sanders dropped to her knees, her keening wail rising, filling the house. Mr. Sanders tried to bring her to her feet, but she struggled against him, shaking her head from side to side, wailing the entire time. "Mom! Get control," Jubal snapped. "It's Gabrielle and she needs you to be strong, not turn away from her."

Traian and Mikhail exchanged an apprehensive glance.

Joie raised her chin. "She is what I am. If you can't deal with Gabrielle as a Carpathian, you'd better know that I'm one and so is Traian. We stand with Gabrielle."

Mrs. Sander's entire demeanor changed. She rose slowly to her feet, her eyes going opaque, her body suddenly fluid and catlike. Her head went down in a classic stalking manner. "Get away from my daughter." She enunciated each word.

"Marissa," Mr. Sanders reprimanded sharply.

She growled at him, a deadly hiss accompanying the warning. Her fingers began to curl and her body stretched, muzzle elongating. Bones cracked and her spine bent.

"Mom!" Joie sounded horrified. "Mom, stop!"

Traian stepped in front of his lifemate, his heavier body shoving her back. At the same time he swept her brother behind him with one powerful arm.

"Mom." Jubal added his plea. "What are you doing?"

Mikhail stepped up to Traian's side. The two Carpathians stood shoulder to shoulder facing the threat. "Mrs. Sanders." Mikhail was calm, trying to reach the mind of Gabrielle's mother.

He found a red haze of anger, a cauldron of fear. Seams burst. Material ripped. Fur burst across skin and she was on the floor, teeth filling her muzzle. Mr. Sanders tried to put a calming hand on her, but she ripped at him with razor-sharp claws.

Traian sprang forward, using preternatural speed, a blur of motion, scooping up Joie's father and shoving him toward his daughter. Mr. Sander's arm bled from the long, deep scratches, and Joie sobbed as she hastily reached for her father.

"Dad, what's wrong with her? You obviously know. Tell us."

"What is she?" Jubal demanded.

"Jaguar," Traian supplied. "She is from a pure jaguar bloodline."

The cat crouched, tail switching in agitation, eyes on the two Carpathian males blocking her path to her goal.

Mikhail, step back, Traian warned. *She is about to attack.*

She is Joie's mother, Mikhail reminded him. *We cannot hurt her.*

There is no we. Get back. Traian edged forward in an effort to protect Mikhail as well as his lifemate and the others.

"She never did that when we were in school and she was really upset with our teachers," Jubal said. "What the hell, Dad? Did you know?"

"Shut up, Jubal," Mr. Sanders snapped. "Now is not the time for levity. She is very dangerous."

"You think? You've got blood dripping all over the floor."

"What triggered this?" Mikhail asked calmly.

Mr. Sanders shook his head. "I have no idea. She seemed to accept everything you told her."

"All of you back out of the room. Let Traian, Mr. Sanders and me handle this," Mikhail ordered.

I am on my way, Mikhail. Wait for me. Gregori, as always, was perfectly calm.

Oh, now you want to help. I think I can take care of one jungle cat.

If you got so much as a scratch on you, your daughter would have my head on a platter. Besides—you are getting old and slow.

As Joie, Jubal, Gabrielle and Gary began to slowly inch their way out of the room, the cat became more agitated, leaping to its feet, running at the two Carpathian males, a roar of rage shaking the house. Her children stopped.

The jaguar exploded into action, leaping over furniture to hit Traian squarely in the chest. Her weight and the suddenness of the attack pushed him over backward. She went for his throat, trying to sink her teeth deep. He caught her between strong hands, holding the snarling cat off.

Gabrielle screamed. "Don't hurt her!"

That's my mother! Joie cried.

Traian hesitated, and the cat raked his chest with her hind legs, tearing great lacerations, all the while driving its teeth toward his throat. It suddenly switched tactics, claws raking his chest, digging in for traction as she gathered power, pushing off with her hind legs to leap at Gary. She struck hard and fast, going in for the kill.

Powerful hands wrapped around her neck, holding her off, and she stared into the black eyes of the prince. He had moved with blurring speed, inserting his body between the jaguar and its prey.

"Mom! Stop!" There was panic in Joie's voice. "What are you doing?"

Traian had no choice. He was sworn, as all Carpathians, to protect their prince. He circled the strong neck in a half nelson, prepared to break the neck should she persist in her attack on Mikhail.

The jaguar fought, using its flexible spine, but neither male yielded.

"Please, Traian, don't. You can't kill her," Joie pleaded, rushing forward to grab his arm.

It was enough distraction that the jaguar twisted, nearly getting away from Traian, the claws tearing at Mikhail.

"Enough!" The command thundered through the room as a tall, broad-shouldered man strode in. His silver eyes gleamed with lethal intent. Ignoring Joie and Jubal's pleas, Gregori reached past Traian and yanked the jaguar's head around to stare into its eyes. "I said enough. If you persist in this action I will slay you immediately. You are human enough to understand me. Go into the other room and regain control now." There was no give, no compassion. He didn't even glance at the others in the room. He simply picked up the jaguar and flung it toward the door.

The cat landed hard against the wall, slid down and lay for a moment, sides heaving. There was a small silence broken only by the jaguar's heavy breathing. Then it turned its head and snarled.

Gregori let out a long slow hiss, eyes glittering. He took one threatening step toward the cat. "I will not tell you again. You attacked my prince and the penalty is death. There are three Carpathians in this room and by all rights you should be dead. Go before I lose what little patience I have."

The jaguar slunk off, and Gregori reached down and helped Mikhail to his feet. "Next time, if you do not protect your prince, you will answer to me. I do not care who attacks him, or for what reason. It is your duty to see to his safety whether he likes it or not." His eyes touched on first Traian, then Joie and Gabrielle. "Do I make myself perfectly clear? Because if I do not, I will go in there and break her neck and show you what one does to keep their prince from harm."

Traian nodded and reached for Joie. Gabrielle kept her face buried against Gary's shoulder. Mr. Sanders rushed into the other room to attend to his wife.

"I was safe, Gregori," Mikhail said quietly.

Gregori whipped around to glare at the prince. "Do not tell me you were safe. She was going straight for your throat. Do you think I couldn't read her mind? She intended to rip it out."

This is fine way to begin our first Christmas celebration. Raven is not going to be pleased.

Raven would not be pleased if that woman had ripped out your throat. This is not finished, Mikhail, and do not make light of it. Traian and Joie have a lot to answer for. I can excuse Gabrielle, but not the others.

"Traian was watching out for me, Gregori," Joie said. "She's my mother."

"Traian does not need to hide behind your skirts, Joie. He is an ancient. Born and bred Carpathian and as such subject to the laws of our people. Above all else, we protect our prince. Without him, our species dies. We are extinct. Our first duty always—*always*—is to protect the living vessel of our people. Mikhail would not have killed your mother to save himself because he is bound to hold our people together. He would have tried diplomacy and she would have ripped out his throat. It was the duty of the three Carpathians in this room to protect him—even from himself." Gregori turned his head, pinning Traian with his cold, peculiar-colored eyes. "Is that not so?"

"That is so. It was bad judgment on my part and I will not fail our prince again."

"And you will not fail our people again," Gregori persisted. He looked to the women. "You must make up your mind whether or not you live as Carpathian. If you do not, I will see to it that you do not live at all."

Gregori. Mikhail's intervention was calm in the eye of the storm. *Enough.*

It is not enough. They will protect you or they will answer to me.

"Why did she do it?" Gary asked, pushing his glasses up and rubbing the bridge of his nose. "I swear she was coming for me, not Mikhail. Gregori, I'm certain she tried to kill me. Mikhail moved so fast I didn't see him, and I don't think she did either."

"Traian needs attention," Gregori ordered Joie. "See to your lifemate's wounds."

Traian's snarl rumbled through the room. "I deserve your reprimand, Gregori, but do not extend your orders to my lifemate. I will not allow it."

Mikhail held up his hand to forestall any further confrontation. "We all forget what is at stake here. Mrs. Sanders is here to celebrate with us and she had accepted Gabrielle and Joie as Carpathians. What we need to find out is what triggered the jaguar into attacking." He gave his second in command a hard look. "And then we're all going to make peace because nothing, and I mean *nothing*, is going to ruin this night for Raven."

Gregori bowed slightly. "Of course." He exchanged a ghost of a grin with Traian. *He is afraid of her.*

She has him wrapped around her finger.

And both of you can go to hell.

Gabrielle sank down onto the couch with Gary on one side of her and Jubal on the other. Joie and Traian shared a chair. Mikhail stood in the corner nearest the door and Gregori stood, arms folded across his broad chest, his body between Mikhail's and the rest of the room.

Mr. and Mrs. Sanders came out together holding hands. She had been crying and was obviously reluctant to face them all. When she saw the marks on Traian's chest, a fresh flood of tears began.

"Mom, it's okay," Joie said. "Please don't cry anymore. Let's just figure out what's wrong and fix it."

"Is it me?" Gabrielle asked. "I don't want to upset you anymore. This is Christmas night and we're supposed to be together as a family. I don't want you upset by what happened to me."

Mrs. Sanders shook her head. "Not you. Never you, baby." Her gaze touched on Gary, and slid away. She gripped her husband's hand tighter. "It's him." She nodded toward Gary. "He's not what you think he is."

"Gary?" Gabrielle looked shocked. Everyone stared at Gary.

"What do you mean, Mrs. Sanders?" Mikhail asked.

"He's jaguar. I can smell his blood. The stench is all over him. He is a jaguar male. They are deceptive and capable of great cruelty. I don't want him anywhere near my daughters. Either of them." She raised her chin, suddenly looking regal. "What I did was wrong, I should have controlled the cat better, but it was such a shock. I haven't encountered a jaguar male in years. I thought that door was long closed. It took me by surprise and brought back painful memories, but I'm under control now. He cannot stay anywhere near them."

Gabrielle gripped Gary's shirt hard. "You're mistaken, Mom. Gary is the sweetest man I know. Kind and good and brilliant. He isn't a shapeshifter. He's human."

"He is jaguar," Mrs. Sanders said harshly. "And he is deceiving you if he has said differently. I am pure jaguar and none can escape my detection."

"Gary?" Mikhail asked, already probing the man's mind.

Gregori had exchanged blood with Gary and could read his thoughts, and did so often. He had never found any evidence of shapeshifting. He looked at Mikhail and shook his head.

"Mrs. Sanders, it is possible Gary shares a bloodline. Many of the women here do, including your daughters and son. But he cannot shift and, in fact, does not know of his lineage. Gregori has shared blood with him and can easily read his thoughts, and many times Gary has volunteered to allow me to do the same. He cannot deceive a Carpathian who has taken his blood."

"He is a jaguar," Mrs. Sanders persisted. "He is not welcome here nor can he be near my daughters."

"Your son is jaguar. Should he be banished as well?" Mikhail asked.

"Mom! What's gotten into you," Jubal demanded. "Dad, stop her."

"You have no idea what your mother has suffered at the hands of a jaguar male," Mr. Sanders retorted. "Don't you dare judge her."

"Not all jaguar males are the same," Mikhail said. "Any more than Carpathian males are. Many of our males turn vampire and many jaguar males turn on their women, but not all. I've known many honorable jaguars—your own son among them, and his blood is far more pure than Gary's. Give Gary a fair chance. He has been with my people for some time now and is committed to helping us. Gabrielle has worked with him and knows his dedication. Use this time to get to know him as an individual."

Before she could protest, Gregori stirred, drawing all eyes to him. "This is a small thing the prince has requested, Mrs. Sanders. You have attacked him, as well as intentionally harming your own son-in-law. Your intention was to kill one of ours. Gary is under my protection and is my friend. I will be responsible for his behavior. All the prince has asked is that you give him a chance and given your own behavior, I think it is a reasonable request."

Mrs. Sanders took a deep breath. "You're right, of course. I was so scared when I scented him. I do apologize for my behavior."

Gary squeezed Gabrielle's hand to forestall any comments. "Thank you, Mrs. Sanders. I honestly don't know if what you say is true, but I'll do my best to find out. As far as I know, I have no psychic abilities whatsoever, and I certainly can't shapeshift. However, I have always been interested in legends and myths, and did at one time try to prove there were such creatures as vampires and shapeshifters. Maybe I was drawn to those things because, as you say, it is my heritage."

"Perhaps," Mrs. Sanders agreed noncommittally.

Mikhail let his breath out slowly. "Our celebration will begin in a couple of hours. I trust you will do your best to work things out so we can present a united front to our guests. And Traian, you will make absolutely certain that our secrets remain safe at all times." That meant taking the blood of Joie's parents, an unpleasant, but necessary task.

"Yes, of course."

Gregori turned deliberately to Gary in front of the others. "If you have need of me, you have only to call out in your mind and I will hear you. Take every precaution. I will not suffer a second attack on you without retaliation. My justice is swift and brutal as you well know." He looked at the others in the room. "Nothing will sway me from my set task should harm come to my friend." He gave a small half bow and followed Mikhail out into the drifting snow.

"You always did know how to leave with a flair," Mikhail remarked.

"I swear, old friend, if you put yourself in harm's way again, I'm going to kill you myself and be done with it."

"I like to keep you on your toes. I'll be by later to see my daughter. I'm heading over to see Destiny. I'd like to hear what her friend MaryAnn has to say about Gabrielle. And if she really is as good as everyone tells me, I want to find a way to get her together with young Skyler. The child is amazing, courageous and smart and way too mature for her age, but so fragile, Gregori. We cannot afford to lose her and Dimitri is very close. Too close."

"I am keeping my eye on him." Gregori said. "You will like Destiny and her Nicolae. She is an amazing woman and a very skilled hunter. Francesca and I are keeping a close eye on her to make certain we removed all the parasites from her blood. We have kept some just in case we find a use for it. An astonishing young woman."

"I am looking forward to meeting her."

Gregori began to shimmer into transparency. "You know there will be trouble over Gabrielle and Gary now that she has been converted."

Mikhail sighed. "Even now, when we are supposed to be gathering for Christmas, there always seems to be trouble."

14

The inn was beginning to fill up with people. Manolito De La Cruz stood in the corner watching the strange scene unfold before his eyes. Chaos. Stupidity. Why would so many people gather indoors and feel safe?

Hunger was sharp and terrible, clawing at his gut, riding him hard, and the sound of so many heartbeats, blood ebbing and flowing in veins, only added to his discomfort. Shadows rose in him, the demon crying for blood, for some small spark of feeling, a momentary rush that would give him back life. Just once. He could almost imagine prey beneath him, heart beating wildly, the rush of adrenaline spiking the blood and giving him a high when he consumed it.

There in the shadows he chose his prey. The man, fit and strong and thinking he was such a big man, telling everyone what to do. Manolito would let him see it coming, death in his eyes, in his heart and soul, and he would sink his teeth deep, feel the struggle for life—always life. A life he no longer had and could never get back.

All around him were Carpathian males who had managed to claim a woman—even two of his brothers. He heard their laughter, felt emotion through them, but it wasn't enough. Too many centuries had gone by. Too many battles. Too many kills. He felt his will slipping into that dark abyss he couldn't seem to drag himself out of. He had stood with the Carpathians against the vampires, had been wounded and had been healed, but rising, had felt the darkness coiled in him, whispering continually every moment until he thought he might go mad—until he thought he would welcome madness.

His gaze shifted to a woman in heels. Women always welcomed his attentions. He could draw them easily with his dark, seductive looks. He knew what women saw when they looked at him: a handsome man, mysterious, wealthy and very, very sexual. He looked the epitome of the predatory male and women followed him, begging to be taken to bed. He used them ruthlessly, leaving behind the impression of sexual prowess, marking them with his teeth, disgusted by their willingness to throw their bodies at him. If they only knew what he really wanted was to drain every drop of blood from their bodies, to leave them a withered shell just so he could feel the momentary rush of life.

Temptation was overpowering, triggering a response, so that his incisors lengthened and grew, filling his mouth even as his body craved the power of the kill. *Just once.* The whispers grew louder, drowning out his thoughts of calling to his brothers for aid. One time only. A taste of life that would have to last him a long while. *Just once.* Who would know?

The heartbeats grew louder until they thundered in his ears. He heard his own heart beating and waited for the sheep around him to follow—and they did, slowly, one by one, picking up his rhythm.

He craved hot blood pouring into his system. He craved the feel of a woman's skin, the thrill of her body submitting to his. Only he couldn't feel it—not for real. His brothers fed him emotions like they would spoon-feed a child. It wasn't enough. Darkness called and he needed to answer. He could almost taste the power in his mouth.

Abruptly, he turned and strode from the inn, out into the night, where he could calm his heart and try to think with more clarity. Hunger beat at him relentlessly, a dark driving obsession he couldn't shake. The night wasn't dark enough to hide in. The snow lit up the ground and kept the shadows from prevailing. He needed the shelter of the woods. Manolito switched directions and headed for deeper forest.

"Nicolae, warrior, brother, it is good to have you home." Mikhail clasped the forearms of the tall, ancient dark-haired hunter, greeting him with the timeless Carpathian tradition for welcoming beloved warriors home.

Nicolae Von Shrieder stood arm to arm, staring into the eyes of his prince, emotion nearly choking him. It was unexpected and shocking to feel the lump in his throat at the admiration and genuine welcome in Mikhail's greeting. He was home and he had served his people with honor and dignity for centuries. "It is good to be home, Mikhail. I serve at the will of my prince, who is the living vessel of our people, and pledge loyalty to him." He paid the ancient homage to his prince.

Mikhail's smile was genuine. "It has been long since I heard those words and felt the meaning behind them. It is truly good to have you home." He turned to the woman standing beside Nicolae. She looked very apprehensive, somewhere between wanting to run—and fight. She had been through so much, her courage and strength honed in the very fires of hell.

He clasped her forearms, looking straight into her startled aquamarine eyes, and repeated the ancient greeting, affording her the highest respect he could give her. "Destiny. Warrior. Sister. It is good to have you home."

She swallowed hard, glanced at her lifemate and nodded, her hands tightening on his forearms. "It is good to be home. I too serve at the will of my prince and pledge loyalty to him."

"You do not have to pledge your loyalty to me," Mikhail said. "The service you have already done is more than any people could ask of you."

"I stand with my lifemate and wish to serve," she replied.

"Then I accept your offer on behalf of the Carpathian people." He let her go, stepping away, his smile welcoming. "I have long wanted to meet the woman who has given and suffered so much for our people. Thank you for coming."

"I had forgotten the feel of our soil," Nicolae murmured. "I cannot get enough of it. Destiny says all I do is roll around in bed, but it is a miracle to me to have the luxury of such richness." He led the way through his family home. As always, the other Carpathians had kept the home clean and in good shape. The moment he had returned he had modernized it, and was proud to show off the changes.

They sat near the fireplace, the one Destiny especially loved, and Mikhail imparted to them all the news he could think of, including his most important find, Syndil. "Do you remember anything of the ancient practices, Nicolae? A woman who could heal the earth?"

"Of course. They were very rare and most honored. She attended all births and healings. The line was old and only the women from that line had the gift. Syndil must be a descendent."

"And the only one we have."

"There were several earth healers I ran across when I was a young man. There could be more. Rhiannon was such a healer. The gift was passed through her mother. Her father was Dragonseeker. She was an incredible talent even as a child. It was a great loss to our people when she was killed."

"Syndil is not Dragonseeker; at least I have not heard she bears the mark of the dragon. She is one of the Dark Troubadours, the lost children Darius managed to save. But we do have Rhiannon's granddaughter, Natalya, whom your brother claimed as a lifemate."

Nicolae smiled. "And Vikirnoff certainly has his hands full with her."

"The two of you have found extraordinary women." A brief smile flirted with Mikhail's mouth. "Although Natalya did not inherit her mother's gift for healing the earth, she is a talented warrior. I believe you will enjoy her company very much, Destiny. Have you met her yet? She taught herself to be a warrior."

Destiny's tongue touched her lips as if they were dry. Once more her gaze flicked to her lifemate before she spoke. "She's a lot of fun. I find myself laughing around her all the time."

Mikhail had the feeling Destiny didn't laugh all that much. He glanced at Nicolae. The ancient's fingers were massaging the nape of her neck, a subtle show of support Mikhail often employed when Raven was in an unfamiliar situation and feeling apprehensive. He flashed another open smile at the woman. "She does love to quote old movies. I told Raven we were going to have to start watching them so I can keep up."

Destiny managed a small, nervous smile. "She loves old movies. Poor Vikirnoff doesn't know what she's saying half the time, but it's good for him." She let out her breath slowly. "I've never been around a prince before. I don't know exactly what I'm supposed to do."

"Most of the time, I'm just an ordinary man, Destiny," Mikhail confided. He looked around and leaned forward, lowering his voice in a conspiratorial manner, although he sent his comments along to his second in command. "Unless Gregori's around, and then I suppose everyone should genuflect to make him happy."

Gregori's retaliation was swift. A clap of thunder shook the house, rattling the windows, and the chair Mikhail was sitting in shifted and bucked, nearly throwing him to the floor.

Nicolae roared with laughter. "That was definitely a Daratrazanoff growling."

"It is not any way for a son-in-law to treat his father-in-law," Mikhail said. A slow grin lit his eyes. "But he will find I have the last word this night."

"You have planned something," Nicolae guessed.

"We need a Santa Claus and I think Gregori Daratrazanoff will fill that role nicely."

Destiny looked from one laughing man to the other. "Gregori is not going to be happy. In all the time he spent trying to heal me, I only saw him smile at Savannah. Well, once he tried to smile at me and it was more a baring of his teeth. The thought of him entertaining a roomful of children is beyond my imagination."

"And everyone else's as well it seems," Mikhail said with evident satisfaction. "How are you feeling? I know you experienced great pain on rising each day with vampire blood in your veins. Was Gregori able to fully heal you both?"

Destiny nodded. "It seems a miracle every rising, to open my eyes and not feel as if razor blades are cutting through my skin. Gregori kept the blood, and mentioned it might be used to infect a warrior to infiltrate the ranks of the undead." Her gaze met Mikhail's. "Don't let them do that. It's the worst thing you can imagine to have that blood in your veins every moment of your existence. It's agony, both physically and mentally. I cannot imagine what it would do to a warrior already close to the edge of madness."

"Nothing has been decided," Mikhail assured. "When we are back to normal, we will all meet together. Your input is very valuable to us and we are hoping you will attend."

Destiny looked relieved. "Yes, of course."

Nicolae slid his arm along the back of her seat. "Destiny has not celebrated Christmas in years. We are going out to get a tree. Would you like to join us?"

Mikhail shook his head regretfully. "I have a few more stops to make before we all gather at the inn. I was hoping I would have a chance to speak with MaryAnn Delaney. I understand she's staying here."

"Yes, she's with a young teenage girl at the moment. Francesca brought her over a few minutes ago and asked that MaryAnn speak with her. We're to take her home shortly."

"Young Skyler. Most of the time, a girl her age would not trigger a response in her lifemate, but she is mature beyond her years and we now have an unrequited male running loose and demanding his rights." Mikhail sighed softly. "Skyler needs protection at all times. If we fail again, her lifemate will bind her to him and I am not certain what Gabriel will do, but it will not be pleasant."

"Francesca warned us," Nicolae said. "Skyler indicated she would like to join us when we get the tree, so we'll leave as soon as MaryAnn has had some time with her. I don't anticipate any problems, but we will be careful. Destiny is a skilled hunter, so young Skyler will be doubly protected."

"Do not let her out of your sight," Mikhail warned. "She has a tendency to wander off. I sometimes wonder why I press Raven to have another child. I have forgotten the trouble they can be."

"See!" Destiny made a face at Nicolae. "I told you they were trouble."

Mikhail rose. "I am off to see your brother. Is there anything you would like me to tell him?"

"Just pass on that you're going to ask Gregori to play Santa Claus. Vikirnoff will definitely enjoy that news." Nicolae stood as well to see the prince out.

"I do not intend to *ask* Gregori, Nicolae. I will give him my first order as his father-in-law."

Nicolae swept Destiny under his shoulder. "I so want to be there when you announce to Gregori that he will play Santa Claus tonight."

"I wish I was there to see Savannah's face. She has such a wonderful sense of humor. I never thought I would become friends with the daughter of a prince. Although, honestly, I think she's just happy she got to fight a vampire so she can have something to hold over Gregori's head."

Mikhail's face darkened and all humor left his face. "The moment something happens to my people—in particular my daughter—I am to be informed. But somehow, this small detail seems to have been omitted. Nicolae, perhaps you would be so kind as to explain, as my son-in-law failed to do so." *Gregori, did my daughter fight a vampire? And why wasn't I informed immediately?* He sent a hiss of displeasure and the image of bared teeth.

Color receded from Destiny's face, leaving her very pale. She turned to Nicolae for reassurance. *Did I say something wrong?*

No, of course not, Nicolae said comfortingly.

Mikhail immediately regained control, forcing a small smile. The last thing he wanted to do was make Destiny uncomfortable. Fighting vampires to her was as natural as breathing. She would have a difficult time understanding why he was considering throttling Gregori.

I had every intention of telling you, but I came home to a battle. I didn't think in the midst of getting my hand cut off that it would be a good time to say, "Oh, and by the way, Savannah was out slaying vampires."

I am considering chopping off your head. You will tell me every detail when we are alone. And don't whine about your hand, it is perfectly fine now.

I take no responsibility for the way you raised your headstrong daughter. I do my best to minimize the damage you and Raven did with your liberal and far too lenient raising.

Mikhail nearly choked. "That son-in-law is going to get taught a lesson he won't forget tonight. Liberal and lenient? I was firm with my daughter." Mikhail waved to Destiny and left with a satisfied smirk on his face.

Destiny frowned, trying to follow the conversation. "Did you understand any of that?"

"I think he was arguing with Gregori over whether or not Savannah was raised properly." Nicolae turned as MaryAnn Delaney and Skyler came into the room. Skyler was dressed in her furred parka, and MaryAnn reached for her own coat. MaryAnn was tall and slender with coffee-cream skin and spiraling curls all over her head. Even dressed in her jeans, she looked far too sophisticated for the woods. Small diamonds sparkled on her earlobes and a thin gold chain circled her neck.

"We're really going to do this?" MaryAnn asked, following the others outside. "Go chop down a tree in the middle of the forest?"

"Are you going to be a big baby? It's not that cold," Nicolae teased. "Didn't you ever have a Christmas tree back in Seattle?"

"Of course I have, but I buy my trees in a civilized manner, you heathen," MaryAnn said. "At the corner right down from my house. And in fact, they deliver them for me each year because my car is too small to get them home."

"Are they always like this?" Skyler asked Destiny.

"They get worse," she answered, drawing the door closed behind them.

"And you don't mind? I thought lifemates were jealous all the time."

Destiny frowned as she made her way across the snow-covered ground. "Is Francesca jealous of Gabriel's friendships?"

"He isn't really all that friendly. Just with Lucian and Jaxon, and he treats Jaxon like his sister. Well, he's good to the housekeeper, but not like Francesca, and he doesn't really like very many men around her." She shrugged. "Earlier, I was with Dimitri and he was being nice to me, but then Josef came along and he changed completely. I was afraid for Josef."

"Jealousy isn't a good trait," MaryAnn said, pulling her hood over her curls. "It shows insecurity."

"Ah but sometimes, when other men look at my woman the wrong way," Nicolae said, leering at Destiny, "they deserve to be scared off."

MaryAnn threw a snowball at him. "You would say that because you haven't joined the modern world."

"And I don't want to either. I like being king of my castle."

Destiny snorted and added her snowball to MaryAnn's. "You wish."

⌒

Manolito moved in absolute silence through the trees. The heartbeats were louder now, thunder in his ears. He could hear blood running, coursing through arteries straight to hearts. His mouth watered and his teeth lengthened. His pulse throbbed as it tuned itself to his prey. Lightning seemed to sizzle in his veins. He tried to reach for Rafael and Riordan, a last effort to remember honor and sanity, but he could not make the effort.

The heartbeats pounded and a single sound broke the rhythm. Laughter. It tinkled in the air, a melodious note that sank into his pores—called to the most basic part of him. Deep within, his demon roared, fighting for release, raking and clawing, demanding he give in. That sound came again, carried on the slight wind, drifting past the snowflakes to reach out to him, to beckon—no—summon him. He turned toward that note and moved with more stealth. He caught the scent now. Three women and a man—not just any man—a hunter. A warrior. He should walk away, get out while he could, but his demon thundered orders, shaking him, demanding he find prey.

A slow hiss escaped. His body was graceful, the body of an ancient hunter who had long battled the vampire and was highly skilled in combat. He moved with the drift of snow, part of nature itself, transparent and fluid, as silent as the flakes falling from the clouds.

~

Skyler pulled her parka closer around her and looked out toward the deeper forest. The world was white and sparkling, snow weighing down the branches of the trees in all directions. Off in the distance she could see the smoke coming from the direction of the inn. She shivered for no reason at all.

"It's beautiful out here, don't you think?" MaryAnn remarked.

Skyler nodded. "Very beautiful—but dangerous."

"And cold," MaryAnn added. "I'm not like the others. I can't regulate my body temperature like they can. Even you do better than I do. And I'm not a particularly adventurous person."

"I love the forest and even the cold. There's something about knowing wild animals are close and everything around me is in its natural state." Even as she admitted it, Skyler's gaze was searching out the darker interior of the woods.

MaryAnn shuddered. "I can see you love this, child, but I'm a city girl. And I'm totally out of my element here. I have to tell you, if any of these men were my man, I'd be bashing him upside the head—and I'm a woman who doesn't condone violence."

Skyler swung her full attention back to MaryAnn, laughing. "I think that's a good idea. I'm going to tell Francesca that's what she needs to do whenever Gabriel gets bossy."

"It's definitely what Destiny needs to do with that bossy man she's hooked up with," MaryAnn said decisively.

"I heard that," Nicolae said. He pitched a snowball at MaryAnn with deadly accuracy.

She laughed as it splattered against her shoulder. "You're so mean, Nicolae. You know I can't retaliate because my hands are frozen."

"You are such a little hothouse flower," Nicolae taunted. "And you couldn't hit me anyway. Your one try hit the tree three feet to my left."

"Just call me Orchid. I thrive best in the warmth of the indoors. As for aim, I never could hit anything, not even a softball and I tried when I was a kid. What about you, Skyler, do you play sports?"

Skyler shook her head. "No. I'm not too good with other kids. Francesca homeschools me."

"I could hit a rock with my eyes closed by the time I was fourteen," Nicolae boasted. "That's what we played with in the old days."

"Did you really?" Skyler was intrigued.

"Yes. We spent a great deal of time seeing who could feel a small attack coming and divert it before it hit. I was darn good at it too. I won't mention my brother, who excelled at it and slipped one or two past me to give me the occasional black eye."

"All this manly beating on the chest is making me weak. I need to fly home soon to my beautiful Seattle," MaryAnn said half-jokingly.

Destiny made a single sound of distress and reached for MaryAnn's hand. "You can't leave me."

"You'll do fine, girlfriend. You know you will. You're strong and whole . . ."

"That's taking it a little too far," Destiny said. "I'm never going to be like everyone else."

"And no one wants you to be. You're Destiny and you're unique. Right, Skyler?" MaryAnn drew the girl into the conversation. "We wouldn't want Destiny to be any other way."

"I like you just the way you are," Skyler admitted shyly.

"I don't know what way I am," Destiny whispered, gripping MaryAnn harder, as if she might be able to keep her in the Carpathian Mountains.

"You accept people the way they are," Skyler said, her gaze too old, memories swirling to the surface before she could stop them. "You just accept people."

MaryAnn put her hand on Skyler's shoulder. "That's right, Destiny. She's right about you. You never ask anything of anyone and you don't expect them to be anything they're not. You're a very accepting person."

"I'm not any different than the two of you," Destiny objected.

MaryAnn blew out a trail of white vapor and watched it float away. "Yes, you are," she said without meeting her friend's gaze. "I could never do what you've done. You have the courage to take on a man like Nicolae. I can't do that. I'll never do that. I intend to remain alone all of my life rather than chance being with someone who is dominating and possibly destructive." She spread her hands out. "I don't want a man in my life and I always judge them too harshly."

"If some handsome hottie came out of the forest and claimed you, you wouldn't accept him?" Skyler asked. "No matter how hot he was?"

MaryAnn shook her head. "Absolutely not. I would catch the first plane back to Seattle."

"Lifemates don't always let you do the things you want," Skyler murmured.

"Ha! Gregori promised his protection, and I'd hide in his house until I could get safely home. I would never, under any circumstances, live with a Carpathian male."

"I feel the same way," Skyler said, and looked out toward the forest, blinking back tears that were suddenly close.

The smile faded from MaryAnn's face as she looked at the other girl and really backtracked in their conversation. Skyler was fighting the pull of her lifemate, and with all the things MaryAnn now knew about their species, she knew it was difficult, if not impossible. "I was being humorous, Skyler," she said softly. "Things we think are forever are often just a short space of time. I have no idea what I'd really do if a Carpathian man came out of the forest and claimed me. How could I really know?"

Skyler shook her head, tears swimming in her eyes in spite of her efforts to keep them at bay.

"Sweetheart," MaryAnn's voice was infinitely gentle. "You feel that way now only because you haven't worked out all of your problems. You need to find out who you really are and what strengths you have. No one can get ahead of themselves and make decisions when they haven't given themselves time to grow. Have patience. Give yourself time to grow up. There's no hurry at all."

Skyler ducked her head. If there was no hurry, why did she feel such a sense of urgency? Why did the woods beckon her every time she looked at them? The pull was strong to go find Dimitri. She hoped it was to tell him she couldn't be what he wanted, but she feared he had already tied them in some way. She couldn't stop thinking about him, and worse, her body reacted when she did—and she *detested* her reaction. Heat spread through her veins, her breasts ached, and lower still, she felt damp and uncomfortable, tension building. She felt his hunger. His need. She felt his silent call to her, even though he tried to suppress his needs and keep a barrier between them. His blood called to her. She knew it was Dimitri. And she didn't want anything to do with a man or what that would entail.

"There's a likely candidate," Nicolae said, pointing toward a particularly full tree. "We could do a lot with that."

The tree was deeper in the woods, and Skyler hesitated to follow as the three adults raced each other across the snow, occasionally throwing a snowball at each other. She was filled with dread when she looked into the shadows. Something lurked there. Something dangerous. It watched them with hungry eyes. Watched and waited for one wrong move. She could feel the waves of menace, and didn't understand how Nicolae or Destiny couldn't feel it as well.

Skyler wanted to run back to the safety of the house, but that meant telling the others or going by herself. If she told the others and it was Dimitri, there would be problems between Gabriel and him again and she couldn't bear that. She'd already caused far too much trouble for both of them. And going back to the house alone was out of the question. She hurried after Destiny and MaryAnn, casting anxious glances toward the thick stand of trees.

For one horrible moment she thought she saw the fiery glow of eyes staring at her, tracking her every move. She blinked and the illusion was gone, but something was there. She was certain of it. And it was watching them with hungry eyes.

~

"Absolutely not. I would catch the first plane back to Seattle. Gregori promised his protection, and I'd hide in his house until I could get safely home. I would never, under any circumstances, live with a Carpathian male." The feminine voice came to him quite clearly, each word distinct, carried on the night itself.

He was blinded. Dazzled by the brilliant white of the snow on the ground. His eyes failed him and he had to cover them, dropping to his knees to keep from crying out at the unexpected pain of such glaring brightness. Color blazed into life, like a living flame, so that he had to squeeze his eyelids shut, yet it still was there, absorbed by his mind. Vivid. Astonishing. Beautiful.

His breath left his lungs in a rush. He tried to look again, his fingers helping to shield against the brightness so he wouldn't be completely blind. There was color in the trees, not a dull gray, but green peeking beneath the coat of sparkling white. *He was seeing in color.* Elation swept through him. It was no wonder his demon was roaring to follow that heartbeat, that melodious laughter.

The woman belonged to him. At last. After centuries of waiting. She was created for him, would be bound to him. He stood, swaying with the strength of the emotions pouring into him. It was overpowering to feel so much, every sense vividly alive. Every cell vividly alive. It was all there, every single emotion he could ever want. From lust to hunger, filling his mind, creating erotic images and testing the years of lost dreams and fantasies. His mouth watered as he thought of the taste of her, the texture of her skin. He had dreamed of her, needed her, and at long last, she was within his grasp.

Even as he moved quickly to catch her, her words sank in. *Protected by Gregori.* A soft growl escaped. She meant to elude him. To deny his claim on her. She was his by right, by law, by everything their world decreed, and he had held out for centuries—*centuries*—waiting for her. No one would keep her from him. No one. He would take her if necessary and damn the consequences. There were few hunters equal to him—or to his brothers, and they would stand with him. The De La Cruz brothers always—always—stood together.

His lips drew back in a snarl and he began to work his way with even more care toward the small group gathered around a tree. The young girl turned several times toward him, a faint frown on her face, and once the ancient male lifted his head to examine the area around him. He felt the mind probe and kept his barriers up, determined not to be discovered. The ancient was good, but Manolito had centuries of experience in hiding his presence to fall back on, and he kept from being discovered by simply becoming the tree nearest to him.

He crept closer until he could see her. She took his breath away. She was everything he had ever imagined a lifemate could be—and more. Tall, slender, with full breasts meant for suckling, curvy hips for cradling his body, and her skin—he could almost feel it even from the distance he was. She had the kind of skin that looked so soft, a man could spend his life just touching her. Coffee-colored, inviting, warm like satin. The hood had fallen back on her jacket and he could see the shoulder-length curls, thick and wild, long spirals and whorls begging for his fingers. Her eyes were large, a dark chocolate, and her mouth was frankly sinful. He was definitely going to be fantasizing over her mouth and the things she would be doing to his body.

His. He still couldn't grasp the reality of it, not even with her standing right there, laughing, her face flushed, her eyes dancing. He sank down and let himself breathe, his brain working quickly to sort out the choices he had. If he took her, as he wanted to, he would bring down most of Carpathian society on him. He had a right to her, but she could ask for protection and from what he'd overheard, she would do just that. He needed a plan. And he needed it fast. He couldn't even reveal to his brothers that he had found his lifemate. They would help him—but if their lifemates got wind of his intentions, they would be angry. He wasn't willing to risk that one of them might betray him.

First, before all else, he had to find out everything he could about his lifemate, without allowing anyone to know he was doing so. And then he had to devise a plan to get her to South America where she would be cut off from all help.

He watched the tree come down and Nicolae drag it across the snow. The young girl took another suspicious look around, and almost immediately one of the women scanned the area for enemies. He did his tree act again, melting into the trunk, becoming part of the growth, until the small group walked back toward the house.

He followed, staying invisible, keeping upwind and out of sight of the youngest girl. She had vision beyond the normal, the ability to sense even the shadow of darkness. Manolito was about to undertake a dangerous entry into the home of an ancient, and the shadow of darkness within him grew enough that it would call to the girl.

He waited until they opened the door to the house, an invitation if he ever saw one. The ancient struggled with the tree. It was awkward and covered with snow, a difficult fit for the open door.

"Is that as wide as you can hold it open, MaryAnn?" Nicolae demanded. "Because there's a lot of tree here. Maybe I should just make it skinny for a second or two. Just enough to get it inside."

"Don't you dare. You promised me we'd do this the old-fashioned way. No cheating. I'll help you," Destiny said.

MaryAnn bowed low as she pushed the door as wide open as possible. "Please do come in."

Beside her, Skyler gasped as a cold breeze blew into the house. Snowflakes from the tree and porch whirled around in a small eddy, and then slowly subsided.

Nicolae and Destiny took several tries to get the very full tree into the house. Snow cascaded everywhere and they both collapsed laughing. "Skyler! Help," Destiny called as the top of the tree hit the couch.

Skyler leapt to lift it over the furniture. Once MaryAnn closed the door and latched it, Skyler thought she would feel so much safer, but she didn't. Nicolae waved one hand and a fire sprang up in the fireplace, almost instantly warming the room. Skyler turned away from them to stare out the window into the forest. Nothing had happened. Was her overactive imagination at work? Why didn't she ever feel safe anymore?

"There's water all over the floor," MaryAnn said. "I'll go get a towel."

"Great idea. Skyler and I will have Nicolae find the best spot for the tree."

"What do you mean, find the best spot for the tree?" Nicolae demanded. "I'm only moving it once if you're making me do this the human way."

"You're taking all the fun out of it," Destiny protested. "Half the fun is seeing that look of total exasperation on your face."

MaryAnn laughed at their antics. It was so good to see Destiny happy. It was worth leaving Seattle and traveling so far from home. The mountains were remote, and she knew she was far out of her depth here, but just to see Destiny settling in, happy with Nicolae and confident in herself, was worth every moment away from home.

She stepped into the bathroom and turned in a slow circle to admire all the tile work. For a room that was never used, Nicolae had paid a lot of attention to detail and it was beautiful. She pulled two of the thickest towels from the rack and turned to the door. It swung shut, the lock snicking in place.

As she reached for the door, Manolito materialized, his mouth at her ear, whispering a command, taking over quickly, wrapping her up in his enthrallment. When she'd held the door open for the other male carrying the Christmas tree and said, "Please come in" under his gentle push of compulsion, she had invited Manolito into her home as well.

MaryAnn, you are my lifemate and therefore subject to my wishes. You will take my blood so that I may call to you whenever I have need of you or I can hear you when you have need of me.

His fingers trailed down the perfect skin of her face. He closed his eyes, savoring how utterly soft she was. He slid his fingers into the collar of her shirt, tracing her collarbone and sliding the buttons open. Her breasts swelled above her lacy bra, an invitation in itself.

He bent his head and kissed the corner of her mouth, his body already tightening. But this wasn't about sex. He would never take something from his lifemate she was not ready to offer him. He kissed his way across her throat and the frantically beating pulse there. Pulling her into his arms, he cradled her body to his and sank his teeth over her breast, allowing the erotic ecstasy of his first taste of her to take him over.

Need slammed him hard, his body swelling in reaction, a hard, painful ache of promise. Her taste was exquisite. He'd never known anything like it, and he took his fill and then some, wanting a true exchange. Their first. He didn't pretend she knew her lifemate was claiming her. He simply took, greedy for what was his, and he damned himself for doing so. But this would bind them together enough for him to get through the dark days ahead, keep him from turning vampire. He would ride the high of lust and need until he could safely take her to his lair.

When he could force himself under control, he closed the pinpricks, leaving behind his mark, his brand, one she couldn't easily remove. He opened his own shirt and slashed his chest, forcing her head to him, commanding her to drink. The moment her mouth moved over his skin and her tongue swirled against him, he nearly shamed himself. His erection thickened, jumped in response, and throbbed with the need to bury itself deep inside her.

"MaryAnn?" It was Nicolae, and there was suspicion in his voice. Manolito felt the quick scan, a hard thrust of a mind probe and then movement in MaryAnn's mind. *The ancient had taken her blood at some time, tying them together.* Manolito hissed his displeasure, kept her brain patterns the same, a woman using the restroom.

Still, the ancient paced outside the door.

With a sigh of regret, when he was certain she had taken enough for a true exchange, Manolito closed the wound, tidied her and placed memories of using the bathroom. It easy enough to disappear, scattering his molecules throughout the room so that when MaryAnn opened the door and Nicolae peered in, there was nothing to see—no way to detect him.

"Are you all right?" Nicolae asked.

MaryAnn pressed her hand against her aching breast. Strangely, she felt flushed—more than that, in a heightened sexual state. She took a slow, deep breath and let it out. "I'm fine, Nicolae. Here are the towels." Had she been daydreaming? For a moment, she couldn't remember going into the bathroom. She thought only of a man touching her skin, sliding his mouth down her throat to her breast. She wanted to open her blouse and look at her skin, touch her body, feel hands on her. But Nicolae was already striding down the hall, casting small suspicious glances over his shoulder, and remembering he could read her thoughts, she hastily followed him forcing inane chatter about Christmas trees.

15

"Natalya, just what are you doing with that hairspray and lighter?" Vikirnoff Von Shrieder demanded. He peered out the kitchen window to the silent sparkling white world surrounding them. "There aren't any vampires around, are there?"

"Don't be silly. I've learned to call down the lightning when I'm fighting a vampire. I needed a flame thingie for the crème brûlée. See, it says so right here on the recipe." Natalya bent forward to reread the card she had on the low-tiled counter.

"Give it up. The silly recipe isn't worth the amount of time you have put into it." Vikirnoff came up behind her and circled her waist with his arms, drawing her back up against him.

"I thought you always wanted June Cleaver cooking in the kitchen with her little apron on," Natalya teased.

"It was you who mentioned June Cleaver, but I do like the apron," he admitted, kissing his way down the side of her face. His hands burrowed under the thin material stretching to cover her breasts. "If you wore this all the time, I might consider trying out one of these strange concoctions you seem to be attempting to whip up."

He nibbled on the back of her neck and let his hands slide down her flat stomach to the junction of her legs beneath the short apron. His palm caressed the short curls, and moved up to cover the birthmark in the shape of a dragon. The pads of his fingers traced the familiar shape, and then moved on around her hips to her firm bare buttocks. *"Ainaak enyém,* you do not have a single stitch on beneath this apron."

She leaned forward just a little more to peer at the recipe and frown at her concoction. The action brought her enticing derrière brushing the front of his body, sending a small electrical charge right through his groin. "I don't think anyone who cooks actually wears clothes. It's too messy. I changed three times and gave it up."

His hands continued their journey, shaping her hips and running over her bottom to slide over her thighs. He felt her shiver of awareness—of answering excitement. "So humans stand in the kitchen stark naked and cook." Once more his hands moved, widening her stance, caressing the inside of her thighs, going higher so his knuckles could brush back and forth across her sensitive core.

"I'm certain of it," Natalya said. "I've discovered their secret." She closed her eyes to absorb the feel of his hands on her bare skin.

His mouth nuzzled her neck, tongue stroking caresses over her pulse, teeth teasing and nipping. "I will ask Slavica's husband if that is why he spends so much time in the kitchen with her. I wondered what they did together in that big room with so many counters."

His teeth sank deep, locking them together, his larger body bending hers forward, pinning her against the low counter and his body. His clothes were gone and his body already hard and aggressive, his fingers pushing slowly, seductively into her body so that she gasped and pushed back against him, already wet and welcoming for him. Already hot. He loved her ready response and the way her body began to ride his hand eagerly.

His hands went to her hips, holding her still, preventing all movement, so she waited for his attentions, unable to bring any pleasure to herself.

"You started this," Natalya complained.

He didn't answer, savoring the spicy taste of her, the way her smaller body waited for his, open and ready, so vulnerable and so willing. It was a heady feeling to be able to take a woman warrior, to wrap his body around hers when she was every bit as lethal as she was beautiful. He held her down with one hand on her back, heightening her pleasure, forcing her to wait for him, breathless, her hips trying to entice him, her body wet and needy. He loved especially when she grew anxious and demanding, yet submitted to his domination—like now.

Vikirnoff swept his tongue across the pinpricks, waited again, waiting for the telltale beat of her heart to accelerate, and he thrust hard, driving deep into her, burying himself all the way. She cried out, a low keen of joy as they joined together. She was so tight, a fist clamping around his shaft, hot and velvet soft, slick with welcoming cream. He took her hard and fast, driving her over the edge without preamble so that her body clamped down and her orgasm rushed over her, rocking her legs, rippling through her belly and crashing through her womb.

He kept the pounding rhythm, moving like a piston, dragging her back with every forward surge so they came together in heat and aggression. He could feel the streaks of lightning racing through her bloodstream, gathering—building, always building, the pressure relentless so that after the first rush to bring more sensitivity to the bundle of nerve endings, he kept her poised on the edge, pushing her higher and higher until she was nearly sobbing for relief.

Vikirnoff could stay there all day, his body buried deep in silk and fire, her tight muscles squeezing and grasping, her body subject to the rule of his. Her hair spilled around her, banded with color, her skin soft and inviting and every square inch of her, every hollow and shadow, his to do with as he pleased.

Right now he felt her tigress close, clawing toward the *surface*, wild and abandoned, adding fuel to the fire, wanting him rough, wanting him to match the cat rising with heat in her. He threw back his head, nearly coming up on his toes, surging deep over and over, so that the friction was nearly intolerable, a pleasure bordering on pain that went on and on because he dictated it so. Because her body was his body when they came together like this. She gave herself to him unconditionally, trusting him to bring her absolute ecstasy, and it was his privilege to accommodate her. Because they needed this sometimes more than anything else, this coming together almost in violence after they had both been alone for so very long.

He murmured softly to her in his own language. "*Te avio päläfertiilam.*

Ainaak sívamet jutta." You are my lifemate. Forever to my heart connected— forever mine.

She answered with one of the few words of the ancient language she knew, her heart in her voice. *"Sívamet."* My love. And she meant it.

Vikirnoff plunged into her until her breath was coming in gasping sobs and his body burned with a kind of fury, until their hunger for each other was so sharp and terrible there was no holding back. Her body tightened around his, clamping down with hard spasms that sent fire racing down his spine straight to his balls. His entire body shuddered as he thrust one more time, hard steel penetrating hot silk, as he emptied himself into her deepest core, further uniting them.

He lay over her, holding her close, kissing her back, nuzzling her neck, all the while trying to struggle for air. Their hearts beat the same rhythm, but the gnawing hunger, so insatiable, was still there. He could feel it in her, stirring and clawing like the greedy cat inside her, and also deep in him, where his demon roared for its mate.

Very slowly, very reluctantly, he separated their bodies and allowed her to straighten up. He crowded close, not giving her space, establishing his intentions with his wandering mouth and hands.

"I always knew you liked the June Cleaver thing. You have a secret food fetish," she told him with a small smile.

"I will admit to a fetish, but I think it's for you." He bent his dark head as he dragged her even closer, forcing her to bend backward so she offered her breasts to him. He lapped at the sensitized nipples, drew her breast into his mouth, sucking with strong pulls, teeth teasing, causing aftershocks to ripple through her body. *"Ainaak enyém,* forever mine," he whispered. "You know you are my heart and soul. My very life."

Natalya loved the way his hair brushed over her skin, the way his mouth was so eager for her. She could lose herself in his body all night, never think of anything—or anyone else. He looked at her and wanted her. One brush of her hand set him on fire. Once he had taken her right in the village, shielding them from prying eyes, but it felt so decadent. She had deliberately tempted him, allowing her fingers to trail over the front of his trousers, rubbing against him, her blouse gaping open to show her breasts—and he had responded in just the way she loved. He shoved her against a wall and took her right there, unable to wait one more second. She loved teasing him, see-ing the heat building in his eyes and that stern mask disappear only for her.

He always told her how much he loved her—how much she meant to him. She found it difficult to put her emotions into words, afraid if she tried to voice the depth of her emotion, that would somehow take it away from her. She had never loved the way she loved him. She hadn't even known it was possible.

Vikirnoff reluctantly released her breasts, skimming her mouth with feather-light kisses before straightening. "Did you hear something?"

"Someone is in the woods near our house." She wrapped her arm around his head and drew him back down, her mouth melting provocatively with his. Heat flared instantly. Her tongue dueled with his, teasing and stroking while her hands slid over his body. Her fingers danced over the hard length of him, satisfaction making her purr as he grew thicker and harder. She wrapped her hand around him and bent down to breathe warm air over him.

His shaft jumped. She licked him much like a cat licking cream. The moist heat of her mouth engulfed him, spreading fire through his belly. He forgot visitors and caught two fistfuls of tawny hair, dragging her closer as he thrust with his hips, surging deep into her mouth. She went to her knees, wrapping her arms around his hips and taking him down her throat, squeez-ing and nibbling and licking until he thought he might go insane from sheer pleasure.

Natalya never did anything halfway, abandoning herself to the joy of serving him, of taking all power through her joy of sex. She loved touching him and tasting him and drawing out every drop of his seed just to see how fast she could bring him back to a fever pitch.

She made a small little purring noise deep in her throat that sent a vibra-tion right through his shaft, and spread out to his entire body. His balls drew tight and hard, and every nerve in his body seemed centered in his groin. Lust was sharp and hungry and raking at his insides as he watched her lips slide over his shaft and he felt the white hot curl of her tongue, the heart-stopping edge of her teeth.

"Harder," he bit out through clenched teeth. She was close to swallowing him, doing something fantastic with her tongue and throat muscles.

She looked up at him and there was so much joy in her eyes. For him. For her ability to give him this gift. If it was possible, she tightened her throat and flicked with her tongue, pushing him over edge just as fast and hard as he had pushed her. Fire streaked through his bloodstream, tore though his body. She milked him with her tight hot mouth, with his fists twisted almost violently in her hair holding her still while he thrust help-lessly, going as deep as he could. His body shattered, from his toes to his head, burst into flames as jet after jet of seed was drawn from him.

Woman, you are killing me. And it felt like it, a beautiful death. He dragged her to her feet, not relinquishing his hold on her hair, his mouth finding her breasts, feeling her heightened desire. He flicked her nipples, felt the ripple of response rush through her body. He bit down gently, felt her jump, her womb clench and spasm.

"I love doing that to you," she whispered. "It always makes me so hot to see you like that, and you always give me what I want. And I want more, Vikirnoff. I want much, much more."

"I am always ready to accommodate you."

Natalya wrapped one bare leg around him, rubbing against his thigh. "Keeping me happy is a full-time job."

He reached down and lifted her with casual strength, turning her so he could rest her bare bottom on the counter. "You have nowhere to run, *sívamet.*"

Secretly, it was one of her favorite things when he spoke his ancient lan-guage and called her his love. His accent was sexy and intriguing and his words seemed a secret world no one else could share. "Was I running? Being in the kitchen, surrounded by all this food, I was hoping you'd be hungry."

Vikirnoff laughed softly, his eyes going midnight dark. "I am always hun-gry for you." He simply pushed her thighs wide, lifting her legs over his shoul-der, and bent his head to the sweet scent of her hot core. He licked her in much the same manner as she had him, a cat lapping at cream. He knew every spot intimately, every secret hollow and what it could do to her. He made slow lazy circles around her sensitive bud, torturing her until she wanted to scream with pleasure. Her thighs jumped helplessly, hips arching toward him, as his fingers slipped into her heated channel adding to the pressure so his tongue could lap at her, suckle and stab with wicked expertise.

He did just what she asked for, but in a manner she could never conceive of. He ate her—devoured her, using his tongue as effectively as he used his shaft. His fingers only added to her slow torment, pushing her far beyond her limits into another realm.

Natalya bucked against his mouth, her body raging for release as he worked his magic. Her head thrashed wildly back and forth. Her body built up pressure fast, needing release, the tension winding tighter and tighter until she thought she might implode. Vikirnoff always held her off, pushing her further than she thought she could ever go, until she was pleading with him, sobbing, almost insane with arousal.

A sensation somewhere between pleasure and bordering on pain gripped her stomach fiercely, tightening her womb, and spread through her body. Her breath slammed out of her lungs and she swore her insides nearly convulsed. She shuddered as the spasms continued and wave after wave of sheer ecstasy washed over her.

Before she had a chance to catch her breath, Vikirnoff brought her hips down, holding her legs apart, and slammed deep into her slick hot folds. She screamed. There was no stopping the cries of pleasure as her body orgasmed again and again.

He pressed down against her small bud, as he slammed deeper and deeper, needing to hear those soft cries, to see her throat working convulsively and feel her body rippling with so much pleasure. He thrust hard, building the friction until her face was flushed and her mouth was open and her eyes wide with shock and lust. Only then did he take her over the edge a second time.

Natalya lay under him, clutching his shoulders, desperate to regain control. Only Vikirnoff could shatter her like that, and it was the only time she felt total release, relaxed and free of all the responsibility she had carried for so long. She turned up her face for his kiss. She loved his mouth and what it did to her. She loved everything about him. "Someone is at the door," she said softly as she kissed the corners of his mouth and ran her lips down his throat to his chest.

"It's just my brother and he can wait," Vikirnoff said, his hands cupping her breasts again, thumbs stroking, sending vibrations through her entire body. "I have far more important things to do."

Back off, Nicolae. I am just a little busy here. He sent the impression of bared teeth for good measure, but his brother only sent back amusement.

Her tongue swirled over his pulse. Her teeth scraped and his entire body contracted in anticipation.

The knock at the door persisted. Vikirnoff swore. "I'm killing him." Abruptly he left her, striding across the room.

"Put some clothes on," she reminded him with a little mischievous grin. "You just might need them."

Vikirnoff just managed to don a shirt and jeans as he jerked open the door. "Did you not hear my . . ." He broke off, recognizing his visitor. One hand raked through his hair. He glanced back at the kitchen. *You knew.* "Mikhail."

Of course. I was looking out for you. Her laughter tightened his body all over again. She even managed to blow in his ear.

I'm thinking of spanking you.

The last time I rather liked it. You were rather wild that night.

His body jumped again, swelling beneath the thin material of his jeans. Her voice was seductive, suggestive, almost purring. He tried to manage a smile of greeting, grateful his shirt wasn't tucked in.

Mikhail's dark eyes slid over him, taking in far too much. "You failed to scan. You should have known it was me and not Nicolae."

"My woman is far too distracting," Vikirnoff admitted. "I think of little else." He stepped back to allow Mikhail entry. *I'm killing my brother. He's probably laughing like a hyena right now. He must have known and could have warned me.*

"Welcome to the club," Mikhail said, but shook his head. "It takes a great deal of discipline to learn to satisfy their needs as well as see to their protection."

Their needs? Natalya sniffed. *You cannot go two hours without sex.*

I take no responsibility for that. You are an addiction.

Natalya's soft laughter brushed through Vikirnoff's mind teasing his senses.

"I just dropped by to make certain you had everything you needed for tonight," said Mikhail. "I have a couple more stops to make before I can go home, and Raven is waiting."

"We're fine. Natalya is making some strange thing." He glanced nervously toward the kitchen. "Unfortunately, it calls for a flame of some sort, and you know how she is so inventive. We could have a fire any minute."

"I heard that!" Natalya called. "For your information, it is working. Well, I did set the curtain on fire and there's a scorch mark or two on the wall."

"She isn't joking, is she?" Mikhail said as the smell of smoke drifted toward them.

Vikirnoff heaved a sigh. "Regrettably, no."

"I will leave you to it then. Let Natalya know Gregori will be playing the role of Santa Claus tonight. She was concerned that no one would be doing it and she volunteered you."

"She what?" Vikirnoff scowled toward the kitchen.

"And she said if they needed an elf for the pageant, that you look rather elvish in tights." Mikhail's features were completely expressionless.

"She said all that?" *I am so spanking your bare little ass.*

Promises, promises.

"I am not certain we have need of an elf, but I'm going to check with Sara and Corrine. They're the ones putting the pageant together, and I'll let them know you offered."

Vikirnoff rubbed the bridge of his nose thoughtfully. "Mikhail, I am fully aware that you are the prince and as such should be protected at all times, but should you deliver that particular message to those women, I will be forced to cut off your head and stuff it somewhere unpleasant."

Mikhail nodded, still without expression. "I think that is a fair reaction and one I myself might have. Suffice to say we understand each other perfectly."

"On the other hand, should you really command Gregori to perform as Santa Claus, I would ask for a front row seat."

Mikhail held out his hand. "Done."

Vikirnoff, I have need of you and Natalya. Nicolae's troubled voice filled his mind as Vikirnoff shook the prince's hand.

He waited for Mikhail to dissolve into vapor and trail through the scattered trees toward Corrine and Dayan's home before responding to his brother. *We are on the way.* "Natalya. Nicolae needs us immediately."

"I was just putting the finishing touches on this thing. It smells funny."

"That's probably the lighter fluid—or the hair spray. I imagine it tastes as funny as it smells."

Do not let on to my lifemate that anything could be wrong, Nicolae warned. *If Destiny thinks for one moment that someone—or something—has tried to harm MaryAnn, she will go ballistic on me. She does not trust many people yet, and MaryAnn is family to her.*

Vikirnoff whirled around, his lazy, casual demeanor gone at once. *And to me. Tell me what you believe.* He shared the information with Natalya.

I have a blood bond with MaryAnn and I can feel something is not right. I thought a vampire had come into my home and taken her blood, but I cannot get a feel for it. Perhaps Natalya's birthmark will roar for us and let me know for certain. MaryAnn remembers nothing, but she seems disturbed, restless, definitely different. And I feel uneasy in my home.

Vikirnoff reached for Natalya's hand as she hurried to join him. *Have you examined her memories?* They both dissolved, shimmering into droplets of vapor and streaming outdoors toward Nicolae's home.

Of course I have. Over and over. Something happened to her right here, in our home. If a vampire has penetrated our defenses, I need to know. There was a moment's hesitation. *And if a Carpathian has used her to feed when she is under my protection and also Gregori's, that is a killing offense. This is a very dangerous situation.*

Vikirnoff could not imagine that Nicolae could be mistaken. If he said something was off, then no doubt it was. What Carpathian would dare risk the wrath of two ancient warriors as well as that of the "Dark One"? Everyone knew Gregori was an executioner. One did not take chances with such a man. The attacker had to be a vampire, but how could a vampire slip past an ancient into his very home?

Vikirnoff and Natalya settled into their normal forms just outside Nicolae's home. They made a circle of the house, looking for tracks, for some sign that an enemy was near. Natalya put her hand over her birthmark and shook her head.

"The dragon is silent, Vikirnoff. There isn't a vampire nearby, nor any evidence that one has been in the vicinity recently."

"But something is off."

"I agree, but I can't figure out exactly what it is."

She inhaled sharply, her eyes going from brilliant green to sea blue and finally opaque. Stripes banded across her hair, orange and black and even white. She dropped to all fours, fur rippled and the majestic tigress paced around the house, using her cat senses to try to find an enemy.

Vikirnoff followed the tiger back into the woods. It padded patiently through the brush and snowdrifts, following an elusive scent he couldn't quite catch. Natalya regained her natural form a few yards from the house.

"Someone watched them from over there." She indicated a thick tree. "I cannot catch his scent. He's very clever. He uses what is natural around him, mimicking whatever he chooses so that only that is seen or smelled. He watched them drag the tree into their home and must have entered at that same time. They were distracted by the Christmas tree and not paying any attention to the something like a wind or small snow flurry. I'm betting he used both. There would have been snow flying from the tree."

"He's smart this one. An ancient with very sophisticated ways. Why would he choose to go after MaryAnn when she is doubly protected?"

"The challenge of it? A dare maybe. Beating Gregori and the ancients protecting MaryAnn?" she guessed.

"And the penalty, if caught, might be death? Certainly, Destiny would kill him. She's extremely protective of MaryAnn. Nor can I see Nicolae allowing such an insult to his house. And if he didn't kill the attacker—I would. MaryAnn saved both my brother and Destiny. She gave Destiny back her life, and in doing so, gave Nicolae life. I will not allow her to be used in this manner."

"Be careful of what you say," Natalya reminded him, taking his hand. "Destiny is very edgy when it comes to MaryAnn."

Both made a long, slow perusal of the area. Were eyes watching? It felt that way, yet for all of their skills, they couldn't ferret out the enemy.

MaryAnn greeted them at the door, her smile genuine. "Vikirnoff. Natalya. It's so good to see you. We've just been putting up the Christmas tree. Skyler is visiting us. Have you met her?" She indicated the young teenager, who stood staring transfixed at Natalya.

Vikirnoff took MaryAnn's hand and bowed low, startling her, his lips touching her skin. He inhaled deeply and allowed her hand to drop away. "You look wonderful."

Natalya stepped close and hugged her, kissing both cheeks. "You do look radiant. Are you looking forward to tonight?"

She does look radiant. She's always been beautiful, but now she has a dangerous allure about her. And a male has definitely been close to her. Very close. His scent is eluding me; not even my tigress can pick it up. I won't be able to track him. But he isn't vampire. He's Carpathian.

MaryAnn smiled at them both. "Yes, of course. Everyone's been so good to me. We were just about to walk Skyler home. Would you like to come with us?"

Natalya crossed the room to the teenager. The girl stepped back avoiding physical contact. Natalya smiled at her. "It's nice to finally meet you. You must have difficult psychic gifts. Can you read people when you touch them?"

Skyler nodded. "I don't like it."

"I don't like it either." She glanced over her shoulder and Vikirnoff took the hint, taking MaryAnn by the elbow and walking with her into the kitchen, leaving Natalya with the younger girl. "You seem a little nervous. Are you really sensitive as well? I often have this dread that swamps me when something dangerous is near."

Skyler nodded. "I hate that too. You never know if you're crazy or if something really is out there stalking you." She glanced uneasily out the window.

Natalya nodded. "It does feel like that. If you tell, people think you're weird, especially if they can't see or find anything wrong. And if you don't tell and something bad happens, you feel like an idiot for not telling."

"That's happened to you too?" Skyler asked. "It's difficult being here because there's so much energy being used all the time and sometimes I can't tell the difference."

"Did you feel something earlier, when you were with Nicolae and Destiny getting the tree?" Deliberately she avoided using MaryAnn's name.

Skyler nodded slowly. "Usually I can tell if something is evil, but it just felt dark and like someone was watching us. It didn't feel good."

"Why didn't you tell Nicolae?"

Skyler looked away. "I didn't want to feel stupid. And none of them felt anything. They're Carpathians—ancients like Gabriel. Shouldn't they know if something is out there stalking us?"

Natalya remained silent for a long moment allowing the teenager to squirm. "That isn't the real reason. Why didn't you tell them?"

Skyler blinked, looked as if she might cry. She turned away, shoving her hands into her pockets. "I thought it might be Dimitri," she admitted in a low voice. "I didn't want to get him into any more trouble on my account."

Natalya gentled her voice, knowing the recent problems through the Carpathians' common path. "I know what that feels like too. Wanting to protect someone and feeling like you're the one causing all the trouble for them." She sighed. "I still don't know how I managed to get together with Vikirnoff. I'm not at all what he wanted." She waited until Skyler turned back to look at her. "Did it feel like him?"

"It just felt like someone was watching us." Skyler frowned.

"Do you feel it now? This minute?"

"That's what's crazy. On and off. Like he's here, but then he's gone. Could someone do that? Could someone be watching me even here in the house?" She shivered. "I just want to go home."

"We'll take care of you, honey. Vikirnoff, Nicolae, Destiny and I are all very capable when it comes to vampire attacks. None of us would let anything hurt you."

"What if it's Dimitri?" Skyler whispered. "He tries to block me out, but I can feel his pain. I caused that. It hurts him so much, but I can't stop it. I can't be what he needs me to be."

"He's a Carpathian male, Skyler. He'll do whatever it takes for you to be happy."

"I don't want to be responsible for him."

"I know." And God help her, she did. Natalya fought Vikirnoff every inch of the way, not trusting who or what he was. "You don't need to think about it yet. You're a child. Let yourself be one. From everything I've heard of Francesca, she will get you through this, and time has a way of working things out."

The others came in, drawing on jackets. "Are you ready, Skyler?"

The girl nodded, casting one more nervous look around the house. Destiny and MaryAnn went out with Skyler between them. Nicolae followed with Natalya, but Vikirnoff slammed the door closed and stood just inside the house, his senses flaring out in an effort to find the intruder. Like his brother, he felt something, but he couldn't find it. Whatever, *whoever*, remained in the house was an ancient and very powerful and skilled.

He turned abruptly and left, slamming the door hard enough to make the windows rattle. *Nicolae. I doubt that it is vampire. It has to be a male using her for blood. Is there any sign whatsoever of any kind of other attack on her?*

The thought that a male Carpathian would use a protected woman—a potential lifemate—and she would not be aware was distasteful to him.

Nicolae sighed. *Many of our unattached males are in the vicinity. There is no telling who it is. I couldn't get a scent.*

We have to be dealing with a very skilled ancient.

Vikirnoff moved up closer to Natalya, scanning, not liking the way the clouds overhead began to swirl and darken. The wind rushed at them, kicking up the snow as they moved in a tight group toward the house where Gabriel was staying. Skyler kept shooting anxious little glances toward the deeper woods.

"Have you ever flown with Gabriel?" Nicolae asked her.

"Or run with the wolves?" Vikirnoff added.

"Or a tigress?" Natalya volunteered.

Skyler's gaze jumped to her face. "I love animals. Wolves especially. But I always wanted to be close to a tiger. Is it dangerous?"

"Whoa!" MaryAnn held up her hand. "I know you're not going to do something crazy right in front of me. I'll go back to the house. My heart can only take so much."

"You wouldn't really like to fly, MaryAnn?" Destiny coaxed. "Or pet a wolf or a tiger? Just once, to say you did it?"

MaryAnn looked at Skyler's hopeful face. She sighed. "Okay, here's the thing. I'm really not adventurous at all. I'm a real city girl, you know, boutiques and girlfriends shopping in a mall, not petting wolves. But if you really want to do this, child, I'll climb one of those trees over there and watch you do it."

Nicolae slung one arm around Skyler and the other around MaryAnn. "We were thinking more of you riding on the back of one of the wolves."

Lightning edged the sky, turned the darker clouds to a fiery orange. A whip lashed out and slammed to the ground, rocking the earth and scorching a long streak in the snow. Thunder clapped directly overhead. In the deafening roar, a beast growled a distinct warning, sending the hair on the back of their necks up.

Skyler stepped away from Nicolae looking anxious. "Was that Dimitri? He doesn't like it if anyone touches me."

Vikirnoff and Nicolae exchanged a long look. "I don't know, honey. We'll talk to him later about it. I can't see him angry over one of us being affectionate. We have lifemates."

"He knows it bothers me to be touched," she admitted.

"Well, if it was him, then he's within his rights to protect you. He would want to keep you safe and happy and if it was bothering you that one of us made you uncomfortable, then he would send a reminder."

MaryAnn moved closer to Destiny, one hand going to a spot just over her breast where it throbbed and burned. She pressed hard with her palm, holding the ache to her. She hated being afraid all the time, and here, in these mountains, she seemed to have lost her usual confidence. In a city she would walk into the worst parts of town and feel in complete control, but here, in this world, nothing was as it seemed. And she wanted no part of wild animals or men who could reprimand others with violent storms.

"Let's just get Skyler to her house and get back home," she said.

16

The sound of music filled the small house Dayan, of the Dark Troubadours, occupied with his family. Two guitars played softly as Dayan's
voice rose in a lullaby. Abruptly, Corinne put down her guitar, leaned
over the crib and shook her head. "She's not going to sleep, Dayan, not even
with that beautiful song you wrote for her. She knows we're having Christmas tonight and she wants to go."

Dayan put his own guitar aside and tried to look stern as he stood beside
his lifemate over their infant daughter. She was tiny, barely fifteen pounds
now, yet she looked back at them with far too much intelligence, and he was
very much afraid she ruled their lives. She was just such a miracle to them
both, and they had fought so hard for her—were still fighting. Her little
body was fragile, although her will was strong.

"Young lady, you are supposed to be taking a nap."

One small hand waved toward his face. His heart lurched in his chest
the way it always did when he looked at his child. She didn't look in the least
bit sleepy as she cooed at him, coaxing him with her wide open eyes to pick
her up. "She takes after you," he murmured. "With that little stubborn
streak. Too beautiful for words, and wanting her own way, even when it isn't
good for her."

Corinne nudged him with her hip, but it was too late; the smile had slipped out and the baby saw it. She smiled back at Dayan and he was lost. He reached down and picked her up, cuddling her close.

"Little Miss Jen, you are so naughty," Corinne said. "I was just about to go for a run too, before all the madness starts. Now what am I going to do with you?"

"She likes to go. We can put her in the pack," Dayan said.

"It's too cold."

Dayan leaned down to nuzzle his daughter's face. "She's getting good at regulating her body temperature and we can dress her warm. We're taking her to the inn later, and that's not much different. She wants to go, Corinne. She loves it when you run with her."

Corinne loved to run. She'd had a bad heart all of her life, preventing her from doing anything physical, and now that she was Carpathian, she couldn't run enough. It made her feel free and whole and so very happy. Back home in the States, she ran with a stroller, so Baby Jennifer could feel the same happiness flowing through her, but here, in the mountains of Romania, the trails were too rough for the stroller and she was afraid of jarring the baby if she used the front-pack.

"I need to run and I do love taking her with me. Running clears my mind and after all this cooking and helping Sara with the children, sewing costumes and rehearsals, I definitely could use some exercise," Corinne explained.

"Baby," he said, one hand curling around the nape of her neck to bring her head to his. He kissed her, a slow gentle declaration of his love. "You don't ever have to make excuses to me. If you want to go out for a run, then we will. It isn't safe to go by yourself, but we don't mind going with you, do we, Jen?"

The baby smiled up at them both, happy to have her way.

"I wouldn't be alone," Corinne tried one last time, reluctant to take the infant out in the cold. "I scanned and Nicolae and Destiny with several others are quite close to the house. I'd be safe with them. You can stay here and keep warm."

"We're going with you, but you have to carry the baby," Dayan said decisively. "It will just take us a minute to get ready." He was already changing the baby's clothes, wrapping her snugly in warm clothes and donning his own outdoor gear. "You know you won't be able to run in the snow like normal. You'll have to use your abilities, to skim lightly over the surface. It takes a little bit of concentration, but you'll get the hang of it. While you're doing it, you'll still have to keep the baby's motion to a minimum."

"You're certain you want to do this with me?"

"Yes." He wasn't about to let her go out alone, and he needed his hands free in order to defend them both should there be need.

Corinne adjusted the front-pack and waited until Dayan had put the baby down into it, securing her and wrapping her up with a tiny hooded jacket. "With all the Carpathians in the area, don't you think it would be suicide for a vampire to attack one of us? Look what happened to the one who went after Juliette De La Cruz. I think he must have had a death wish. The De La Cruz brothers are just plain scary."

"The De La Cruz family was always very powerful, according to Darius. He says they are ancients, somewhat secretive, and have very incredible skills. He has a great deal of respect for their power, and coming from Darius, that's saying a lot."

"So why would a vampire target a De La Cruz woman? I'm telling you, none of this makes sense. Most of the women here are probably descendents of the jaguar line. Juliette definitely has stronger blood ties to that lineage than most, but still, the vampire drew her out. Didn't he? Wasn't he specific to her fears?"

"I don't really know. There's been some talk about it, but no one really knows what's going on. But that was the second attack, Corinne," Dayan reminded. "Lesser vampires are often used by much more powerful ones. I'm not willing to take any chances. I think we've got one hanging around waiting for an opportunity and it isn't going to be with my family."

"I still say they'd be utterly stupid to hang around here with so many Carpathian hunters gathered in one spot. Why would they do that?"

Dayan shrugged. "It's an old battle tactic. Harassing the lines continually eventually weakens them. And they are definitely striking at our women now." He glanced at the baby. *And our children.*

Maybe we shouldn't go then. I can do without running this evening. I just was cooped up for so long with all those children. I don't know how Sara does it. One is enough for me.

Ours is a handful. Dayan bent to brush a kiss across the back of the baby's head. "We take precautions, Corinne. We don't change our lives. You want to go running, we'll go. And like you said, it's good practice for you. The more you practice using Carpathian methods, the better you'll be at them. We'll be safe enough with all the others in the area as well. We'll head toward them."

"Falcon dropped by to take most of the food to the inn already, so nearly everything is done," Corinne said, as she opened the door. "He and Sara were going over the last minute rehearsals with the kids. The children are so excited. Even for Falcon, they wouldn't calm down, and they adore him."

"I noticed Jen really responds to him as well," Dayan said, turning back to add safeguards around the house. He didn't want any surprises when they returned. Corinne had embraced the Carpathian life, his way of life, and she'd never looked back, seemingly had no regrets, but it was important to him that she never did. He had come so close to losing her—losing both mother and child—and he wanted her life to be smooth and happy—to give her anything he could.

Corinne put her hand on his arm and smiled up at him, her heart in her eyes. "Falcon's gentle like you and the children respond to that. You're such a poet, Dayan."

He groaned softly, tucking away the fact that he was secretly pleased she saw him that way. "Don't let Darius hear you say that. I'll never hear the end of it."

She laughed as she began a slow jog, skimming over the snow, trying to get the feel of how to place her feet to stay on the surface. "You're all so afraid of Darius. Have you even watched him with Tempest? He's a total pushover. He just can't be that scary."

"You even say that about Gregori," Dayan pointed out, keeping pace with her.

"He was wonderful to me and to the baby. The man is a teddy bear."

Dayan snorted. "I've heard him called a lot of things, but teddy bear is not one of them."

She shot him a small loving smile. Dayan felt his heart melt. She did it so easily. A look. A touch. And his world was right. All those years on the stage with so many women throwing themselves at him, not seeing him, not caring who he was. And then Corinne. She'd given him life.

"You gave it to me," she said softly, showing him she was becoming adept at being a shadow in his mind. "You gave me life." For a moment she reached out to take his hand, connecting all three of them. Baby, mother and father.

Dayan's heart swelled. He loved having a family. He would always love it.

Corinne shot him a mischievous smile. "Keep up, music man." She bolted, running like a machine, smooth and fluid, her body moving easily, heart and lungs in perfect synchronization. Dayan ran behind her because he loved to watch her run. It was something she had wanted more than anything, something that had been denied her all of her life. Others took it for granted, but Corinne enjoyed every single step she took. He could always feel her enjoyment, and he knew the baby felt it too. Jennifer always loved to go running with her mother, and Dayan knew it was the waves of happiness rolling off Corinne that both he and his daughter wanted to bask in.

Corinne was impervious to the cold, but not to the sparkling beauty around her. The trees were transformed, branches laden with white crystals, so that they glittered with millions of gems. She felt like she was running in a fairy-tale world with her handsome prince. Her daughter snuggled tightly against her chest, rocking gently, as if in a cradle, adding to the surreal effect.

Corinne flung out her arms. "I love my life!" She shouted it to the sky, happiness bursting through her until she couldn't contain it.

Dayan smiled, even while he was scanned the area around them for enemies. They were closing the distance to Nicolae and Destiny and the small group of people with them. He could tell the couple and their friends were walking in the general direction of Francesca and Gabriel's home, so the young girl had to be Skyler. He was beginning to know individual scents now and it helped ease his mind. He was used to living in the much smaller family of the Dark Troubadours. Even that had grown recently as each had found a lifemate. He was the only one of the Troubadours with a child, but he hoped that would change soon so Jennifer would grow up with other children around her.

Corinne listened to the steady beat of her heart. It always amazed her to hear that rhythmic beat, to feel strength in her arms and legs and be able to breathe easily even while she was running. She took a step, blew air out and her heart skipped. Missed a beat. She heard it clearly, felt the invasive weakness slide into her body. The breath left her lungs in a rush and she faltered, stumbling. Her heart missed another beat. She stopped running, wrapping her arms around the baby, holding her close, her mind racing, terror gripping her.

Was it possible her heart had been so damaged that even conversion to a Carpathian couldn't keep it going? She heard it distinctly, the beat, a skip, two beats, another skip. Fast. Slow. She turned to Dayan, eyes wide with shock.

"What is it?" He stepped back away from her, turning in a circle, searching the area around them for any enemies.

"Can't you hear it?" Her voice shook.

Dayan listened to the night, sorting the sounds muffled by the snow. He could hear voices in the distance, knew Nicolae and his brother were close. *Something is wrong.* He sent them the message on the common telepathic path.

There was a moment of silence. *We're coming to you from the south.* Nicolae responded. *We have MaryAnn and Skyler to protect.*

We have the baby.

Dayan felt edgy, troubled, but he couldn't find a blank spot that might indicate a vampire. They weren't alone, someone or something was watching, but he couldn't find a location. It didn't appear a vampire was the threat. He swore under his breath, startling Corinne.

"Can you hear it?"

He didn't want to hear it. The baby had a regular heart rate, faster than an adult, but Corinne's heartbeat was irregular. Even when he put his hand over her heart and tried to regulate the beat, it was all over the place. He forced calm when he really felt panic. He would not lose her. Not to anything or anybody.

"Do you think my heart is failing?"

"I want to wait for the others to get to us before I check. If I go into your body and we are attacked, the vampire would have the advantage."

"Do you think we'll be attacked?" Corinne tightened her hold on the baby, her arms wrapping around the infant protectively. She looked carefully around the area, up into the trees and along the snow-covered ground. "Why can't I feel a vampire if there's one close? And how would a vampire affect my heart? It must be failing. The healing was only able to last a couple of months, Dayan."

He kept his palm over Corinne's heart, in order to keep her heart beating in rhythm with his. "That isn't true, Corinne. I don't know what's going on, but when the conversion was completed, Gregori made certain your heart was whole and healthy."

Nicolae and Destiny came striding through the trees, MaryAnn and Skyler in between them. Destiny was to the young teen's right, several feet between them, her restless eyes searching the ground while Nicolae searched the terrain. Above them flew two owls, circling the warriors, working their way through the canopy to try to spot an enemy from above.

Nicolae reached Corinne and Dayan, his gaze jumping to the protective way Dayan had his hand placed over Corinne's heart. In the muffled silence of the snow, they could hear the irregular heartbeat overly loud. "Vikirnoff and Natalya search from above. What is it?"

"I don't know," Dayan said. "I feel something out here, Nicolae, but I cannot find it. And whatever it is, Corinne's heart is responding."

Vikirnoff and Natalya spiraled down to earth, taking their natural forms, Natalya in leather, weapons everywhere. The warriors spread out, keeping MaryAnn, Skyler and Corinne with her baby in the center. Corinne's heart faltered and her legs went out from under her.

MaryAnn caught her before she could fall to the ground. She helped her to sit and knelt beside her, screening the baby from anything that could be close and intend harm. "We need Gregori," she said. "Someone call him."

Skyler lifted her face to the sky and spun around, an alarmed look on her face. MaryAnn flung out a restraining arm when she went to move outside the circle, but Skyler avoided contact and stepped outside the circle to face toward the inn. "It's here again. I feel it. A steady current of energy." She shuddered and wrapped her arms around her stomach, distaste flickering across her face. Her palm crossed over her wrist and she rubbed as if it was aching.

Vikirnoff frowned, watching her, as the others tried to identify what the younger girl was feeling. "Let me see," he said, and reached for her wrist.

Skyler screamed and backed away from her, sheer terror on her face. She put her arm behind her back, turned and ran. Natalya signaled the men off and she went after the girl, moving with blurring speed, catching her before Skyler could get away from the protection of the warriors.

"What is it? What did you think Vikirnoff would do?" she asked gently.

Skyler stilled in her arms, her heart thundering, her mouth dry. She shook her head. "I don't know. I don't know what happened."

Natalya touched her mind very lightly, a soft probe, and found blankness, an impenetrable wall hiding memories.

"Do you feel it?" Skyler asked, her eyes pleading with Natalya. "I'm not crazy. I can feel it disturbing the air. It's so subtle."

Natalya inhaled sharply, opened her mind, utilizing more than her Carpathian senses. She dug down, reached for her lineage, the part of her that was mage. Her cat roared, bared teeth and lunged for the surface.

"Oh, yeah, honey, I feel it," Natalya assured her. She hissed out a long slow breath of displeasure, turning in a wide circle, palms up in the air. "I definitely feel it."

Is it vampire? Vikirnoff asked.

Natalya shook her head, her face paling. She turned to look at Vikirnoff, despair on her face. She stepped back away from the Carpathians as if she suddenly couldn't bear to be in their presence.

Tell me now! It was a clear command from her lifemate.

Natalya bared her teeth at him, snarled and turned away. Vikirnoff looked from her to the teenager, who was once more rubbing her wrist as if in pain.

Vikirnoff stalked Natalya with long, purposeful strides, one hand coming down hard on her shoulder, spinning her around, the other up defensively to prevent the rake of her claws. "Tell us now."

Natalya looked up at him in utter desolation. "Mage." She whispered the word. "I think Razvan is alive. This is a mage spell. It is why Carpathians are finding it difficult to detect. A mage is working a destruction spell. It is subtle, but I can feel it. Whoever is wielding the magick is very skilled."

Vikirnoff felt the sorrow, the devastation in her. Razvan was not only her brother, but her twin. She had been the one to throw the sword to end his life. They had not recovered his body and no one knew for certain if he had died. Razvan was a terrible enemy. Part Carpathian, part mage and now vampire as well, he was able to do what no other had done. He had formed an alliance with the vampires and he had fathered children when it was thought impossible.

Vikirnoff brought his hand up to the nape of Natalya's neck, joining them together. *We do not know if it is Razvan. It could be Xavier, our mortal enemy, or any of his trained followers. And if it is Razvan, how would Skyler feel him? How would she ever detect a mage spell? She was the one earlier in the woods recognizing the flow of power. Only then was Alexandria able to feel it. Mikhail sent the word to all of us.*

Natalya took a deep breath and turned to the teenager. She knelt down in front of her, taking both hands. "I know it is hard to touch others, and to remember much about your past, Skyler, but sometimes it is necessary."

Skyler shook her head and tried to back away. "I can't. I don't want to."

Ask her about her wrist. Why it is aching when she is feeling the weaves of the dark mage.

Natalya held Skyler firmly, preventing her from moving. "Just answer a couple of questions. Why does your wrist ache?"

"My wrist?" Skyler looked confused.

"Yes, you're rubbing it whenever you talk about the feeling of power in the air. Does your wrist hurt?"

Skyler frowned. "It burns and throbs as if . . ." She trailed off and cradled her wrist close to her body, glancing uneasily at Vikirnoff.

"As if someone had torn it open and used you for feeding?" Natalya persisted.

Skyler shook her head. "I want to go home. Right now." *Gabriel! Lucian!* She struggled against Natalya's hold on her, tears forming in her eyes.

"Okay, honey. We're going to take you home, but something is wrong with Corinne's heart. You don't want her to die, do you?" Natalya persisted. "Not if we can help her."

Dayan swore aloud. "I've called the healer. Corinne can't maintain her heart alone. I'm doing it for her. Someone take the baby."

Skyler choked back her tears. "I don't know how to help her."

"Do you have a birthmark?"

Skyler drew in her breath sharply and shook her head again.

"Any mark at all? Like a tattoo? Of a dragon maybe?"

Skyler burst into tears, shame on her face. "How did you know? Nobody knows. I've never told anyone, not even Francesca. It's faded most of the time. My father said he branded me because I was his property to rent out and everyone would know to give me back." Her voice was so low it was barely audible.

Natalya sank back on her heels, the tiger in her struggling for supremacy as her anger rose. Her hair banded with color and her eyes began to change color. "That man was not your birth father, Skyler, and he didn't brand you. The rotten bastard."

"He was. He was always with me." Skyler nearly shouted it, this time, shaking off Natalya's restraining hands. "He was my father."

Gabriel and Lucian materialized on either side of the girl, and she flung herself into Gabriel's arms. He wrapped his arms around her and held her close. "Would someone like to explain?"

Vikirnoff did so. *What could have traumatized her even more than the brutality of the father she had that she dare not remember it, Gabriel?*

You think Razvan fathered her?

We know he was alive that entire time and that he fathered Colby Jansen. We know he had other children, that he wanted them for their blood. If she carries the mark of the dragon, she is Dragonseeker. It would explain so many things about her.

But why would we not know, Vikirnoff? Francesca and I have often been in her mind, distancing her from the brutality of her childhood.

"Gabriel," Skyler looked up at him. "I know you're talking to them about me. What is it? What do they think about me?"

He stroked back her hair. "They think you are from a very special lineage among our people. That is why you are so rare a talent."

Natalya stood up, glancing over to where Gregori had materialized beside Corinne. The young woman lay in the snow, her face pale, beads of sweat dotting her brow while she struggled for every breath.

"Her heart appears to be normal," Gregori said. "Yet it is not functioning as if it is. I can breathe for her, but it is impossible to reverse what is not wrong."

Natalya moved away from the others. "Take Skyler and go. She should be guarded at all times. Send word to Rafael to guard Colby. Just in case. I will do battle with this mage and see which of us is the stronger." There was determination on her face. She put more distance between them.

She lifted her hands and sketched a sign in the air. At once they could see a grid of arcing light pulsing in the snow-filled sky. It was faint but there, a trace of brightness with veins everywhere, scattered across the sky like a giant net.

Skyler shook her head. "Don't let her do it. Stop!" She wrenched herself out of Gabriel's arms and ran to Natalya. "He's aware of us. If he knows who you are, where you are, he'll find you. He can always find you."

"I'm aware of him," Natalya said. "And I can find him. It's no good living your life afraid, Skyler. Whatever he's done to you, whatever anyone has, you have to take your life back. You're strong enough and you have Gabriel and Francesca to guide you. Go with Gabriel and trust me to do this."

Skyler hesitated, then shook her head. "If you do it, then I will too."

Natalya smiled at her. "I am the granddaughter of the dark mage. I have Dragonseeker blood in my veins and I am well versed in the magick of the old ways. Even if it is Xavier, my grandfather, I am a match for him. Don't be afraid for me." She avoided her lifemate's gaze. Both knew if it was her twin brother, she might hesitate at the wrong time. She felt Vikirnoff moving in her, coiling to strike should there be need.

"Get it done," Gregori ordered. "Dayan and I cannot hold this failing heart forever."

Natalya turned back to the sky and examined the flickering veins of light stretching across the sky. Each was faint, but she could follow the threads, all leading back to one source. One primary source.

"They're different weaves," Skyler pointed out.

"Gabriel," Natalya called. "If it is either Xavier or Razvan, I could be in trouble and so could Skyler. Don't allow this."

"I have to do this," Skyler pleaded. "I've been afraid every minute of my existence. I don't even know why some of the time, but it's tied to this." She rubbed her wrist where it burned and throb. "I try to remember why I'm afraid, but then my head hurts and I can't."

Natalya spun around. "Vikirnoff!" His name was a cry for help. "It *was*

Razvan. That is what Xavier did to us, hid our memories of him behind a wall of pain. Razvan took Skyler's blood. He fed off his own child. And somehow her mother ran, got them both away from him and that's how she ended up with that brute of a man, another monster she couldn't get away from."

Vikirnoff circled her waist, drawing her back against him in an effort to comfort her, but she stepped away, furious with her twin, so furious her tiger leapt to the surface, all claws and teeth, banding her hair and turning her eyes blue and then opaque.

Natalya didn't wait for the others to get clear. She didn't wait for Gabriel to give permission for his adopted daughter to participate; she simply looked to the sky, wove a response and sent it slamming through the veins of light, crashing each and every vein, destroying the entire network.

Sparks of light lit the sky and rained down. Lightning edged the clouds and whips scorched the ground. The earth trembled beneath their feet. Somewhere, far off, they heard a scream of agony. At once there was silence as shock registered.

"Get back," Natalya ordered her lifemate. She actually shoved him with one arm, trying to put distance between them. She sprinted to her left and ducked, just as lightning struck where she'd been standing. The sound was deafening. Ice arrows rained down, slamming to the ground with a terrible rhythm.

The men rushed toward her, but Vikirnoff waved them back. "See to the others. She is mage, and she can defeat our enemy. We will only get in her way."

Natalya kept running, drawing fire away from the others, her hands weaving a complicated pattern in the sky. At once the arrows melted. Droplets of water fell harmlessly. She drew clouds from the sky, blew warm air and spun it between her palms, all the while whispering to Mother Nature. Clapping her hands suddenly together, she sent it skyward. At once a thundercloud burst into the air, climbing high, shooting upward rapidly, building speed until it became a whirling vortex, spinning rapidly and spawning vicious destructive winds.

Natalya continued to weave her spell, drawing the bitter cold from the snow, the ice from the trees, spinning it together into a long solid spear of ice. She sent it upward, straight into the middle of the raging thunder-cloud.

Skyler's gasp was audible as Natalya sent the tornadoes slamming to earth, aiming them precisely, using the flow of energy from their enemy. "She hit him," she whispered. "I felt it. She hit him hard. The ice spear was in the tornado and he didn't see or expect it. She hit him dead center. His influence is gone. Is Corinne all right?"

"He's not finished," Natalya warned, already moving from her position. "Never think its over, Skyler." *Vikirnoff, cover the others, he'll retaliate there.*

The men hastily wove a shield as fire rained from the sky, hot embers that sizzled and hissed as they hit the trees and landed in the snow.

Natalya knew the enemy was on the move. She'd wounded him and he was simply trying to gain time. She took to the air, Vikirnoff with her, wings beating strongly to try to find him before he crawled back into whatever hole he'd come out of.

"I want to be able to do that," Sklyer said in awe. "Can I do that, Gabriel? Am I capable?"

"If you are what Natalya suspects, then there's a good chance you have a natural ability."

"She wasn't afraid of him. I could see it on her face. And I could feel his fear. *He* was afraid of *her.*"

"Yes, he was," Gabriel agreed. "And with good reason." He didn't point out that as strong and as powerful as Natalya was, so was their greatest enemy. Instead, he wrapped his arm around his daughter. "I think you're going to stay with me every second until we make it to the inn for our celebration."

"I think he's staying at the inn," Skyler said.

Gabriel exchanged a long look with Lucian. "We checked it out once, honey, but we will again. Lucian will go. Now that Natalya has scored a hit on him, maybe he will be easier to identify."

Lucian immediately shimmered into transparency, became mist and streaked in the direction of the inn.

Gregori helped Corinne to her feet. "I have examined you and your heart is perfect. There is no further need to fear anything could go wrong with it."

"Was it really an illusion? The mage trading on my worst fears?" Corinne asked. "How could he know?"

"He is already gone and left behind nothing to identify him." Vikirnoff and Natalya returned, hand in hand, striding to Corinne's side.

"He doesn't actually know your worst fear," Natalya explained. "The spell works on each person it touches differently. Whatever *your* particular fear is, that is what takes hold of you. In your case, you fear something will happen to your heart, so it did. In Alexandria's case, she relived the attack on her and thought that the vampire was still alive and stalking her. Each person will see what they fear and yes, it can become real enough to kill."

"What should we do in the future if something like that happens?" Corinne asked.

"Mage spells, especially if they know what they are doing, are difficult. Half of the safeguards used are mage spells—more than half," Natalya explained. "Fortunately, over the years, since the war with Xavier, they have been changed enough and personalized enough that most mages couldn't figure them out without you knowing, but so many of the other spells are quite lethal. You're all going to have to take that into consideration now, when you feel an attack. I'll start working on simple reverse spells that will have to do until I can see what we're up against. But it's obvious the mages are working with the vampires."

"Do you really think I'm like you?" Skyler asked.

"Let Francesca examine you. Show her the mark, Skyler, and don't be afraid of it. If the dragon is a birthmark, it is a good symbol, not a bad one. Razvan was once a great man. Anything he did as a vampire, was not the true man."

"Why are there so many monsters in the world?" Skyler burst out. "Why can't everyone just get along?"

"I don't have the answer to that," Natalya said, brushing back the girl's hair. "You've been through a lot and most of it was not good, but you have the opportunity to become whatever it is you would like. Don't let fear stop you. Let Gabriel and Francesca find out what's behind that wall in your mind. Once you know, it can't hurt you anymore. Isn't that right, MaryAnn? Isn't it better to have the knowledge and just deal with it than lock it away and not understand why we're afraid?"

MaryAnn kissed the baby's brow and carefully put her back in the front-pack so she could snuggle against her mother's chest. "I believe it's better. I'm a great believer that the more knowledge one has, the more empowered they are. You think you don't have courage, Skyler, but you found a way to survive when few others could have."

"And you aren't alone," Destiny said. "There are millions of survivors. We refuse to be victims. We rebuild our lives, and maybe we aren't ever what is considered normal, but we're strong and we lead happy lives. Don't let your past take that away from you."

"Don't ever think you don't belong," Corinne added. "All of us"—she gestured to encompass everyone there—"we all stand together. And you belong here with us."

Gabriel hugged her again. "Francesca is anxious to see you." He lifted her into his arms and took off into the night with her.

"Are we going to pull this party off tonight?" Dayan asked.

"We'd better," Corinne said. "After all the work that went into it. And the children are really anxious. We can't let them down. Fighting off vampires and now, mage attacks, is just part of our lives, just like you told me earlier. Now that we know what is happening, we can find a way to prevent it. I don't want them to stop us from living our lives, any more than we want Skyler not to be living hers."

Dayan slung his arm around Corinne and pulled her close to him. Now that her heart was beating just fine, his was accelerating overtime. "I'm thinking, just for a while, I might wrap the two of you up in that bubble wrap and keep you safe on a shelf. Thank you, Gregori. I'm sorry to have interrupted your evening."

"It was an interesting puzzle," Gregori said. "I want to get together later with you, Natalya, so we can begin working together to keep such things from happening."

Natalya nodded. "Of course. Right now I'm heading over to the inn to see if I can help Lucian spot any likely candidates. Skyler was very certain he had come from there. We want to make certain that this party will be safe for all the children."

"I think I'll go back to the house and hide under the covers," MaryAnn declared. "All this excitement is just a little too much for me."

"You never think of yourself as brave, MaryAnn," Gregori admonished. "But you always manage to find the courage to go to a fellow woman in need, no matter what the cost to you."

She gave him a small smile. "Anything for my sisters."

Gregori suddenly swung his head around, looking toward the trees, his silver eyes narrowed as he carefully examined the area around them. Mary-Ann shivered and pressed her hand over the small spot right above her breast that seemed to be aching from the cold.

"Are you all right?" Destiny asked.

"Just a little tired," MaryAnn confided. "Your late night hours are a little hard on the human here."

17

Manolito De La Cruz filtered through the trees in a slow, steady stream, careful not to disturb the air around him. There was something exhilarating about being so close to so many hunters, his prey in the middle of their tight circle, and none of them even saw him. He couldn't leave her until he was certain she was safe. He wanted her out of the woods and back in the shelter of Nicolae's house until the party. The ancients were suspicious, doubling back several times trying to figure out where he was—who he was.

Euphoria could be as dangerous as feeling nothing at all. He felt alive, giddy with it, staring in awe at the colors, absorbing emotion that seemed to bombard his entire system. He had waited in vain for so long, living only with his memories, only with honor, and now this woman had given him life. They would not keep her from him, no matter the cost. He had lived centuries risking his life—his very soul—asking nothing in return. Until now. MaryAnn was his, and he would not give her up.

Manolito? Have you a need of me?

His brother's voice stilled the wild chaos in his mind. He needed to be cold and deliberate, planning out his campaign each step of the way. Even as Rafael reached out to him, he felt Nicolae probing, thrusting hard in an effort to catch the unwary's mind open for invasion. It had been centuries since he was able to enjoy himself, to actually feel anything, and playing hide-and-seek, as dangerous as it was, was giving him a rush of adrenaline, a powerful high. He used his hunting skills, playing cat and mouse with them all, not leaving so much as a scent or a hair to tip them off. As a Carpathian male without a lifemate, he would naturally fall under suspicion, but there were several gathering with the couples to attend the celebration. He had to appear indifferent, not so much as brush up against her, not even noticing that she was near.

Manolito. Where are you? Have you need of me? Rafael called out to him again, this time much more insistent, alarm in his voice. His brothers knew how close he was, how the beast crouched and roared and the darkness spread covering his soul.

I checked the inn for our enemies and have scanned the forests. I will be returning as soon as I ensure Juliette and Riordan are safe. I want to double their safeguards. Manolito made certain he sounded matter-of-fact, expressionless, simply a man going about his duty. His brothers, Rafael and Riordan, would definitely help him carry out his plan, but enlisting them would put them in a terrible position with their lifemates—and he didn't altogether trust the women to stay silent. None of them seemed to understand it was a saving of the soul—far more important than a life.

Rafael heaved a small sigh. *That is a good idea. Juliette was so upset over her sister and cousin refusing to join us for this holiday. They never come to any of the family functions. Colby says Juliette is so unhappy, Riordan is considering leaving the ranch and going into the jungle where Jasmine and Solange live so she can be closer to them.*

Manolito was silent for a moment, weighing whether or not to use this opportunity to plant a seed. He took it. *It is too bad we do not have a counselor such as this woman visiting with Nicolae and Destiny. Nicolae mentioned she had helped both Destiny and the young teenager, Skyler. Perhaps Riordan should try to find someone similar near the ranch.* He kept his voice as always, flat and uncaring, merely a suggestion to solve a problem. He didn't betray that his heart was accelerating or his eyes nearly blinded by the vivid brightness of the world around him.

There was another small silence. *That is a good idea. I hadn't thought of that. I heard Destiny was nearly lost and this woman brought her back. Perhaps*

Juliette's sister would benefit from counseling as well. See to Riordan and if possible, come back before the party. I do not know if you were paying attention, but the word went out that there is a mage at work.

I have heard. He had seen Natalya do battle, and he'd stayed close to watch over MaryAnn. Now she was finally safe, back in Nioclae's house, and he could relax his vigil somewhat. Twice he had glimpsed the black wolf he knew to be Dimitri watching over young Skyler, and he felt sympathy for the man. Dimitri didn't have the choice to snatch a child from the safety of her parents. Even Manolito would draw the line there.

He made his way back toward the inn, trying to get a feel for the mage who had attacked earlier. A mage spell such as the one that had been used wouldn't work on a hunter without a lifemate. They had no emotions to play on. This was directed at the women. And that meant all the women were in great danger. Urgency gripped him. He wanted to simply kidnap MaryAnn and rush her back to his ranch in South America. With his four brothers and their ranch hands available to help see to her safety, there would be no chance of anything—or anyone—harming her.

Away from Nicolae's house—and temptation—Manolito shifted into mist and streamed through the forest toward the cave of healing. He knew the safeguards had been woven, but with enemies so close, he wanted to take extra precautions. Maybe he was simply uneasy with so many other Carpathians around. The De La Cruz family was used to relying on one another, and he wasn't taking chances with his youngest brother's life. He had a nagging feeling that just wouldn't go away, and he never ignored those feelings.

He streamed into the cave through one of the narrow chimneys and dropped down to the main floor. There was a network of chambers and pools and instead of going directly to the chamber where Riordan and Juliette rested, he moved slowly through the others, trying to feel with every sense, wanting to rid himself of the plaguing feeling that something wasn't quite right. The mage knew Juilette was injured. He had set her up for the vampire to make the kill. He would know her lifemate would rest with her in the healing soil, and if he knew where the caverns were that were routinely used, wouldn't it be the perfect place to strike? That's what Manolito would have done.

He took his time, hiding his presence as he examined each chamber. He was adept at concealing himself, and he assumed his enemies would be as well. He looked for a small anomaly, a rift in the natural harmony, one small sign of malignancy. To his shock, as he entered the chamber where his brother lay, Mikhail Dubrinsky stood examining the walls and floor of the cavern, a small frown on his face. He turned his head at Manolito's approach, moving into a better defensible position.

Manolito took his human form, striding across the cavern floor, automatically checking on his brother as he did so. Riordan appeared to be resting peacefully beneath the ground with Juliette. "You should not be out here alone," Manolito said. Already he was moving to protect the prince, reaching to Rafael, concerned that their prince was so exposed. "Where is your second?"

Mikhail gave him a faint smile. "I do not need a bodyguard to travel in my home territory, Manolito."

"I disagree and cannot imagine that Gregori would want you traveling alone. What are you doing here anyway?"

"I began to worry that Riordan and Juliette might be attacked as they lay in their resting place." Mikhail raked a hand through his dark hair. "I suppose I second-guess our enemy far too much."

"I had the same thought. I did not like that the dark mage has sent an emissary or come himself. He uses things we do not have adequate safeguards against." Manolito studied the prince's face. He looked older than Manolito remembered him even the week before. There was sorrow in his eyes, and a trick of the light made him look as if the weight of the world was on his shoulders.

"We have certainly learned we have to protect below ground as well as above. Our resting places are no longer the safe havens we thought them," Mikhail agreed. "How are you feeling? I know your wounds were quite serious. Has Gregori examined you to ensure that you are completely healed?"

"I'm fine. I have been wounded many times and will be again." Manolito examined the walls of the cavern. "Do you believe Xavier has been able to unite the vampires against us?"

"Whoever has united our enemies, whether it be the Malinov brothers or Xavier and Razvan, doesn't really matter. They have come together and we have no choice but to deal with them." Mikhail added a complicated weave to the safeguard already surrounding the couple in the earth. "I can find no evidence in here, or throughout the network of caves, that our enemy is lying in wait. Have you?"

"No." Manolito admitted with some reluctance as he added his own strands of safeguard, peculiar only to his family, one that would be difficult—and slow—to unravel, with serious consequences if it were done improperly. Riordan would recognize his handiwork immediately. He had found no evidence, but he still wasn't convinced his youngest brother was entirely safe—and that didn't sit well with him.

The two walked together out of the chamber and started down the narrow passageway leading back up toward the surface. Manolito tried to move just ahead of the prince, still uneasy, still feeling edgy, in spite of his examination of the entire cavern.

"I have to see Falcon and Sara, and then head over to touch base with Gregori and my daughter," Mikhail said. "I will be glad when this night is over. Did you check the inn? Skyler has indicated several times that she thinks the surge of power is coming from that direction."

"Yes, but I will go back again. Falcon told me he was bringing the children there in about an hour. I want to make one more sweep before all the women and children arrive," Manolito replied. "Just to be sure they are safe."

His restless gaze moved over the ground, the walls, the roof of the cavern as they walked quickly through the passage. The sound of the water dripping was relentless. It seemed overly loud in the chambers, the endless rhythm blocking out any whisper of sound that might alert him to danger. He tried to tone down the volume, but the sound only seemed louder, almost booming through the caves.

Manolito halted, placing his body between Mikhail's and the cavern. "I don't like this."

"I haven't liked any of this for a long time," Mikhail answered.

They both studied the passageway. They were only a few feet from the entrance. Light from snow and ice spilled along the opening for several feet as if in invitation. Small formations of ice had formed on the ceiling of the passageway, long, narrow spears of various colors.

Manolito shook his head, holding up his hand. "Let me go first. Just wait here and see if I trigger a trap, or perhaps we can move through as vapor and see what happens."

"If they're here, we want to know it. Your brother lies asleep with his lifemate. One of our women is about to give birth. We have to know if our enemies have invaded our chambers as well."

Manolito nodded and took several cautious steps, keeping an eye on the ice spears overhead. With each step he took, the ice rippled as if a vibration had gone through it.

"Go to mist," Manolito instructed the prince, concern shadowing his mind.

Dirt and ice spewed into the air right at the prince's feet, a geyser of soil spraying high between the hunter and Mikhail, opening the earth where Mikhail would have stepped.

"Go! Get out of here," Manolito ordered, swinging back.

The hole widened and deepened with blurring speed, a yawning crevice cracking beneath the prince even as he began to dissolve into vapor. A clawed hand reached from the dark hole and wrapped around Mikhail's ankle, talons biting deep into flesh. The hold prevented the change and the creature jerked hard, determined to drag the prince beneath the ground.

A collective gasp went up from the Carpathian people. It was Mikhail who connected them together. Mikhail who provided the common path of communication, and it was Mikhail who held the past and future together with the present for the Carpathian people. They all knew the moment he was in trouble—under attack.

Raven's soft cry of distress only added to the alarm and shock.

Manolito ignored it all, dissolved into vapor, sliding through the geyser of soil to the other side. Mikhail struggled to stay out of the gaping hole ripped in the floor of the passageway. The talons had torn two holes in his ankles. Mikhail could feel the razor tips of the vampire's claws meeting in his very flesh. The creature gulped his blood, teeth trying to tear at his flesh for more, all the while making hideous noises, as he wrenched at Mikhail's leg in an effort to drag him below to his lair.

Vampire, yet not. Mikhail sent to Manolito.

Manolito dove straight into the ground, aiming for the creature's upturned face. At the last instant before contact, he shifted form into that of a harpy eagle, the great curved beak, razor-sharp talons curved and wicked. He went straight for the eyes. As he entered the killing grounds of the unknown creature—a mixture of vampire and something hideously evil, he thought of MaryAnn. *I am sorry.*

For one brief moment he felt her awareness, bewildered and frightened. He touched her mind, one brief caress, and he let her go. Better not to have found her than to take her with him to the grave. And entering the burrow of an unknown enemy was tantamount to suicide. The prince had to be protected and there was no hesitation on his part. If his life was forfeit, his people would still go on.

The eagle ripped at the vampire's red-rimmed eyes, shredding skin over the throat and chest, digging deep and fast in an effort to force the creature to give up its prey. It had no choice, not if it wanted to survive. The abomination wrenched its claws from Mikhail's ankle and stabbed viciously at the eagle.

Go! Go! Get out of here! Manolito shouted at Mikhail as the dirt and rocks began pouring in over his head. One rock hit the eagle hard, knocking it sideways so one great wing crumpled. Manolito switched forms, trying to get a purchase in the soft dirt to get out before the rapidly filling dirt could close over his head. He used his hands to catch at roots to hold himself up as he kicked at the clawing creature with his foot. The dirt and debris rained on his head, filled his mouth so that he spat and closed his eyes, once more shifting to stay alive beneath the dirt.

Mikhail swore as the hole closed, trapping the hunter beneath the ground. He shifted to the body of a badger, plowing his way through the layers of soil, reaching for Manolito, all the while sending waves of tremors through the earth, hoping to disorient the monster.

Both hunter and hunted were blind now, the eagle having done its work. Manolito tried to utilize the senses of the giant mole he had become in order to find his way to the top. He heard the prince digging, felt the earth shake and knew Mikhail hadn't left him. He began frantically tunneling toward the prince.

It was the mole that sensed the creature coming up behind it, but Manolito went silent, shrinking the mole to normal size, waiting until he felt the hot breath on the mole's face before he struck hard, leaping forward, ripping with his own claws, a savage attack that scored. He couldn't see it, but he could feel the blood burning through his body, heard the horrible howl of pain, and suddenly it was gone, dropping through the soil where Manolito had no hope of following it.

The dirt above him was nearly gone, thanks to Mikhail's efforts. He made short work of it and as he broke through the surface, he shifted once more, throwing himself across the top of the ground, breathing in fresh air.

"Your blood or his," Mikhail demanded.

"Mostly his," Manolito answered, desperately trying to regain his control. He couldn't afford for the prince to realize he'd regained emotion and for the first time in his life, he had experienced claustrophobia. "It feels like vampire blood, it burns like acid, yet he did not act as any vampire I have ever encountered. He didn't seem experienced in an actual fight." Manolito sat up slowly, buying a little more time. "He laid a great trap, but he cannot really fight. He was relying on poison to stop us. It's in his claws."

"Are Juliette and Riordan safe beneath the surface?"

"I don't think he can get to them. He cannot get past the safeguards. Don't you find that strange? He can do so much, yet he falls short when it comes to finishing."

"I fear Razvan was not slain as we had hoped." Mikhail reached out and circled his ankle, inspecting the damage. "He is good at the planning of a battle, but from what I understand he was unable to make up his own spells and safeguards. That would mean he could not unravel them." *I am tired, Raven. So very tired.*

Gregori comes to you, my love. Her voice was a soft caress. *There have been so many battles lately. This is my fault. I should not have insisted on bringing everyone together. The responsibility of their safety weighs on you.*

Gregori tore into the passageway, a thundering cloud of vapor, already shifting. He came striding toward them, his silver eyes blazing, his long hair streaming behind him, his face a grim mask. Muscles ran like steel beneath his skin and he moved with fluid grace. He simply bent and ran his hands over Mikhail, looking for every scratch that could have opened a doorway for poison. "Our people are grateful to you, Manolito. We cannot thank you enough for your intervention."

Ah, old friend. Must you treat me like a child in front of the children?

Do not make a joke. How many times is this now that our enemies have set traps for you? Raven and Savannah are both distressed, both in tears. For that alone I could tear out your heart. His hands were extraordinarily gentle as he examined the prince.

"Manolito has several burns and claw marks," Mikhail said.

Gregori eyed his prince warily. Mikhail always responded to his outrageous threats, but this time he didn't even attempt a quip. Alarmed, Gregori went over his body a second time to make certain he had assessed the damage correctly. "I will take you home to Savannah to heal your ankle, if you do not mind, Mikhail. It will do her good to see you and I will be able to spend more time making certain I have all the poison out."

"Whatever is best for you, Gregori."

Gregori's dark brow rose and once again, his slashing silver gaze probed the prince. He finally turned to Manolito and cleansed the burns from the acid blood, healing the few claw marks on his face and chest, checking to make certain he had pushed all the poison from his body. "You should rest," he advised.

"I will go to ground after the celebration. I think every warrior should be close just in case," Manolito said.

Gregori nodded. "Thank you again for your service to our people."

"The allegiance of the De La Cruz family has always been pledged to our prince," Manolito said. He sketched a small salute and left the two alone.

"Are you all right, Mikhail? Really all right?" Gregori asked.

Mikhail was silent for a few moments. "Yes, of course. I am just tired of so many of my people having to make a decision to exchange their life for mine. It is difficult to live with oneself after a time." He didn't wait for Gregori to reply. He shimmered into mist and streamed from the caverns toward his daughter's home.

Savannah waited anxiously for them, her thick blue-black hair a long rope down her back, anxiety in her deep blue—almost violet—eyes. She threw her arms around Mikhail's neck and held him tightly. "Papa, we were all so worried."

"I know, *csitri*," he replied. "I'm sorry. I'm fine, just a scratch."

"You've always called me your little girl, but now that I'm grown"—Savannah reached for Gregori, clung to his hand—"you only do so when things aren't very good. How bad are you hurt, really, Papa?" She looked up at her lifemate. "Gregori?"

Gregori framed her face with his large hands, thumbs brushing gently over her mouth. "You know I would never allow anything to happen to your father. He has a torn ankle and I'm going to take a good look at it." His silver gaze slid over Mikhail.

"Do not look at me like that," Mikhail snapped, his hand sliding down to his ankle. The pain was nearly impossible to block. "What would you have me do? Stand by and watch a man who risked his life for me die?"

Gregori waved his hand and a cushioned stool slid in front of Mikhail. "Yes. That is what I would have you do. I would not expect it of you, but yes, I would prefer it. One of these days, you are not going to survive these continual attacks on you. If you cannot think of yourself or your lifemate, perhaps you might think what would happen to your people." His voice was mild as he delivered what was definitely a reprimand.

Savannah ducked her head, flinching a little, her protest dying under Gregori's slashing gaze. She brushed back her father's hair with gentle fingers. "It was courageous of you, but you could have been killed."

"And what of the hunter, Manolito De La Cruz, who risked everything to save me? He went willingly into the burrow, knowing what it was, knowing he probably would die. I am to ignore that? I cannot, Gregori. I will not."

Gregori shrugged his broad shoulders. "I suppose you could not. That is why you are the prince. But in truth, De La Cruz did his duty to his people. He has his honor and he can live with that. It is what we all do, Mikhail, and even you have to live within the rules of our society. We cannot exist without you."

"There is Savannah."

"We do not know if she is a living vessel for our people. And she is female. She is needed to provide children. If she ruled, we could not chance it." Gregori bent to examine the wounds in Mikhail's ankle. "This is very similar to the attack on Natayla's ankle just before the big battle. Razvan attacked her from below ground and injected her with poison using the tips of his claws. How are you feeling?"

"Like he tore a hole through my ankle clear to the bone," Mikhail admitted. When Gregori continued to look at him, he sighed. "The leg is weak and I feel sick."

Savannah went to wipe the blood away, using a soft wet cloth. "This should help a little with the pain," she explained. "I know you're having a difficult time controlling it and I put a soother in the water."

Before she could touch her father, Gregori caught her arm and pulled her away from the wound. "I think we will treat this as if it is poison."

Savannah glared at him. "You're going to go into his body and destroy the poison, aren't you? So big deal if I help my father feel a little better."

Gregori paused, his black brow shooting up. "It is unlike you to snarl at your lifemate, Savannah. Perhaps you are more upset than you realize that your father has been injured. And you wept over that ridiculous dish your mother asked you to make."

Color stained her cheeks. "I did not cry over it. I told you that." She glared at him. *Don't tell my father that. He'll tell my mother and then she'll feel bad. And stop giving me orders. I just don't feel like putting up with it today.*

Gregori caught both her arms and pulled her into the shelter of his body. "You are near tears again. What is wrong with you? Is it the baby?" His hand brushed over her hair with exquisite gentleness.

"Baby? What baby?" Mikhail asked, shifting position so he could look at his daughter's stomach. Savannah was small, like her mother. Now that Gregori had spilled the news, he could see that she was definitely thicker around the waist and he found himself smiling in spite of the pain.

She gasped and hit Gregori's shoulder with her clenched fist. "You weren't supposed to tell. I was going to tell them."

"What is wrong?" Gregori demanded, catching her fist and opening it, to place a kiss in the center of her palm. He cast a swift glance at Mikhail. "I can always remove your father's memories."

"Oh, I'd like to see you try that," Mikhail scoffed. "And if you're making my baby girl cry, you're going to see what a prince can do when he's angry."

"I'm having twins," Savannah announced. "Girls."

"We only heard one heartbeat, felt one life," Gregori objected, giving her a narrow-eyed glance. "She's having a baby. A boy."

"The other was there, hiding behind her sister. There are two of them, both girls and I'm going to be as big as a house. And you're going to be just awful, ordering me around. If you think he's bad about giving you orders, Papa, trust me, he's way worse with me."

Gregori shook his head. "Not girls, Savannah. We need sons. Warriors. Daratrazanoffs guard the prince."

"Well I'm sorry to tell you this, but they are definitely girls. Not sons. Daughters. I connected with both of them. There's no doubt."

Mikhail leaned back with a satisfied smirk on his face. "And you so deserve this, Gregori. You cannot imagine how much I'm going to enjoy watching you survive, not one, but two little daughters."

Gregori simply stood there looking as shocked as he was capable of looking. "How could I not know? I examined you myself." He shook his head again. "You must be mistaken. I cannot be wrong."

"She hid."

His brows drew together. "That is unacceptable."

Mikhail laughed. "I'm certain your infant daughter will do exactly as you command, Gregori. And as toddlers, they will really listen to you."

"Savannah, I am serious. You talk to them," Gregori commanded. "I cannot have one hiding from me when I make certain they are healthy."

"Your manner was gruff and you frightened her."

"I'm her father and I shouldn't frighten her."

Mikhail sighed. "I'm bleeding and I have to be up and running in good form in a few minutes, so I suggest you get over your shock that the world doesn't do everything you dictate and get on with healing me."

Gregori swung around, all cool elegance and danger. "You put her up to this, didn't you, Mikhail?"

"Put her up to giving you twin girls? If I had thought of it, I would have, but my imagination doesn't stretch quite that far." Mikhail shifted his leg and tried not to wince.

At once Gregori was all business. "Savannah, stay away from the blood just in case it is as poisonous as I believe it to be." He shed his body fast, becoming pure white light, a glowing energy that entered Mikhail's body and moved quickly to the wound. As expected, the poison was a problem. He was thorough, making certain to chase down every drop, push it out of Mikhail's body and heal his ankle from the inside out.

"It is done, but it will be weak for a while. Stay off it as much as possible until you can go to ground and allow the soil to rejuvenate you."

"Of course."

"I don't suppose you'd agree to lie down for an hour or two now and skip a small part of the festivities."

Mikhail felt Raven's light touch brushing in his mind. *Perhaps you should do as he says.* She sounded anxious.

"No." *I am fine, Raven, just a little tired. I want to come home and hold you for a while. That will do me more good than going to ground.*

Then come home.

Did you hear the news? Did Savannah tell you? She carries twin girls.

I heard. She is very excited. Raven didn't add anything more and he knew she was trying to sound happy and brave for her daughter. Carrying twins would be much more difficult than a single child and Raven was fully aware of that. She didn't want the sorrow of losing children for her daughter.

"I need to get home to Raven," Mikhail said. "Savannah, sweetheart, as always you are so beautiful. I think pregnancy agrees with you. Have you kept this secret for long? To know if they are girls or boys you must be several months along."

"We didn't want to say anything until we were certain I had a good chance of carrying." She smiled up at Gregori and once again he leaned down to kiss her.

"Son," Mikhail said softly, putting a hand on Gregori's back.

The Dark One stiffened and spun around, his silver eyes going molten. "Son?" he echoed. "Since when does my prince address his second in command and oldest friend in this manner?"

Mikhail's lips twitched. Inside, where only Raven could hear, he was roaring with laughter, but he managed to keep his mask intact. "You are family—my son-in-law, and I think of you as son upon occasion," Mikhail said rubbing his temples as if they ached, looking as pitiful and tired as he could.

"Oh, you do, do you?" Gregori folded his arms across his chest and cast a suspicious look around the room. Colorful flies and beetles clung to the walls and windowpanes. Some crawled from beneath the door to join the others. He glared at the insects and swung his gaze back to his father-in-law. "There seems to be an inordinate amount of bugs invading my home. I think we need a particularly venomous pesticide. Your sudden paternal feelings don't have anything to do with the insects, do they?"

Mikhail groaned softly.

"Gregori!" Savannah scowled at him. "My father is in terrible pain. He's treating you like family and you're not at all being nice. Get him a pillow for his back."

"Thank you, sweetheart, but I cannot really stay. I need to finish up the details for tonight. I'm certain whatever you made will be fine, and if it isn't, there will be plenty of other dishes." Mikhail swung his legs back down to the floor and waited a moment for the pain to subside. Gregori was right. He had healed the wound as best he could and removed the poison, but it was tender and raw. He needed to go to ground to complete the process and until morning, he would have to live with the ache.

"Here, *Dad*," Gregori said with heavy sarcasm, "let me help you up. Is there anything else you need?"

Mikhail allowed him to help him to the door. "Now that you mention it, son, yes." He wrapped his arm around Savannah and kissed her cheek. "Congratulations, honey, I will look forward to having granddaughters." He smiled at Gregori. "I'd like you to play the role of Santa Claus for the children tonight. It's a big responsibility and obviously you're the best choice for the job." He pulled a red cap topped with a white knitted snowball out of the air and plopped it on top of Gregori's head. "I've brought along the costume, although there's some controversy over whether Santa wears red tights or not." He waved the tights under Gregori's nose.

Gregori snatched the tights from Mikhail's hand and the hat from his head. "Mikhail . . ." His teeth came together in a loud snap of warning. "You wouldn't dare do that to me." He looked around the room at the insects decorating his walls. "I see now why my brothers have decided to visit." He waved his hands creating a wild wind that blew like a cyclone through the house.

The insects wavered, shifting into men, all laughing uproariously. Lucian clapped him on the back and Gabriel ruffled his hair. "Congratulations, little brother, you drew the short stick."

"You all knew about this?" Gregori demanded. He made a grab for Mikhail, but the prince was already out the door with a cheery little wave.

Darius touched fists with Julian, the pair of them grinning at each other. The others whooped with laughter.

"Out," Gregori ordered. "Every last one of you."

"I wouldn't mind seeing the cap on your head again." Darius wiggled his fingers as if Gregori should spin around and model for them.

"Put on the tights," Jacques encouraged.

"Get. Out." Gregori enunciated each word.

"Sure, sonny boy," Julian snorted. "We'll leave you to practice for your command performance tonight."

Another whoop of laughter filled the house, threatening to take off the roof. Gregori held open the door and simply pointed. The men filed out, large grins on their faces.

Gregori kicked the door closed and turned to his lifemate. "I'm killing your father. I've decided the Carpathian people can do without him just fine."

Savannah pressed her hand tightly over her mouth. "It's really an honor." The words came out muffled as she choked on her laughter.

He held up his hand. "Don't. Do not say another word."

She slipped her arm around his waist and leaned into him. "Is it really so terrible?"

"You saw them. Every single male in the territory was here. Your father set me up."

Savannah was silent for a moment. "Then I guess we have to figure out a way to turn the tables on them all, don't we?"

He wrapped a fistful of hair around his hand and stared down into her upturned face, always so beloved to him. "Just what are you thinking?"

A slow smile lit her eyes. "They want Santa Claus? I'm a magician aren't I? The great Savannah Dubrinsky? And you are Gregori, commander of earth, spirit, fire and water. You call down the weather and make the earth tremble. Santa Claus is going to be a piece of cake. I do wish they had given us a little more time to prepare. But we'll give them the best Santa Claus ever. No child will be afraid of you and you won't be falling on your face like they all expect."

"Are you certain it wouldn't be simpler just to do in your father and bury his body somewhere in the forest?" Gregori sounded hopeful.

She went up on her toes to press kisses against his mouth. "You are so bloodthirsty."

He placed his hand over her rounded stomach. "There are really two little girls growing inside of you?"

She nodded, placing her hand over his. "Yes. We really managed to shock you, didn't we?"

"I'm a healer, *ma petite*. I should know what is going on inside your body at all times. How else will I keep you healthy?"

She brought his hand to her mouth, nibbling on his fingers. "I like that we can occasionally surprise you."

"Oh, you do that, Savannah," he assured her. "You always do that."

18

"Sara, I can't find my wings," little Emma said, running down the hall, her curls bobbing. "I looked everywhere."

"Trav took them," Chrissy volunteered. "He said Emma was no angel and he was going to throw her wings away." Her too-large eyes were very solemn, waiting to see what terrible punishment the adults would mete out over such a crime.

Sara rolled her eyes when Emma started to wail. "I am an angel. I am! Trav is a bad, bad boy, isn't he, Falcon?"

Falcon scooped her up and whirled her around before her wail could turn into a serious crying jag. "I think Trav is a mischievous boy, not a bad one. What could you possibly have done to keep him from thinking you're an angel?"

"He always wants food and I took his sandwich and gave it to Maria's dog. Trav doesn't need the sandwich as much as Maria's dog does. Trav can just go in the kitchen any time. That's what Sara said, right Sara?"

"That's right, Emma," Sara agreed. "There's always plenty of food to go around, but you shouldn't take Trav's sandwich. If you want to give Maria's dog something to eat, get it from the kitchen."

Falcon cleared his throat. *That could be downright scary. She's liable to give the dog a roast next time.*

"What I mean, Emma, is ask Slavica or Maria before you take anything from the kitchen. They know what dogs should eat," Sara hastily added.

Emma was four, and Sara was fairly certain the argument would go on forever if she didn't find a way to change the subject. "We have to hurry and get all of you children over to the inn. Everyone is waiting to see the show."

"I need my wings, Falcon," Emma declared. "I can't be an angel without my wings." Her lower lip began to tremble.

"We'll find your wings, little one," Falcon assured her. He looked across the room and smiled at Sara.

She had done this, created a miracle for these children. Now they were on the road to health and slowly beginning to believe they wouldn't have to steal for food and would always have a roof over their heads. It was never easy. Sara had rescued seven gifted children who had been living in the sewers in Romania and brought them to the Carpathian Mountains. Sara and Falcon rose as early as possible, and stayed up as late as they could in order to be with the children. They were lucky enough to find several human women willing to work for them, caring for the children during the hours they had no choice but to be asleep.

Falcon had never imagined he could love so much, but sometimes, like now, it seemed it spilled out of him and fill all the empty spaces in the room. He hugged Emma again, ignoring her squeals, and led the little group to the chair where Travis sat, trying to glare at the others. Falcon winked at the boy and held out his hand. "Let's go. This is a celebration *dinner* and the quicker we get the play out of the way, the quicker you get to eat. I know Corinne and Mrs. Sanders are fantastic cooks. You won't want to miss this meal."

Travis sighed and stood up, dragging the wings out from under his bottom. "At least I don't have to be the angel." He suddenly grinned up at Falcon. "I get to be king."

Falcon dropped a hand on the boy's shoulder. Travis was the oldest and at eight, had carried a lot of responsibility over the others, picking pockets, trying to get food to feed them, always trying to protect them from the older, larger bullies on the streets and in the sewers. He was tall for his age and very thin, with a mop of dark hair he refused to cut. When Falcon had wanted to insist on having the hair cut, Sara had pointed out the boy was trying to be like him, so he left it wild and untamed. After that, Falcon spent time trying to give the boy a few pointers on keeping his long hair groomed. Tonight it seemed he had done a better job than usual. Even Emma didn't have anything to say about Travis's hair.

"You look great tonight."

"Sara said everyone was coming from the church to the inn."

"Yes, they went to midnight service and they will be coming for the dinner. Did you want to go the service?" He glanced at Sara, trying hard to keep a straight face.

Travis scowled at him. "Not me. I'm not going."

"I didn't think you wanted to, but figured I'd better ask, just to keep your options open. We'd better get going or we'll be late."

"Falcon," Emma asked as they headed out the door. "Is St. Nick really going to come? Will he have a present for me?"

There was a sudden silence, and he realized his answer was important to all of the children as he looked down at their upturned, expectant faces. Even Travis looked hopeful, although he tried to appear indifferent. They'd never had a Christmas tree, or enough food or even a roof over their heads, let alone a Christmas present.

"I certainly believe he is coming," Falcon said, a lump in his throat threatening to choke him. He exchanged another look with Sara. It was easy to understand why she had needed to rescue at least these children. She could only save so many, and she had done her best to provide a good home for them.

"Come on, everybody, let's go. We're riding in a sleigh this evening," Sara announced. "Make certain you have your hats and coats and gloves."

"Like Santa's sleigh?" Chrissy asked. At five, she was the oldest girl and took her role very seriously. There was wonder in her voice, and Sara was instantly grateful Falcon had thought of a sleigh ride.

"Well, we'll have horses instead of reindeer," Sara said, "but it should be fun. When you get in, pull the heavy blanket over you, so you stay warm."

They couldn't put seven children in one sleigh, so Sara rode with the four boys so they could "take care of her" while Falcon looked after the three little girls. Travis took the reins and, looking very grown-up, gave the command to start the horses. Jase, the youngest boy, only three, gripped

Sara hard and squealed with delight as they skimmed across the snow toward the inn.

Falcon scanned the area around them. He knew there had been several attacks on the women and one directed at the prince, and his apprehension grew as they proceeded through the heaviest part of the woods. A flutter of movement overhead pulled his gaze upward and he saw several owls winging their way overhead. The horses snorted, blew streams of vapor into the air, heads tossing as they eyed the wolves pacing along beside them, the leader running parallel, ice-blue eyes blazing.

"Our escorts," Falcon called out, laughing. Warriors everywhere, flying above them, running beside them, watching over the children and Sara. He saluted them as the sleigh raced over the snow, runners gliding easily.

The sleigh bells tinkled with every step the horses took. The children's cheeks were red and rosy, eyes wide with excitement, and their laughter was music to his ears. *I love you, Sara. Thank you for giving me life.*

I love you right back, Falcon. Thank you for being you. No other would have taken on these children and embraced them the way you have. You are a remarkable man.

The inn was lit up, colorful lights shining from the balcony and around the door. The horses pulled right up to the entrance and the innkeeper, Slavica, one of the women who often cared for the children, came out to greet them. Hugging each, she took them into the huge dining room where they had set up the stage. Falcon and Sara took their seats, Sara gripping his hand hard, fingers crossed that the children would have fun putting on their performance for all the adults.

The pageant went off with only a few hitches. The play went well, although the angel kicked the king in the shins, and he jumped around the stage for a minute before remembering he had an audience. Josef sang a stirring rap song, his own Christmas version of "Jingle Bells," which was actually quite good and had the audience clapping along until, in his enthusiasm, he nearly fell off the makeshift stage.

Falcon wrapped his arm around Sara's shoulders and put one hand over her stomach where their unborn child rested. "You are an incredible woman. How did you put this all together? The children are so happy and look at them up there. They're all little performers."

Mikhail nodded his head. "It was a fantastic performance, Sara, I had no idea. You must have put in so much time preparing them." He looked around him at the faces of his people, all smiling, the worn, grim faces of his warriors relaxed and happy, most of them saluting the children with a thunderous applause.

"Didn't they do a wonderful job?" Sara was beaming for her children. "What did you think of Josef's rendition of a rap Christmas carol? He really worked hard on that number. And Skyler sang beautifully. I was shocked when I heard her voice for the first time. Paul and Ginny did a great dance performance, and of course no one plays the piano the way Antonietta does. I'm just so happy about all of this."

"And having the Dark Troubadours sing for everyone went over big," Falcon added. "I think our guests were very happy with the show."

"In all honesty, Sara, I never expected anything near this production," Mikhail admitted. "When did you have time to put it all together? I knew you were practicing with the children, and even the teens, but this really was a far larger performance than I ever imagined."

"It was fun, Mikhail. And the children really needed to feel a part of the event. I don't want them to feel different. Any of them. It's important that the adults see them and acknowledge their accomplishments."

"Don't they do that?" The smile faded from his face. They didn't do that. As important as the children were to them, as treasured and as precious, the rest of the Carpathian community saw to their health and safety, but not necessarily anything more. It hadn't always been like that.

"Not just their parents," Sara said. "Carpathian males have struggled alone for so long without families they've forgotten what it is like to have them. Their life is war, not home, not wife and children. There is education, not just books, but teaching them the ways of the Carpathians, how to shapeshift, safeguards and even battle. Who does that? We've never established that. The children are so few and no one thinks to bring them together like this where they can all get to know one another, become friends and have adults accept them."

Mikhail remembered his own youth, the warriors stopping to give him a word of advice here and there, a gem caller taking him into the caverns to show him how it was done, others working with him on shapeshifting and even battle tactics. Sara was right.

"I will give what you say some thought, Sara," he said. "It makes sense. The children look happier than I have ever seen them. I had a brief visit with Joie's mother, Mrs. Sanders, and she mentioned that you hand-sewed those costumes. I would have provided help had you asked."

"I had help. Corinne sews as well. And we wanted to sew by hand rather than the Carpathian way in order to show my girls and boys how it can be done. Falcon and I try to integrate the two worlds as much as possible. Colby De La Cruz told me she and Rafael do the same thing for Paul and Ginny."

Mikhail took Raven's hand and brought it to his mouth, teeth scraping gently back and forth over her knuckles. "There seems to be many things I haven't considered. We've learned a lot from your party, Raven. Several of our people do have to incorporate the human ways along with the Carpathian ways. As more of our warriors find mates among human women, it will happen with more frequency. It's best if we learn how to integrate human and Carpathian families now."

He drew her away from the others over toward the tall Christmas tree. Several people had made ornaments to hang on it, bringing them to Slavica from all around the village. He leaned over to brush the corner of his lifemate's mouth with a kiss. "Look around you, Raven. You did this. It is the first time in centuries I have seen so many Carpathians gathered in one place with our neighbors. The children are laughing and running around, all excited, and the men are relaxed. Well," he amended, "alert as they should be, but so much more relaxed than I have seen them." His gaze went to Lucian. "Look at him, Raven. That man has spent his entire life in battle, yet now, he is at peace."

Raven's answering smile was gentle and filled with understanding. "Of course you needed to see this. You have to be reminded occasionally what you're fighting for, Mikhail. All the effort you make is for them. If you never see a payoff, the workload begins to weigh far too much."

He felt the ache in his throat as he stared around the room. There were so many of them, his warriors, tall and straight with their signature long black hair, eyes restless, but laughing now. He looked beyond them to the other males, some in the dining hall, a few in the bar, most outside where he could feel them. On the edge. No lifemate to bring them out of their barren existence. Would this help them? Give them hope? Or would the gathering only accentuate their loneliness?

Raven leaned against him, sharing the warmth of her body. "We're not just a people, we're a society. But how can we be a society if we never interact with one another?" She reached up to touch his face, so lined with worry. "The old ways are gone forever. They are, Mikhail, as sad as that is. We have to find a way to bring these people together with new traditions. We have to make our own history now. We have enemies, yes, but we have this." She swept her hand around the room to encompass all the Carpathians as well as their human friends. "We have so much and you've done that. Gregori used to snarl about your friendship with your priest, Father Hummer, yet now, one of his best friends is Gary Jansen."

The mention of his longtime friend, a priest murdered by members of the society for his association with Mikhail, saddened him. He forced his mind away from the past.

"Sara mentioned that we've fought so many battles and been so long without children, we are not giving them the proper tools they need. Do you think she's right?" Mikhail's black eyes rested on Raven's face. Lifemates did not lie to one another, even if the telling was painful. He saw the answer in her face, the way her fingers tightened around his and she looked momentarily distressed.

"You cannot think of everything, Mikhail."

"I have no choice, Raven. That is my duty, my responsibility. These children are all Carpathian, and those who are not yet—soon will be. You are right in saying we're not just a people. We are a society and we need to start acting like it. Our enemies have managed to keep us focused on them, instead of paying attention to the details of our lives that are important. Our children are everything. Rather than be annoyed by their antics, as I have been with Josef, we should all be helping them learn."

"Honey," she said softly. "Josef would try the patience of a saint."

A small smile flirted with his mouth. "Okay, I'll concede that point. That boy is so old in some ways and so young in others. None of us have dealt with children, not in centuries, and trying to find the tolerance and patience is going to have to become a priority, especially now that some of our women are pregnant."

Raven nudged Mikhail as Jacques and Shea entered the room. "She looks strained. Do you think she's in labor?"

"Jacques told me she's been fighting it. I asked Syndil to choose a birthing place and to enrich the soil for Shea and the baby, hoping that would help Shea relax enough to give birth."

"I'm surprised she came."

"She was to meet an online friend here tonight. One of the guests. Eileen Fitzpatrick is her name. Have you met her?"

"No, but Slavica mentioned her. Apparently, right before she came she had an operation for cataracts and she's spent most of the time in her room. She only came to meet Shea and would have put it off, but she's up there a bit in age and was worried this might be her only chance."

"Jacques told me Aidan investigated her. She's supposedly legitimate, but I want to take extra precautions with Shea. At this point, I do not trust anyone near her—not even harmless old ladies with cataracts."

Shea and Jacques made their way slowly through the crowd toward Mikhail and Raven. Mikhail stepped forward to greet his sister-in-law with a kiss on the cheek.

"You are certain you shouldn't be resting?" he asked, looking at Jacques, one brow raised in inquiry.

"I'm definitely in labor," Shea admitted. "This baby has decided he will come tonight whether I want him to or not. It's easier and faster if I stay on my feet as long as possible. I wanted to see the performance, but I moved a little too slow."

Raven hugged her. "I can show it to you in my mind, every detail, especially the fun parts. The little ones were so cute and I had no idea the teenagers were so talented. Josef really does have a good voice and he's always so inventive."

"Josef sang? And I missed it?" Shea asked.

Mikhail sighed. "If you call what he did singing. He does have a good voice, and I cannot understand why the boy doesn't sing a song one can actually understand. And what were all those gyrations he was doing up there?"

"Gyrations?" Jacques echoed, looking to Raven for an explanation.

"He looked like he was having a convulsion," Mikhail explained.

"He was dancing," Raven said, sending Mikhail a quelling look.

"Is that what it was? I couldn't decide whether he was doing striptease without stripping or needed medical aid immediately. As no one raced to his aid, I remained in my seat. He spun on the floor and threw his body around like a caterpillar on the floor."

"Break dancing," Raven interpreted for Shea.

"And the striptease?" Shea asked.

"That would be freak dancing without a partner, I think," Raven said. "I'm not exactly up on the terms, but he did look as if he was . . . er . . . Well, you know."

"I don't know." Mikhail shrugged. "He nearly fell off the stage at that point."

Shea laughed, one hand pressed to her stomach. "I knew I should have been here, just for that."

"It was worth seeing," Mikhail agreed, "although I didn't understand a word he was saying or why he was spitting and grunting while he sang."

"You're not with it," Jacques stated.

Raven and Shea laughed together. Mikhail looked injured. "With what? I'm with it. I happen to know that is not dancing. Paul and Ginny were dancing and Antonietta played real music and Skyler sang like an angel. The Troubadours sang a couple of wonderful ballads and no one, not even Barack, spit while they did it."

Jacques shook his head sadly. "There's no hope of modernizing you, bro."

Shea pressed one hand to her stomach and reached for Jacques's hand. "The contractions are really beginning to strengthen. Laughing is making it worse."

Both men looked so panic-stricken Raven had to hide a smile. "She'll do fine, Jacques. You're so pale. You did feed tonight, didn't you?"

"He's just being a baby," Shea said. "He fed. He wanted to be prepared in case I needed blood." She smiled at him. "Which I won't. Everything is going well."

"Not for me," Jacques admitted. "I have no idea what it feels like to give birth. Sharing the experience is plain frightening."

Mikhail nodded in agreement, but he was looking to his warriors, the unattached Carpathian males. They were the guardians tonight, as they so often were in foreign lands, only this time, they had the responsibility of guarding one of their women about to give birth. The men moved through the room, probing and scanning and searching the surrounding region for enemies.

"I actually am very excited to meet one of the guests who flew in from San Francisco. Her name is Eileen Fitzpatrick and she may be a relative of mine. We're both interested in genealogy and since I don't really have any relatives from my side of the family, I'm really hoping she is related to me," Shea said. "She sent word through Slavica that she wasn't feeling very good tonight and wanted me to meet her up in her room so she wouldn't have to be down here with all the chaos. I thought it was a very good idea."

"Absolutely not," Jacques said.

"No!" Mikhail was adamant.

Shea made a face at them. "I'm not made of porcelain. She's elderly and she just had an operation and she came all this way. The least I can do is climb the stairs and go see her."

"Not alone. She'll be here more than one night, Shea," Jacques coaxed. "You do not need to see her tonight." He placed his hand over her stomach, rippling once more with a contraction. "You have other things to do tonight. Raven, if you would be so kind as to ask Slavica to send word that Shea is in labor and will arrange a visit in a day or two."

"Well, I'm not going to miss out on Gregori playing Santa Claus," Shea said firmly, aware that the stubborn set to Jacques's jaw meant he wouldn't change his mind. "So don't think you can hurry me out of here."

Gregori. In spite of the gravity of the situation with Shea so near her time, Mikhail couldn't keep the taunting laughter from his voice. *Shea is close to her time and she wishes to see you parading around in your jolly red suit before she has the baby. So get on with it, my son.* Mikhail gave the order on their private mental path established centuries earlier through a blood bond.

You cannot rush St. Nick. This is a busy night for him, Mikhail. Even you, my prince, cannot command his time.

Mikhail flashed Jacques a small grin and tugged at Raven's long hair. "I need to speak with some of my men. It will not take long. You can walk around with Shea and see that she behaves herself."

"As if I could do anything else," Shea replied.

Mikhail sauntered away, moving through the villagers, guests and his people to reach the ancient he had spotted. Dimitri was in the bar, in the shadows, his cold eyes following Skyler's progress as she moved around the room.

"How are you doing?" Mikhail asked.

"I am better. She is not so distressed and it helps. I thought I would torment myself for a few minutes and then go back to my patrol. If I can do nothing else, I know I can keep her safe."

"If she is Dragonseeker as Natalya suspects, she is much more than a powerful psychic. It would explain the things Francesca says she can already do."

"And it also means she suffered far more trauma even than we already know."

Mikhail clapped Dimitri on the back. "You are an honorable man, Dimitri, and more than deserve a rare gem as no doubt our Skyler will be."

"Let us hope you are right."

Mikhail left him alone, standing in the shadows where he lived most of the time. Sadness seeped into the prince, sorrow for his warriors, so alone, most without much hope, but living their lives to the best of their abilities.

Manolito De La Cruz was standing just inside the door, and Mikhail approached him. "Do you suspect any of these men of being the mage? You came closest to him, entering his burrow and possibly finding his scent."

Manolito shrugged his shoulders. "I cannot find a single man who could be the mage we seek. All of us have been through the rooms, listening and scanning and even probing, but all the guests appear to be legitimate."

"What do your instincts say?" Mikhail asked.

"That the enemy is close," Manolito answered.

"Mine say the same thing." Mikhail shrugged. "Keep looking. Tell the others to do the same. We cannot afford any mistakes."

Manolito nodded and made his way once again around the room, giving the prince's message verbally to the warriors present. He didn't trust their common path of communication not to be overhead if the mage was in league with a vampire. As he neared Nicolae and Vikirnoff with their lifemates, he risked a quick glance at MaryAnn.

The sight of her took his breath away. She sat at a table near Colby and Rafael, talking to Ginny, Paul and Skyler, laughing at something they were telling her, and she looked so beautiful it hurt his eyes. Her skin seemed to glow and he was mesmerized by her mouth and eyes. The sound of her voice played down his spine. Need slammed into his body, tightening his muscles, hardening his groin so that he stopped moving and stood still, forcing his gaze away from temptation. It wouldn't do to be caught staring at her, or even thinking about her. He had to keep his mind fixed on his objective—ferreting out the dark mage.

"Mikhail still feels the threat is very real with Jacques's woman so close to her time. He asked that you both remain on high alert." He delivered the message, keeping his mind in battle mode, knowing both would test him. They had been probing the minds of as many of the unmated males as they could. Several times they had touched his thoughts.

Colby looked up and smiled at him. "Are you all right? Rafael told me you were injured defending the prince."

"It is nothing, little sister, a scratch, no more." He had felt nothing for this woman other than through his brother when Rafael had first brought her home, yet now he could remember all the little things she did for him and his brothers. She often shared her thoughts of laughter and warmth with them and the antics of Paul and Ginny, hoping to make their existence a little brighter. Now he could feel real affection for her.

He casually dropped his hand onto Colby's shoulder. "I checked on Riordan and Juliette. Nothing has disturbed their slumber." His gaze flickered to Paul and Ginny. "Juliette would have loved to see you two dance. She always mentions that her sister used to enjoy dancing so much. Hopefully she will get a chance to see you perform." He glanced at MaryAnn, gave a slight bow and walked away without a flicker of expression on his face.

MaryAnn stared after him. "My God, that man is handsome."

Colby nodded. "He is, isn't he? All of the De La Cruz brothers are. There are five of them and when they're all together they are quite the sight. Most women just drool around them."

MaryAnn stared after the man, feeling a little jealous over the missing women. Manolito certainly had the attention of the single women in the room, but he never so much as glanced their way. It wasn't that she wanted a man of her own, but she wouldn't have minded being noticed by him. "What did he mean about Juliette's sister? Why doesn't she dance anymore?" She wondered if Manolito had ever seen Juliette's sister dance. And she wondered why it bothered her to think that maybe he had.

Colby sighed heavily. "Juliette's younger sister, Jasmine, was kidnapped by a group of jaguar males. They . . ." She broke off, looking at her brother and sister, and shook her head. "Did things to her. She won't come out of the jungle or come near the ranch. She refuses even to see Juliette if Juliette is with Riordan. Juliette is so distressed she's been talking about leaving the ranch, our home, to try to help her sister. Rafael was just saying to me that you'd helped Destiny so much and maybe we could find Jasmine a counselor. Although, out where we live, that might be very difficult."

MaryAnn found herself watching the tall Carpathian as he glided through the room with utter confidence stamped in the very line of his body. He was fluid and graceful, almost elegant. The spot over her breast was aching again and she pressed her hand tightly over it. The sensation spread, making her breasts tingle and her nipples tighten. Warmth spread down her belly and between her legs. She swallowed hard, trying to tear her gaze from the sensual mouth and the image of it moving over her body. "I guess there aren't too many counselors near your ranch."

"No." Colby frowned. "From what Juliette says, Jasmine was never a strong person. And they have a cousin, Solange. She detests men and Juliette hasn't been able to combat her influence. It's all very sad."

"Perhaps I'll have a word with Juliette when she rises," MaryAnn ventured.

"Would you? That would be so helpful. Maybe you could just try to give her some advice on how to approach Jasmine to at least accept the men in our family. They would die to protect her. That's just the way they are."

"I'll be more than glad to help," MaryAnn said, her gaze once more straying to the tall, handsome Carpathian who was obviously on guard.

"Excuse me, Colby," Paul interrupted, "but you promised to introduce me to Gary Jansen. After all, he could be my uncle."

Colby squeezed Rafael's hand. "I did, didn't I? Let's go talk to him and see what he has to say." She led her brother over to the table where Gary

Jansen sat with Gabrielle Sanders, her brother Jubal and her sister Joie. Joie's lifemate, Traian, rose when she approached, as did the other two men.

Gary stared at Colby, shaking his head. "You look so much like my sister it's amazing. She was older than me by quite a few years and left home when I was about ten. I never saw her again. But I swear, you look just like her."

Colby sank down in the chair beside him after introducing Paul. She noticed Gabrielle's mother walked away quickly, a small scowl on her face. "I'm sorry, did we upset her?"

"No, I'm afraid she doesn't like anything jaguar, although in all honesty, I don't believe I am," Gary said. "I never heard that we had jaguar blood. In fact, I never heard of the jaguar race until I became friends with Gregori."

"Don't worry about Mom," Gabrielle added. "She'll come around. She just has to get used to all of this."

The double doors from the dining hall leading to the balcony suddenly swung open, and a short woman dressed as an elf with pointed ears and a wealth of blue-black hair stood in the center of the open doors. "Ladies and gentleman, may I have your attention, please? Many of you may not know this, but I happen to be a magician. Come here to me children. May I have the children here on the balcony? I'm about to show them one of the greatest magicians of all times. He is a well-kept secret."

All the children, both Carpathian and from the village, pushed forward and the adults crowded behind them. Paul lifted Emma onto his shoulders, and Skyler took Baby Tamara while Josef lifted young Jase up. Travis grabbed Chrissy by the shoulders and held her close, while Ginny held the hands of Sara and Falcon's other two young boys. Josh, feeling quite grown up, had the responsibility of the last girl, young Blythe.

As she spoke, small pulses of colored lights twinkled all around her and snow drifted down without ever touching her. The world around her appeared dazzling and majestic, swirls of fog covering her feet as she danced along the balcony railing with her little elf boots, her hair swinging around her like a cape, her face a little fey in the silver moonlight. Crystals hung from the eaves and pulsed with the same colors, soft reds and greens and blues and yellows, turning the night into a light show.

A collective gasp went up from the children, and Travis had to grab

Emma as she wandered out onto the balcony, staring in awe up at the lights. Savannah turned in a little circle and jumped back down in front of the children. "Oh, dear, I think I've forgotten my wand. I need it to reveal St. Nick to you." Her voice lowered dramatically and she looked right and left as if confiding only in them. "He always comes in under cover of the cloak of night using storms like this one to keep children from spotting him." She looked around again. "If only I had my wand."

"But Savannah," Chrissy ventured, "it's in your hand."

"It is?" Savannah managed to look surprised and she raised the glowing wand, swiveling it in a small circle. It rained sparkling pixie dust all over the snow-covered balcony. "Oh, good. It's working. Let's see. Look up to the sky and I'll try to remember how to do this. I've only done it once, you know, but for you, I'll try again."

Savannah waved the wand in a sweeping gesture as she danced across the railing again. The falling snow drew back like a curtain. A large snow-man with coal for eyes and a carrot for a nose whirled around, looking guilty, and raced away over the ground into the village.

"Oh, dear, that's the wrong one. That was Frosty the Snowman. Let me try again," Savannah said.

The children laughed as Savannah brought back the snow, did another whirling dance and once more sent pixie dust flying as she opened the curtain of snow.

The children—and even most of the adults—gasped again, some of them putting their hands over their mouths, in an effort to stay quiet. Up in the sky, where the stars twinkled and the moon shone, a gleaming sleigh raced across the night, drawn by reindeer. A man with a white beard dressed in a fur-trimmed red suit commanded the deer. In the sleigh was an enor-mous bag bulging with toys. Bells on the sleigh chimed softly, and the puls-ing lights that lit the snow now lit the sky around the reindeer-drawn sleigh, so that one moment Santa's jolly face could be seen clearly, and the next it was softened by a pale pastel strobe.

His eyes appeared to be as black as coal. There was snow in his beard and on the fringed and silver-studded red saddles of the reindeer. The sleigh circled above their heads. A hush fell on the crowd as the deer descended lower and lower in a wide circle to finally settle to earth on the roof above them. No one moved. They could hear the sound of hooves prancing above their heads. Silence. Then heavy boots walking.

Everyone turned their heads to see Santa by the tree, piling presents everywhere. He stopped once to grab a handful of cookies as well as some carrots Sara had her children set out for his reindeer.

Emma was the first to move, wiggling until she was put down to race across the room to Santa Claus. She halted, rocking back on her heels, staring up at him. "Did you bring me a present?"

Santa rummaged in his bag. "I believe I did. Now where did that go? Elf! I need you to help find Emma's present."

Savannah put her finger to her lips. "Santa Claus thinks I'm a real elf," she whispered to the children. "I'd better go help him." She tiptoed through the crowd, her elf hat bobbing, her little green boots making no noise on the floor.

Santa sat down and beckoned to the children forming a line. As little Tamara was placed in his lap, yanking at his beard, Santa sent a smoldering glare to the elf. *I'm so getting your father back for this.*

19

Shea leaned against Jacques, turning away from the crowd gathered to watch Santa distributing the presents to the children in the dining hall. Her fingers gripped Jacques's arm as she breathed her way through the contraction. "You know how we can set aside pain most of the time? This is like the conversion. There's no setting it aside. You just have to go with it. I was hoping, as a Carpathian woman, it would be a little easier."

A burst of laughter captured her attention and she turned to see Baby Jennifer spitting up on Santa's pristine, white beard. For a moment the coal-black eyes glinted silver, like a wolf, and rested on Mikhail. Just as quickly Santa recovered his jolly state and handed the baby back to Corinne.

Shea smiled up at Jacques. *I wouldn't have missed this for the world.*

If I were Mikhail, I'd be expecting lightning to strike. "Let's get you to the birthing chamber," Jacques said aloud, wrapping his arm behind her back to support her. He could feel the pain rippling through her body, growing stronger with each contraction. Stronger—and of longer duration.

Shea brushed her fingertips over his strong face. "Don't look so anxious. Millions of women have done this."

"But not you, little red hair," he whispered, leaning down to brush kisses on the top of her silky head. "Not us. You're my world, Shea."

"We'll be fine. Look." She indicated the back of the room with her chin.

"Oh, they've done this little show for the children right. Trust Savannah to know how to work a crowd with her magic. Before Gregori claimed her she was a mistress of illusion, working magic shows all over the world, and she certainly hasn't lost any of her skill. She has the crowd in the palm of her hand. Now the children will never believe, for a single moment, that that is Gregori in that sleigh."

Even as "Santa" finished handing out presents, Gregori appeared at the back of the room, frowning at his lifemate. "Savannah! Why in the world are you dressed like that? What do you think you're doing?"

Children giggled when Savannah turned around with a mock guilty look on her face. She held a finger to her lips and made a little face. "I've got to go, and I'll have to bring down the curtain on St. Nick before I do. We wouldn't want to reveal his secrets to the entire world."

Santa Claus gathered up his sack and hurried over to the fireplace. Although the flames burned hot, he simply disappeared up the chimney. Another gasp of awe spread through the room.

"Savannah makes magic wherever she goes," Jacques agreed. "Those children will never forget this night."

Savannah waved her wand just as the footsteps overhead indicated St. Nick was climbing back into the sleigh. He swung his black boots expertly over the edging and picked up a long whip, cracking it over the head of the reindeer. They took to the air. The sleigh and bag of toys, now considerably less filled, lifted into the air and glided away to the sound of Santa's laughter.

Another ripple of pain slid maliciously through Shea's body. Her fingers clamped down hard around Jacques, even as she breathed slowly in an effort to control it. This time the pain was hard enough and lasted long enough to make the other Carpathians in the room fully aware that she was in active labor. Heads turned. Warriors, lifemates and even some of the children turned their attention to her.

Shea tried a small smile and nodded. "It is time. Where is Slavica? I must thank her for such a wonderful evening. It was filled with delightful surprises."

Francesca and Mikhail with several others closed rank around Shea.

"We need to get you to the birthing chamber now," Francesca declared. "We can do this, don't be afraid."

"I'm anxious, but not afraid. Jacques won't let anything happen to us, will you?" Shea asked, holding her lifemate's gaze.

"Not a single thing. This is going to be a beautiful, unforgettable birth," he assured her.

Shea took a few more steps toward the door and stopped, one hand pushing at her hair to get it off her brow as the swelling pain tightened across her stomach and down through her back. "Do you realize the latest report on babies is that they are sitting in a terrible chemical brew, just the way the animal and bird young have been doing, which is what is putting so many species on the endangered list?"

"Shea," Jacques cautioned. "Now isn't the time to think about that."

"No, Jacques. We all have to think about it." She gasped as the pain rushed over her, stealing her breath. She grit her teeth and recited statistics. "Cord blood reflects what the mother passes to the baby through the placenta. Of the two hundred and eighty-seven chemicals detected in umbilical cord blood, one hundred and eighty of them are known to cause cancer in humans or animals, two hundred and seventeen are toxic to the brain and nervous system, and two hundred and eight cause birth defects or abnormal development in animal tests. And I'm quoting a report done by an environmental group out of Washington," Shea added, taking a breath as the pain subsided. "Everyone should be paying more attention to it. Among the chemicals found in the cord blood were methylmercury, produced by coal-fired power plants and certain industrial processes. People can breathe it in or eat it in seafood and it causes brain and nerve damage."

"Shea, our baby isn't going to have brain or nerve damage."

"You haven't read this report. The researchers also found polyaromatic hydrocarbons, or PAHs, which are produced by burning gasoline and garbage; flame-retardant chemicals called polybrominated dibenzodioxins and furans; and pesticides including DDT and chlordane."

"I don't know what half those things are," Jacques said, trying to soothe her. He ran his hand over her arm, but she shrugged him off.

"That's exactly why no one listens. Because they don't know what it is, they figure they don't have to pay attention." Panic filled her voice. "I know that's what's been happening to our children. We're so connected to the soil and the earth has become so toxic that we're now on the endangered species list as well."

"It's time to go," Jacques urged.

Get her out of here now, Mikhail ordered his brother. *We cannot afford to have her overheard by the villagers.*

It is her way of coping with pain and fear, Mikhail.

I am aware of that, Jacques.

"I have to thank Slavica first," Shea insisted, fighting back another swelling pain.

Mikhail leaned down to whisper to Raven. "Find her fast. We need to take Shea out of here before anyone else figures out what is happening."

"She's coming now and she has that older woman from San Francisco with her," Raven said, relief in her voice.

Mikhail swept his hand to help part the crowd, making it easier for Slavica and the woman to make their way across the room.

Raven hurried to them. "Shea has gone into labor and we need to take her home. She wants to quickly say good-bye and thank you for the lovely evening, Slavica," she said. "And of course, say a quick hello to you, Ms. Fitzpatrick. She's been waiting to meet you."

"I'll just wish her good luck, then, dear," Eileen said, leaning heavily on Slavica, using her cane to feel her way, her body bent slightly as she hobbled toward Shea and Jacques.

Aidan, standing across the room, frowned as the woman halted in front of Shea and stretched out her hand toward her.

"Finally. It is so good to meet you, my dear, and at such an eventful time." She tapped the floor with the cane twice, judging the distance between them. "I'm afraid I have to wear these terrible dark glasses and I'm having trouble seeing you. I was hoping you would have an unmistakable family resemblance."

Warriors. Using the common link of communication, Aidan called out to the others, his voice echoing his alarm. *This makes no sense. The woman I met in San Francisco is the same as this one, but different. Old, yet not elderly. She walked spryly with a spring in her step and not at all bent.* He was already moving, trying to use his speed to get through the crowd to Shea.

At once there was a stir as the men rushed toward Shea.

Jacques stepped in front of his lifemate as Eileen swung the cane straight up from the floor, stabbing at Shea's rounded stomach. Manolito, who had positioned himself closest to the couple, shoved Jacques aside and took the sharp needle buried in the cane deep in his abdomen. He stood for a moment staring at the mild-looking old woman, noting the nearly blind eyes and the wrinkled face. For a moment she wavered in his vision and he could see another face superimposed over hers, a face bearing long rake marks and torn eyes from a harpy eagle.

The creature from the burrow. She has been possessed. Manolito gasped. *The mage dwells within the same body as the old woman.* His body had already gone numb, and agony ripped at his chest as his heart seized. Blood seeped from the corner of his mouth, his eyes glazing over as the air stilled in his lungs and his heart ceased to beat.

Across the room, MaryAnn grabbed her chest with both hands to still the sudden twisting pain spreading through her body. Her legs went out from under her and she sat down abruptly. As suddenly as the pain started, it ended, leaving her feeling empty and lost, grieving, but for what—she didn't know.

Rafael leapt to his brother's side, crouching over the dead body, reaching with his spirit to force air through lungs, and blood through an uncooperative heart.

Mikhail and Jacques dragged Shea back, thrusting her behind them. Other hands caught her and thrust her even further away so that they made a wall of warriors around her. The cane arced toward Raven.

"Mother!" Savannah screamed and rushed toward Raven.

Gregori was there first, wrenching the cane out of the withered hand. *Natalya!* He kept his body between the old woman and Raven and Mikhail.

Natalya was already weaving a complicated sign in the air, murmuring softly, insistently. Vikirnoff picked the chant from her mind and added the power of his voice. Nicolae and Destiny joined with him, pouring their combined strength into Natalya through Vikirnoff.

They used throat chanting and mage spell, a combination of Carpathian and mage power. Eileen's mouth drew back in a snarl as the mage fought to maintain his shield. They could not attack him without killing Eileen. Her body bent almost double. The warriors ringed her, watching as her face contorted, showed a mouthful of teeth, elongated, and then went back to that of an older, refined woman.

Shea's pain swept through the Carpathian people, nearly paralyzing the men. *Jacques, take her to the birthing chamber.* Gregori commanded. *Francesca, we must go now. She's too close. We cannot wait.*

Mikhail took Syndil by the elbow and pushed her toward Gregori. *They need you there as well. We will join you as soon as possible. Get the children home. The Von Shrieders will deal with this mage.*

Eileen will need a healer, Gregori cautioned, even as he bent to lift Manolito. Rafael was keeping his brother's heart beating and he remained close to the master healer as they all moved into action.

I will see to her, Darius volunteered.

It is done then, Mikhail said as Jacques swung Shea into his arms and strode from the inn, Francesca close on his heels. Gregori and Rafael followed with Manolito.

Natalya's voice grew more commanding, more insistent. She pointed to the floor, ordering the mage out of the body and onto the floor, to crawl like a dog.

Eileen's body rippled with unease, stretched and twisted until it appeared warped. Her throat bobbed and undulated as growls swelled in volume and spittle ran down her face. She slowly turned her head until she was staring straight at Natalya, the eyes deep pits, wells of hate. The mage stared out at her, the wide, distorted mouth shaping one word. "Traitor," he accused, the voice a demonic rumble.

Her voice never faltered, although Vikirnoff put his hand on her back to steady her, a gesture of complete solidarity.

A shadow slid from Eileen's body, a dark oily substance, insubstantial, impossible to hold in one's hand or to kill. Several warriors tried, punching through the shadow to try to find a heart, even stabbing at it, but it continued to slink along the floor toward the door. Darius caught the elderly woman before she could hit the floor and lifted her into his arms, taking her back up the stairs to her room.

How do we kill it? Vikirnoff asked Natalya.

I don't know. It isn't a shadow warrior so I cannot send it back to the realm of the dead. It is a lost soul doing the bidding of the mage. Only he can really control it, give it peace or send it away. I have never run across a spell to kill one. I tried a few and maybe, over time, I can come up with something, but it is going to go back to its master.

Dimitri returned from escorting Gabriel with Tamara and Skyler back to their home. "I can try to follow it, see if the mage is close."

Natalya nodded. "Do not let them see you. The mage is strong and his knowledge is very ancient. I remember some of these spells, but they are faded from memory."

Natalya watched the Carpathian male shift on the run, a fluid, easy change almost in mid-stride. One moment he was walking tall; the next he was running on all fours as a shaggy, black wolf. "Good luck to you," she whispered, pressing her hand to her stomach as another wave of pain hit them all. "We'd better get to the birthing chamber if we're going to be of any use to Shea."

Deep below the ground in the warmest chamber of the cavern, Syndil called to the Earth, singing softly to enrich the soil, preparing it as Shea settled down into the soft bed of the richest loam, her head pillowed in Jacques's lap.

Several feet away, Gregori and Rafael worked on Manolito, trying to draw the poison from his body and at the same time, keep his heart beating and his lungs working.

All around them, candles sprang to life and the soothing aromatic scent of herbs and spices filled the air. The great healing chant swelled in volume as Carpathians everywhere, including Shea and Jacques, sang to keep the great warrior from slipping away, while Gregori undertook the journey to recover his spirit and escort him back to the land of the living.

Shea breathed through the contractions, using Jacques as her focus. She simply crawled into his mind and stayed there as contractions increased in duration and strength. In between she chanted with the others, feeling the camaraderie, being part of something so much larger, in harmony with the earth around them. Sisters and brothers coming together as family to heal one of their fallen—a warrior who had voluntarily given up his life to keep Shea and her unborn child safe.

The healing was difficult and slow, Gregori struggling against a poison meant to give a quick death. Twice he had to stop, pale and swaying with weariness, to be rejuvenated by Rafael and then Lucian. Darius joined them, indicating Eileen was sleeping comfortably. Vikirnoff and Nicolae, Destiny and Natalya entered the chamber, reporting Dimitri was trying to follow the shadow back to its master.

Through it all, Shea remained quiet in Jacques's arms, breathing through each contraction until she gasped and gripped Francesca's hand. "He is coming soon," she whispered.

"We're ready," Francesca assured her.

Shea's gaze went to Gregori, already back in the warrior's body. Francesca swept her arm to encompass all the Carpathians in the chamber and without. "You are not alone. The child will be helped into the world, assisted by our people, welcomed by all and protected by all. Gregori will join us the moment he is able. Let your baby into our world, Shea."

Shea nodded and waited for the next contraction before pushing.

Gregori stepped away from Manolito. "He needs blood," he announced softly, "and several risings in good soil, but he will live."

It was Mikhail who stepped forward to offer blood to Manolito, an offering from the prince in respect and honor for Manolito's sacrifice. It was Rafael who opened the earth to receive his brother, weaving safeguards to ensure Manolito's rest would be undisturbed.

Gregori brushed his hand over Shea's head in a gesture of affection. "So, little one, you are, at last, bringing your son to us."

"I waited for you."

He smiled at her. "I am here now."

"Can you feel him? Are you touching him, making certain he is okay to breathe on his own?" She looked anxiously from Francesca to Gregori, her hands gripping Jacques tight.

All around her she could hear the birth chant, and the beautiful sound nearly overcame her fears—nearly. "You checked him for pollutants, Gregori? You made certain his blood is strong?"

"It is done and all is well. Give him to us and then you can rest. You have been too long worrying. Let him come so you can hold him in your arms."

Her gaze clung to his glittering silver one, and he gave her another nod of encouragement. "Trust me, *ma petite,* trust in your people and your lifemate. Release him."

She turned her head and looked up at Jacques. "I love you. Whatever happens, no matter what. I love you and I've never been sorry, not one single moment."

He blinked back tears and moved so she could stay looking him in the eye. Mind to mind, they reached for their son. They took a breath and she pushed, never looking away from her anchor—away from Jacques—the love of her life.

"Stop. That's good. Just breathe through it, Shea. He's looking around, take a look at him. He's excited to see his new world," Francesca encouraged.

"Not yet. Tell me he's breathing and he's healthy," Shea panted, still clinging to Jacques's mind, afraid if she let go she would simple shatter with fear for her child.

"Push again," Gregori instructed. The baby slipped out into his hands and he cradled the child to him, immediately leaving his own body to examine the child thoroughly in the way of their people.

Francesca clamped off the cord and Jacques cut it, separating mother and child.

Silence fell in the cavern. Candlelight flickered over their faces, as everyone stayed very still waiting. Suddenly, a squalling cry split the air.

Gregori smiled at Shea, held the baby high, out toward the prince. "Welcome our newest member into our world. A son for all to cherish."

Mikhail stepped up and laid his hand on the child's head. "A fine healthy boy. He couldn't be more beautiful. Welcome, son. Nephew. Warrior. Your life is linked to our lives for all time. We live as one and we die the same way. When one is born, it is cause for all to celebrate, and when one dies, we all feel the loss. You are brethren. Carpathian. It is an honor and privilege to welcome you."

Gregori held the boy above his head, and a cheer thundered through the birthing chamber. He turned and slowly, gently, put the infant in his mother's arms. She looked down into her son's face, tears in her eyes, one hand clinging to Jacques's. "He's so beautiful. Look at him, Jacques, look what we did."

Jacques leaned down to brush kisses over her face, his lips tasting her tears. Tears of happiness. "He's perfect, Shea."

Mikhail swept his arm around Raven and looked around the cavern at the happy faces of his people. Even Dimitri had returned to get a peek at the baby. Many of the unmated warriors crowded close, wanting to see what they had been fighting so many centuries for. They were together again after so many years and so much struggle. He kissed his lifemate, happiness sweeping through him. "We have every reason to celebrate, Raven. And all of it is right here, in this chamber. We're not only celebrating life, but hope. There is hope for our people again."

DARK DESSERTS

By Christine Feehan Readers

Walnut Moons

Submitted by: Slavica G. Kukich-Ostojic
Phoenix, AZ

This recipe has three layers, the first layer is the cake layer, the second layer is the egg yolk icing, and the third layer is the chocolate glaze icing.

FIRST LAYER, CAKE
8 egg whites
1 cup sugar
2½ sticks butter
4 cups finely ground walnuts
2½ cups flour
powdered sugar

Take 2½ sticks of butter and 1 cup sugar and mix well in the electric mixer. When that is done, add the egg whites, 2 at a time, until you have all 8 egg whites mixed in. Mix well. Next, add 4 cups of ground walnuts and mix in using a wooden spoon. Add 2½ cups flour mixing well with the wooden spoon. When the cake batter is well mixed, take a large rectangular cake pan and grease it well with butter. Pour the cake mix into the pan and bake at 350° for 25 minutes. When done baking, let it cool. When cooled, top with egg yolk icing.

SECOND LAYER, EGG YOLK ICING
8 egg yolks
1¾ cups powdered sugar

Take the 8 egg yolks and 1¾ cups powdered sugar and mix well with electric mixer. Then pour over the cake. Place it back in the oven at 250°

until dry. Keep an eye on the icing and check it periodically. When dry, take it out of the oven and pour the chocolate glaze icing over it.

THIRD LAYER, CHOCOLATE GLAZE ICING

1 cup milk

1 cup sugar

4 chocolate squares (for cooking)

3 cups ground walnuts

½ stick butter

Take 1 cup milk, 1 cup sugar, and 4 chocolate squares for cooking. Place all ingredients together and cook on top of the stove for about 15 minutes until blended, smooth and thickened. When thick, add 3 cups of ground walnuts and ½ stick butter. Mix well, and while still warm, pour over the cake on top of the egg yolk icing. Let cool and let chocolate become firm. When cooled, cut with half-moon cookie cutter into moons. Serve cooled.

Love Bites

Submitted by: Stephanie Schmachtenberger
Riverside, CA

2 cubes butter, softened

1 can sweetened condensed milk

2 (1-lb) boxes powdered sugar

1 (16-oz) bag coconut

2 cups chopped walnuts

¾ stick parowax

32-oz semi-sweet chocolate chips

1. Combine butter and milk, add powdered sugar, coconut and nuts. Roll into rounded teaspoon-size balls and refrigerate 12–24 hours until firm.

2. Melt wax and chocolate chips in top of a double boiler. Turn flame down to a simmer. Dip balls in chocolate (one at a time) and set on wax paper. It is easier to dip with a 2-pronged fork.

3. Refrigerate 6–8 hours until chocolate has set.

Carpathian Reading Snack

Submitted by: Tempe Hembree
Murphy, NC

1 package of dark chocolate chunks
dried sweetened red cranberries (Craisins)
lightly salted peanuts

Mix equal portions into a lidded container and scoop out about a cup. This is a good serving and is so delicious together. For some reason, the chocolate doesn't melt . . . maybe because of the dryness of the peanuts and cranberries.

For those of us who: love to snack and read, love the salty and sweet together and want to be healthy at the same time. Enjoy!!!!!

Chocolate Trifle

Submitted by: Kim Smejkal
Sugarland, TX

1 box Duncan Hines Devil's Food Cake
8–10 tablespoons Kahlua
3 small boxes instant chocolate pudding
2 tubs Cool Whip
6 Heath Bars (frozen)
½ cup chopped pecans

Bake cake in 9 × 13-inch pan as directed and let cool. Make the pudding and set aside. Break up the frozen Heath Bars into small pieces. Crumble the cake into a large bowl. Start layering into a trifle bowl in order of: cake, drizzle Kahlua, Cool Whip, and Heath Bar pieces. Your last topping should be Cool Whip, and then top with more Heath Bar pieces and chopped nuts.

Dark Sun Cheesecake

Submitted by: Sabine Reichelt
Wiesbaden, Germany

Before you can take the cake out of the form, make sure it is cold. Use a plastic knife to loosen the cake from the form edges.

5 eggs (separate yolks and whites)

125 grams (½ cup) margarine

250 grams (1 cup) sugar

100 grams (½ cup) sugar

1,000 grams (4½ cups) cream cheese 20 percent rich (Quark)

100 grams (½ cup) wheat semolina (Weizengries)

1 level tablespoon starch

1 level teaspoon baking powder

½ glass lemon aroma

juice from 1 lemon

1. First, put the white of the eggs and 100 grams sugar in one high bowl. Use a mixer (liquidizer) to stiffen it. Stand it apart.

2. Put 125 grams margarine and 250 grams sugar into a big second bowl and beat it until frothy. One by one, put the 5 egg yolks into it. It looks bright orange like the rising sun.

3. With a wooden spoon, stir the cream cheese under. Now is the time to add the rest of the ingredients (NOT THE EGG WHITES). Stir it all thoroughly. Carefully stir the egg whites under it.

4. On the bottom of a springform pan, lay down a piece of baking paper. After baking, it's easier to take the cake out of the form. Fill the springform pan with the dough and lay another piece of baking paper on top of it. Bake at 200° C (390° F) in oven for 60 minutes.

Chocolate-Covered Cherry Bon Bons

Submitted by: Julie Badtke
De Pere, WI

If the cherries haven't all been eaten the first day, I put them in pretty tins and store them in the refrigerator. This is one of my family's favorite traditional choco-late Christmas recipes. It has been in our family for the last 3 generations that I know of, and is now being passed on to the 4th generation, as I am teaching my daughters how to make them! Enjoy!

2-pound bag of powdered sugar
1 teaspoon real vanilla
1 stick butter
1 (14-oz) can sweetened condensed milk
1 large bag of semi-sweet chocolate chips
2/3 bar of paraffin wax, broken into small chunks
2 (10-oz) jars maraschino cherries (with stems) drained

In a double boiler, melt wax and the bag of chips over hot water until smooth. Reduce heat. Cream the sugar, vanilla, butter and condensed milk until well blended. Roll sugar mixture into ½ inch balls and shape it around each cherry until covered. Holding each cherry by the stem and using a spoon, dip and coat the cherry with chocolate until it is completely covered. Set the cherries on wax paper until chocolate is cool and firm.

Dark Hedgehog Slice

Submitted by: Elizabeth Woodall
Melbourne, Australia
SERVING SIZE: 10 OR MORE PIECES
COOKING TIME: ABOUT 15 MINUTES

Slice can be made up to four days ahead of need. It stores well in a sealed, airtight container in your refrigerator.

Approximately 300 g (1⅓ cups) graham crackers, coarsely chopped
1 cup chopped walnuts
½ cup desiccated coconut
250 grams (1 cup) butter, chopped
1¼ cups caster sugar
⅓ cup cocoa powder
1 egg, lightly beaten
150 grams (⅔ cup) of DARK chocolate, melted (or more to taste)
½ teaspoon vegetable oil

1. Grease a 20 cm × 30 cm (8 × 12-inch) pan; line base and two long sides with baking paper, extending paper a small amount (say 2 cm) (1 inch) above the edges of the pan.

2. Combine graham crackers, walnuts and coconut in a large bowl.

3. Place butter, sugar and sifted cocoa in a medium saucepan and stir over medium heat until butter is melted and sugar is dissolved. Remove saucepan from the heat and whisk in the egg.

4. Pour the melted butter/cocoa mixture over the dry crackers/nuts

mixture and mix them together well. Press combined mixture into the prepared pan.

5. Cover with cloth or paper and refrigerate overnight.

6. Turn slice out onto a chopping board and cut into pieces. Spoon combined warm, melted chocolate and oil in a small snap lock bag. Squeeze chocolate into one corner, twist the bag, then snip the tip off. Drizzle the chocolate over the top of the slice and refrigerate for another 15 minutes, or until chocolate is set.

Evil Indulgence

Submitted by: Wendy Ellis
Limerick, PA

1 package regular Oreo cookies
1 (8-oz) package cream cheese, softened
1 package dark chocolate chips

1. In food processor, crumble cookies and add cream cheese until blended. Remove from food processor and roll into small balls.

2. In saucepan, melt dark chocolate on low. Dip each rolled cookie into chocolate and let cool on wax paper.

3. Sprinkles, powdered sugar or any other decoration can be added before chocolate cools.

Sinfully Sweet Bouillie

Submitted by: Suzanne LeBlanc
Terrytown, LA

This old-fashioned Cajun custard is a family favorite. Served at all family gatherings. It never seems to be left alone.

2 (12-oz) cans evaporated milk, any brand
½ gallon milk, any type
5 tablespoons cornstarch, heaping
½ cup water
6 eggs
1½ cups sugar
2 tablespoons pure vanilla extract
1 angel food cake

1. Cut the angel food cake into chunks in a large serving bowl and set aside for later.
2. In a large saucepan, put evaporated milk and milk to boil.
3. In a blender, add sugar, eggs and vanilla. Blend until smooth.
4. In a medium bowl, dissolve the cornstarch in water. Make sure that the tablespoons of cornstarch are heaping.
5. Once milk begins to boil, add blended mixture and stir until thoroughly mixed. Then, add water/cornstarch mixture to saucepan and cook on low heat, constantly stirring until mixture thickens. As you stir, the thickness will feel like the consistency of custard or porridge.

Pour mixture over angel food cake; best served hot.

Optional: Add 2 cups of fruit, mixed nuts or some other additional ingredient to give bouillie that lagniappe. Use without angel food cake as a pie filling or, sweet tart filing. Add bananas for banana pudding or other confections.

Le bon bouillie du tout la mon!

Dark Decadence

Submitted by: Felicia Slack
Almont, MI
SERVES FOUR

4 packages hot chocolate mix
4 shots Kahlua
1 (2-oz) semi-sweet dark chocolate bar, grated
4 tablespoons Cool Whip

Make cocoa as directed. When hot, add 1 shot of Kahlua, top with 1 tablespoon of Cool Whip. Sprinkle with dark chocolate shavings.

Dark Delight

Submitted by: Anita Toste
Ukiah, CA

1 box dark fudge cake mix
1 box chocolate pudding mix
4 eggs
¾ cup oil
¾ cup Kahlua
powdered sugar

Combine cake mix and pudding; add eggs and oil, mix for about three minutes. The batter will be thick. Then add Kahlua, make sure to mix well. Pour mixture into Bundt pan that has been greased. Bake at 350° for 45 minutes. Let cool. Sprinkle with powdered sugar.

German Chocolate Cream Cheese Brownies

Submitted by: Marcella Brandt
Federal Heights, CO

I rarely make a single batch of these brownies. Because of the divided amounts, I write the doubled amounts in parentheses beside the divided ingredients both in the ingredients list and in the recipe.

1 (4-oz) package German chocolate
5 tablespoons butter (divided)
1 (3-oz) package cream cheese
1 cup sugar (divided)
3 eggs (divided)
½ cup plus 1 tablespoon flour (divided)
½ teaspoon baking powder
¼ teaspoon salt
¼ teaspoon almond extract
½ cup chopped walnuts
1½ teaspoons vanilla (divided)
8 to 9-inch square pan

1. Melt chocolate with 3 tablespoons butter over low heat. Stir occasionally, and let cool.

2. In a small bowl, combine cream cheese and 2 tablespoons butter. Cream until smooth. Add ¼ cup sugar. Beat until fluffy. Blend in 1 egg, 1 tablespoon flour and ½ teaspoon vanilla. Set aside.

3. In larger bowl, beat 2 eggs until light colored. Gradually add ¾ cup sugar. Beat until thickened. Add baking powder, salt and ½ cup flour. Blend in chocolate mixture, 1 teaspoon vanilla, almond extract and nuts.

4. Grease pan. Spread ½ chocolate mixture in pan. Spread white mixture evenly on top. Drop remaining chocolate by spoonfuls over chocolate and cut through with a knife to marbleize.

5. Bake at 350° for 40 minutes. Brownies will be very moist. Cut into squares as soon as removed from oven. Remove from pan and cool on a rack.

Chocolate Passion Bowl

Submitted by: Kelley Granzow
Reynoldsburg, OH
MAKES 16 SERVINGS, ABOUT ⅔ CUP EACH

My husband likes this with all chocolate but it makes it very rich. But hey, a dessert even I can make!

3 cups cold milk

2 packages chocolate flavor instant pudding (4-serving size)

1 tub (8-oz) whipped cream french vanilla topping (or chocolate) thawed, divided

1 baked 9-inch square brownie layer, cooled, cut into 1-inch cubes

1 pint (2 cups) raspberries (or strawberries; if you use strawberries, cut them)

Pour milk into large bowl. Add dry pudding mixes. Beat with wire whisk 2 minutes or until well blended. Gently stir in 1 cup of the whipped topping.

Place half of the brownie cubes in the 2-quart serving bowl; top with half of the pudding mixture, half of the raspberries and half of the remaining whipped topping. Repeat all layers.

Refrigerate at least 1 hour or until ready to serve. Store leftover dessert in refrigerator.

Dark Moist Chocolate Cake

Submitted by: Brenda Edde
Englewood, CO

2 cups sifted flour
1 cup sugar
5 tablespoons cocoa
2 teaspoons baking soda
1 cup water
1 cup mayonnaise
1 teaspoon vanilla

Sift together all dry ingredients. Mix all liquid ingredients. Pour liquid into dry mixture and blend thoroughly. Pour batter into 9 x 11-inch cake pan. *Tip: You should pound pan on counter a couple of times to get air bubbles out.* Bake 30 minutes at 375°. I like to frost cake with powdered sugar frosting.

Chocolate Caramel Diamonds

Submitted by: Eddie L. Thacker
Kerrville, TX

Estimated Times:
Preparation, 45 minutes
Cooking, 20 minutes
Chill, 30 minutes

YIELDS: 42 SERVINGS

CAKE

4 ounces fine-quality bittersweet chocolate (not unsweetened)

1 stick (½ cup) unsalted butter

¾ cup sugar

3 large eggs

¼ cup all-purpose flour

¼ cup unsweetened cocoa powder

GANACHE

5 ounces fine-quality bittersweet chocolate (not unsweetened)

⅓ cup sugar

⅓ cup heavy cream

CARAMEL TOPPING

¼ cup sugar, MELT SLOWLY

MAKE CAKE

Preheat oven to 375°. Butter a 9-inch square baking pan and line bottom with wax paper. Chop chocolate into small pieces. In a double boiler or a metal bowl set over a saucepan of barely simmering water, melt chocolate and butter, stirring until smooth. Remove top of double boiler or bowl from heat and whisk sugar into chocolate mixture. Whisk in eggs 1 at a time until combined well. Sift flour and cocoa powder over chocolate mixture and whisk until just combined. Pour batter into baking pan and bake in middle of oven until a tester comes out clean, about 20 minutes. Cool cake completely in pan on a rack and invert onto a baking sheet lined with wax paper.

MAKE GANACHE

Chop chocolate. In a dry heavy saucepan, cook sugar over moderate heat, without stirring, until it begins to melt. Continue to cook sugar, stirring with a fork, until a deep-golden caramel. Remove pan from heat and add cream (mixture will bubble up and steam). Simmer mixture, stirring, until caramel dissolves. Remove pan from heat and add chocolate, stirring until mixture is smooth. Pour ganache over top of cake and smooth with a spatula. Chill cake, uncovered, at least 30 minutes and, covered, up to 3 days.

MAKE TOPPING

Lightly grease a baking sheet. In a dry small heavy saucepan, cook sugar over moderately low heat, stirring slowly with a fork (to help sugar melt evenly), until a pale-golden caramel. Continue to cook caramel, without stirring, gently swirling pan, until golden. Remove pan from heat and pour caramel onto baking sheet. Cool caramel completely. Pry caramel from baking sheet with your fingers and in a food processor pulse caramel until coarsely ground. Sprinkle the ground caramel evenly over top of cake and with a sharp knife cut cake into 1¼-inch diamonds.

Black "Carpathian" Forest Stuffed Cupcakes

Submitted by: Tammy Taylor
Nashville, TN

Preparation time, 10 minutes
Total time, 45 minutes

MAKES 2 DOZEN CUPCAKES

1 package (2-layer size) chocolate cake mix (the darker, the better)
1 package (8-oz) cream cheese, softened
1 egg
2 tablespoon sugar
1 can (20-oz) cherry pie filling, divided
1½ cups Cool Whip, thawed

Preheat oven to 350°. Prepare cake batter as directed on package and set aside. Mix cream cheese, egg and sugar until well blended. Remove ¾ cup of the pie filling for garnish and set aside. Spoon 2 tablespoons of the cake batter into each of 24 paper-lined medium muffin cups. Top each with 1 tablespoon of the cream cheese mixture and remaining pie filling. Cover each evenly with remaining cake batter. Bake 20–25 minutes. Cool 5 minutes and remove from pans to wire rack. Cool completely. Top cupcakes with Cool Whip and remaining pie filling to garnish just before serving. Cupcakes should be stored in tightly covered container in refrigerator for up to 3 days. *Great substitute—use Cool Whip <u>Chocolate</u> Whipped Topping.*

Per cupcake:

Calories, 220	Carbohydrates, 25 g
Total fat, 13 g	Dietary fiber, 1 g

Saturated fat, 4.5 g · Sugars, 18 g
Cholesterol, 45 mg Protein, 3 g
Sodium, 240 mg

Jaxon's Jell-O Cake or Jaxon's Blood Cake

Submitted by: Su-Pei Li
Hilliard, Ohio

Enjoy! If not completely enjoyed in one sitting, cover loosely and refrigerate.

1 box white cake mix, prepared per package instructions
1 large package (6-oz) Jell-O mix in a red color (raspberry is my favorite)
1 tub Cool Whip

1. Make and bake cake in a 13 x 9-inch pan.
2. Add 2 cups boiling water to dry Gelatin mix. Note that this is only half the water called for in making regular Jell-O. Do not add the 2 cups cold water, only hot.
3. Cut slits all the way to the bottom into warm (just slightly cooled) cake every few inches with a butter knife.
4. Pour warm gelatin liquid over warm cake.
5. Refrigerate to cool completely.
6. After completely cooled, top with Cool Whip.

Dark Chocolate Profiteroles

Submitted by: Nancy A. Staab
Saint Albans, WV

Profiteroles are little puff pastries filled with ice cream. They are surprisingly easy to make and are guaranteed to dazzle your guests. First, prepare the pâte à choux (puff pastry):

$^1\!/_2$ cup water

$^1\!/_4$ teaspoon salt

$^1\!/_4$ cup unsalted butter, cut into pieces

3 large eggs, room temperature

1 ounce unsweetened baking chocolate, broken into small pieces

$^1\!/_2$ cup plus 1 tablespoon flour

1. Preheat oven to 400°. Line two baking sheets with parchment paper and lightly butter the paper.

2. Heat the water, salt, chocolate and butter. Bring to a boil and remove from heat.

3. Immediately add the flour and stir quickly with a wooden spoon until smooth.

4. Set the mixture over low heat and stir for about 30 seconds. Remove and allow to cool for a few minutes.

5. Add 1 egg and beat it thoroughly into the mixture. Beat in the second egg until the mixture is smooth.

6. In a small bowl, beat the third egg. Gradually add enough of this egg to the dough until it becomes shiny and soft enough to just fall from a spoon.

7. Shape the dough, while warm, into mounds of about 1½ inches.

Gently push down any points, because they will burn. Bake 30 minutes or until puffed and brown.

8. Remove from oven and allow to cool completely. The puff pastry will have a hollow center.

9. When you are ready to serve, open the pastry by making a small opening and fill with a quality chocolate ice cream, drizzle with raspberry sauce and garnish with a few raspberries.

Dark Chocolate Cool Whip Cookies

Submitted by: Soemer Simmons
Normal, IL
MAKES APPROXIMATELY 4–5 DOZEN COOKIES

1 German chocolate cake mix
1 egg
1 (8-oz) container of Cool Whip, thawed
powdered sugar

Put several cups of powdered sugar into a mixing bowl. Put aside. In a separate bowl, beat together dry cake mix, egg and Cool Whip as well as possible. Take ¾ batter and roll it into a ball in the powdered sugar. Place balls 2 inches apart on an ungreased cookie sheet. Bake at 350° for 11 minutes.

Midnight Delights

Submitted by: Marie Ohngren
Croswell, MI

1 cup washed blueberries
2 cups sliced strawberries *mixed with* ½ cup sugar and ½ cup grenadine
2 cups cubed angel food cake
4 ounces shaved dark chocolate
1 carton Cool Whip

Alternate berries with cake, in 4 glass goblets, ending with strawberries. Top with Cool Whip. Drizzle with strawberry juice and finish with shaved dark chocolate.

Sinful Confections

Submitted by: Deborah J. Macklin
Biloxi, MS

1 jar smooth peanut butter
1–2 boxes of powdered sugar
1 package of chocolate chips
½ bar of paraffin wax

Mix peanut butter with powdered sugar—enough to form mixture into 1-inch balls. Melt package of chocolate chips and ½ bar of paraffin wax in a double boiler. Dip peanut butter balls into chocolate and set on waxed paper to dry.

Festive Punch

Submitted by: Stephanie Azmoudeh
Tampa, FL

12 cups brewed vanilla nut coffee
½ cup sugar
1 gallon vanilla ice cream
1 gallon chocolate ice cream
¾–1 cup Frangelico liqueur
1 can Redi-Whip cream
Hershey's special DARK syrup

Brew coffee; add ½ cup sugar while hot. Make sure that the sugar is dissolved. Cool coffee.

Thirty to forty-five minutes before serving, put both ice creams in punch bowl. Add coffee over ice cream. Add Frangelico (can use Kahlua or Bailey's Irish Cream instead). Top with whipped cream. Drizzle chocolate syrup over top.

Prussian Dark Chocolate Cherry Cake

**Submitted by: Margee Ott, great-granddaughter of Prussian immigrant
Baldwin, WI**

*From my German immigrant great-grandmother Magdalana Von Krusemark.
Due to DARK chocolate and little sugar, this dessert has a BITE!*

2½ cups flour
1 cup sugar
1 cup cacao powder
1½ teaspoons baking soda
¼ teaspoon baking powder
2 eggs
1 teaspoon vanilla
¾ cup butter (or shortening)
1 (20-oz) can cherry pie filling
1 tablespoon red food coloring

Mix all ingredients well and pour into greased baking pan(s). May use rectangle 8 x 12-inch, or two round 9-inch pans. Bake 40 minutes at 350°.

FROSTING
Frosting is made from melting 16 ounces of DARK or bitter chocolate and then gently pouring over the cake, allowing liquid to freely flow. May garnish with maraschino cherries. The red tones from pie filling and food coloring add rich tones to the dark brown chocolate cake. Very appealing in layered effect, using cherry pie filling between layers.

Blackberry Wine Cake

Submitted by: Cathy Smith
Lynnwood, WA

1 package white cake mix (has to be white)
2 small packages Raspberry Jell-O
1 cup oil
1 cup blackberry wine
4 eggs

Preheat oven to 350°. Generously grease a Bundt pan. Pour mixture in and bake for 50–55 minutes until toothpick comes out clean. Remove from oven and allow to partially cool before removing from pan.

FROSTING INGREDIENTS
1 cup powdered sugar
¼ cup blackberry wine

Mix together and drizzle over cooled cake. Allow cake to stand and cool all the way before covering (this will give the outside a crust).

Heaven and Hell on Earth Torte

Submitted by: Cindy LaFrance
Phoenix, AZ

1½ cups well-chopped cashews
1½ cups crushed vanilla wafer cookies (38 cookies)
1 cup packed brown sugar
1 cup butter or margarine, melted
Dark Cocoa Cake (see below)
Heaven and Hell Mousse (see below)
Natural or Chocolate Glazed Leaves (optional)

1. Heat oven to 350°. Place cooking parchment paper or waxed paper in bottoms of 2 round pans, 9 x 1½ inches. Stir together cashews, crushed cookies, brown sugar and butter. Spread about ¾ cup mixture in each pan; reserve remaining mixture. Make Dark Cocoa Cake (below). Pour about 1¼ cups batter in each pan; refrigerate remaining batter.

2. Bake about 20 minutes or until tops spring back when touched lightly. Immediately remove from pans to wire rack and peel off paper. Repeat with remaining cashew mixture and batter. Cool completely.

3. Make Heaven and Hell Mousse (below). Place 1 layer, cashew side up, on serving plate; spread with about ¾ cup of the mousse. Repeat with remaining layers and mousse. Or place mousse for top layer in decorating bag; choose a design you like for fancier decorating; garnish with natural or Chocolate Leaves (below). Cover and refrigerate about 4 hours or until chilled. Cover and refrigerate any remaining torte.

DARK COCOA CAKE INGREDIENTS

2¼ cups all-purpose flour

1⅔ cups sugar

⅔ cup baking cocoa

¾ cup shortening

1¼ cups water

1¼ teaspoons baking soda

1 teaspoon salt

1 teaspoon vanilla

¼ teaspoon baking powder

2 eggs

Heat oven to 350°. Beat all ingredients in large bowl with electric mixer on low speed for 30 seconds, scraping bowl constantly. Beat on high speed for 3 minutes, scraping bowl occasionally.

HEAVEN AND HELL MOUSSE INGREDIENTS

12 ounces cream cheese

1¾ cup confectioners' sugar

2 cups peanut butter

¾ cup heavy cream, at room temperature, divided use

In a bowl, with an electric mixer, whip the cream cheese until light and creamy. Gradually beat in the confectioners' sugar, then the peanut butter. Continue beating until thoroughly incorporated and fluffy. If mixture looks lumpy, add 2 tablespoons of the heavy cream. It may not smooth out, but it will be easier to blend. Set aside. Place the remaining heavy cream in another bowl, and using an electric mixer, whip until stiff. Being careful, combine both mixtures thoroughly. Set aside.

CHOCOLATE LEAVES INGREDIENTS

5 to 6 nonpoisonous (unsprayed) leaves (lemon, grape or rose leaves work well) *or*
   pliable plastic leaves

¼ cup dark chocolate chips *or* 1 ounce semi-sweet baking chocolate

½ teaspoon shortening

Wash and dry leaves. Melt chocolate chips and shortening. Brush chocolate about ⅛-inch thick over backs of leaves using small brush. Refrigerate at least 1 hour until firm. Peel off leaves, handling as little as possible. Refrigerate chocolate leaves until ready to use.

My thoughts on the top design are finishing off with a layer of mouse, then covering it with dark cocoa cake crumbles (to represent the earth). Add well-placed leaves of choice and a possible design or formation of some sort with any leftover mousse. I know your wonderfully creative mind can think of something.

Or:

Keeping it DARK, with the dark chocolate glaze on top of a layer of mousse, finishing off with optional garnishes done in mousse with a decorating bag and chocolate-covered leaves.

DARK CHOCOLATE GLAZE INGREDIENTS

4 ounce dark chocolate

3 tablespoons butter

1 tablespoon milk

1 tablespoon light corn syrup

¼ teaspoon vanilla

1. In a small, heavy saucepan or microwave oven on medium, melt broken chocolate with butter. Stir frequently until smooth. Remove from heat.

2. Stir in milk, syrup and vanilla. Place cake on rack over a baking sheet. When glaze is cool, pour onto center of cake. Let glaze run down sides. Chill about 10 minutes to set glaze.

The Next Best Thing to . . . Feehan Novels

Submitted by: Diana M. Dennison
Oxford, ME

1 stick margarine or butter
1 cup flour
1 cup pecans
1 (8-oz) package cream cheese
1 (16-oz) carton Cool Whip
1 cup sugar
3 cups milk
1 large chocolate instant pudding
1 large vanilla instant pudding
extra pecans and chocolate shavings for top

1. Mix margarine or butter, flour and pecans. Press into 9 x 13-inch pan. Bake in 350° oven for 15 minutes. Let cool.
2. Mix cream cheese, ½ of Cool Whip and sugar. Spread over crust. Mix milk, chocolate and vanilla instant puddings until stiff.
3. Spread over first layer. Spread remaining Cool Whip over top.
4. Garnish with pecans and chocolate shavings.

Dark Molten Chocolate Cakes

Submitted by: Abby Leavitt
Veyo, UT

6 ounce (1½ package) dark bittersweet chocolate baking bars
1½ cups powdered sugar
½ cup flour
3 whole eggs
3 egg yolks
raspberries (or other fruit)

Preheat oven to 425°. Grease 6 (6-oz) custard cups or soufflé dishes. Place on baking sheet.

Microwave chocolate and butter in a large microwaveable bowl on medium (50 percent) for 2 minutes or until butter is melted. Stir with a wire whisk until chocolate is completely melted. Add powdered sugar and flour; mix well. Add whole eggs and egg yolks; beat until well blended. Divide batter evenly into prepared custard cups.

Bake 14 to 15 minutes or until cakes are firm around the edges but soft in the centers. (Centers should be oozy.) Let stand 1 minute. Run a small knife around cakes to loosen. Carefully invert cakes onto dessert dishes. Sprinkle lightly with additional powdered sugar and garnish with a fruit, such as raspberries. Drizzle with hot fudge or add to the side.

Serve immediately, best when warm.

Sunset Pumpkin Bars

Submitted by: Liz Kreider
Fargo, ND

BAR INGREDIENTS
2 cups sugar
¾ cup oil
4 eggs
1 can (15-oz) pumpkin
2 cups flour
2 teaspoon baking soda
1 teaspoon salt
3 teaspoon cinnamon

FROSTING INGREDIENTS
8 ounces cream cheese
½ cup butter
2 teaspoons milk
1 teaspoon vanilla
½ teaspoon maple flavoring
1 cup powdered sugar

Mix bar ingredients together and bake in a 9 x 13-inch pan at 350° for 20–25 minutes. Let cool. Mix frosting ingredients together and frost before cutting into sunset bars.

Chocolate Cherry Bars

Submitted by: Peggy Barker
Suquamish, WA
MAKES APPROXIMATELY 3 DOZEN

My grandmother used to make these yummy bars. She died in 1997 and I just recently found the recipe again. They are even better than I remembered them.

BAR INGREDIENTS
1 package fudge cake mix
1 can (21-oz) cherry pie filling
1 teaspoon almond extract
2 eggs, beaten

FROSTING
1 cup sugar
5 tablespoon butter (no substitutions)
⅓ cup evaporated milk
1 (6-oz) package chocolate chips

Grease and flour 13 x 9-inch pan. In a large bowl, combine first four ingredients. By hand, stir until well mixed. Pour into prepared pan. Bake at 350° for 25–30 minutes or until toothpick inserted in center comes out clean.

In small saucepan, combine sugar, butter and milk. Boil, stirring constantly, 1 minute. Remove from heat; stir in chocolate chips until smooth. Pour over bars.

Dark Chocolate Tapioca Pudding with Strawberries

Submitted by: Amanda Brown
Utica, MI

MAKES 8 SERVINGS OF ½ CUP EACH

1 egg

⅔ cup sugar

3 tablespoons Minute tapioca

3½ cups milk

2 squares of DARK baking chocolate

1 teaspoon vanilla

4 large strawberries (cut into slices)

Beat egg lightly in medium saucepan with a wired whisk. Add sugar and tapioca. Mix well and gradually add milk, beat well after each addition. Let stand 5 minutes. Add dark chocolate. Bring to a boil on medium heat, stirring constantly. Reduce heat to medium-low; cook until chocolate is completely melted, stirring constantly. Remove from heat. Stir in vanilla. Cool 20 minutes. Then stir. It starts to thicken as it cools. Serve warm or chilled. Put a few slices of strawberry on top of each serving of pudding.

Dark Devil Chocolate Cheesecake

Submitted by: Franny Armstrong
Brighton, Ontario, Canada

This cake is very rich and will make about 10 servings. You'll definitely want to "sink your teeth" into this one!

FILLING INGREDIENTS

12 ounces cream cheese, at room temperature

1 cup sugar

pinch of salt

1 tablespoon chocolate liqueur (having a drink of it on the side is optional)

1 teaspoon grated lemon rind

4 eggs, separated

½ cup all-purpose flour

¼ cup cocoa

½ cup whipping cream

CRUST INGREDIENTS

1 (8-inch) chocolate Oreo crumb crust mix

2 tablespoons margarine or butter

DECORATE WITH

whipping cream

cherry pie filling

shaved dark chocolate

Preheat oven to 325° F (165° C)

1. In a medium bowl, beat the cream cheese, ½ cup sugar, liqueur and lemon peel together.

2. Beat egg yolks into mixture one at a time.

3. Beat in the flour.

4. In a separate bowl, beat the whipping cream until soft peaks form.

5. Fold whipping cream into the mixture.

6. In a medium bowl, beat the egg whites until they are stiff.

7. Beat in the remaining ½ cup of sugar into the egg whites, 1 tablespoon at a time. Keep beating until stiff and glossy.

8. Fold the egg-white mixture into the cream cheese mixture only until mixed. Do not overwork it.

9. Oreo crust: melt the margarine or butter and mix with the crumbs.

10. Using either an 8-inch springform pan or a Bundt cake pan, grease the pan and press the Oreo crust mix into the bottom. Leave the greased sides of the pan clean.

11. Pour filling over crust and bake in preheated oven for 1 hour, 15 minutes or until a toothpick comes out clean.

12. Cool and let sit for about 4 hours before serving.

13. Spoon the whipped cream or use a cake decorating kit to create a circle on the top of the cheesecake. Spoon the cherry pie filling in the center and shave dark chocolate over the whipped cream.

Carpathian Moonlight Blood Fruit Pizza

Submitted by: Elaine Kollias
Castro Valley, CA

This unusual and gorgeous dessert is not too heavy and terribly easy to make. When made with all berries, it sparkles like a ruby or garnet jewel, or perhaps even like Carpathian blood in the moonlight!

CRUST INGREDIENTS

¾ cup butter

3 tablespoons powdered sugar

1½ cups flour

FILLING INGREDIENTS

8 ounces softened cream cheese

⅓ cup sugar

1 teaspoon vanilla

assorted fruit: raspberries, strawberries, cherries (pitted and halved), blueberries, and/or sliced bananas, kiwis, peaches, and grapes (halved)—fresh preferred.

GLAZE INGREDIENTS

½ cup sugar

1 tablespoon cornstarch

⅛ teaspoon salt

½ cup pomegranate juice (for dark berry fruits) *or* orange juice (for lighter fruits)

2 tablespoons lime juice

1. *Crust:* Heat oven to 350°. Melt butter, add sugar and flour and mix well. Pat crust onto a 12-inch round pizza pan. Bake until golden brown, about 10–15 minutes. Remove from oven and let cool.

2. *Filling:* Cream together the cream cheese, sugar and vanilla and spread over the cooled crust. Slice the strawberries and arrange fruit/berries in concentric rings, alternating colors and textures for a striking design.

3. *Glaze:* Combine all ingredients in a saucepan and boil until thickened. Cool before spooning evenly over entire fruit pizza. Chill 2–6 hours to set before serving. Cut into wedges with a pizza cutter and garnish with a sprig of fresh mint and optional shaved bittersweet chocolate.

Chocolate Cups

Submitted by: Jill Purinton
Lamar, MO

I used these for a baby shower. No leftovers.☹

dark chocolate cups
key lime yogurt
fresh berries (raspberries, blueberries or strawberries)

Fill chocolate cups with key lime yogurt. Top with fresh berries. Serve.

Delectable Darkness

Submitted by: Susan Schreitmueller
Elon, NC

CRUST INGREDIENTS
1 (8½-oz) package chocolate cream-filled cookies, finely chopped (2½ cups)
2 tablespoons melted butter
1 teaspoon Chambord

Combine and press into bottom and 2 inches up sides of 9-inch spring-form pan. I usually use a food processor to crush the cookies.

FILLING INGREDIENTS

1½ pounds cream cheese, room temperature

½ cup sugar

6 ounces bittersweet or semi-sweet chocolate, chopped, melted and fairly cool

½ cup Chambord

½ teaspoon vanilla

4 large eggs

½ cup whipping cream

1 cup strained seedless raspberry jam

Beat cream cheese in a large bowl until smooth. Add sugar, chocolate and liqueur and beat until well blended. Add eggs one at a time, beating each addition until just combined. Mix in cream. Swirl in seedless jam. Pour into crust. Bake in preheated oven at 350° until filling is almost set but center still moves slightly when pan is shaken (about 55 minutes). Place on a rack and cool completely.

TOPPING INGREDIENTS

½ cup sour cream

2 tablespoons Chambord

6 ounce melted/cooled chocolate chips

Chocolate curls or fresh raspberries rolled in cocoa with mint leaves (optional)

Combine thoroughly and pour over *completely cooled* cheesecake and then chill to set.

Old Fashion Dark Fudge

Submitted by: Amy McKinney
Vincent, AL
MAKES 1 POUND

2 cups sugar
⅓ cup cocoa
1 small can (5-oz) evaporated milk
2 tablespoons unsalted butter
1 teaspoon vanilla extract
walnuts (optional)

In a heavy 3-quart saucepan, mix together sugar and cocoa. Add milk and cook over medium heat until mixture reaches softball stage (236° on a candy thermometer), stirring as necessary to prevent sticking.

Take off heat and add butter, vanilla and nuts if desired. Put boiler in a pan of cool water and stir until it starts to firm up. Pour into a buttered pan. Cut into squares.

Chocolate Éclair Cake

Submitted by: Susan L. Farrell
Pine Grove Mills, PA

2 small packages of Vanilla Jell-O Instant Pudding
1 tub of EZ-Spread Chocolate/Fudge frosting
1 (16-oz) tub of Cool Whip
3 cups milk
graham crackers
9 ×13×3-inch pan *(a pan this deep lessens the loss of the frosting)*

1. Mix packets of pudding and milk. *(Easier if done with mixer, but whisking/stirring by hand works too.)* Then slowly mix in Cool Whip.

2. Line bottom of pan with graham crackers. Pour half of mixture over crackers. Add another layer of graham crackers. Pour remaining mixture over crackers. Add final layers of crackers.

3. Remove foil from frosting tub. Microwave frosting tub 15–25 seconds. Spread frosting over final layer of crackers.

4. Cover and refrigerate for four hours or overnight for best results. *Enjoy!*

Christmas Mice

Submitted by: Susan Maluschka
Houston, TX
YIELDS 70 MICE

1 package chocolate almond bark
1 large jar cherries with stems, drained
1 bag Hershey's Kisses
1 small bag almond slivers

1. Put water in the bottom of a double boiler.
2. Spread out foil on the countertop next to stove.
3. Break chocolate almond bark into pieces and melt in double boiler.
4. Pat cherries dry on paper towels and unwrap the Kisses.
5. Hold cherries by the stems and dip in chocolate until cherry is covered. Lay cherry on its side on the foil (forms body and tail).
6. After dipping 4 or 5, prop up a Kiss with the flat part of the Kiss against the bottom of the cherry (forms head with pointed nose).
7. Then go back and place two almond slivers between Kiss and cherry (forms ears). If the chocolate has dried too much already, put a little chocolate from the double boiler on the almond slivers and hold them in place until they stay.

Appendix 1
Carpathian Healing Chants

To rightly understand Carpathian healing chants, background is required in several areas:

- The Carpathian view on healing
- The "Lesser Healing Chant" of the Carpathians
- The "Great Healing Chant" of the Carpathians
- Carpathian chanting technique

1. THE CARPATHIAN VIEW ON HEALING

The Carpathians are a nomadic people whose geographical origins can be traced back to at least as far as the Southern Ural Mountains (near the steppes of modern day Kazakhstan), on the border between Europe and Asia. (For this reason, modern-day linguists call their language, "proto-Uralic," without knowing that this is the language of the Carpathians.) Unlike most nomadic peoples, the wandering of the Carpathians was not due to the need to find new grazing lands as the seasons and climate shifted, or the search for better trade. Instead, the Carpathians' movements were driven by a great purpose: to find a land that would have the right earth, a soil with the kind of richness that would greatly enhance their rejuvenative powers.

Over the centuries, they migrated westward (some six thousand years ago), until they at last found their perfect homeland—their "*susu*"—in the Carpathian Mountains, whose long arc cradled the lush plains of the kingdom of Hungary. (The kingdom of Hungary flourished for over a millennium—making Hungarian the dominant language of the Carpathian Basin—until the kingdom's lands were split among several countries after World War I: Austria, Czechoslovakia, Romania, Yugoslavia, Austria, and modern Hungary.)

Other peoples from the Southern Urals (who shared the Carpathian language, but were not Carpathians) migrated in different directions. Some ended up in Finland, which accounts for why the modern Hungarian and Finnish languages are among the contemporary descendents of the ancient Carpathian language. Even though they are tied forever to their chosen Carpathian homeland, the wandering of the Carpathians continues, as they search the world for the answers that will enable them to bear and raise their offspring without difficulty.

Because of their geographical origins, the Carpathian views on healing share much with the larger Eurasian shamanistic tradition. Probably the closest modern representative of that tradition is based in Tuva (and is referred to as "Tuvinian Shamanism")—see the map at the front of the book.

The Eurasian shamanistic tradition—from the Carpathians to the Siberian shamans—held that illness originated in the human soul, and only later manifested as various physical conditions. Therefore, shamanistic healing, while not neglecting the body, focused on the soul and its healing. The most profound illnesses were understood to be caused by "soul departure," where all or some part of the sick person's soul has wandered away from the body (into the nether realms), or has been captured or possessed by an evil spirit, or both.

The Carpathians belong to this greater Eurasian shamanistic tradition and shared its viewpoints. While the Carpathians themselves did not succumb to illness, Carpathian healers understood that the most profound wounds were also accompanied by a similar "soul departure."

Upon reaching the diagnosis of "soul departure," the healer-shaman is then required to make a spiritual journey into the nether worlds, to recover the soul. The shaman may have to overcome tremendous challenges along the way, particularly: fighting the demon or vampire who has possessed his friend's soul.

"Soul departure" doesn't require a person to be unconscious (although that certainly can be the case as well). It was understood that a person could still appear to be conscious, even talk and interact with others, and yet be missing a part of their soul. The experienced healer or shaman would instantly see the problem nonetheless, in subtle signs that others might miss: the person's attention wandering every now and then, a lessening in their enthusiasm about life, chronic depression, a diminishment in the brightness of their "aura," and the like.

2. THE LESSER HEALING CHANT OF THE CARPATHIANS

Kepa Sarna Pus (The "Lesser Healing Chant") is used for wounds that are merely physical in nature. The Carpathian healer leaves his body and enters the wounded Carpathian's body to heal great mortal wounds from the inside out using pure energy. He proclaims, "I offer freely, my life for your life," as he gives his blood to the injured Carpathian. Because the Carpathians are of the earth and bound to the soil, they are healed by the soil of their homeland. Their saliva is also often used for its rejuvenative powers.

It is also very common for the Carpathian chants (both the lesser and the great one) to be accompanied by the use of healing herbs, aromas from Carpathian candles, and crystals. The crystals (when combined with the Carpathians' empathic, psychic connection to the entire universe) are used to gather positive energy from their surroundings which then is used to accelerate the healing. Caves are sometimes used as the setting for the healing.

The lesser healing chant was used by Vikirnoff Von Shrieder and Colby Jansen to heal Rafael De La Cruz whose heart had been ripped out by a vampire in the book titled *Dark Secret*.

Kepä Sarna Pus (The Lesser Healing Chant)
The same chant is used for all physical wounds. "sívadaba" ["into your heart"] would be changed to refer to whatever part of the body is wounded.

Kuńasz, nélkül sivdobbanás, nélkül fesztelen löyly.
You lie as if asleep, without beat of heart, without airy breath.
[Lie-as-if-asleep-you, without heart-beat, without airy breath.]

Ot élidamet andam szabadon élidadért.
I offer freely my life for your life.
[Life-my give-I freely life-your-for.]

O jelä sielam jörem ot ainamet és soɲe ot élidadet.
My spirit of light forgets my body and enters your body.
[The sunlight soul-my forgets the body-my and enters the body-your.]

O jelä sielam pukta kinn minden szelemeket belső.
My spirit of light sends all the dark spirits within fleeing without.
[The sunlight-soul-my puts-to-flight outside all ghost-s inside.]

Pajńak o susu hanyet és o nyelv nyálamet sívadaba.
I press the earth of our homeland and the spit of my tongue into your
     heart.
[Press-I the homeland earth and the tongue spit-my heart-your-into.]

Vii, o verim soɲe o verid andam.
At last, I give you my blood for your blood.
[At-last, the blood-my to-replace the blood-your give-I.]

To hear this chant, visit: http://www.christinefeehan.com/members/.

3. THE GREAT HEALING CHANT OF THE CARPATHIANS

The most well-known—and most dramatic—of the Carpathian healing chants was **En Sarna Pus** ("The Great Healing Chant"). This chant was re-served for recovering the wounded or unconscious Carpathian's soul.

Typically a group of men would form a circle around the sick Carpathian (to "encircle him with our care and compassion"), and begin the chant. The shaman or healer or leader is the prime actor in this healing ceremony. It is he who will actually make the spiritual journey into the nether world, aided by his clanspeople. Their purpose is to ecstatically dance, sing, drum, and chant, all the while visualizing (through the words of the chant) the journey itself—every step of it, over and over again—to the point where the shaman, in trance, leaves his body, and makes that very journey. (Indeed, the word "ecstasy" is from the Latin *ex statis*, which literally means "out of the body.")

One advantage that the Carpathian healer has over many other shamans, is his telepathic link to his lost brother. Most shamans must wander in the dark of the nether realms, in search of their lost brother. But the Carpathian healer directly "hears" in his mind the voice of his lost brother calling to him, and can thus "zero in" on his soul like a homing beacon. For this reason, Carpathian healing tends to have a higher success rate than most other traditions of this sort.

Something of the geography of the "other world" is useful for us to examine, in order to fully understand the words of the Great Carpathian Healing Chant. A reference is made to the "Great Tree" (in Carpathian: *En Puwe*). Many ancient traditions, including the Carpathian tradition, understood the worlds—the heaven worlds, our world, and the nether realms—to be "hung" upon a great pole, or axis, or tree. Here on earth, we are positioned halfway up this tree, on one of its branches. Hence many ancient texts often referred to the material world as "middle earth": midway between heaven and hell. Climbing the tree would lead one to the heaven worlds. Descending the tree to its roots would lead to the nether realms. The shaman was necessarily a master of movement up and down the Great Tree, sometimes moving unaided, and sometimes assisted by (or even mounted upon the back of) an animal spirit guide. In various traditions, this Great Tree was known variously as the *axis mundi* (the "axis of the worlds"), Ygddrasil (in Norse mythology), Mount Meru (the sacred world mountain of Tibetan tradition), etc. The Christian cosmos with its heaven, purgatory/earth, and hell, is also worth comparing. It is even given a similar topography in Dante's *Divine Comedy*: Dante is led on a journey first to hell, at the center of the earth; then upward to Mount Purgatory, which sits on the earth's surface directly opposite Jerusalem; then farther upward first to Eden, the earthly paradise, at the summit of Mount Purgatory; and then upward at last to heaven.

In the shamanistic tradition, it was understood that the small always reflects the large; the personal always reflects the cosmic. A movement in the greater dimensions of the cosmos also coincides with an internal movement. For example, the *axis mundi* of the cosmos also corresponds to the spinal column of the individual. Journeys up and down the *axis mundi* often coincided with the movement of natural and spiritual energies (sometimes called *kundalini* or *shakti*) in the spinal column of the shaman or mystic.

En Sarna Pus (The Great Healing Chant)
In this chant, ekä ("brother") would be replaced by "sister," "father," "mother," depending on the person to be healed.

Ot ekäm ainajanak hany, jama.
My brother's body is a lump of earth, close to death.
[The brother-my body-his-of lump-of-earth, is-near-death.]

Me, ot ekäm kuntajanak, pirädak ekäm, gond és irgalom türe.
We, the clan of my brother, encircle him with our care and compassion.
[We, the brother-my clan-his-of, encircle brother-my, care and compassion full.]

O pus wäkenkek, ot oma śarnank, és ot pus fünk, álnak ekäm ainajanak,
    pitänak ekäm ainajanak elävä.
Our healing energies, ancient words of magic, and healing herbs bless my
    brother's body, keep it alive.
[The healing power-our-s, the ancient words-of-magic-our, and the healing
    herbs-our, bless brother-my body-his-of, keep brother-my body-his-of
    alive.]

Ot ekäm sielanak pälä. Ot omboće päläja juta alatt o jüti, kinta, és szelemek
    lamtijaknak.
But my brother's soul is only half. His other half wanders in the nether
    world.

[The brother-my soul-his-of (is) half. The other half-his wanders through the night, mist, and ghosts lowland-their-of.]

Ot en mekem ŋamaŋ: kulkedak otti ot ekäm omboće päläjanak.
My great deed is this: I travel to find my brother's other half.
[The great deed-my (is) this: travel-I to-find the brother-my other half-his-of.]

Rekatüre, saradak, tappadak, odam, kaŋa o numa waram, és avaa owe o lewl mahoz.
We dance, we chant, we dream ecstatically, to call my spirit bird, and to open the door to the other world.
[Ecstasy-full, dance-we, dream we, to call the god bird-my, and open the door spirit land-to.]

Ntak o numa waram, és mozdulak, jomadak.
I mount my spirit bird and we begin to move, we are under way.
[Mount-I the god bird-my, and begin-to-move-we, are-on-our-way-we.]

Piwtädak ot En Puwe tyvinak, ećidak alatt o jüti, kinta, és szelemek lamti-jaknak.
Following the trunk of the Great Tree, we fall into the nether world.
[Follow-we the Great Tree trunk-of, fall-we through the night, mist, and ghosts lowland-their-of.]

Fázak, fázak nó o śaro.
It is cold, very cold.
[Feel-cold-I, feel-cold-I like the frozen snow.]

Juttadak ot ekäm o akarataban, o sívaban, és o sielaban.
My brother and I are linked in mind, heart, and soul.
[Am-bound-to-I the brother-my the mind-in, the heart-in, and the soul-in.]

Ot ekäm sielanak kaŋa engem.
My brother's soul calls to me.
[The brother-my soul-his-of calls-to me.]

Kuledak és piwtädak ot ekäm.
I hear and follow his track.
[Hear-I and follow-the-trail-of-I the brother-my.]

Saɣedak és tuledak ot ekäm kulyanak.
Encounter-I the demon who is devouring my brother's soul.
[Arrive-I and meet-I the brother-my demon-who-devours-soul-his-of.]

Nenäm ćoro; o kuly torodak.
In anger, I fight the demon.
[Anger-my flows; the demon-who-devours-souls fight-I.]

O kuly pél engem.
He is afraid of me.
[The demon-who-devours-souls (is) afraid-of me.]

Lejkkadak o kaṅka salamaval.
I strike his throat with a lightning bolt.
[Strike-I the throat-his bolt-of-lightning-with.]

Molodak ot ainaja komakamal.
I break his body with my bare hands.
[Break-I the body-his empty-hand-s-my-with.]

Toja és molanâ.
He is bent over, and falls apart.
[(He)bends and (he)crumbles.]

Hän ćaδa.
He runs away.
[He flees.]

Manedak ot ekäm sielanak.
I rescue my brother's soul.
[Rescue-I the brother-my soul-his-of.]

Alədak ot ekam sielanak o komamban.
I lift my brother's soul in the hollow of my hand.
[Lift-I the brother-my soul-his-of the hollow-of-hand-my-in.]

Alədam ot ekam numa waramra.
I lift him onto my spirit bird.
[Lift-I the brother-my god bird-my-onto.]

Piwtädak ot En Puwe tyvijanak és saɣedak jälleen ot elävä ainak majaknak.
Following up the Great Tree, we return to the land of the living.
[Follow-we the Great Tree trunk-its-of, and reach-we again the living
    bodie-s land-their-of.]

Ot ekäm elä jälleen.
My brother lives again.
[The brother-my lives again.]

Ot ekäm weńća jälleen.
He is complete again.
[The brother-my (is) complete again.]

To hear this chant, visit: http://www.christinefeehan.com/members/.

4. CARPATHIAN CHANTING TECHNIQUE

As with their healing techniques, the actual "chanting technique" of the Carpathians has much in common with the other shamanistic traditions of the Central Asian steppes. The primary mode of chanting was throat chanting using overtones. Modern examples of this manner of singing can still be found in the Mongolian, Tuvan, and Tibetan traditions. You can find an audio example of the Gyuto Tibetan Buddhist monks engaged in throat chanting at: http://www.christinefeehan.com/carpathian_chanting/.

As with Tuva, note on the map the geographical proximity of Tibet to Kazakhstan and the Southern Urals.

The beginning part of the Tibetan chant emphasizes synchronizing all the voices around a single tone, aimed at healing a particular "chakra" of the body. This is fairly typical of the Gyuto throat chanting tradition, but it is not a significant part of the Carpathian tradition. Nonetheless, it serves as an interesting contrast.

The part of the Gyuto chanting example that is most similar to the Carpathian style of chanting is the midsection, where the men are chanting the words together with great force. The purpose here is not to generate a "healing tone" that will affect a particular "chakra," but rather to generate as much power as possible for initiating the "out of body" travel, and for fighting the demonic forces that the healer/traveler must face and overcome.

APPENDIX 2

The Carpathian Language

Like all human languages, the language of the Carpathians contains the richness and nuance that can only come from a long history of use. At best we can only touch on some of the main features of the language in this brief appendix:

- The history of the Carpathian language
- Carpathian grammar and other characteristics of the language
- Examples of the Carpathian language
- A much abridged Carpathian dictionary

1. THE HISTORY OF THE CARPATHIAN LANGUAGE

The Carpathian language of today is essentially identical to the Carpathian language of thousands of years ago. A "dead" language like the Latin of two thousand years ago has evolved into a significantly different modern language (Italian) because of countless generations of speakers and great historical fluctuations. In contrast, many of the speakers of Carpathian from thousands of years ago are still alive. Their presence—coupled with the deliberate isolation of the Carpathians from the other major forces of change in the world—has acted (and continues to act) as a stabilizing force that has preserved the integrity of the language over the centuries. Carpathian culture has also acted as a stabilizing force. For instance, the Ritual Words, the various healing chants (see Appendix 1), and other cultural artifacts have been passed down through the centuries with great fidelity.

One small exception should be noted: the splintering of the Carpathians into separate geographic regions has led to some minor dialectization. However the telepathic links among all Carpathians (as well as each Carpathian's regular return to his or her homeland) has ensured that the differences among dialects are relatively superficial (e.g., small numbers of new words, minor differences in pronunciation, etc.), since the deeper, internal language of mind-forms has remained the same because of continuous use across space and time.

The Carpathian language was (and still is) the **proto-language** for the Uralic (or Finno-Ugrian) family of languages. Today, the Uralic languages are spoken in northern, eastern and central Europe and in Siberia. More than twenty-three million people in the world speak languages that can trace their ancestry to Carpathian. Magyar or Hungarian (about fourteen million speakers), Finnish (about five million speakers), and Estonian (about one million speakers), are the three major contemporary descendents of this proto-language. The only factor that unites the more than twenty languages in the Uralic family is that their ancestry can be traced back to a common proto-language—Carpathian—which split (starting some six thousand years ago) into the various languages in the Uralic family. In the same way, European languages such as English and French, belong to the better-known Indo-European family and also evolve from a common proto-language ancestor (a different one from Carpathian).

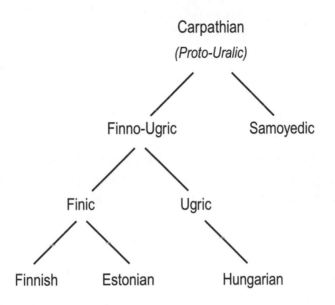

The following table provides a sense for some of the similarities in the language family.

Note: The Finnic/Carpathian "k" shows up often as Hungarian "h". Similarly, the Finnic/Carpathian "p" often corresponds to the Hungarian "f."

Carpathian (proto-Uralic)	Finnish (Suomi)	Hungarian (Magyar)
elä—live	*elä*—live	*él*—live
elid—life	*elinikä*—life	*élet*—life
pesä—nest	*pesä*—nest	*fészek*—nest
kola—die	*kuole*—die	*hal*—die
pälä—half, side	*pieltä*—tilt, tip to the side	*fél, fele*—fellow human, friend (half; one side of two) *feleség*—wife
and—give	*anta, antaa*—give	*ad*—give
koje—husband, man	*koira*—dog, the male	*here*— drone, testicle (of animals)

wäke—power	*väki*—folks, people, men; force	*val/-vel*—with (instrumental suffix)
	väkevä—powerful, strong	*vele*—with him/her/it
wete—water	*vesi*—water	*víz*—water

2. CARPATHIAN GRAMMAR AND OTHER CHARACTERISTICS OF THE LANGUAGE

Idioms. As both an ancient language, and a language of an earth people, Carpathian is more inclined toward use of idioms constructed from concrete, "earthy" terms, rather than abstractions. For instance, our modern abstraction, "to cherish," is expressed more concretely in Carpathian as "to hold in one's heart"; the "nether world" is, in Carpathian, "the land of night, fog and ghosts"; etc.

Word order. The order of words in a sentence is determined not by syntactic roles (like subject, verb and object) but rather by pragmatic, discourse-driven factors. Examples: *"Tied vagyok."* ("Yours am I."); *"Sívamet andam."* ("My heart I give you.")

Agglutination. The Carpathian language is **agglutinative**; that is, longer words are constructed from smaller components. An agglutinating language uses suffixes or prefixes whose meaning is generally unique, and which are concatenated one after another without overlap. In Carpathian, words typically consist of a stem that is followed by one or more suffixes. For example, *"sívambam"* derives from the stem *"sív"* ("heart") followed by *"am"* ("my," making it "my heart"), followed by *"bam"* ("in," making it "in my heart"). As you might imagine, agglutination in Carpathian can sometimes produce very long words, or words that are very difficult to pronounce. Vowels often get inserted between suffixes, to prevent too many consonants from appearing in a row (which can make the word unpronounceable).

Noun cases. Like all languages, Carpathian has many noun cases; the same noun will be "spelled" differently depending on its role in the sentence. Some of the noun cases include: nominative (when the noun is the subject of the sentence), accusative (when the noun is a direct object of the verb), dative (indirect object), genitive (or possessive), instrumental, final, supressive, inessive, elative, terminative and delative.

We will use the possessive (or genitive) case as an example, to illustrate how all noun cases in Carpathian involve adding standard suffixes to the noun stems. Thus expressing possession in Carpathian—"my lifemate," "your lifemate," "his lifemate," "her lifemate," etc.—involves adding a particular suffix (such as "*=am*") to the noun stem ("*päläfertiil*"), to produce the possessive ("*päläferti-ilam*"—"my lifemate"). Which suffix to use depends upon which person ("my," "your," "his," etc.) and whether the noun ends in a consonant or vowel. The following table shows the suffixes for singular nouns only (not plural), and also shows the similarity to the suffixes used in contemporary Hungarian. (Hungarian is actually a little more complex, in that it also requires "vowel rhyming": which suffix to use also depends on the last vowel in the noun; hence the multiple choices in the cells below, where Carpathian only has a single choice.)

	Carpathian (proto-Uralic)		contemporary Hungarian	
person	**noun ends in vowel**	**noun ends in consonant**	**noun ends in vowel**	**noun ends in consonant**
1st singular (my)	-m	-am	-m	-om, -em, -öm
2nd singular (your)	-d	-ad	-d	-od, -ed, -öd
3rd singular (his,her,its)	-ja	-a	-ja/-je	-a, -e
1st plural (our)	-nk	-ank	-nk	-unk, -ünk
2nd plural (your)	-tak	-atak	-tok, -tek, -tök	-otok, -etek, -ötök
3rd plural (their)	-jak	-ak	-juk, -jük	-uk, -ük

Note: As mentioned earlier, vowels often get inserted between the word and its suffix so as to prevent too many consonants from appearing in a row (which would produce unpronounceable words). For example, in the table above, all nouns that end in a consonant are followed by suffixes beginning with "a."

Verb conjugation. Like its modern descendents (such as Finnish and Hungarian), Carpathian has many verb tenses, far too many to describe here. We will just focus on the conjugation of the present tense. Again, we will place contemporary Hungarian side by side with the Carpathian, because of the marked similarity of the two.

As with the possessive case for nouns, the conjugation of verbs is done by adding a suffix onto the verb stem:

Person	Carpathian (proto-Uralic)	contemporary Hungarian
1st (I give)	-am (andam),-ak	-ok,-ek,-ök
2nd singular (you give)	-sz (andsz)	-sz
3rd singular (he/she/it gives)	—(and)	—
1st plural (we give)	-ak (andak)	-unk,-ünk
2nd plural (you give)	-tak (andtak)	-tok,-tek,-tök
3rd plural (they give)	-nak (andnak)	-nak,-nek

As with all languages, there are many "irregular verbs" in Carpathian that don't exactly fit this pattern. But the above table is still a useful guideline for most verbs.

3. EXAMPLES OF THE CARPATHIAN LANGUAGE

Here are some brief examples of conversational Carpathian, used in the Dark books. We include the literal translation in square brackets. It is interestingly different from the most appropriate English translation.

Susu.

I am home.

["home/birthplace." "I am" is understood, as is often the case in Carpathian.]

Möért?

What for?

csitri

little one

["little slip of a thing", "little slip of a girl"]

ainaak enyém

forever mine

ainaak sívamet jutta

forever mine (another form)

["forever to-my-heart connected/fixed"]

sívamet

my love

["of-my-heart," "to-my-heart"]

Sarna Rituaali (The Ritual Words) is a longer example, and an example of chanted rather than conversational Carpathian. Note the recurring use of *"andam"* ("I give"), to give the chant musicality and force through repetition.

Sarna Rituaali (The Ritual Words)

Te avio päläfertiilam.

You are my lifemate.

[You wedded wife-my. "Are" is understood, as is generally the case in Carpathian when one thing is equated with another: "You-my lifemate."]

Éntölam kuulua, avio päläfertiilam.
I claim you as my lifemate.
[To-me belong-you, wedded wife-my.]

Ted kuuluak, kacad, kojed.
I belong to you.
[To-you belong-I, lover-your, man/husband/drone-your.]

Élidamet andam.
I offer my life for you.
[Life-my give-I. "you" is understood.]

Pesämet andam.
I give you my protection.
[Nest-my give-I.]

Uskolfertiilamet andam.
I give you my allegiance.
[Fidelity-my give-I.]

Sívamet andam.
I give you my heart.
[Heart-my give-I.]

Sielamet andam.
I give you my soul.
[Soul-my give-I.]

Ainamet andam.
I give you my body.
[Body-my give-I.]

Sívamet kuuluak kaik että a ted.
I take into my keeping the same that is yours.
[To-my-heart hold-I all that-is yours.]

Ainaak olenszal sívambin.
Your life will be cherished by me for all my time.
[Forever will-be-you in-my-heart.]

Te élidet ainaak pide minan.
Your life will be placed above my own for all time.
[Your life forever above mine.]

Te avio päläfertiilam.
You are my lifemate.
[You wedded wife-my.]

Ainaak sívamet jutta oleny.
You are bound to me for all eternity.
[Forever to-my-heart connected are-you.]

Ainaak terád vigyázak.
You are always in my care.
[Forever you I-take-care-of.]

See **Appendix 1** for Carpathian healing chants, including both the *Kepä Sarna Pus* ("The Lesser Healing Chant") and the *En Sarna Pus* ("The Great Healing Chant").

To hear these words pronounced (and for more about Carpathian pronunciation altogether), please visit: http://www.christinefeehan.com/members/.

4. A MUCH ABRIDGED CARPATHIAN DICTIONARY

This very much abridged Carpathian dictionary contains most of the Carpathian words used in these Dark books. Of course, a full Carpathian dictionary would be as large as the usual dictionary for an entire language.

Note: The Carpathian nouns and verbs below are word **stems**. They generally do not appear in their isolated, "stem" form, as below. Instead, they usually appear with suffixes (e.g., "*andam*"—"I give," rather than just the root, "*and*").

aina—body
ainaak—forever
akarat—mind; will
ál—bless, attach to
alatt—through
alə—to lift; to raise
and—to give
avaa—to open
avio—wedded
avio päläfertiil—lifemate
belső—within; inside
ćaδa—to flee; to run; to escape
ćoro—to flow; to run like rain
csitri—little one (female)
ekä—brother
elä—to live
elävä—alive
elävä ainak majaknak—land of the living
elid—life
én—I
en—great, many, big
En Puwe—The Great Tree. Related to the legends of Ygddrasil, the axis mundi, Mount Meru, heaven and hell, etc.
engem—me
eći—to fall
ek—suffix added after a noun ending in a consonant to make it plural
és—and
että—that
fáz—to feel cold or chilly
fertiil—fertile one
fesztelen—airy

fü—herbs; grass

gond—care; worry (noun)

hän—he; she; it

hany—clod; lump of earth

irgalom—compassion; pity; mercy

jälleen—again

jama—to be sick, wounded, or dying; to be near death (verb)

jelä—sunlight; day, sun; light

joma—to be under way; to go

jörem—to forget; to lose one's way; to make a mistake

juta—to go; to wander

jüti—night; evening

jutta—connected; fixed (adj.). to connect; to fix; to bind (verb)

k—suffix added after a noun ending in a vowel to make it plural

kaca—male lover

kaik—all (noun)

kaŋa—to call; to invite; to request; to beg

kaŋk—windpipe; Adam's apple; throat

Karpatii—Carpathian

käsi—hand

kepä—lesser, small, easy, few

kinn—out; outdoors; outside; without

kinta—fog, mist, smoke

koje—man; husband; drone

kola—to die

koma—empty hand; bare hand; palm of the hand; hollow of the hand

kont—warrior

kule—hear

kuly—intestinal worm; tapeworm; demon who possesses and devours souls

kulke—to go or to travel (on land or water)

kuńa—to lie as if asleep; to close or cover the eyes in a game of hide-and-seek; to die

kunta—band, clan, tribe, family

kuulua—to belong; to hold

lamti—lowland; meadow

lamti ból jüti, kinta, ja szelem—the nether world (literally: "the meadow of night, mists, and ghosts")

lejkka—crack, fissure, split (noun). To cut; hit; to strike forcefully (verb).

lewl—spirit

lewl ma—the other world (literally: "spirit land"). Lewl ma includes lamti ból jüti, kinta, ja szelem: the nether world, but also includes the worlds higher up En Puwe, the Great Tree

löyly—breath; steam. (related to lewl: "spirit")

ma—land; forest

mäne—rescue; save

me—we

meke—deed; work (noun). To do; to make; to work (verb)

minan—mine

minden—every, all (adj.)

möért?—what for? (exclamation)

molo—to crush; to break into bits

molanâ—to crumble; to fall apart

mozdul—to begin to move, to enter into movement

nä—for

ŋamaŋ—this; this one here

nélkül—without

nenä—anger

nó—like; in the same way as; as

numa—god; sky; top; upper part; highest (related to the English word: "numinous")

nyelv—tongue

nyál—saliva; spit (noun). (related to nyelv: "tongue")

odam—dream; sleep (verb)

oma—old; ancient

omboće—other; second (adj.)

o—the (used before a noun beginning with a consonant)

ot—the (used before a noun beginning with a vowel)

otti—to look; to see; to find

owe—door

pajna—to press

pälä—half; side

päläfertiil—mate or wife

pél—to be afraid; to be scared of

pesä—nest (literal); protection (figurative)

pide—above

pirä—circle; ring (noun). To surround; to enclose (verb).

pitä—keep; hold

piwtä—to follow; to follow the track of game

pukta—to drive away; to persecute; to put to flight

pusm—to be restored to health

pus—healthy; healing

puwe—tree; wood

reka—ecstasy; trance

rituaali—ritual

saγe—to arrive; to come; to reach

salama—lightning; lightning bolt

sarna—words; speech; magic incantation (noun). To chant; to sing; to celebrate (verb).

śaro—frozen snow

siel—soul

sisar—sister

sív—heart

sívdobbanás—heartbeat

soŋe—to enter; to penetrate; to compensate; to replace

susu—home; birthplace (noun); at home (adv.)

szabadon—freely

szelem—ghost

tappa—to dance; to stamp with the feet (verb)

te—you

ted—yours

toja—to bend; to bow; to break

toro—to fight; to quarrel

tule—to meet; to come

türe—full; satiated; accomplished

tyvi—stem; base; trunk
uskol—faithful
uskolfertiil—allegiance
veri—blood
vigyáz—to care for; to take care of
vii—last; at last; finally
wäke—power
wara—bird; crow
weńća—complete; whole
wete—water